A. A. Gill was born in Edinburgh in 1954 and studied at the Slade School of Art. He is the restaurant and television critic for the *Sunday Times*, for whom he also writes a weekly opinion column. He is the author of *Sap Rising* and *The Ivy Cookbook*. He lives in London.

Sap Rising:

'He writes brilliantly.' *Evening Standard*

'Extremely funny.' *Time Out*

'Among the most original novels of the year.' *Financial Times*

'Funny, well written and saucy.' *Woman's Journal*

'Fine comic scenes . . . readers will have trouble putting *Sap Rising* down.' *Daily Express*

'Imagine Barbara Pym writing for *Penthouse*.' *Literary Review*

Also by A. A. Gill

SAP RISING
THE IVY COOKBOOK

STARCROSSED

A.A. Gill

Doubleday

LONDON · NEW YORK · TORONTO · SYDNEY · AUCKLAND

TRANSWORLD PUBLISHERS LTD
61–63 Uxbridge Road, London W5 5SA

TRANSWORLD PUBLISHERS
c/o Random House Australia Pty Ltd
20 Alfred Street, Milsons Point, NSW 2061, Australia

TRANSWORLD PUBLISHERS
c/o Random House New Zealand
18 Poland Road, Glenfield, Auckland, New Zealand

TRANSWORLD PUBLISHERS
c/o Random House Pty Ltd
Endulini, 5a Jubilee Road, Parktown 2193, South Africa

Published 1999 by Doubleday
a division of Transworld Publishers Ltd
Copyright © A.A. Gill 1999

A catalogue record for this book is available from the British Library.

ISBN 0385 409001

Typeset in 11/14pt Sabon by Falcon Oast Graphic Art

Printed in Great Britain
by Mackays of Chatham plc, Chatham, Kent.

1 3 5 7 9 10 8 6 4 2

For Nicola

The Minstrel Boy to the war has gone,
In the ranks of death you'll find him;
His father's sword he has girded on,
And his wild harp slung behind him.
Land of song, said the warrior bard,
Though all the world betrays thee,
One sword, at least, thy right shall guard.

                                    Anon

JOHN DART, POET, WOKE EARLY TO FIND THAT HIS HAND, HIS LYRIC hand, was still asleep. This happened quite regularly. John was a messy sleeper. Bits were always folding themselves away and dying in the dark. He reached across with his other, sentient, non-rhyming, bottom-wiping hand and squeezed – nothing. He began to bend the fingers back, waiting for the tingle of sensation. The sonorous hand said, 'Ahhh fuck!' and got out of bed. A number of thoughts jostled to the top of John's sticky consciousness. The one that sprang most lucidly was surprisingly not that his hand had somehow become disengaged from his arm, or that it spoke, or even that it spoke profanely, but that it was American. As far as he'd ever considered it, he imagined all his hands were English. Both his parents were English, his grandparents had all been English – with just the merest embarrassing smear of Welsh.

But before he had a chance to question the hand, a third hand grabbed his sensate wrist and a fourth hand – the bed was all fingers and thumbs this morning – hit him painfully across the bridge of the nose. He did two things: first he let go of the Yankee hand, then he bit the face-thumper. And two other things, in the Newtonian way, happened simultaneously. One, a severe shock of pain ran up his arm, and two, a hand – he was beginning to lose track – turned on a light.

John Dart sat up, took his own artistic wrist out of his mouth, looked, and saw that he had been well and truly fingered by the fifth, invisible hand of fate.

'My God! You're Lee Montana.'

The naked woman in front of him massaged her fingers.

'Jeez, it's five thirty olde worlde time. And you need to take

9

lessons in waking up. Are you always this violent first thing?'

'Sorry. My hand went to sleep and I didn't remember I'd gone to bed with anyone.'

'No, it came as a shock to me, too. God I feel lousy.' She pushed her hair back from her face.

'I'm hungover. Last night's a haze,' John said by way of apology.

'Ah ha! Well, in case you're thinking of writing your memoirs, we didn't do it. But we could do it. In my vast experience, a fuck's the second best thing for a hangover. The best thing is not waking up. Cock's not still asleep, is it?' She pulled back the bedclothes. It wasn't. 'Oh, impressive. All yours or surgery?'

'I beg your pardon?'

'I beg your pardon! I love it. Come to Mommy.'

She got back into the bed and lay across him. She was warm and heavy and hard. She slid a hand behind his head and kissed him gently and slowly on the lips. 'Usually at this point I make you sign a no-publicity agreement, but I can't be bothered to get my agent over.' She pushed her tongue into his ear. 'Only joking. But, please, no Sunday confessionals.' She rolled off him and onto her back. 'OK, straight sex. No foreplay, no interval, no talking. I'm going straight back to sleep after. Wake me at eight. Right, off you go.'

She reached down and waggled the unaugmented cock. 'By the way, what's your name? I've got to scream something.'

'John Dart.'

'Good to have you aboard, John.'

John let himself into the shop. It was still only seven thirty. They didn't open for a couple of hours. He walked, in the dark, past the tables of hardback fiction, biography and crime to the small staff room at the back, flicked on the light and filled the kettle from the hissing Ascot, then slumped onto a box.

Shit. He felt dreadful. Hungover. Exhausted.

Yesterday's clothes hung damply; his socks felt as if they were full of congealing fish paste and his underpants nested clammily. Looking up he saw his own face staring back at him from the neon-bright pane of mirror over the sink, sandwiched between the disapproving, bespectacled gaze of T. S. Eliot and the altogether more understanding one of Oscar Wilde.

A pale, thin face. Not a bad face: hooded bleach-blue eyes, smudged darkly; quizzical arched brows; a thin straight nose; a big mouth, too full perhaps; strong bones. It was a pallid, empty face. An Art teacher with a tickly moustache, who had once kissed his neck furtively, had said it was a Renaissance face: Florentine, Sienese, an arrogant Medici face. Perhaps. But it didn't have the hero's look; it didn't wear the laurel or the helm; it was just an extra's face; a watching face; a face in the crowd; a spear-carrier; a waiter who glances sideways over a tray; a man playing dice in the foreground, who holds the reins as the pageant passes. John Dart's face – poet's gaze, bookshop assistant's smile, pessimistic romantic's frown, poor relation's scowl, overdue lodger's grin and now, hungover, unfaithful boyfriend, brazen and blank.

Twenty-six and a lost boy. Not so much lost perhaps as an aimless boy, a stalled boy. Early promise settled into the past tense.

He ran his hand through his long black hair, damp with sweat and drizzle, and smelled the faint, throat-catching scent of wet rust and sea urchin: the smell of sex and a woman's groin. He scalded his dip-stick finger on the kettle and took his cup back into the shop, which, in turn, smelled of sour lees and ashtrays.

The detritus of last night's party was scattered over the room. John collected glasses into boxes and tipped prawn heads and fag butts into a rubbish bag. Lee Montana watched him, with sultry wet lips parted to whisper something, dark eyes following him around the room. She watched from tables and counters. Her reflected gaze shone from the pyramid display in the window, the drizzle trickling down her face like tears.

John picked up one of the books and sat behind the till. *Lee Montana: Fame. Black and White* across the page. Overleaf her face huge and solemn, absolutely symmetrical, with perfect features, all set as if by a jeweller, or drawn on vellum. A face that had never looked over a tray, never cleared glasses, or held the reins while the parade passed. It was a face-the-music face, a face-the-camera face, a face-the-applause face, a centre-of-the-frame face. It

11

was the focus of all sight lines, the vanishing point. It was mathematically precise. Perfect. Over.

'Lee Montana. Fame.' Two columns written by America's most famous serious novelist, who had come out of the most-notorious, most-written-about writer's block, lasting two decades, to pen his adoration of this face.

'Lee Montana. I can't remember the first time I saw Lee's face, but then, I can't remember a time when I didn't know her face. I can't remember when it was first carved on the prow of my lust and adoration.'

Christ, he was better off with the block.

It went on in the same vein. An old Jewish penis writes, 'A new Helen of Troy, a post-modern Marilyn, the most famous woman in the world, a star all her life, a star before life. Her mother, a famous television comedienne of the late Forties, briefly married to an equally famous bandleader, co-star of *Ranch Montana*, had been outrageously photographed, decorously naked whilst pregnant with Lee. From famous baby to America's favourite toddler, Lee had her first gold disc at nine; her first big movie, *Stowaway*, at ten; and her first Oscar at nineteen for *A Private Shame*.

Then there were the rebel years: the famous falling-out with her parents, the famous *Playboy* centrefold, the engagement to a South American dictator's son, the famous photograph with a black eye, and the ditched wedding which became a famous diplomatic incident. The famous Back on the Tracks tour with her band, Montana, who played live to more people in the world than had ever been together to hear one person before, and sold more records than anyone else ever before. John flicked through the pages of photographs. Lee Montana was famous and sexual as an actor and sexual and famous as a singer, but most of all she was famous for being the benchmark of her gender's sexuality.

John stopped at a photograph of Lee lying on her stomach, asleep on a big white bed, everything sun-bleached. In the cleft of her bottom was a small mole, a famous mole, a small round famous mole. A couple of hours ago he'd seen it, real time. He'd watched it in the faint dawn, stroked it and remembered the raised velvety sensation of the tiny inconsequential thing, private and personal.

Now, here, he touched the page. It was smooth and cool and drew the heat from his finger, leaving a smudge.

John thought two things at once. Well, he thought one thing and felt another. He thought he might just have done the most memorable thing in his life, that nothing he accomplished would ever be as noteworthy or interesting as having fucked Lee Montana, and he felt a huge wave of depression. It was as if he hadn't known what to feel about the night before, as if his head had been waiting for a sign and now, having ordered the event and weighed the ramifications, the pros and cons, he'd decided it was to be baptized a sad thing. John knew that he could just as easily have dubbed it exciting, that fucking the most famous woman in the world like a dog could equally have been a cause for huge celebration and big redletter boasting, but it was in his nature to weave a cloak of misery and disappointment from the most unpromising material.

John stared at the sleeping Lee and picked up a bottle of Tippex. Carefully dipping the crusty, pubic brush he dabbed the mole away and blew on the page. A faint Braille texture rose on her glossy rump.

He snapped the book shut. Putting it back on the pile, he walked over to the poetry section – four thin shelves elbowed in by reference books, obese dictionaries and encyclopedias. Fat fact bores, hogging the attention with regimental-blazer covers, droning on from aardvark to zygote. The poets, slight and shabby, huddled in their pale, badly designed jackets, tight-lipped with false modesty. He picked out a familiar spine, pressed tersely and apologetically between Cowper and Day-Lewis. John Dart. *The Failed Stone*.

There was a small tear on the cream wrapper and the edges of the paper were smudged with a repetitious thumb, the author's thumb. He flicked through the thirty-two pages. These twenty-eight poems, one hundred and four verses, three hundred rhymes, twenty-six half-rhymes, fifty analogies, twenty-seven similes, fifty-two metaphors, a sunset, eighteen landscapes, five beds, one mangle, four thousand words, two buggers, six fucks and one bubo had taken four years to write, and it had been two years since publication. It had sold ninety-eight copies. Sarcophagus, his publisher, who still had 500 available copies, said they were quietly happy with the good reviews. 'A quiet new voice' – the *Poetry Review*;

'Assertive yet tentative' – the *Literary Review*; 'A puritan ear' – the *Yorkshire Post*. Not including fucking Lee Montana, this was his life's work. If the shelf of self-help alternative medicine, women's studies and comparative religion fell on his head this is all that would be left to mark an assertive, yet tentative life.

He took the book back to the chair behind the till and opened it, trying to see the over-familiar words for the first time, to resurrect the intense pleasure and pride he had felt when he'd first held it. It was altogether a pale, light thing; the sense of achievement a diminishing return, like a love affair that had become mostly memories and guilt. He picked a poem, 'Loaves and Fishes', and settled back.

My dad cast troubled bread on calm waters,
Fretted offerings to a heathen pike,
That hung in solitary darkness.
I, beside him, mother-huddled, only child,
I, too, cast hard pellets to the saw jaw.
Kneaded silent prayers to hang on his hopeless hook,
Dreading the jerking, thought-dragging line,
Bone-head breaking the familiar tension,
Gaping in air, ripping our element,
Wordless eyes, sky blind, stone live, thrashing the cold.

John finished gloomily. It wasn't a very good poem, really. It was only a poem because he said it was, and some of the lines were shorter than others.

The shop door opened. It was Clive.

'Christ, you gave me a shock. I thought I'd forgotten to lock up.'

'No. Hello. I got up early, so I thought I'd clear up.'

'Great, I owe you. God, I feel dreadful. Wasn't it amazing last night? Isn't she fantastic, I mean, in the flesh. Amazing. I've been wanking myself stupid over that book all night.'

Clive put a brown paper bag on the till and fished out a styrofoam cappuccino, three Danish pastries and a bottle of aspirin. He was a big Scotsman, fat actually, with thinning red hair and beady sultana eyes.

He was also a novelist, an unpublished novelist, who kept his manuscript in a blue folder beside the lavatory rolls and vacuum cleaner in the back room. John had read it. A seminal erotic fantasy about a deep-sea diver who comes across a nymphomaniac mermaid. He came across her thirty times in the first twenty pages. Clive would sit out the back in his lunch hour, and, with one hand down the front of his trousers, consider the mechanics of coupling with the bottom half of a fish.

'John, I've got a bit of a problem. Where do you think a mermaid keeps her snatch? I mean, I've got him giving her one from behind, dogfish style, but do you think it's possible?'

'Clive, mermaids are mythical.'

'Yeah, I know. But if they weren't?'

'Well, if they weren't I expect they'd lay eggs on seaweed and he'd have to cover them in sperm.'

'No, that's no good. It's not very sexy, jerking off onto kelp. You see, up until now, it's just been snogging and blow jobs. The top half's fine, but the bottom half's a worry.'

'I can see that.'

'Be a help, John,' Clive had pleaded. 'I've got to get the logistics right or no-one's going to believe it.'

'Well, I'm not sure anyone's going to believe a subaquarian welder called Garth McTavish knocking off Ciara, unnatural daughter of Neptune and a haddock, anyway.'

'Oh, very funny. What, in your poetic opinion, would be the biggest problem with shagging a mermaid then?'

'Oh well, now you ask, um, I don't know that getting an erection in the North Sea would be that easy.'

John often wondered at the need, the pressing desire of bookshop sales assistants to augment the stock. He was a poet; Clive was a sex-and-shipping popular novelist; Dorothy was compiling a women's psychic political self-help manual; and Mrs Patience, who owned the shop, was slowly eating her way through her grandmother's recipes with a view to publication. This didn't happen in other retailers. Clothes shops weren't staffed by people who knocked up underwear in their spare time, chemists weren't attended by little Marie Curies and Dr Jekylls. Only around books did the statement 'I'm a shop assistant' come with the qualifying 'but', and a

15

shy manuscript. It was rather pathetic; touching, but pathetic.

Clive stuffed half an apricot Danish in his mouth and flicked through Lee Montana's pages. He put the coffee cup down on *The Failed Stone*. John quickly rescued it and put it back between Cowper and Day-Lewis.

'Christ, what wouldn't you give to get up that?' Clive sprayed Lee's neat pubis with sticky crumbs. 'I mean, what wouldn't you give?'

John realized that here was a crossroads. At this point he could take a deep breath and say, You mean, do it again. Actually, I had her last night. And there would be the fleeting pleasure of watching Clive asphyxiate, and then the disbelief and the questions. Yeah, it was great. Oh well, you know, it was sex, what can you say? Yeah, she did. Yeah, I did. Yeah, we both did. Very beautiful. Look, I don't really think I should talk about it. Well, OK, she asked me. I don't know, I think they're real. The questions going on and on and on. Passed from mouth to mouth, down the phone, out of the door and along the street. The same questions, sly and then brazen, stretching on and on over the days, weeks and years, and the answers becoming automatic, word-perfect. The act becoming a routine, repeated over and over, like a one-hit pop star dogged by the medley of his hit. John looked at *The Failed Stone* and realized that this tiny mote of a thing would disappear under Lee's hard-backed fame, that the guttering flame of John Dart, poet, would be replaced by John Dart, the shop assistant who once got lucky, who won the sex lottery, and he realized that no-one must ever know about last night. He didn't need to say anything. The question was rhetorical. Clive answered himself.

'Christ, I'd give up everything for just one feel.'

That, thought John, is what it would cost you.

'I'd even give up the royalties for *Fins of Desire*.'

John laughed.

'It's OK for you to laugh, but don't tell me you didn't put her to the pork sword last night.'

John's stomach lurched. 'What?'

'Yeah, yeah, I can tell, Mr Higher Poetic Things. You went home and shagged the arse off Petra while thinking of Lee. You shut your eyes and thought of this great arse bucking in your face, and you gritted your teeth so you wouldn't say the wrong name.'

John smirked with relief.

'You're lucky, you've got someone to lay your fantasies. She might be a nagging bitch, but at least she lets you deposit the genetic slime. I've just got Mrs Palm and a pair of Dorothy's knickers.'

'How on earth did you get them?'

'She brought in her laundry last week. I had away a pair of white Marks & Sparks; not exactly the stuff of dreams, but then, masturbators can't be choosers.'

'You're disgusting, Clive. Actually, it's not just that you're disgusting, it's that you're just so predictably, unimaginatively disgusting.'

'Hang on, I'd say a thousand words on anal sex with a mermaid was pretty imaginatively disgusting.'

'Well, it would be if it weren't impossible. Mermaids don't have bottoms.'

'They do.'

'No, they don't. They're fish from the waist down, and fish have one vent – a cloaca – that does the lot.'

'You mean they get fucked and buggered at the same time?'

'If you think of it like that, yes.'

'Oh, that's really disgusting. I'm going to have to completely rethink the sixty-nine oral sex scene. Here, you won't tell Petra, will you?'

'What, that fish only have one hole?'

'No, about the knickers.'

'Probably not.'

'Oh, John, please. Not the old "probably not", just "not" not.'

What was he going to tell Petra? She wasn't going to ask where he'd been last night as a rhetorical question. Clive was right, she was a nagging bitch, and she was also persistent, mean, furious, nosy, humourless, unforgiving and prone to projectile violence. In two years John had never successfully lied to her. He'd tried, of course, in the beginning. Little lies, just to see. Just testing: I'm late because I had to help a Sardinian organ-grinder catch his monkey;

17

I swapped the shopping money for a handful of magic beans; I did put the rubbish out, that's different rubbish; I'm looking after it for a friend. What on earth was he going to tell her? Sod it, something would turn up. If the worst came to the worst she'd think he'd slept with someone else and dump him.

John tried on the idea of being dumped to see how it felt. Not great. Then he thought that this was odd, because if he met Petra for the first time today he'd reckon she was a pretty thorough-going nightmare, which indeed she was, but she was his girlfriend, and girlfriends aren't really for liking, they're there because not having one is worse than having one, because if you didn't have a girlfriend you'd have to nag yourself. He knew why he had to have a girl-friend. If you don't have a girlfriend you become Clive and have fantasies about fish. He just wasn't at all sure why he'd chosen this one, and the answer was that he hadn't chosen Petra at all, she'd chosen him. She and Dorothy.

Dorothy and Petra were best friends. John had got the job here, and after his first day Dorothy and Clive had taken him out for a drink and he'd been given to Petra in the pub, just like that. Dorothy had taken a look at him and thought, You might do for my friend Petra, who works in the photographic studio up the road. She hadn't said that, of course, but John knows that's the way girls work. Girls hunt in pairs. She'd thought, I can't use him at the moment – I've got Slim, the ghastly plasterer – but my friend Petra, she might fancy you for a summer. You can't waste a spare man.

He'd woken up in Petra's bed the next morning to a new job and a new girlfriend.

Petra was fierce. It was her fierceness that kept John attracted to her. Not the fear of it, although there was that, but the heat of it, the burning intensity of her livid filament of commitment. Petra had never had a tepid reaction to anything, never shrugged her shoulders and said, Who cares? Petra cared; she cared for, about and on behalf of everything. Her life was a clenched fist and John was amazed and entranced by that. He was so much the opposite, his life one long shrug, an open palm. Why would this small, wild, urgent, angry, electric girl, day in day out, dash herself on his laconic sighing apathy? John was, he supposed, another of her

18

desperate causes, like the tramps she'd give her taxi fare to, like the articles of grim foreign beastliness she'd cut out of the paper to rant and weep over, like the petitions she'd carve her name in, another lame underdog that warmed itself on Petra's burning ire. And perhaps it was because Petra loved being Petra and John couldn't find it in himself to love being John. She loved her life, not in a self-regarding way, but with an obsessive commitment. She gulped at it, sucked its marrow; she burrowed for the shreds of it with her nails. It was all she had. She wouldn't be passing this way again. Life was a daily jihad, a sworn covenant.

The door opened and Mrs Patience bustled in. It was Mrs Patience's shop. She was a plain, pink woman in her fifties, who, in middle age, had taken to dressing like a teenager, not for any particularly nubile or flirtatious reason; quite the reverse: she didn't have anyone to dress like a grown-up for. Jeans, trainers and a sweatshirt were cheap, comfortable and didn't need ironing. She'd been forced by circumstance to grow into her name. The bookshop had come to her via her husband, a man who had been congenitally ill-suited to the name and who'd run off with a weekend assistant after a month of Saturday nights. Mrs Patience had little interest in books, and as far as anyone could tell she'd never read one. Occasionally she'd open a volume that had been particularly lavishly reviewed or hyped, and would apparently be surprised that it contained merely the same old print. What she really yearned for was to live in the country, to grow soft fruit and win Women's Institute jam-making contests, and live with Peter Bowles.

Although utterly uninterested in the written word herself, she was sensible enough to employ young, over-qualified, but essentially lazy graduates who knew and respected the stock. Clive (Hull, third, Liberal Studies) handled the bulk of enquiries on popular fiction; Dorothy (Exeter, 2.2, Women's Studies and Journalism) did reference and biography; and John (Oxford, 2.1, English) got the difficult ones – classics, poetry, foreign and old men who came in and said, 'There was this book I remember reading on a train going south from Perth, and it's about a man with a huge mole, who hangs himself in Thailand,' and John would say, 'It's a birthmark; he shoots himself and it's in Burma, and it's by George

19

Orwell and it's over there.' For some reason he also got lumbered with children's books, as if poetry were just a step up from nursery rhymes.

'Morning, boys. Oh good, you've tidied up.' Mrs Patience said it as if it were their bedrooms. She treated the staff like the children she'd never had; that is, she bullied them and was embarrassingly inquisitive about their sex lives and ladled out guilt like Salvation Army soup.

'Well, we're never doing that again. I hold you responsible, Clive. You encouraged me. All those ghastly people, and the mess and photographers. Oh no, from now on launches will be strictly Booker Prize possibles, they don't have extravagant private lives and cabinet ministers' memoirs. Well, they may, but they keep them quiet.'

'Oh, Mrs P., it was great. Don't you think Lee was fantastic? Here in the flesh. And it was so exciting. Better than Roy Hattersley spitting all over everyone and signing all of Stephen Hawking's books by mistake.'

'Yes, come to think of it, that was pretty ghastly. Did we ever get any of those back? Thank God nobody ever actually reads them. No, Clive, no more personalities. I understand why you liked her; those absurd breasts.'

'Come on, Mrs P. There's nothing absurd about them; they're fantastic.'

'Clive, dear boy, they're plastic.'

'They weren't.'

'Oh, really, of course they were plastic. So much static she was picking up lint.'

Clive turned to John. 'They weren't plastic, were they?'

John was straightening classics, Aristophanes to Xenophon. He felt himself blush. 'I don't know, I didn't notice.'

Mrs Patience huffed, 'Oh don't be daft. You couldn't take your eyes off them. When you were helping her sign copies I thought you were going to dive down her cleavage. You must have noticed all those scars.'

'No, really, Mrs P. I can't say that I did.'

'Anyway, at her age' – Mrs P. opened the till with a flourish –

'they can't have been real. No, none of it: face, breasts or bottom. I mean she's only a couple of years younger than me, and you don't see me walking round in a bottom like that, Clive.'

Clive caught John's eye and puffed out his cheeks.

'God, what a lot of cheques.'

'Yes, we sold loads of paper tits last night,' said Clive.

'Richard Briers bought one. Well I never, I thought he'd have more taste.'

The door opened and a customer hesitantly stepped in, with that half-witted grin that people reserve only for dentists' waiting rooms and bookshops. Their conversation stopped. Mrs P. didn't like the staff talking out loud when punters were in the shop. Bookshops should be contemplative, so they spent most of their day hoarsely whispering, making the atmosphere uncomfortably tense.

'Put some music on, Clive dear, would you.'

'Not *The Four Seasons*,' added John. He went back to straightening classics and thought that maybe he could make a fortune out of producing a tape of bookshop music. 'Winter' from *The Four bloody Seasons*; 'The Slaves' Chorus'; Ella Fitzgerald singing Cole Porter; Dave Brubeck and Philip Glass. It was Ella, the first note instantly making mid-morning feel like the middle of the night. She started telling the solitary customer about the man she loved as he flicked over Lee's breasts.

The door banged open again and Dorothy and Petra barged in, panniered with canvas bags and rucksacks.

'Sorry I'm late, Mrs P.,' Dorothy shouted without looking.

She said this every morning, and Mrs Patience smiled and raised her eyebrows.

Daughters!

Dorothy and Petra went into a huddle in the alcove, shielded by interior design and cookery. John watched them from the corner of his eye. Petra hadn't said good morning – a bad sign. After a minute's finger-jabbing and head-nodding she walked over.

'So?' Her small dark eyes glared from under heavy brows.

Boyish is how you'd probably describe Petra. Slight, flat-chested, thin-hipped, bony-ribbed, long-jawed, thin-lipped, with spiky, cropped black hair and a weak-tea complexion, running to dirty

21

mauve under her eyes. She had the nervous look of an Algerian urchin. She bit her lip, a habit not of nerves but of anger. John put down a pile of Balzac and smiled far too broadly.

'Hello, darling,' he whispered. 'Nightmare last night, wasn't it?' Shit, he shouldn't have started talking about last night; it sounded guilty. 'Is that the jersey I gave you? It looks great.'

'Where were you?' she hissed.

'No, really, it suits you.'

'John, where were you?'

'When, darling?'

'Don't lie to me, you shit.'

'I haven't lied. I only said the jersey—'

'No, but you're about to. Oh God, I can read you like a book.'

John almost said, 'Well, I do work as a bookshop assistant,' but didn't. Being facetious wasn't going to help. 'You mean last night. God, I got drunk. I was going to—'

'We waited an hour for you. I ordered you a pizza.'

'I'm really sorry. It took longer to get them all out than I thought, and then Berryman from the *Literary Review*, of all people, asked me to have a drink with him. He said there might be some reviewing.' The lying came suspiciously easily; he hadn't thought it out until it was past his teeth. John examined Petra's face fretfully.

A pause.

'Fucking hell, John. You're such an idiot. He doesn't even commission; he's a sad old queen who's after your bottom.'

'Do you really think so? Blimey.' She'd bought it – his first successful lie in the back of the net. Yes. Come the hour, come the mendacity.

The telephone rang once.

'Where did you sleep?'

Shit, shit, shit. Where did I sleep? Where did I sleep?

'John, it's for you.'

Apologetic smile. Not that damn apologetic. Saved by the bell. John walked over to the till and picked up the phone.

'Hello.'

Phone calls in shops are communal; they belong to everyone or anyone who wants to listen.

'Hello, John.'

'Yes.'

'It's Lee.'

All John's organs leaped for their closest orifice. For one hellish moment his insides were like a bomb warning in a mortuary. He could feel the intense, hot glare of Petra's eyes on the back of his head.

'John, are you there?'

'Yes, yes. Hello.'

'Hello. It's Lee, you remember, from last night.'

'Yes.'

'Right, would you like to have lunch?'

'What?'

'Lunch, today.'

'Oh!'

'Well?'

'Ah . . .'

'John. You do remember who I am, don't you?'

'Yes. Er, yes to both.'

'To both what?'

'Never mind.'

'Look, do you want lunch?'

'Yes please. Yes.'

'Good. Where?'

'Where?'

'Yes. Any ideas?'

'No.'

'Oh, right. You only live here.'

'Right.'

'Well, what about my hotel?'

'Yes.'

'One o'clock?'

'Yes.'

'You're not on medication, are you, John?'

'No.'

'Good. OK. Look, do me a favour. Read a book or something before you get here. It would be nice to have a conversation.'

'Yes, of course. Bye.'

John carefully replaced the receiver. He looked round and five pairs of eyes intently met his. The customer held Lee's book, frozen.

'A customer,' John said, in the direction of Mrs P. 'Foreign, I think. No, well, definitely foreign. Japanese, I would imagine, or perhaps Chinese, Malaysian or Indonesian.'

'What did they want?'

'Want? Want? Oh, she . . . she wanted . . . actually she wanted to know if I had Lee Montana.'

PEOPLE WITH MONEY, PEOPLE WHO CAN HAIL A TAXI WITHOUT feeling in their pockets first, think London is big in two dimensions, like the map says it is, but for poor people, people for whom hailing a cab is to hock lunch, London is bigger than that. It's arranged in layers. There are places and parts of London they can't go to, and which are terrifying if you don't have money. The Connaught is one of these places. After a sweaty jog up Park Lane, John arrived at the hotel.

Nobody will actually stop you walking into the Connaught, or places like the Connaught, but if you're poor you'd be better off if they did. If there were a door policy, like a club, if a man on the door in a folderol greatcoat said, 'You, you and you,' and told the rest of us to piss off and try again next week, we'd know where we stood in the order of things. But they don't. You walk in and your shoulders prickle, waiting for the tap and the muttered, Can I help you, sir? and the restraining hand on the upper arm. There's no place more aggressively foreign than a grand hotel in your own town when you're wearing yesterday's socks and have seventy-eight pence in your pocket.

John got to the restaurant without being fingered. He got to the lectern with the reservations book, like a low-church Bible, and its list of the elect. The tail-coated maître d', who studiedly didn't look him up and down, whose eyes never strayed from John's, who smiled easily and said, in a quiet, unilaterally European voice, 'Can I help you, sir?' didn't click his fingers for security, but everything about him was forbidding.

How could all the outward signs be so fawning and proper and polite, but the essence so unequivocally hostile?

'Miss Montana. Er, expecting me for lunch.'

'Of course, sir. Your name? Would you mind waiting here?'

The waiter moved on electric castors into the dining room and returned a fleeting moment later with apparently the same smile on his face, but somehow its message was different. Less. More. Servile, but felinely welcoming.

'Miss Montana is expecting you, sir. Now, I am sorry, but you'll need a tie.' He managed a look of mild apology, as if to say, Of course you and I don't give a fig for petty sartorial rules, but the rest expect it, whilst at the same time implying that arriving without a tie was an act of infantile rebellion. A tie of simply stupendous hideousness appeared, as if by magic, between his manicured fingers. It was fat enough to be an elephant's condom and bright enough to attract swarming bees. It was made of some slippery material which had never seen field or beast. Miserably John tied it inexpertly round the soft collar of his polo shirt. The thinner end hung down to his crotch. The waiter smiled like a father watching his son go on a first date, and also like a waiter who has better things to do. How can this man smile in so many different ways without moving a muscle? thought John.

'And the jacket, sir. I'm afraid that it's not acceptable. We have one here.'

Again, as if out of the thick, static atmosphere, he produced a sports jacket that had plainly been left behind by a jocular twenty-five-stone Hawaiian bandleader. It was a vile shade of lemon and John resignedly handed over his denim coat and disappeared up to the tips of his fingers, which just made it past the gold-buttoned cuffs. The waiter gave a quick, appreciative glance at his deft piece of ritual humiliation and picked up a menu, 'We'll ignore the jeans, shall we, sir?', and led the way into the dining room.

John felt as if he were stark naked, being led to the stocks with a pig's bladder tied to his willy. Rich, bored eyes fell on him like hungry magpies, avaricious for *schadenfreude* and disgrace. The room watched, with huge pleasure, this ignorant hobbledehoy, paraded in the tar and feathers of a civilized polite society, and then they realized where he was being led and their dish of hot humiliation was cruelly ripped away and replaced with the thin gruel of envy.

Lee sat at the head of the room. She looked sensational: cool, poised, unbelievably handsome and palpably exuding a let's-do-it-on-the-table sexuality. John was immensely pleased to see her.

'John, you got here. My God, where did you get that coat?'

'Sorry, um, they made me wear it.'

'Oh, don't be silly. Alonzo, take it away.'

'Madam. I'm afraid . . .'

'Don't be afraid, Alonzo,' she flashed him a hooded hint of a look, which lasered through his sponge-bag trousers and poached his scrotum. 'You don't want me to have to look at a thing like that over my Dover sole, do you?'

'Of course not, Miss Montana. I'll get the gentleman's coat.'

'Oh, John, take that tie off. This country, can you believe it? You know, you go and invade or invent the most laid-back people on the planet – Australians, West Indians, Christ, even Americans – and you still haven't learned how to undo your top buttons.'

'Only in places like this, and this is only here to remind Americans and Australians and West Indians what they're missing. The rest of us are actually pretty relaxed.'

'You do have some other clothes, don't you, John? You're not going to be one of those fans who never wash because they've touched a star?'

'I had to go straight to work, I haven't been home yet.'

Alonzo returned with the jacket. 'Can I get you a drink?'

Lee said, 'I'll stick with water.'

But John took a deep breath and said, 'I'll have a large whiskey, no ice.'

'Oh well, if you're going to get smashed, I'll have a Vodka Gibson,' said Lee.

'What on earth's a Vodka Gibson?'

'A martini with an onion.'

'Sounds foul. I'll have one of those too.'

'Instead of the whiskey?' Alonzo's pen hovered.

'No, as well. At the same time.'

'God, how wonderful, a man who still drinks. Do you smoke too?'

'Rather. And I don't take any exercise. A day isn't over until I've had a full alphabet of additives and a pig's bottom of saturated animal fat.'

'Perfect. A real English dude. Well, John, here's to an intense and, in all probability, short friendship.' Lee leaned forward and raised her glass in a small, ironic toast, but she didn't drink. She held John's face with a gaze and bathed and stroked him in her full, concentrated attention for a long moment. It felt like a convection heater, and he saw for the first time what film buffs meant when they said the camera loved a face. Without the prophylactic of a lens Lee's gaze was like turning your own to the sun. He bathed in it and felt it soaking through his skin.

'It was fun last night, wasn't it?'

'Yes, wonderful. All those people. I suppose you're used to the photographers and—'

'No, I meant us. Fucking; that was fun. The book thing was work.'

'For both of us.'

'Oh? Sorry?'

Lee caught his face again, but with a glacial look. He realized that she could shut it down as easily as she could turn it on.

'Sorry, I'm still, well, rather . . . I can't really believe we, you know, slept together.'

The look remained alabaster.

John stumbled on, 'I mean, why me? Why did you choose me?'

'John, we chose each other. If you mean, how come you got lucky with a film star, well, film star is my job. I'm famous for a living; I fucked you for fun. What do you want to eat?'

There was a long pause.

'OK, I'm sorry. I chose you because you're my type: sort of lost, rangy, awkward, uncomfortable, with nice hands. OK. And you're not in the business, you're not going to want a part or to be my agent or anything. You work in a bookshop and you've already got my book.'

There was another long silence. The menu was a particularly

27

impenetrable document, with the dishes named after old stars of the Forties and Fifties, as if they were daffodils. John humped his back against the covert glances of the rest of the room. Alonzo came back.

Lee glowered, 'What the fuck's Sole Cole Porter? Look, never mind, give me a fish that doesn't have a plaque on Hollywood Boulevard or has been arranged by Joe Loss.'

'And to start, madam?'

'Another Gibson.'

'I'll have the same,' said John, 'and chips.'

'So, what else do you do, John?' Lee asked, searching in her bag for a cigarette.

'Um, well, I write a bit.'

'Write a bit. What? Novels, journalism, begging letters?'

'Poetry.'

'You're a poet.' She looked up and studied him and then broke into deep chuckles. 'Of course you are, what else.'

'I'm pleased that makes you laugh. It's always a pleasure to bring a little added happiness to already exciting lives.'

'Oh, don't be pissed; it's a private joke. I just split with someone.'

'Con Mackintosh. I know, I read about it.'

'Yeah, old Con. God, may all his shorts shrink in the wash. A man so vain that when the wind changes he spins round. Anyway, when I dumped the bastard he couldn't believe it, that's how vain he is. And I told him he had all the poetry of a sumo's moist-wipe, and he said, "Well OK, honey,"' she did a deep, drawling impression, '"you go to jolly old England and get fucked by a fucking poet," and I have. That's funny. Are you good?'

'As a fucking fuck or a fucking poet?'

'As a poet.'

'I don't know. Yes, perhaps. I could be, maybe.'

'Give me one.'

'What, here on the table?'

'A poem, poet.'

'I can't just do it; it's embarrassing.'

'Come on, just slip me a couple of verses. I've never been wooed in verse. That's what you poets do, isn't it? Woo. Well, lay some of that woo on me, goddamn it.'

28

John slugged back his drink and furrowed his brow, took a deep breath and said, 'You left a tampon in the loo.'

'Is that the title?'

'No, it's called, "All I Have to Offer". That's the first line. Shut up.'

> You left a tampon in the loo,
> Lid down,
> An elegant billet doux.
> And a stain on the sheet,
> A rusty, Jungian blot on our copulation book.
> Tears on the pillow,
> Sour, musk sweat,
> No need to lipstick on reflection.
> Got the message,
> No strings attached.

'God, that's some wooing.' Lee reached across and took his hand. 'Phew, sanitary stuff on a first date, you really cut to the chase.'

'OK, your turn now.'

'I don't do poetry.'

'No, you do what you do.'

'You want me to act?'

'No, sing something.'

'Oh, John, come on. I can't. Not in the goddamn Connaught.'

'Yeah, yeah. Coward.'

'OK.' She bent her head and thought, and then, in a low, warm, husky voice, she sang 'Miss Otis Regrets'. Slowly the voice grew stronger. Slowly the hum and clatter of the restaurant died away. By the last verse the room was silent. John felt the bitterness, humour and sadness in the song through his skin, and his scalp prickled. When she finished there was a ripple of applause.

'Perhaps we should have had the Sole Cole Porter.'

After that, lunch was fine. Better than fine. There was a slight awkwardness over the bill. John reached tentatively for his cheque book.

'Hey, don't be an idiot. Poets don't pay. I asked you; that's the etiquette.'

As they got up to leave John looked around the room and thought it must be the most charming and cosily sophisticated dining room in London. He simply loved it. He beamed at Alonzo, shook his hand, and Alonzo beamed back.

'Come on,' said Lee, taking his arm, 'let's go shopping. Show me the tills of old London town.'

'Lee, I can't. I've got to go back to work. What's the time? Oh Christ, I'm already an hour late; she'll kill me.'

'Oh, go on. I don't know anyone here. Please call in sick or something.'

'Lee, I can't.' But he did.

'WHERE DO YOU WANT TO BE?'
Where indeed. John caught the brown eyes of the driver in the rear-view mirror. They were alone in the car: Lee and her shopping had been left at the hotel. John sat in the vast expanse of inhuman-looking leather of the Mercedes.

'Oh, a tube station. Anywhere really. I can walk from here.'

'Don't be a twat.'

John didn't know much about conversing with chauffeurs. Indeed, he didn't know anything, but he didn't think being called a twat was how these things usually started. He examined the eyes again. They were still brown and impassively questioning. 'If you went down a hole in the ground, queued for a ticket, waited on the piss-slick platform and then crammed yourself into a carriage, where would you finally emerge?'

'Oh, Shepherd's Bush, I expect.'

'Right. Why don't we cut out the messy bit and I'll take you straight to Shepherd's Bush?'

'OK.'

'OK.'

'Thanks. If it's not too much trouble.'

'It's not too much trouble.'

30

John looked again at the eyes, but they'd gone. Just the white lights of the road shuffling away behind him. The big car slipped through the chaotic streets. Most people drive in competition; traffic is the enemy. This man drove as if the traffic were another element. He surfed with a languid ease, with minimal, smooth movements, undulating around the eddies and shoals. John came to the great limousine truth: a man driving in rush-hour traffic is teetering on the edge of cardiac meltdown and psychosis, but a man sitting in the back, being driven through the rush hour, is a zenned-out calm bubble of *que será será*. It's all in the control. There's a great peace in letting go, abrogating responsibility. Delivery vans and taxis, bike messengers, cream saloons, become an environmental variable, like rain or traffic lights. John went with the flow, handed it over. The car smoothed into the kerb on Shepherd's Bush Green.

'This all right for you?'

'Yes, thank you.'

The driver got out and opened his door. He was a tall man in a double-breasted suit; a long, smooth brown face; symmetrically fine features, like a mask, unlined, relaxed, without expression; neither enquiring, servile or threatening. Just brown eyes which had a hint of resigned sadness, a veiled memory.

'Right then. I'm Hamed.' He held out a big hand.

John took it, surprised. Was this what chauffeurs were supposed to do? 'Hamed, hello, thank you. John Dart.'

'Yeah, poet. I'll be seeing you.'

'Yes, I'm sure.'

There was a moment as the brown eyes searched his face for something. 'Look after yourself.'

The car purred away. John watched its tail lights blend into the river of traffic with a childish sense of loss, because it was in his nature not to feel anything without examining it afterwards, like a vegetarian staring into the lavatory, and he walked slowly and considered it had been a good day.

Lee, of course, was remarkable, wonderful, beautiful, funny, confident and famous. John was amazed at how succulent fame was, just on its own. It didn't have to be accompanied by anything

– talent, humour, kindness, interest – it just was. It was like the pheromones that moths follow; it was like the auroras that only batty women called Doris, with sixth senses, can see.

There had been a lot of firsts today. The first time he had seen that shopping could be anything other than the plughole of poverty, that buying things could be entertainment, that it was a game with prizes for everyone. He had been to Bond Street before, of course, with his parents at Christmas to look at the lights, but never like this, not going in past those terrifying doormen. He'd never pushed a doorbell to get into a shop, never been given a glass of champagne by an assistant, never seen the vast variety of things, stuff, this and thats, all the artifice and imagination laid out to entertain and divert. Shopping was quite different when it wasn't hunt-the-reduced-ticket. The bag swayed happily at his side, like a soft, mute pet.

He turned into a side street, the yellow streetlights turning the tulips and laurels of pretentious little terrace gardens a dirty brown. Televisions flickered through the curtains, studio laughter leaking irony.

In the distance the Maggie O'Doone was lit up like a National Trust folly. Two years ago Maggie's had been the Earl of Grafton, but he'd undergone major surgery to emerge from a rather frayed and unfriendly aristocrat into a large-breasted, tipsy Irish peasant, a not altogether happy or successful transformation. Where the Earl had affected a risible, genteel hospitality, Maggie had attempted to become the good time that was had by all. Both had been effortfully repellent. Maggie's was John's local only because it was the closest pub to Petra's house, and therefore where he spent most of his time.

Dorothy's bike was chained to a bench beside the penicillin-green door. Damn! They were already here. Petra would be here, and Clive and all the rest. The bag weighed heavily in his hand. He'd hoped to be first, so he could hand it covertly to Sean behind the bar, but there was no way he could explain away a £1,000 burgundy velvet jacket as an impulse buy. Oh, I was just passing Oxfam, and you know what, a millionaire had just died and his widow brought in all his ninetieth-birthday presents. I got this for a fiver. No way.

John opened the bag and pulled aside the tissue paper. The velvet was soft and thick, as soft and thick as ... He searched for the simile. As soft and thick as I'm being. What was he thinking of? A velvet jacket? When would he wear a sodding red velvet jacket?

'Because you're a poet,' Lee had said, as she pulled it off the rack. 'Please, just try it on.'

And he'd said, 'No,' in an agony of embarrassment and awkwardness.

'Just put it on, for Christ's sake. For me.'

And so he had, and he'd looked in the mirror, with her behind him, smoothing the back, pulling the hem, and then leaning her chin on his shoulder and offering a professional smile. The reflection was a shock. They looked like a lifestyle photo in a glossy magazine; the sort of snap you might find in the middle of the thin layer of photographs in a hardback biography. Good together – blonde and dark. That was surprising, but the real shock was himself, the John he saw grinning a big easy grin. He never grinned, never even smiled at mirrors or cameras, but here he was, curls of hair falling onto his claret collar, a beautiful girl, chin resting on his shoulder, staring back with this cheesy, confident, canary-got-the-pussy grin. Lee had taken his cheeks between her hands and kissed him on the lips, her tongue just dabbing his mouth. It was the first time they'd kissed that day. He'd assumed they weren't on kissing terms, that the sex had been what famous, beautiful film stars did and that it didn't count as an introduction.

'You're very handsome,' she'd said. 'Velvet. It's your writing coat. Your wooing coat.'

John put the tissue back and paused, and then, with a sigh, he pushed the bag roughly into a dustbin. It wasn't him; it wasn't real. Not part of his life, this life. Not needed on the voyage. It wasn't fair.

Then he kicked the door and the pub lurched out to embrace him. The bright, confused light; the sour smell of rancid beer towels and sodden ashtrays; the noise of football on the telly, Queen on the jukebox and bollocks at the bar; the chunk, chunk of the fruit machine; the turd-brown tables and chairs; the cowpat-flock banquettes; the phoney bog-Irish mickery on the walls – hurling sticks and peat shovels, green-eyed colleens and red-faced piggy-eyed boyos with bony fingers, gripping thin stout; the crusty carpet and the rancid-butter paint; and it all yelled a big, slurred, Hello. Welcome home.

'Look who it isn't.'

There in the regular corner sat Petra and Dorothy, flanked by Clive and Dom and Pete, dole-poor performance artists. Shepherd's Bush's sadder Gilbert and George in identical school suits, Doc Marten's and oily, military haircuts.

'Ho. The wandering troubadour returns. Where the fuck have you been? You're in for such a bollocking Monday,' shouted Clive, happily.

'Sorry, I just couldn't face it, you know. I felt really rough.'

'Yeah, yeah. It's OK. Actually, she hardly noticed. It was pretty quiet. Here, what are you having; it's my round?'

'Pint, thanks.'

Clive swayed off to the bar. John slid in beside Petra and waited to see what the reaction was going to be. He always took his cue from her mood; it was like going out with a praying mantis. She turned to him.

'Hello, lover. Where have you been?' she said in a whiny, childish voice. 'Missed you,' and she kissed him, big and hard on the mouth.

Petra always kissed him as if he'd just been pulled out of the Thames, her mouth wide, her teeth locked, and he got her whole, flat, cold, lagered tongue, which lay on his like an exhausted dab. Disengaging, she drained her glass and squeezed his thigh.

'Have a good time?' Dorothy asked beadily. She considered herself Petra's better half, her protector, her hard man. She played bad cop to Petra's good cop, and vice versa. That's what she considered sisterhood and feminism were all about: protecting your mate's back; kicking ball while she snogged.

'Yeah, sort of. I just went for a walk and then I went to the Tate, you know.'

'What was the Schwitters show like?' Dom chipped in.

'Well . . .'

'Mind your backs.' Clive came back with the beer and slopped it onto the slippery table.

'Lived under a table and barked like a dog, didn't he?'

'Connor Mackintosh? Really? I didn't know that,' said Clive.

'No, Kurt Schwitters,' said Dom and Pete together.

'Who the fuck's Kurt fucking Schwitters? Thought she was going out with Con Mackintosh,' said Clive.

'She does. Did,' said Dorothy. 'She got dumped, according to the *Guardian*.'

'Oh well, then it must be true. He's the dog's bollocks, though.'

'Connor Mackintosh is?' asked Clive.

'No, dummy. Kurt Schwitters.'

'Who the fucking Christ is crappy Shitters? I thought we were talking about Lee Montana.'

'We were. Now we're talking about Kurt Schwitters, at the Tate, where John spent a solitary, cultural day communing with art,' said Dorothy, as if talking to a simpleton.

'Oh, I see,' said Clive, seeing nothing at all. 'So, I still don't know who he is.' He looked enquiringly at John.

'Um, he's an artist. Interesting really. Er. Lives under a table and barks like a dog.'

'Fuck. At the Tate. There's some bloke under a table at the Tate, barking? Is he naked?' Clive added.

'Er, yes, sort of. Except for his collar, of course. He didn't do a lot of barking when I saw him, just sort of growled a bit.'

Dom and Pete snorted and rocked.

'No. That's outrageous. Has he got a big cock? I mean, does he growl at the birds? I mean, can you go and stroke him?'

Dom and Pete erupted, spitting beer and jogging the table.

'What have I said?' said Clive.

'You plonker. He's dead,' choked Pete.

'Dead. There's a dead, naked geezer under a table at the Tate. That's outrageous.'

Petra sighed and looked at the ceiling. 'He's been dead for years, Clive. He's a dead artist. His paintings are on at the Tate. John's pulling your leg.'

John sank back into his seat and took a long gasp of beer. It tasted thin and chemical and cheap. He tried to remember what a Gibson tasted like, but couldn't. A wave of miserable exhaustion descended on him. Petra's hand on his thigh felt like lead. His head ached. The argument got louder and more pointless. Childish swearing, posing, posturing non sequiturs, unfinished sentences, unanswered questions, stupid repetitions. A typical evening in the pub, with Clive taking up his favourite position as the voice of *Daily Mail* reason, and the other four beating him down, like furious rolled-up copies of *Time Out*. Because it was art and not football they thought it counted as debate. The evening shunted towards closing time. The rounds of beer, the swaying visits to the bog, the broken cigarettes, the final pooling of change for shorts, the double vision and stumbling. Clive ending up under the table, barking, Petra's slurred tongue in his ear.

Sean came and took away the glasses and they barged, unsteadily, into the street. Dom and Pete went off to get a doner, Clive said he'd sleep on Dorothy's sofa if that was all right, and they began to move home. Petra took his arm and snuggled into his side.

'Miss me, babe?'

'Fucking hell. Look at this!' Clive shouted. He was swaying under the lamp post, holding something up. 'Look at this.'

'Put it down, idiot. You can't go through bins,' Dorothy sneered.

'No, no, it's new. It's still got the label on it. Fuck. A thousand fucking quid.' He struggled to put the jacket on, but kept missing the arm. It was too small and bunched up under his pits, the vent gaping over his fat buttocks. 'Perfect fit. It's velvet. I'm having this.'

'Who'd throw away a new jacket?' Dorothy asked suspiciously.

'Fuck knows. Some old poof. Colour clashed with his knob end probably.' Clive did an exaggerated queer mince up the street, holding a limp hand out like a teapot.

'Squirt-shitters. You look like a nice boy.' He blew a kiss at John and burped.

John said nothing. There was nothing to say.

'Are you coming back for coffee?' said Petra.

Although they'd been going out for over a year now, and slept together most nights, this invitation had become a little ritual. It had started as a small bonding joke, but now it annoyed him. It was a reminder of who held the controls, an affair by invitation and Nescafé.

'You had a nice day, though,' she added.

John sat in the tiny, mildew-smelling bathroom and waited for the furious immersion heater to dribble a stuttering four inches of water into the gritty bath. In the kitchen Petra and Dorothy argued with Clive about the correct way to make toast. Finally he lay in the tepid, greasy water, which lapped his knees, and stared at the rail of grey bras, T-shirts and knickers over his head. He smeared his junctions with a cat's tongue of soap, sluiced himself like a cold otter and dabbed himself dry on a clammy towel which imparted a faint smell of pickled poodle. Then he went, as invited, to Petra's bed. She sat, propped up with pillows, eating cheese on toast and reading.

The room looked like a Hendon Police College search-warrant-training area. John had no idea what colour the carpet was, even if there was a carpet. It would have been quite redundant. What always amazed him was how much of the stuff seemed to be under-wear when Petra rarely wore any, and when she did it was always the same pair.

The other thing was the colours. The room looked as if it had been smeared with a wet parrot, yet all she ever wore was faded black. John picked his way up the shallow gradient to the promon-tory of bed. Petra lit a cigarette. Smoking in this room added a devil-may-care frisson of danger.

'I've been thinking' – she brushed the crumbs onto his side – 'did you ever get on to the *Literary Review*?'

'No, why?'

'You should try to get some more reviewing.'

'You said I shouldn't bother.'

'God, John. You're so lacking in ambition; you're such a wimp.'

'But—'

'Your whole life is a series of buts. Sometimes I think you spend your entire day just thinking up reasons not to do things. Like today. If you're going to take a day off, why don't you do some-thing useful with it, something that might make some money?'

'Oh,' John sighed, 'money,' and turned off the light.

The cigarette cast a faint orange glow that rose and fell as Petra inhaled. There was a hiss as she dropped it into that morning's teacup.

'It's no good just sighing about money. We . . . Oh shit! What's the use? Let's fuck.'

John hunched his shoulders. 'Petra, please. I'm dead tired.'

'No, come on. I want to shag.'

'Darling, in the morning. I really don't feel like it.'

'Just quickly. What's the point of having a prick for a boyfriend?' She pulled him roughly onto his back, like a shepherd about to geld a sheep.

'And switch the light on.'

Fucking with the light on was an inviolate article of liberation for Petra. She was certain that her parents, back in the dark ages, had never done anything but couple in coal-hole blackness, face to face, eyes shut, fingers in their ears. Shagging in a spotlight was proof that she wasn't her mother, when so much else of her life told her she probably was. Illuminated sex and frequent sex. Petra wasn't particularly libidinous by nature: she didn't seek out fleshly pleasures or care what she ate; she didn't yearn for the sensuality of satin and fur; she refused to pamper herself, even by her own meagre resources – she wouldn't even put Radox in the bath; she didn't polish her nails, or pluck her nipples, and she shaved her armpits and legs only when her tights sparkled with static. But sex wasn't so much about pleasure as her membership card to the late twentieth century. Sex was proof that she was a healthy, modern, liberated, functioning person. She devoured magazine articles on sex and read manuals in the shop, not for the mechanics but for the statistics. She couldn't afford to join in with most of the glittering, giggling culture that rushed by, but she could get her gutful of the sexual revolution. So, if 30 per cent of the population had orgasms, she'd be one of them. If 20 per cent of women instigated sex, she'd be there. If the average couple normally had sex two times a week, she'd have it four. Copulation wasn't so much the entertainment of the poor as their one tenuous, slim, slippery hold on the consumer society.

Petra sat on John's thighs and tugged at his supine penis. He folded his arms over his eyes. She tugged and waggled for a couple of minutes, sighing and imploring under her breath. Nothing.

'Oh, come on, John. You're not trying.'

She bent over and fed the thing into her mouth, like a stick of gum, mumbling and vacuuming for as long as her growing irritation could bear. Oral sex wasn't really Petra's forte. As a couple, mouth stuff wasn't their strong suit. Palate-to-genital contact isn't a matter of aptitude, or desire, or credit, so much as hygiene, and hygiene is one of those everyday niceties that count as a luxury if you're poor. That's not to say that poor people are dirty – heavens no – but cleanliness is a virtue, like a front room, more for show than use. Petra spat it out.

'Come on, John, for Christ's sake. Concentrate. You do it.'

Apologetically, and with an irritated familiarity shorn of embarrassment, he manipulated his unoffending cock. Petra sat back and mumbled her pudenda with two fingers, like a tired bank clerk counting fivers. And for a moment they quietly fiddled so that romance might burn; the separate, voyeuristic foreplay of young moderns. If it's worth doing, do it yourself.

'What are you thinking of?' Petra asked.

'Nothing.' John really was thinking of nothing. A dark-brown sense of limpness and weariness.

'I'm imagining a biker who came to the lab today. Black, great dreads under his helmet.'

This was Petra's unique selling proposition in bed. She didn't do blow jobs, but she did do fantasy. She had great fantasies. She'd read that it was important and had taken to imaginary sex like a chief inspector to fishnets.

John, needless to say, wasn't that good at it. It embarrassed him; it tapped into his shame and awkwardness. If really pressed he could undress and précis plots from books and films, animate pictures from the National Gallery and bra advertisements, but not with any conviction, and certainly with no erotic effect.

'All in black: leather trousers, boots, gauntlets. He asks me to sign for his package, so I take the clipboard and write "I want you to fuck me" in the box. He smiles and, gently but firmly, takes my

39

head and kisses me. His tongue is long and hard and tastes of mint. We don't say anything, but he pushes me to my knees in the middle of the shop. It's difficult to undo his flies. I put my hand in. It's hot and damp, and then, Christ; it's amazing, huge. It just goes on and on, as thick as . . .'

'As a magnum? A jeroboam? A methuselah? A bitter pump?'

'A fucking huge salami. Shut up, John.'

He sighed at the predictability of her metaphor.

'It struts out of his trousers.'

'It can't strut. Technically, strutting—'

'Shut up. It struts. And he pushes my head down, and, like, I'm really frightened by it, but I open my mouth as far as it will go and I can just get the end in; and it tastes like . . .'

'Bassets Allsorts? Dreft and TCP? The last girl he delivered to?'

'Shut up. Salty and sort of animal.'

'Ah, smoky-bacon crisps.'

'OK. I suck him a bit and he takes his clothes off until he's just wearing his boots. I hook my nails into his really taut bottom and he pumps and nearly chokes me.'

'How did he get his trousers off over his boots? I mean, does he take his boots off and put them back on again?'

'Shut up. I pull my dress off and I'm naked. He reaches down and roughly grabs me between the legs. I can feel his long, bony finger slip inside me. His thumb slides into the crack of my bottom and lifts me like . . .'

'A bowling ball? A six-pack?'

'Like I was light as a feather. I'm on my back on the table, and it's just the right height. My legs are spread wide. No, my legs go over his shoulders, and with both hands he fits, no inserts, his huge, purple-headed, hard, hard, hard, African thing into me, and fucks me long and slow, at first, and then harder. All the boys in the office are watching, and they get their cocks out and start wanking. They're really weedy and pasty and white compared to my black biker and . . .'

Petra's voice grew huskier and higher, her head was thrown back and her fingers had finished with the fivers and were now rapidly flicking small change.

'Oh, for Christ's sake, John, just bloody well fuck me.'

Despite the tacky monologue he was approaching something resembling seaworthiness. Petra lay on her side with her back to him and pushed her bottom at his groin. Lifting one leg, she put her hand on her pubis. John shuffled round. With a bit of rootling and squeezing, and a couple of bent false starts, this weedy, white-boy, suety apology of a thing slipped and skidded through Friday night's fatty swing doors. He waited a couple of beats for Petra to adjust to an old house guest, and then started the rhythmic pushing and pulling, trying to magnify the small twinges of sensation into sensual ardour.

They usually fucked like spoons, cold and mottled. It had grown, through habit and without consultation, to be their congress of choice, after a process of slow elimination. They'd stopped screwing standing up against the front door, with all their clothes on, treading on the shopping, and they'd stopped screwing with her on his lap on the armchair in the living room. They'd stopped doing it bent over the bath and leaning on the kitchen table and they'd stopped doing it like dogs in bed, because Petra had thought it too submissive. They'd stopped doing it with her on top because they'd lost the mutually agreed rhythm to selfishness, and they'd rarely ever done it missionary – face to face – because it made her think of her parents. So they ended up in this cul-de-sac of fucking, side by side, but separate; with the light on, but without eye contact. The libidinous equivalent of couples eating dinner together in silence, except it wasn't silent.

Petra kept up her wishful prattle with her hand pressed into her mean, unkempt front garden, with John digging away in the back. He held her bony hips, closed his eyes and tried to fill his head with nothing. He never thought of anything when he had sex, not even the sex.

The grey polyester sheets corrugated under his thigh, he felt the grit of crumbs and the sticky spirals of dead skin, navel lint, toe jam, cock curd and bed mite dung roll into black rubber shavings to burnish his jagging body. His breath grew rapid, spit abseiled from the corner of his mouth, sweat trickled into his eyes and hung like dew in the hair on his chest and the tendons of his knees. The

41

room grew warm and fetid with the smell of vinegar pits and warm, meaty groins, with piss and beer breath and glum laundry. The weekend aroma of a thousand transient bedrooms. Through the wall a television clucked and chuckled.

Petra's mumbles sounded like an angry, exhausted child. Just the words now; the monosyllabic, limited lexicon of love: stuff, wet, thrust, stuff, fill, big, wet. She came, all in a rush, falling over herself to get to the screwed-up moment when all the synapses fire at once. That short, stabbing, blacked-out, blissed-out second. She hissed through clenched teeth. John felt the constriction without excitement. He plugged on, shortening his run up. Petra's prune-fingered hand, nails scoured and bleached clean, moved round and cupped his hanging, mossy scrotum.

Her touch was surprisingly tender and unexpected. It flashed a memory. Lee turned over and smiled. It was just a glimpse – the big eyes and white teeth, through a veil of shiny blond hair, a hand on his thigh – but it was enough. John emetically spurted a drizzle of thick sperm, which felt like a fish bone, and it was all over.

Welcome to the weekend.

They lay for a long moment. Petra took back her hand, her body sloughing his cock. She switched off the light and lit a cigarette. The orange tip glowed like a distant watchtower. John turned over and drew up his knees. The bed was chilly and uncomfortable. Exhaustion numbed him. The image of Lee turning faded in the dark. Petra blew her nose and took a drag. A long, blue, last gasp of smoke.

'I do love you, you know,' she said, in a brittle, clear voice.

John woke late. He got up, sprinted to the lavatory and covered the seat, wall and floor with a fine drizzle of pee. Why does the penis become a dysfunctional garden sprinkler after you've fucked with it? He quietly ferreted through the clothes in the bedroom for something cleanish to wear. Pulling on a pair of jeans he watched Petra with a burglar's fearful attention.

Urchin pretty, the back of her neck vulnerable, her hair half-term boyish, her little, pinched, elfin face still tense and furious. Even in sleep her heavy brows were furrowed and her teeth ground slowly.

On her dark-rimmed eyes the long lashes rested like nervous insects. John was almost overwhelmed by a great wave of emotion; it crashed onto him in a roaring, suffocating minute of deep fondness and pity, flecked with the spume of guilt. He came up with a gasp. He almost got back into bed to kiss the white nape of her neck, but he didn't.

He was just gingerly letting himself out when the sitting-room door opened and Clive staggered into the hall, wearing a piss-stained pair of Y-fronts. He scratched his fat tummy.

'Morning. Are you going to get some milk?'

All over poor Saturday-morning Britain these are the first words spoken. Milk, the currency of rented accommodation, the cause of rows, bitter feuds and that hideous corner-petrol-station chore. Whoever called human kindness milky never shared a flat.

'No, I'm going home to write,' John whispered. 'Will you tell Petra I'll call later.'

'Oh God, be a mate, get some milk. I'm dying.'

'OK. I'll leave it on the doorstep.'

'And some cornflakes. I don't think there's any coffee, and, oh, a packet of fags. And a paper.'

JOHN LET HIMSELF INTO THE LARGE SOUTH LONDON HOUSE WHERE he had lodgings, praying the landlady wasn't in. He owed rent. It wasn't a lot, but it was more than he had, and Mrs Comfort wouldn't evict him in any case, which sort of made it worse. She was his aunt's best friend; they'd been in the chorus line together.

His Aunt Sonia, the only romantic member of his family, had been a Bluebell Girl, who'd travelled the world in plumes and G-strings and could still do the splits if plied with enough gin, and whose breasts were still impressive. It was said, though not out loud, that his father had fallen in love with her and married the other, younger, plainer sister as a sort of consolation. Aunt Sonia now lived with a conjuror turned hotelier in Hoccombe.

'We did them all, love, but I wasn't like Sonia. I was just tits and bums and a big grin in the back row. Sonia was real talent,

43

wonderful. Men just loved her, like your dad. Lor, she had every-one. Not in a nasty way, not sordid; she just liked having fun. We all did. It was a grim time, the Fifties – bomb sites, tinned ham.'

Mrs Comfort had kept the memories but lost the figure. She was a big, pear-shaped woman, given to elasticated waists, fry-ups and a sweet, silent West Indian tailor called Des, who had grizzled white hair and huge hands which could thread the tiniest needle. He would cup her vast bottom in his huge palms with a painful tenderness and shake his head as if he couldn't believe his luck.

John's room was on the top floor. There were three other rooms let out. The occupants, mostly foreign students, seemed to change monthly, and apart from the odd dinner with Mrs Comfort and Des John kept himself to himself.

He could hear a radio in the basement kitchen, and Des's deep baritone singing along. Quietly he crept up the stairs. The house was cosy and tasteless in equal proportion, with shiny, pastel, pudenda-pink paint and thick, glans-purple carpet, framed the-atrical posters, paintings of girls with cats and French vases with Japaneseish birds.

His room, under the eaves, was in marked contrast. White and sparse, with an iron-and-horsehair bed, militarily neat, and grey blankets; a hideous but comfortable hessian armchair; a chest of drawers; a cupboard and a gas fire. Nothing on the walls but a bookcase. There were neat piles of books in the corners and a tin trunk that passed as a coffee table was full of more books. Books were John's hardbacked comfort, his identity, and also a musty reproach.

Against the far wall, with its back to the window, was a desk. A great Victorian bureau, with drawers and finial brass right-angles and keys, and things that slipped and folded and stuck and stuttered and smelled of Latin declension. There was a neat stack of white paper, two biros and a postcard of Philip Larkin. He wasn't quite sure why he had Larkin there; he wasn't particularly a favourite poet, but he seemed to fit the ascetic dreariness of the room – those glasses, the absence of expression. John would have liked to have had Byron, in colour, in Greek kit, but, well, he really wouldn't have gone.

Petra had given him a framed picture of *The Death of Chatterton*. John had been silently furious. Chatterton, the mock poet, the tragedy and manqué, the sentimental faker of doggerel, romanticized to show that poetry was indeed a blood sport. Chatterton would have made the room a sitcom set. She didn't realize, none of them realized, how tenuous the life of a poet really is, how fragile the gap between truth and wishful thinking. Sometimes the only thing that made it live was the sound of saying, I am a poet. Like shouting, I believe in fairies. The death of poets isn't that poisoned, languid rigour with wilted petals on the bed, it isn't the spot of blood on the handkerchief, it's the slow drip, drip, drip of confidence ebbing away, the encroachment of life until the observed overwhelms the observer and the words stick in your throat. There would come a day when someone would ask, What do you do? And instead of saying, 'I'm a poet,' 'I work in a bookshop' would come out, and he'd be reduced to just writing thank-you limericks and verses for retirements and weddings. He'd no longer be a poet, just a bloke who might have been one. Once you give in there's no going back. John Dart, Poet, needed a poet's room; he needed everything that could staunch the slow dribble of disbelief and self-doubt.

He sat at the poet's desk, picked up the poet's biro, lit the poet's cigarette, kicked the poet's bin, looked at the stubbornly pristine, poemless, blank paper and tried to see poetry with a poet's eye. He thought of Petra asleep and wrote, 'I thought of you asleep,' and then he crossed out 'thought of' and wrote 'watched', and then crossed out 'watched' and wrote 'saw', and crossed out the 'a' from in front of the 'sleep' and then crossed out 'I' and put back 'watched' and wrote 'slumber' instead of 'sleep', but crossed it out immediately and wrote 'sleeping', and then crossed out the whole lot, screwed up the paper, threw it in the bin and started again. 'I thought of you in bed,/You thought of a black messenger in leather.'

There was a soft knock.

'John?' Des slowly opened the door. 'Hi. Long time. There's a phone call for you. A chick called Lee.'

Lee sat, or rather spread, over the back seat of the big Mercedes in

a sea of magazines, water bottles, scripts, handbags, tissues, tele-
phones and faxes. Hamed opened the door and John got in.
Through the smoked windows he saw Des standing on the steps
and Mrs Comfort in the front-room window. John thought it was
probably the way people looked when aliens landed in their
gardens. He was glad they couldn't see into the car.

'Hi, again.'

'Hello.'

'John, before we start, do you want to see me?'

'Well, of course.'

'You're not just being polite or anything?'

'Heavens no. I . . .'

'You see, you haven't called and, you know, generally, when I go
to bed with someone they, like, phone or something. You do want
me? Sex wasn't some weird, British good-manners deal, was it?'

'Lee, no, no, really. No, absolutely not. It's just, well actually—'

'Well, John, why don't you kiss me hello.'

'Sorry, it's just that, well, you know.'

Lee leaned across the seat, pushing stuff onto the floor and offering her mouth. He kissed her politely; she kissed him back less
politely. They kissed for a long time.

'So, why didn't you phone me? Or kiss me?' She kissed him
again.

'Well, it sounds silly, but it's your . . . well, it's because you're so
famous. I don't know. I don't know what the form is; I don't know
any other famous people.'

Lee smiled. 'I understand. It's awkward for both of us. I don't
know any infamous, or unfamous or not-famous people. Well, I do.
My maid's not famous. Actually, she is famous, for being my maid.
Anyway, I don't know anyone else here. My PR people gave me a
list of actors who'd love to see me or be seen with me, but Christ,
I know the type – phoney, cool Royal Shakespeareans, with badly
capped teeth, who patronize you by the yard. They turn up in
Hollywood in droves on every economy flight, and sneer at everything, grovelling for any job at half the going rate. I'd much rather
have you.'

'Where are we going?'

'Out to lunch, somewhere. Where is it, Hamed?'

'Lower Swell, by Stow-on-the-Wold.'

'There. Do you know it?'

'No.'

'We're seeing Oliver Hood. Do you know him?'

'Only by name. He's in the theatre, isn't he?'

'Right. He's got a project. We're going to see if we like each other.'

'Why am I here?'

'You're my accessory, my handbag-holder, my drink-getter, change-carrier, cab-fetcher. Oh, for Christ's sake, John, you're here because I want to spend a day with you. No, I want to spend a night with you. I rather fancy sleeping with you again. I wasn't going to mention it, but seeing as you're so goddamn suspicious' – she laughed – 'I thought you wouldn't mind being my boyfriend for the weekend.'

'Sorry I'm being such a git. It's just hard to believe. This sort of thing doesn't really happen to me.'

It happened. They got past the crawl of traffic waiting to get onto the M25; Hamed moved into the fast lane and the Mercedes shot west smoothly on a hiss of tyres. The CD played a compilation of road music. Bruce Springsteen ran incongruously towards the Cotswolds. Lee, elegantly slumped back in the car, draped her feet over John's thighs and read *Variety*. John watched the smoked landscape stream past and felt the almost manic elation you get only when you're leaving a city at speed to a basic quadraphonic rhythm. He realized how rarely he left the pavements. If you were poor, getting away from the city was a weary prospect of bus stations, bruised muscles, luggage grating your shins, running down escalators, queues and loonies, beery breath and snivelling children. Except for the biannual exodus home for Christmas and bank holidays, the last time he'd left the city to go anywhere new had been to his grandfather's funeral in Leeds. This sense of release and freedom was almost painful. How easy it was with a Mercedes and a Hamed, how damned pleasant. John ran his hands up Lee's silky thigh and felt his peripheral vision expand.

'How do I look?' Lee said.

John reluctantly pulled his head from the window.

'Fabulous. You know you look fabulous.'

'Of course. But do I look appropriate? Do I look like a Saturday afternoon in Lower Swell with theatre folk?'

She was wearing a light-mauve cashmere suit, with gold buttons and a skirt that stopped just above her knees, and a pink satin shirt.

'Well, the last time Larry and Vivien had me down to tiffin we were all in blazers and cravats. God, how should I know if it's appropriate?'

'Because this is your damned country. Is this how intellectuals playing at the rural look dress? This meeting is very important.'

'Well, perhaps you're a bit overdressed. I'm really not the person to ask, but it looks a bit, I don't know, a bit Barbra Streisand.'

'Barbra Streisand!' Lee shrieked and kicked his thigh. 'Oh my God, my God. Hamed, stop the car now. I can't.'

'There's a service station in a mile, Lee. Will that do?'

'Quickly. You bastard.' She laughed and pouted. 'Anyway, you look pretty nerdy. Did you get that T-shirt off a dead person?'

Hamed parked the car and opened the boot. It contained two huge suitcases and half a dozen shopping bags spewing with clothes, shoes, hats, tissue paper and cardboard boxes. John grinned.

'This is the most expensive car-boot sale in Britain.'

'A what?'

'Doesn't matter.'

'What about this?' She held up a leather miniskirt.

'No, definitely not.'

'What about this? This? John, tell me what I should wear.' She looked at him with real desperation.

He laughed, not believing that anyone could be this concerned about clothes on a Saturday.

'Fuck you,' Lee shouted. 'Fuck you. Help me, please.'

'OK, OK. Let's see. Have you got any jeans?'

'Jeans? Like blue jeans? Yes. I don't know. Sure.' She buried her head in the clothes and came up with a faded pair of men's Levi's which had holes in the bottom and the knee.

'Those are great.'

'These are the jeans I wore at high school. I only keep them to prove I can still get into them.'

'They're perfect. And this.' John pulled out a sawn-off, white Lycra top with no sleeves.

'But that's what I wear to the gym.'

'And this.' He produced a gossamer white lawn shirt with baggy sleeves.

'You mean I should look like a slob, as if I was at home?'

'Exactly. Look like you're at home. Walk into any English room and generally the person with the worst clothes is the most important.'

'You're not pulling my leg? Promise? Let's get a cup of coffee anyway. I'll change in the john.'

They walked through the carpark, past the lines of weird First-World refugee cars, hunkered down on their exhausted rear axles, which you only see at motorway service stations. Inside the canteen were the gormless, dispossessed drifting of England on the move. Fat women in sweat pants beating surly children; huddles of permed pensioners; gents in pale-blue-and-white sightseeing caps; humpy-backed youths phut-phutting at video machines; families from building-society posters; frantic, school-bullied children on treats; country women with bursting, shit-desperate labradors; a few mired bikers; lads on a spree; young girls with old eyes; married men fishing for casual boys; lorry drivers with prison tattoos of women who'd got under their skin and then pissed off; root-faced, Northern, ooh-ah lads; runaway Scotsmen with their hearts in their mouths; wanted men; unwanted men; women meeting their husbands' bosses; fat-arsed women called Maureen and Doreen and Shirleen, starting again on hard shoulders. A great crusade of democracy, freedom, consumption, boredom and disappointment, a pervading sense of irritability and repressed violence. Pissed off with road maps and fetid air and the rattling fourth-hand car, with nothing on the radio, and cones and roundabouts and travel sickness and wasted time and somebody else's rural idyll outside and the waste of the sunshine and each other. The grim, crappy transit cameo of enjoying yourself, getting out and going for a spin.

49

Lee walked confidently, obliviously, through it all, with Hamed close by her side. She was stranger than a creature from another planet. She was from the place that was more unreachable than Mars, she was out of films and TV, out of fantasy, out of thin air.

They sat at a table full of tomato-ketchup-smeared plates, plastic cups and snot-screwed napkins. Lee leaned forwards and took John's hands.

'You're sure you're right? The jeans? It's not a bit Marilyn and Strasberg? Trying too hard? You're sure?'

'Look, it's lunch in the country. You'll look fabulous. They won't notice what you're wearing, you're a star.'

'Oh yes they will. I'm sorry to come on so weird about this, but it does matter.'

'Oh, it doesn't matter,' said John. 'I mean, it doesn't matter that you've come on weird. Not that . . . anyway.'

'Thanks. Now, what about my hair? Off my face.'

John smiled.

Over her shoulder he saw a table of men huddled together; they were staring at Lee. All around them John caught the blank, hard glares on the slowly chewing faces. A couple walked past; she looked, and looked again, and tugged at her partner's sleeve and hissed. The mutter of conversation dropped an octave and grew sibilant. John looked around. Dozens of eyes, unembarrassed and blank, looked back. Lee went on talking about her hair.

'Does this always happen?' John interrupted.

'What?'

'The staring strangers watching you?'

'I don't know. Yes, I suppose. They recognize me. You're absolutely sure about my hair?'

'Doesn't it bother you?'

'My hair? Oh God, constantly. I cannot tell you.'

'No, the staring.'

'I don't really notice. Yeah, sometimes it's annoying. Don't catch anyone's eye. I'm used to it, all my life. I usually wear shades, but I left them in the car.'

The room watched, as if waiting for something to happen, for a narrative, a script, music, lights and a camera. Confirmation. The collective look wasn't pleasant; it was borderline threatening, unsure. Who did this girl think she was, teasing them by looking like Lee Montana? *The* Lee Montana. And if it was Lee Montana, why was she here, surprising them like this, when they weren't ready, didn't have their cameras, hadn't shaved, washed their bottoms, bought condoms, had a drink? They had places to be. It was confusing motorway fact with their glittering fantasies. They stared and waited. John's skin prickled.

A little girl of seven or eight, no more, started walking across the room. Her mother bent down, blowing smoke and instructions into her ear, and pushed the child hard in the small of her back so she stumbled and then walked slowly past the other tables. Halfway she lost her nerve and, with a sour look, turned back to her parents. Her father, presumably, the *loco-parentis* man, mouthed a swear word and flicked the air with the back of his hand. The girl continued on her mission. She was an unprepossessing child, overweight, with a fat little tummy and thighs, in a dirty pink towelling jumpsuit with a teddy bear on the front. She had tiny red nails and plastic pearl earrings. She got to their table and stared at Lee.

'Are you Lee Mont . . . ?' Frowning to remember the rest, on the verge of tears.

'Sure am, honey.'

'Will you write your name?' She plopped a napkin and a chewed eye-liner pencil on the table.

Lee smiled and wrote quickly. The stubby wax stuck in the paper, tearing it. The little girl grabbed the napkin and ran for her mother.

'It's her, Mum.'

It was as if everyone in the room breathed out at once. Hamed came back with a tray. The group of men were up on their hind legs, stretching their necks like hounds scenting a corpse. Someone started tunelessly humming one of Lee's songs, someone else laughed. Children began to edge forward in twos and threes, chivvied by parents.

Suddenly there was a woman hyperventilating with excitement and nerves beside them. She had long, lank hair, dyed a liver purple, a tiny miniskirt and thick pale piqué thighs.

51

'Oh, I love you,' she said, in a mad, whiny voice. Her eyes were bleak and intense. 'You changed my life; you're an inspiration. I'd be dead if it wasn't for you.'

She punched two grubby fists towards Lee. John thought she was going to hit her, but she turned them over at the last minute and held them out in a gesture of supplication. The wrists were criss-crossed with smooth white scars.

'I'd be dead if it weren't for you. I love you.' Imploringly, 'I love you.'

'I think we'd better go.' Hamed took Lee's elbow and led her from the table.

'Love you.' Desperate, accusatory.

John stumbled to his feet. The tray slipped and splattered on the floor.

'Oh please.'

The movement triggered the room. Chairs scraped and fell, knives and forks tinkled. The volume expanded with shouts of, 'Lee. Lee. Over here, Lee.'

They moved to the exit and the sunshine. People barred their way, pushed and stumbled.

'Lee. Over here. Lee. Lee. Wait.'

Faces leered out of the scrum, blank mouths opened, working, shouting. 'Over here. She's over here.'

'Oi, oi, oi. Lee, suck my cock,' bellowed from just behind them. 'Suck my cock. Fuck your arsehole. Arsehole.'

People pushed and thumped. Hamed had his arm round Lee's shoulder, the other hand outstretched, palm flat, pushing. Lee kept her head down, eyes fixed to the floor, shoulders hunched, arms crossed, making herself as small as possible.

John was quickly elbowed aside. He was punched heavily in the kidneys. Something tried to work its way under his armpit. He looked down and it was a very small, very old man, his mouth pulled and fixed in a panting grin, pushing away, stumbling over the kerb. A child fell at his feet screaming; he tried to reach down, but couldn't.

'Lee, Lee. Please, please. Shag me, shag me.'

Just ahead of him a woman strained over a wheelchair, as if it were a battering ram. The front wheels caught ankles. 'Excuse me, excuse me.' The invalid in it was bent over, almost at right angles, a huge, flabby head rocking back and forth, eyes rolling, mouth wide, tongue mewing, bent claw arms flailing.

Hamed reached the car and, in a surge of panic, John thought he might be left there in this insane Gadarene crusade, and that the crowd, furious that their goddess had transubstantiated into a German motor, would turn on him and tear him to shreds out of love and devotion.

He shouted, 'Lee, Lee, wait,' and pushed and elbowed like the rest of them, clouting a teenage girl in the back of the neck. He wriggled his body towards the car. Hamed saw, reached out and reeled him in. He levered open the car door and piled in. With a finger-shearing ferocity it slammed shut. Lee was sitting back on the tan leather seat. She wrinkled her nose and gave him a big smile.

'I thought you'd got lost.' She smoothed her hair.

Hamed started the engine. It was dark inside. The windows were entirely obscured by pressed faces, cheeks, hands and nostrils smeared against the glass, a small Bruegel tableau. Beside John, a middle-aged man with huge blackheads opened his mouth wide and, lips inverted, suckered onto the pane like a guppy. He licked the glass with long circles of glutinous, mucus-yellow tongue. Another face winked maniacally. The car rocked and thumped, like a muffled tattoo, 'Bang, bang. Lee, Lee, Lee.' Slowly they edged through the crowd, Hamed expertly negotiating the other parked cars.

'How're we doing for time, Hamed?'

'Fine.'

As they picked up speed the people fell away. John turned and saw them out of the rear window, shouting obscenities; gaping, livid faces gesticulating obscene semaphore. The car turned onto a slip road. There was only one left, sprinting behind them: the scarred girl, her thick thighs juddering, a stream of snot smeared across her cheek. They accelerated back onto the motorway and she came to a juddering halt and hoiked up her skirt, pushing out a thick black pubic triangle in a final, panting exclamation.

'Jesus Christ! Does that happen all the time?'

'What? The fans? Yeah, mostly. If I go out without protection. You know, I don't spend a lot of time in service stations.' Lee was supremely unconcerned.

John felt adrenalin-sick.

'That's not the worst we've seen, is it, Hamed?'

'Lord no. They were really quite well behaved.'

'I'm sorry to be so pathetically naive,' said John. 'It was horrible.'

'Oh, sweetheart, don't be sorry. I like it that you're shocked. It is shocking. I'm just used to it.' Lee took off her jacket. 'The worst are the Italians. They try to fuck you standing up on the move, all of them, even the women and kids. Pizzas, everything. In Italy it's just jig-a-jig up against you. *Bellissima, bellissima.*' She unzipped her skirt. 'The Spanish are worse actually; they smell. They get really aggressive, and they don't frot you, they grope. It's like a million untrained gynaecologists.' She slipped her shirt over her head. 'Oh, but they're nothing to the Argentinians. Argentina. I took one look out the hotel, ordered an armoured car and went back to the airport.'

Lee had taken off all her clothes. She put her hands behind her head and pointed her stark body at John. 'Now, before I become the girl next door, why don't we make love?'

'What? Here? Now?' John shot a look at Hamed.

'Hamed's seen worse, haven't you, Hamed?'

'Never seen anything in the back, love. Not even when I had Def Leppard and the black hookers.' He laughed.

John had, of course, made love in the back of a car before – his father's Cortina with Helen Dibbs, his plain, scrotum-shrivellingly intelligent girlfriend for one term at university. He'd gone out with her principally because she would sleep with him with negligible emotional and, more importantly, economic outlay. She was the daughter of a bishop and had an appetite for sex on a par with her hunger for thirteenth-century ecclesiastical Latin. His mother had insisted on separate bedrooms, giving Helen his one, with the plastic Spitfires and the nightlight, and John had slept on the army camp bed in the utility room. But after dinner Helen had dragged him to the garage and the hurly-burly of the Cortina. He remembered the smell of the lawnmower, and the dog hairs and crisp crumbs that stuck to her bottom.

The memory was tinged with humiliation. His mother, cheery and terrified of his university chums and the sudden strange cuckoo her son had become. His mother in her faded best apron, in the kitchen that smelled of bleach, asking if they'd had a nice walk, and Helen smirkingly saying, 'Lovely, Mrs Dart. John showed me a short cut.' And his mother apologizing for everything, and saying, 'No, not those glasses,' to his father. 'Not those napkins,' and putting a new cake of Imperial Leather in the loo. And his father starting every sentence with, 'In our day,' and talking about the University of Life and quoting Kenneth Clarke.

After the sex in the Cortina they'd hiked round Greece for the summer, which was where Helen had told him she was staying behind in Mikonos to have better sex with an Australian photographer, a Greek waiter and two German lesbians.

'You're sweet, but you're provincial,' she'd said as they'd separated the contents of their rucksacks. 'It's not just the sex. Well, I suppose it is. It's not that you're not any good at it, although you're not actually terrible, it's just that you're frightened of it. You think that someone's going to ask you to sit an exam in fucking. You're a revisionist swot in the sack. Sorry. Look, I know you're trying to get away from your roots, but you wanted to dig them up and plant them somewhere sunnier, and I'm not somewhere sunnier.'

John remembered all this as he pulled off his trousers. Yes, he'd had sex in a car before, but never one that was moving. Not one that was bowling through the sunny Gloucestershire countryside, and not with a naked megastar with perfect breasts.

Hamed thoughtfully put Lee's platinum album on the stereo, so her soaring voice could camouflage her soaring voice. It was fantastic, not because the sex was great, which it was, but because he was putting a prettier picture in an old frame, drawing a thorn. Now, if someone were to say, 'Have you ever done it in a car?' he could smile and say, 'Well, yeah. In a chauffeur-driven limo with Lee Montana,' and not, 'Yeah, in my dad's Cortina, in a garage, with a bitch who left me.'

'We'll be there in ten minutes, ma'am,' said Hamed.

'Do I look OK?' Lee asked as they pulled into the small road and then onto a smaller farm track.

'You look delicious, like you've just been fucked.'

'And my hair?'

'That's particularly fucked.'

'Great. It's a really difficult look to fake, that. And one that's particularly good on me.'

They stopped outside a largish, half-timbered farmhouse beside a mill-race, with a long, glossy, sloping garden, which had a trestle-table set for lunch, and a louche group of people, surrounded by newspapers, looking Bloomsburyish. A tall man sauntered across the lawn towards them.

Lee arranged her bosom. 'Just relax, act naturally. You're my boyfriend. This is important, so don't get drunk, insult the host or make a pass at the ducks.'

Hamed opened the door and Lee got out for her alfresco entrance.

'Lee Montana. How wonderful,' Oliver Hood declaimed, as if he were introducing an act at the Palladium. 'You found us all right?'

'Oliver! Well, it's a pleasure to meet you at last. This is John Dart, Oliver Hood.'

'Nice of you to come.' A cursory handshake and a pat on the upper arm.

John recognized Hood, of course. The most famous impresario in the theatre. He'd been the Sixties *enfant pétulant* of the Royal Court, and had staged a year that was still mentioned as being a golden season. Well, it still was in his programme notes. He'd moved on to a national theatre, where his petulance had grown grey and grizzled. He had completed ten years which were generally considered by people who consider these things to have been a reasonably good fist. He then left to direct a great and saccharinely lachrymose musical, which was essentially a *tableau vivant* with carnival effects, set to bowdlerized Puccini. It and its worldwide clones made him a millionaire. From this vaunting height he'd stepped down to pluck Hollywood. However, Hollywood didn't fancy plucking with this supercilious, thoughtlessly snotty, histrionic Limey nobody. He made, at vast personal expense, a version of *The Odyssey*, set in the deep South in the Sixties, with a black Odysseus. Hood had returned to London, leaving behind his third wife and a new lexicon of sworn enemies. Blooded, but better balanced, he returned to the boards as an impresario, having grown the obligatory beard, collected a new wife from the stage door and worked full time at getting his peerage.

'Come and meet everyone. Can we do anything for your chauffeur?' He pronounced the word the way he imagined Molière might have said it.

'Don't mind me, mate,' Hamed said cheerily, in a cor-blimey accent. 'I know a great little boozer just down the road, I'll get a bag of scratchings. Give us a bell, doll.' He turned and touched an imaginary peak to Lee.

'Right, everyone, you hardly need telling, but let me introduce Lee Montana.'

The Bloomsbury Group looked up with varying degrees of ennui.

'Gilbert Frank you probably know for having had the most sensational season at the old National.'

Frank was a short actor with a big head. He was blandly, symmetrically handsome, with a large nose, which made the public think he was upper-class.

'And my wife, Betsy, and daughter, Skye.'

They might have been sisters; Skye looked the older and definitely plainer. She was an overweight girl, with a roll of tummy hanging over her tight shorts, her sagging bosom squeezed into a bikini, thin lips and a precipitous absence of chin, as if the bottom half of her face had been eroded. Betsy was slim and had that sinewy, gym-starved look. John wondered what she was in training for: the weekly bout of holding back the clock, or holding on to her husband? She looked at Lee from under her brows, the way a boxer might size up an opponent at a weigh-in, with the sudden realization that she'd been mismatched.

'And John, sorry.' Oliver looked at him apologetically.

'Dart,' said Lee.

'Dart, of course. Sit, sit. Drinks are on the way. Stu's just mixing some more Pimms. That all right for you both?'

A man walked across the lawn carrying a tray and glasses.

'Here he is. Stu Tabouleh.'

Stu put down the tray. 'Nice to meet you.'

'Hello, Stewart. I haven't seen you for years,' said John quietly.

'Good gracious. John Dart. Well, hello. How bizarre. I mean, how simply fabulous. You look wonderful . . . different. Dear heart, sorry,' he said. Looking round at the ensemble, 'We were at Oxford together. Well I never, what a shock. Are you still a poet?'

'Yes, and obviously you're still in the theatre.'

'I'm up to here in theatre, darling. Still hanging round carnival folk.'

'Stu is the most talented director of his generation. You must both go and see his *Volpone*. Stunning,' Oliver added smoothly.

John remembered Stewart at college. They'd both hung around the Dramatic Society. John had been rather intimidated and had spent a year trying to pluck up the courage to see if anyone was interested in a one-act monologue he'd written in quatrains. Stewart, on the other hand, arrived a silent, spotty, long-haired Geography student looking for artistically topless girls. John threw his play into the Isis early one morning in a spray of Byronic tears and Australian lager, and then spent a term being an ASM before drifting back to pubs and solitary, secret poetry. But for Stewart the Drama Soc. had been a complete conversion. Amongst the plastic coffee cups, dusty costumes, papier-mâché props and towering pseudery he'd discovered the makings of, if not the person he was born to be, then a person he could live with. He threw off the surly cynicism of too-clever-by-half Northern provincialism and donned the motley as if it were a Californian religion. Within a term he was wearing make-up and kimonos to lectures and calling the beadles Nellie. John and he had never really been friends, they'd rather despised each other, one for his book-and-pint dowdiness and the other for his screaming arch-phoniness. But John had always secretly envied Stewart for being able to turn from a provincial grub into an urbane butterfly. It was, after all, what they'd all come to university for. The hope that they'd slip the earth-bound expect-ations of their parents and headmasters and the little rows of shops where everyone knew their name. To be able to leave all that behind like the first stage of a rocket, and watch the first nineteen years of your life fall away and burn as you soar. Stewart had done it, becoming a show queen by simply averting his gaze from breasts to chests. A simple twist of orientation and he'd been free, but John had remained like an astronaut, waiting for a spaceship that looked less and less likely to come. This Stewart, handing round Pimms on a Gloucestershire lawn, had changed again. He'd cropped his hair and wore a baggy straw-coloured suit. The sibilant operatic drawl had been replaced by a soft Radio-4 approximation of his original Northern accent, and again John felt the envy of someone who could slide from major to minor. John sat at the far end of the long table, between a scowling, muttering Skye and Betsy's empty seat. She spent most of her time ferrying food back and forth across the grass.

Skye used a brief dramatic silence in a story of some old, dead, theatrical knight, who'd wet himself on stage as Hotspur to whisper, loud enough for the upper circle to hear, 'I've had as much of this as I can stand, why don't we go down to the river.'

'Yes, what a good idea, darling.' Oliver smiled. 'Take John down to the mill pond. We really ought to talk some business here, wonderful though all this banter is. Betsy, sweetheart, when you've cleared up will you bring out the Armagnac?'

Skye led John in silence across the lawn, through a rickety gate and down to a hot, reeded river. It was a dark pool surrounded by willows, a secret, beautiful place; a complete, tiny, perfect canapé of England. A rotting punt clagged in weed, a water vole stretching a perfect arrow in its wake. Words and rhythms swam lazily into John's head. A pheasant cackled over the water, midges and dragonflies swarmed and dipped their thin strata; it was all so utterly pristine and perfect, so quietly confident, so . . .

'Do you have any coke?' Skye slumped heavily onto the bank.

'No, sorry.' John sat beside her.

'Shit. I could really do a line. I was praying you'd bring some. Hollywood people usually do. Bitch Betsy does her nut if I do it, but film people bring it, so it's OK. I'll roll a joint. OK?' She pulled the makings out of a back pocket. 'You're not really Hollywood, are you?'

'No, I'm Shepherd's Bush.'

'Well, you've certainly fallen with your knob in the butter. How did you manage that?'

'What?'

'Well, getting hold of Lee Montana. Fuck, she's great. They're just so much better in America, aren't they? Women. Stars. They're proper stars. Really fucking huge, not the scraggy, tight-snatched wannabes like Betsy. Can you believe that over here they think she's a fucking sex symbol.'

'You don't like her?'

'I don't mind her, she can be OK, it's just all that theatrical bollocks. I hate all that luvvy crap. Listen to that divvy, Gilbert. What a tosser. He's famous for making a sherry commercial. You'd think he was fucking Johnny Depp. And he's a lousy shag,' she added as an afterthought. 'Give me a break. They're all such crap, all that theatre stuff.'

She passed the joint to John. He took a drag. It was thin and tasted of dried tobacco and cardboard.

'I suppose you've grown up with it; it just seems ordinary to you.'

'Yeah. Perhaps. Listening to Dad spunk; it's such a wank. I wish we'd never left LA; it was great there. It was great. And now we're in the fucking back of fucking beyond, doing fucking pantomime. He's such a selfish bastard, my dad. I hate him for it.'

'What do you want to do then?'

'I'm an actor.'

'But I thought you hated it.'

'Oh no, only the stage. I don't want to be a fucking glove puppet. Films. Back in Hollywood. As soon as I've fixed an agent I'm going back. There are a couple of projects in the pipeline. Dustin said he wanted to work with me.' Skye unhooked her bikini top and took it off. Her large breasts sagged with relief, the pale, flat nipples squinted at the ground. 'I'm going to be a star. A tarot reader on Venice beach told me. "Honey, you're going to be famous." It's the only thing, you know, being famous, being a star. I've been sort of famous all my life, with Dad and my mother, we've always been a famous family.'

John looked down at this grotesquely miserable fat teenager with

60

her soft, stretch-marked flesh, her red shaving rash, the butterfly tattoo on her thigh, her stubby, spatulate feet, her thick, dimpled knees, the gritty sweat in the folds of her stomach and the tide mark of orange foundation round her neck. This whole ghastly, fleshy edifice arranged like a gross cartoon Venus in Arden, this perfect, subtle, beautiful place.

'How old are you?'

'Fifteen. I know I look older, right?'

'Yes, yes, you do.'

'I know what you're thinking, but I'm not going to fuck you, OK.'

'OK.'

'But we can fool around if you like. I give really good head; I learned it in Beverly Hills. My Dad used to make me give it to him when I was young.'

'Really?'

'Yeah. I don't remember it, but I had a friend who said I had Repressed Memory Syndrome, because everyone with anorexia has it, and I had anorexia one summer. What's Lee like in bed?'

'Much the same as she is standing up.'

'No. You know what I mean.'

'Yeah. But it's not polite to ask.'

'Fuck you. I bet she's amazing. I bet she gives great head and you've got a massive knob. Film stars only go for massive ones. Only the best. Here, do you want a suck then?'

'Not just at the moment, but thanks for the offer.'

'It's no big deal. Just sex, just networking. So you're a poet then?'

'Yes.'

'And you've got a treatment for Lee?'

'No.'

'You want to direct?'

'No.'

'Act?'

'No.'

'You don't want to be famous?'

'I don't think so.'

61

'Fuck me! Shit or get off the pot, man. Why are you shagging Lee Montana then?'

'I think it's time we got back.'

'Yeah, I need a drink.' Skye wriggled back into her bikini top. She hefted herself to her feet and leaned on John's shoulder. A nail-bitten, childish hand groped the top of his thigh. She smirked, 'Yeah, pretty impressive,' and walked on ahead.

John turned back to look at the mill pond. The black water had turned quite gold. A squadron of swallows did victory rolls just for the hell of it, just because they could, and a pigeon rhythmically cooed in the vaunting summer sublimity of it all.

'Ah, here come Skye and John,' Oliver boomed, 'just in time for tea. Did you have a dip, love?'

'Don't be ridiculous, Dad. The water's disgusting. Can't you build a pool, like we had before?'

Oliver turned to Lee. 'You see, spoiled by Hollywood. It's exactly what we've been talking about. That's the absolute metaphor. Hollywood is a chemical, transparent, hygienic pool. Over here the theatre is an ancient mill pond, dark, mysterious, deep and endlessly variable. Dip into us and you'll have to get your hands dirty.'

'We've got muddy bottoms,' added Gilbert, helpfully.

Lee gave John a fierce look. 'Did you go far, John? You were a long time.'

'No, not far. It was very beautiful.'

'John, could I have a word?' Stu got up, took his arm and walked him into the house.

They stood face to face across a narrow corridor.

'Look, it's really very good to see you again; it's rather sad the way we lose touch with old college mates. Life gets so hectic, in the theatre particularly. You know how it is, hail fellow one day and who the hell's he the next. Look, I won't beat about the bush. I know it's a bit much to cadge a favour on an old friendship when we've only just met again, but this project we're discussing with Lee – of course she's told you – it's just that it's really, really important, artistically, of course. What I want is to direct films, and this is exactly the sort of thing I need to get a toe in. Look, I wouldn't be asking if Lee weren't obviously very keen, but I know what it's like, there'll be agents and managers and minders and press officers and God knows who to get through, and they'll all have reasons for her not doing it, and they'll expect obscene amounts of money and Winnebagos and five-day weekends and all that stuff. And it would be just great, well, if you wouldn't mind putting in a good word. Obviously you're in a position to. Look, I'm sorry to . . .'

'No, I'm . . . really, I'm flattered you think I could make a difference. I don't really have anything to do with Lee's work. I'm just her boyfriend.' The word made him blush.

'OK, I understand. But please be positive. Tell her it'll be really good for her. I mean, it really will be.'

'Of course. I'll be positive.'

'Oh, you're an angel. Look, I wasn't making it up. It really is nice to see you again. You're just as handsome as you were in the wings.'

'And you look much the same.'

'Oh Lord, you're being kind, I've lost most of my hair.'

'And about a pound of make-up.'

'God, the slap. Yes, you remember that.' Stu put his hand on John's chest. 'It's just all such a dream now, university, isn't it? It was fabulous. We were fabulous, weren't we?'

'Well . . .'

'We were. Did we ever . . . you and I. You know?'

'No.'

'Oh. I seemed to do it with an awful lot of people. Did I ever try?'

'Yes,' John lied.

'Ah well, better luck next time.'

'Tea, I think.'

'That's a terrible exit line,' Stu laughed. He linked arms with John and they walked back into the garden. 'I've got to ask, what's she like in bed?'

'Oh, much the same as she is standing up: famous, a star.'

'She truly is a huge star, isn't she?'

Over tea Gilbert did more stories, voices, prat falls, bits of business.

Stu whispered, 'Christ, whoever said Variety was dead?'

Betsy clapped her hands and said, 'Why don't we all do a turn?'
Skye groaned.

'Oh, come on, it'll be fun. All this talent. Oliver, darling, do your party piece.'

'No, no really.' He waved his hands, getting up from the chair. 'OK. This is from the first production I ever played in as a small boy, and I remember hearing this from the wings, from the great, great Ron Moody.'

A gentlemen's-club grunt from Gilbert.

'I was transfixed, wonderful, and you know, thirty years later it could still be my song.' He pulled a grotesque face and growled 'I'm Reviewing the Situation' with a cartoon Jewishness that would have brought a warm glow to Martin Bormann's heart.

When he'd finished Stu sang 'There's Nothing Like a Dame', high and flat and badly. Betsy did 'Rosalind', with a lot of gush and hand wringing, and Gilbert fell over himself trying to be both characters in the balcony scene from *Brief Lives*, and then everyone looked at Lee.

This is what they really wanted. They could see themselves writing the introduction to their memoirs. 'I remember the evening in Gloucestershire – Lee Montana singing "In the Gloaming".'

Lee didn't demur or sigh or dissemble. She got up and walked away until she was framed in the landscape. England rolling behind her, the old oaks arched down the valley in the curve of the river. Whatever they thought they were going to get they didn't get it. She started to sing:

> The Minstrel Boy to the war has gone,
> In the ranks of death you'll find him;
> His father's sword he has girded on,
> And his wild harp slung behind him.
> Land of song, said the warrior bard,
> Though all the world betrays thee,
> One sword, at least, thy right shall guard.

She sang it with such restrained power and clarity, splicing every plain note with utter craft and assurance. It's a short and dreadful song, and as soon as the shock of the sound of it was out of her mouth and registered in their ears it was over.

John looked at their faces, rapt. A sort of childish awe, mouths slightly parted, dreamy-eyed, spongy heads sucking up every note, every move, all the atmosphere, to pack it in tissue and store it away to be taken out and re-examined with friends and people they wanted to impress. A memory that would grow sticky and soft with the retelling. These people, so soigné and self-confident, so blasé about their profession and their business, were reduced to little more than fans, faces in the dark, bathing in starlight. Perhaps not reduced, but elevated to acolytes.

Gilbert broke the silence, left his seat, grabbed her hand and planted a fervent kiss on her knuckles. 'Oh, I'm speechless. Quite, quite speechless. Overcome.'

He was about to explain quite how speechless and overcome he was when Oliver cut in with a booming, 'Bravo, bravo. We have to put this on the boards.'

Lee smiled and retrieved her hand and looked at her watch. 'You're kind. Look, the fat lady's sung, we should be getting on.'

The car picked its way through the dark lane. Lee snuggled close and kissed his neck.

'How did I do?'

'You were wonderful. That song was amazing. They were eating out of your hand.'

'That Gilbert almost ate my hand. God, what a bore. He's got to go. What do you think of Oliver and Stu?'

'Well, perfectly nice. Oliver seems, well, you know, jolly and expansive. I think he, well, wanted something.'

'Of course he wanted something. He wants me. His career's in the crapper; he's broke and he's got a reputation that's still wearing flares and sideburns. Nothing he's done has made a red cent for a decade. I'm his best hope to get back in the game.'

'Oh.'

'I thought he was flaky.'

'Flaky?'

'Yeah, no confidence, no bottom line, a bit of a jerk.'

'You looked as if you were his new best friend.'

Lee moved away and lit a cigarette. 'That's how it is. That's the business. What do you think of the shrew wife?'

'Well, I didn't really take to her, and I must say, she didn't look too happy. I thought she was rather jealous of you.'

'She's a bitch. You know she's fucking Gilbert?'

'No! How do you know?'

'Everyone knows. And what were you doing with the troll by the lake?'

'Oh, she wanted drugs, and then when I couldn't oblige she tried to shock me.'

'You didn't oblige her at all?'

'No, of course not.'

'But she made a pass, right?'

'Yes, she did.'

'She'd make a pass at a cigar-store Indian. She's had more prick in her mouth than an alterations tailor. And that Stu, what do you make of him? You knew him at college?'

'Vaguely. It was a surprise seeing him. I had no idea he was still in the theatre. Actually, he made a pass too.'

Lee laughed. 'Well, aren't you the popular one. Can't take you anywhere.' She was only half joking. 'But do you think I should work with him?'

'He's very keen. He asked me to use my influence.'

'And he thought a spot of sodomy might help. Well, he's very hot at the moment; the word is he's going to be the best.'

'What actually is the project, if you don't mind telling me?'

Lee thought for a moment. 'It's exciting. A classic. It's exactly what I've been looking for. You know I've never done theatre act-ing – what that doofus Gilbert would call proper acting. It frightens the shit out of me but, you know, it's there and I haven't done it. The people who think theatre's the fucking apex of every fucking thing are a load of deadbeats, but there you go. I just want to do it, so I can tell them all to go and take a running jump, because it's no big deal, because I've done it. And, well, my dad always wanted to do the stage, classics. All that art schtick. But he never did, just vaudeville and television. He used to recite Falstaff to me in bed.

66

Can you imagine?' Lee smiled at her reflection in the window and blew a thin jet of smoke over the memory.

'Well, which one is it?'

'Which Falstaff? Oh God, I can't remember. Beer and pussy, that's what Dad and Falstaff were into.'

'No, which classic do they want you to do?'

'*Antigone.*'

The Greek girl's name fell with a great thudding shock.

'*Antigone*?' John repeated, trying to keep his voice as neutral as possible.

Lee picked up the backsqueak of incredulity. 'You know it?'

'Yes, of course. I mean, yes. I did it at school. In fact, I played the Chorus.'

'And?'

'And what?'

'And what do you think? Do you think it's a good part for me?'

'Antigone?'

'No, the fucking maid. Yes, of course Antigone.'

The correct answer here was yes with an exclamation mark, or absolutely yes with two exclamation marks, or even Sophocles could have written it with you in mind without the exclamation marks, but John made a mistake common to people who come upon fame and stardom for the first time. They imagine that a person who is surrounded by adoration, sycophancy and yes-men would really value an honest, critical answer. He didn't stop to consider that sycophancy is one of the most sought-after, precious and elusive perks of fame.

'She's very young, Antigone,' he said.

This wasn't just the wrong answer; it was the wrongest possible answer.

Lee's shoulders straightened. She shifted to the farthest corner of the seat and swivelled her chest like battleship guns.

'And just how old do you think I am? Just how fucking, god-damn old do you think I should play? I'm thirty-four, for Christ's sake.' This was almost the truth; it was just within the 10 per cent allowed for error by most popular surveys. 'I don't exactly look like I'm ready to advertise condos in Arizona, do I?'

In the faint glow of the passing streetlights John saw the flint in her face. He felt rejected from the warmth of her goodwill, heard the steel shutters descend, and still she looked beautiful, and he realized he'd say almost anything to get back into the warmth – jettison all criticism, all honesty, if that was the price of a smile.

He backpedalled furiously. 'It's a very long time since I read it, and I think you could do anything: you're so wonderful; you're such a great actress. You know, I don't know anything about the theatre, but it's a fantastic play and you're hugely popular. When you sang for them they were completely captured, and that's supposed to be a boy, and they do know. I think you could recite the phone book dressed as Shirley Temple and they'd queue round the block to look.'

'All right.' She turned the big guns away. 'All right, John, but you've got to be supportive. If we're going to go on being friends.' She twisted her fingers through his. 'If we're going to be more than friends you've got to be one hundred per cent with me. This is a very insecure business; there are thousands of cretins' – she pronounced the word as if they all lived in Crete – 'out there, just waiting for me to fail. I've got to have a lot of positivity. If you write a bad poem who gets to know? Who cares? If I fluff a line it's headlines round the world. Do you understand?'

John understood. He was being read his contract, his terms of employment. He leaned across and kissed her neck. The subject's kiss of abasement, the acolyte's kiss, the apostle's kiss. He kissed the box marked 'Yes'. Her neck smelled of amber and mimosa and frankincense.

'Yes,' he whispered.

'Good.'

The hotel was not so much tucked away as dumped in a small valley behind a hill at the end of an avenue of beech trees. It had been built by an Edwardian newsagent, who had wanted to be mistaken for a medieval robber baron. The building boasted crenellations and a good deal of ornamental plaster work. Through the headlights a lexicon of signs swam: 'Deliveries', 'Guest Parking', 'Tennis Court', 'Please Drive Anti-Clockwise Round the

Drive', 'Long Walk', 'Short Walk', 'Kitchen', 'Stables', 'Reception'. They were met by a man in a dinner jacket and sponge-bag trousers, a boy in a pillbox hat, a girl in an Armani suit and another man in tweed. They looked like exhibits in a history of rural hospitality. The man in tweed welcomed Lee with a spout of genuflecting gush that would have been embarrassing anywhere but in an English country house hotel.

'You must please, please treat this place exactly as if it were your own home.'

Apparently this was a commandment, a mantra which was tattooed on every member of staff's heart, from the lowest pastry chef's to his very own, that guests were to be allowed to do exactly, exactly, precisely whatever they wanted. It was utterly, utterly relaxed, and if anyone wasn't as completely and totally unwound as a stringless yo-yo he wanted to know why. They could do as they wished in any of the snuggly-puggly, cosy-wosy public rooms, where every employee from the meagrest bootblack to his own, good, tweedy self would see it as an unforgivable, suicidal rebuke if they'd failed in their one true heart's desire, which was – at the risk of repeating himself – to feel supernaturally, narcotically relaxed and cosmically comfortable with little velvet buttons on.

'Please, please, please.'

Now, gentlemen, jackets and ties in the dining room and smoke by all means, but only in the conservatory. No cigars or pipes. No stiletto heels on the parquet floor. Tennis, swimming, clay-pigeon shooting, brass-rubbing and cycling arranged by the staff if given twenty-four hours' notice. Breakfast from six thirty to nine thirty, lunch from twelve to two, picnics by prior arrangement, vegetarians and religions or allergies catered for, but only on thirty-six hours' notice. Drinks on an honesty basis – please fill in the book in capital letters, including your name, number of room and a signature. Dinner from seven to ten. Unfortunately, they'd just missed it, but a light supper of moreish comestibles and exotic sweetmeats might be served in the Eau-de-Nil Drawing Room, the Chinese Library or the Hunters' Den. By all means read the books in the library – the key to the original breakfront bookcase was available from reception – but don't take any of them to your room or to the garden or swimming pool. Wellington boots, umbrellas, overcoats and a selection of walking sticks available if the staff were given sufficient notice. They were more than welcome to make use of the dog, called Bottom, who of course needed twenty-four hours' notice, and please don't teach the parrot to swear.

'So the only rule here is relax and enjoy yourself. Well, two rules: relax *and* enjoy yourself.'

Lee and John stood with fixed grins, waving away two glasses of champagne being offered by the man in the dinner jacket, a cup of tea with chocolate truffles from the Armani woman and a menu from the boy in the pillbox hat. Bottom offered a crotch examination.

'Thank you so much,' Lee finally said. 'We'll have a chicken sandwich, a bottle of vodka and a pot of coffee in our room. Please give my driver whatever he wants, and if that fucking parrot comes anywhere near me it'll have to learn Braille.'

John stood in the bathroom and regarded his nakedness in the repeated reflection of the four mirrors. The room was a picture-book illustration done by someone who knew England only from Merchant-Ivory films and Barbara Cartland novels. He wondered how many thousands of eider ducks had given their lives to stuff this little pastel, chintzy place with so much softness. The cushions had cushions, the curtains looked like duvets, everything was plump. The carpet snogged his feet, the white towels sat as fat as Christmas geese on the rail, the soap was a little cushion of pink-ness, the labial luxury of everything stroked and snuggled up to him. What really seduced him was the heavy, velvety warmth. John had never stood naked in a bathroom before and been warm. This inconsequential thing stunned him, not just the pleasure and the freedom of it, but the shock that such a small, unimportant pleasure should have eluded him until now. How dare naked com-fort in a bathroom not be a basic human right in a civilized society? Why wasn't it available on demand from the welfare state? He stepped into the Victorian ball-and-claw tub and almost sank. Where his feet should have touched the other end there was just more water. The point where his bony knees would have emerged like hairy atolls was now just a cloud of bubbles. He lay back and looked at the blameless ceiling through the rising steam and picked up a flannel as thick as a miner's sandwich. He hadn't used a flannel since he was a child but now he placed it over his face and felt the heat leach away all worry and care, through the pit-pat of the softly expiring bubbles.

John got out of the bath and wrapped himself in a bed-sized towel. Lee was sitting cross-legged, picking chicken out of brown bread. The image of Petra eating cheese on toast flicked briefly. That and a crumb of guilt; this was the first time he'd thought of her. The television was on.

'I was offered a part in this movie. Thank God I didn't take it. You know she hasn't done one since. Advertises dandruff shampoo now.'

They ate silently.

'Rub my back, will you, honey?' Lee stretched out on her stomach.

He'd never rubbed anyone's back before, and imagined it was the sort of thing Californian boys learned at junior school. They always seemed to be giving each other neck rubs and massages and fiddling with their feet. He tentatively began doing what he'd seen people do in movies; his long fingers felt Lee's vellum skin. It was as if she were part of the soft furnishings, made of the same luxurious stuff. He leaned forward and kissed the back of her neck. She half turned.

The next day they got up late, missed the bay window of opportunity for breakfast, found that the dog had been double-booked and put their name down for a cancellation. The country was pretty in an undemanding way – neat organic fields, Sunday-gentleman farming. There were strategic copses and stands of oak for shooting. This place was bisected and coursed into fields of fire, enflayed and deflayed to facilitate a great avian Somme in the shortest possible time. Pretty acres of killing zone. To John and Lee it seemed as quietly peaceful and cutely English as a tablemat. The middle distance was arrowed with steeples and there was thatch and blousy hedges and bounding bunnies. They walked arm in arm, and found, to their huge mutual relief, that they could chat.

The ability to chat is the next great hurdle for a love affair after finding out that the sports equipment works. Can you do the inconsequential is the question? Anyone can declaim, but can you do asides? Everyone's got their big pulpit pieces committed to memory, the 'Will you sleep with me?' scene, the 'I know you've slept with someone else' scene, the 'It was nothing, just a physical thing; she meant nothing' scene. Anyone can do the 'I'm not spending Christmas with the in-laws' row, the 'That's just typical of you, you never listen; you're selfish, what about me?' argument and the old 'We need to talk, I feel claustrophobic; you're so needy, I want some freedom and space' monologue. And all of us have the script for the chilling, more in sorrow than in anger, 'I've grown up, we've grown apart; I still love you but not in that way, I just want to be friends' soliloquy. And somewhere, in the bottom drawer of your life, you've also got the shaming, gut-stripping, whining bit that comes next, the 'I'm sorry, sorry. Look, I can be whoever you want really. I'll give you more space, you can sleep with other people, honestly, I don't mind; I've got enough love for both of us. Please, please don't dump me.' Oh yes, oh yes, don't deny it, you've got that one tucked away somewhere. We can all do a set piece with conviction, timing and a certain amount of extemporized business, but it's the one-lump-or-two, getting-in-and-out-of-rooms stuff that's difficult, that takes effort and dedication and talent.

John and Lee walked through the unfamiliar woods and over the cunning stiles and twittered about nothing very much. They wove a nest of verbal twigs and straw, and by the time they'd trudged back up the lane to the hotel they'd achieved a fragile something out of nothing of any consequence, and neither had had to say, 'Tell me what you're thinking,' because 'Tell me what you're thinking' is an admission of failure.

After lunch they read the papers. After a long, late tea Lee paid the bill, Hamed brought the car and they crunched down the gravel to join the dotted line of red tail lights going back to town. John watched Lee's face flare and fade in the on-coming headlights. They

72

held hands and listened to a play on the radio. As they got back to the familiar West London streets he felt a light pall of depression. The familiar Sunday-evening feeling of people who have resistible things to do on Mondays. The *Stars-on-Sunday*, beans-on-toast, can-of-lager feeling, ironing a shirt, phoning your mum.

'I've really loved this weekend, you know.' He sounded flat and polite. 'Really.'

'Yeah, it was kinda fun. Look, can I drop you anywhere?'

'No. I'll get a cab from the hotel.'

'OK. Look, you don't mind not staying the night?'

'No, of course not.'

'I've got an early flight and some things to do. If you're there I won't get any sleep and I'll look like shit in LA.'

When they pulled up in front of the Connaught it was late and spitting with rain.

'Thank you for being my boyfriend for the weekend. Hey, don't look so long in the face. I'll be back soon. If I'm going to do this play later in the year I'll call you.'

John sensed that she was already gone. Her eyes flickered over his shoulder.

'Lee, it was special, wasn't it?'

'Oh come on, honey, of course it was. I'm just bad at all this goodbye shit. Write me a poem.'

He hadn't meant to, but he slid his hand round the back of her head and pulled her face towards him. It was the first time he'd instigated anything in their short, lop-sided affair. He felt her resist; her beautiful blue eyes flashed at his. She put her hand on his chest and then, what the hell, she kissed him back, mouth wide, hot tongue running across his teeth, soft breath, long fingers pressed on his heart. A bright, fierce moment of everything.

White light pricked through John's closed eyes. Lee pulled away. A string of spittle hung between their lips.

John saw the photographer out of the corner of his eye, and a second bright, white bolt covered them. Lee was already moving past him, blind-siding the lens.

'It's the first rule: never kiss in public. Bye, John.'

It was final; she didn't look back. Her hunched shoulders pushed through the revolving doors. A small, bald man with a grizzled beard, dressed in an expensively stained leather jacket, held his camera with the professional nonchalance of a gunslinger. He let her go. There were a million snaps of Lee Montana. He smiled at John. There weren't any of her new boyfriend. John smiled back, the polite reflex, a little boy's smile for his daddy's holiday Brownie, squinting into the sun.

And here it was. This was the flickering kilowatt moment when John Dart the poet's life changed irrevocably. This sliver of celluloid and emulsion, the trapped beams, the trick of chiaroscuro, cast the die, crossed his Rubicon, burned his bridge. He was about to spin off a dangerous corner.

Ronnie fox, celebrity photographer, 'not paparazzi, please, no long lenses, all up close, front work, in your face, in the street, on the level. Nothing private, nothing intrusive; if it's public then the public's got a right to see it, but I'm a reasonable man. You see me right, I'll see you in the glossies,' walked back to the BMW, dumped his camera on the passenger seat and drove to a twenty-four-hour developers. Three rolls today.

Damp negatives put on the light box, fish-eye magnifier. Scratched faces, caught mid-canapé at a party at a jeweller's shop; one TV presenter looking fat and a lot of journalists no paper would print. A politician's book launch, full of politicians looking like politicians. Who wants the social page to look like *The News at Ten*? There was one cabinet minister's daughter, a bit of a 'hello, how's your father, high tits and short skirt' he'd had hopes for, but the pictures weren't good. No eyes, no look. And then, at the end of the roll, there was Lee and, oh yes, yes. He took them to the picture editor.

'I've got something for you. Look at that.'

'Oh yes, Lee Montana and snog. Very nice, very nice. Who is he?'

'No idea. John somebody.'

'That's a bit of a story. Hasn't she just split up with that beef-on-the-bone? Who's she kissing now? Who's this mystery John? Might make front of the first edition; there's no fucking news. Nice snap, Ronnie. Anyone else got it?'

'Nope.'

'Great.'

It didn't make the front page. A small gas explosion in Camden, not many hurt, saw to that, but it made page three.

Clive sat on a broken swivel chair in the back room; it was his tea break. Arranged in front of him on a box of cookery books was a large cappuccino with extra chocolate, two Danish pastries, a Twix, twenty Silk Cut, the *Evening Standard* and a folder containing his thumbed and frantically scribbled novel. Clive's brow was furrowed; he was not happy. The muse was not running like a clear mountain stream for him; he was struggling.

A blond Adonis called Dicky, who was a bit of a disposable git, the sort of white-toothed bird-magnet that really got Clive's goat, was about to get his come-uppance. Raped by a fey squid, which had been turned predatorily homosexual after eating the puffy, poofy corpse of a man who'd died in a nuclear-power-station accident.

Dicky did a lazy backstroke in the clear blue, no, azure ocean, no, lagoon. The sunlight glittered, no, sparkled on his bronze pectorals, and his blond curls waved like wet yellow hair. Life didn't get better than this, he thought smugly.

Well, it was about to get a whole lot better, if you're into cross-species sex, that is. If you're into queer cephalopods, it was going to get much, much, much better. If not, then it was the starter from hell.

With a start, no, with a little shriek, yeah that's gayer. With a little shriek, Dicky felt something slide up the leg of his Pierre Cardin swimming trunks; something hard and rubbery, something textured, something prehensile and purposeful, something not unlike a novelty condom with a dirty mind. He thrashed, but his legs and arms were twined and pinioned, and a suckered arm roughly pulled off his shorts. His little floppy willy was stroked, his bollocks were puckered in a lustful embrace; more arms encircled

75

his chest, sucking his nipples. A slimy lavatory plunger splattered on his mouth and Frenched him. His clenched buttocks were firmly spread and he felt the blind eye winking like a shy anemone. It was tenderly insinuated by a stiff probe, which grew to the width of a man's arm. Fourteen inches of pulsing Greek hors d'oeuvre was served up his jaksi and began to rhythmically give him the shafting of his life.

In horror he looked down into the deep, and beneath him, undulating in the clear water, was the gaping beak and round eye of his sodomistic ravisher. It winked slowly at him and slipped up another six inches, rhythmically tossing a lather of foam.

Oh God, thought Dicky, is this just a holiday fling or is he serious?

No, the end wasn't quite right. It didn't live for him; it didn't leap off the page as a shared experience. That magic moment when the imagination of the author melds across time and space with the reader and they are as one. A single narrative thought shared. Clive shut his eyes and tried to imagine floating on a blue lagoon with tentacles up his bottom. His fat buttocks squeaked on the rickety chair. It wasn't as bad as he'd hoped – quite nice really. He imagined the little suckers tugging at his scrotum, like being gently shot with children's arrows. The firm, cool slippery teasing of his nipples. The firm but tender rhythm of being wanked by a hoover attachment, and just floating in the warm water, the taste of salt on your lips, the sun patting your fat tummy. The keening of the gulls, the soft plop-plop of the enquiring suckers. The full-up, enema-probed, prostate-feeling, gloriously suspended sensation, and it didn't mean you were a poof or anything. Nothing nancy about copping a zipless squid-fuck.

Whoa, Clive! Whoa boy! Get a grip. Pull for shore, man. Feet on terra firma. Don't get carried away. That was the trouble with having a literary bent, the old imaginative juices could carry you away. Clive shook his head, slurped the scum off his coffee and picked up the *Standard*. 'Small gas explosion in Camden – not many hurt.' He turned over and took a big bite of pastry.

Lee and John took up most of page three. Clive didn't so much do a double take as slide into momentary suspended animation and then do a passable rendition of a man having a major stroke.

It was a good picture; the kiss had an added erotic charge. It was the hands, John's fingers in her hair, Lee's pressed on his chest. They looked taut and passionate. Clive's imaginative brain ran hither and yon. Klaxons howled. And the impossible became improbable, and then, because light travels in straight lines and never deviates or lies, it has to be the truth, it became a fact.

At the bottom of the page was an insert of John smiling in a gormless, embarrassed sort of way. 'Lee's mysterious John. Do you know him?' Clive held the picture close, took it all in and ran through all the possible explanations: John had a twin brother; it was taken in Madame Tussaud's; it was aliens.

'Fucking bloody right I know him,' he bellowed, and a raisin lodged in his windpipe.

John was in the children's books section, trying to impose some order on the thin, bright, hyperactive lines of kiddies' books. They skittered and slid out of his hands and along the shelf, falling over themselves in a giggling game of tag.

There are two sections of children's books: the expensive, hard-back, elegantly designed classics about ballet dancers and kindly uncles in crumbling castles and holidays in Cornwall. They're supposed to be subtly addictive, soft-drug literature, to lure innocents into the hard stuff of Austen, Brontë and intravenous Hardy before their balls drop or they grow out of their first training bra. You just know they are never opened and that you could print *The Story of O* or the *Kama Sutra* in them and no-one would ever notice, but oddly they do teach children something about books; something even more important than the dubious benefit of reading. They teach them about books as status, as accessories. Every smart munchkin past the age of five knows that a matching set of Beatrix Potter in its own wooden box, like miniature Folio Society editions, says something about them that grown-ups appreciate.

The other section is full of books that children choose themselves, invariably books that pretend not to be books. They are comics or mobiles, or they have bits of string or fluffy moles, or smelly patches or beepers and buzzers and tiny electronic quacks attached to them. Children buy them as a sort of second-division toy.

'You can have anything you like,' mothers say, too loudly. 'What about this? I loved this when I was your age.'

Why do parents bother? What's so great about books that mean you have to work your way through *Decline and Fall of the Roman Empire* when you're a quarter of the age that Gibbon was when he got round to writing it? Why is literature so different from all other adult pleasures? Parents spend most of their time trying to stop children picking up adult pleasures. What is it about books? It is, John thinks, because parents see children as being like coffee-table books, and childhood like an Edwardian story.

He became aware that, over the Dave Brubeck, there was a muffled commotion coming from the stockroom.

'Go and see what Clive's doing in there.' Mrs Patience looked up from the till.

Clive was bouncing off the walls and packing cases, trying to give himself the Heimlich Manoeuvre, his face the colour of mottled afterbirth. His cake-mulchy mouth hung open, his little parrot's tongue flapped, his eyes swam and bulged, his knees buckled. In one hand he held the crumpled paper and with the other he furiously and futilely beat himself on the back of the neck. John opened the door just in time for the now frankly desperate Clive to lurch into the handle with some force. It clouted him fairly in the solar plexus, exploding a turkey's crop of tacky pastry at a poster of Martin Amis, where it clung to a sneering nostril. Clive collapsed like a landed porpoise.

'Are you all right?' John asked, rather pointlessly.

Clive wagged a furious, fuck-off finger at him, turned himself over and lay propped against a filing cabinet, hawking for breath.

'Can I get you anything?'

'Jam.'

'Jam?'

He shook his puce head and coughed, wiping his spit-flecked chin. 'Jammy cunt.'

'Jammy cunt?' John looked around. 'Is that what made you choke?'

Clive snorted and wheezed, a sort of guffaw. 'You, you jammy cunt.'

'Me? Why me?'

Weakly, Clive handed over the crumpled paper.

'"Small gas explosion in Camden – not many hurt"?'

'Over.'

The photograph came as a shock of quite a different kind to John.

'Oh Christ.'

'Jammy cunt. Why didn't you tell me?'

'Oh Christ. Has anyone else seen this?'

'That's a stupid question. It's in the fucking *Evening Standard*. A million people will see it. Do you know who this jammy cunt is?' Clive stabbed at the portrait.

'Oh Christ. Petra. Do you think she'll notice?'

'Notice? Notice? You . . . you . . .' Clive was about to asphyxiate himself again. 'You shag the most beautiful woman in the world. You did shag her, didn't you? didn't you? Of course you did. Oh God, I can't even think about it. And then get a picture of the sweaty act printed in the evening paper, and you think Petra won't notice.'

'Well, it's not actually the act. We could be just, like, friends.'

'What? Are you fucking addled? Look at the two of you, I can almost smell the sheets. If you were pressed any closer together you'd be organ donors. And don't try and tell me that's not tongues.'

'Oh Christ, Clive. What am I going to do?'

'Retire, mate. Everything's downhill from here. You have, at the age of twenty-six, reached the highest peak possible to mankind. You've shafted Lee Montana, stuffed the dream, porked Helen of Troy. Live out your life in a rocking chair, mate, drooling over the memory. First sue her for a million in palimony, of course, and sell your story to the *News of the World*.'

'Clive, shut up. What am I going to say when Petra sees this?'

'Petra? Forget her, man. You're in a different league now. She's the before, this is the after.' Clive coughed on Lee's hair. 'Petra's before you were a bit of rough to the stars, a tabloid legend.'

'Clive, just fuck off, OK. This is serious.'

'OK, OK. I understand. It hasn't sunk in yet. Well, it hasn't for me either. You sank it in all right, though. God, I still can't believe it.'

'I'm going back in. You're no help, you're supposed to be my mate.'

'Fine, fine, OK.' Clive pulled himself up, brushed the front of his shirt and then pinned John to the door with a big sticky hand on each shoulder. 'Just tell me one thing, *mano a mano*.'

'Don't ask.'

'It won't go any further than this room.'

'Clive, don't ask.'

'I've got to; I've got to know. I'll die a bitter man. Please, please, I'll never mention it again. It'll just be between ourselves, but you've got to tell me. Was she as good as she looks?'

'Clive!'

'Of course she was, of course she was. Just make it live for me?'

'Clive!'

'Oh God, a crumb, anything. You know. Was it tight? You know, really tight? And wet? Does she shave round her bits?'

'Clive!' John tried to push him away.

'Tell me. No, you don't have to say anything, just nod. Just look blank if it's true. Did she go down on you? Did she? And then did she stick a finger up your arse and twiddle your prostate like a giant squid?'

'I haven't got a prostate like a giant squid. Jesus, Clive.'

'That's it! Just say, "Jesus Clive", if it's true. Did you have her on her hands and knees? Were her perfect buttocks spread and her tight, wet vulva pouting at you like a soft clam? And when you stuck it in her did she make a mewing noise, like a hungry herring gull? Did she? Did she, John? Did she beg you, John?' Clive's voice was a hoarse whisper. 'Did she beg?'

John put his hand over his face and groaned.

'Don't leave me, John. Stick with it.' Clive shook his shoulders. 'We're getting something here. Look, I'm never going to get this close to a goddess again. This has got to last me a lifetime of winter wanks. I know it's sad, John. I'm sad. Have pity on a sad boy.

Orgasms, John? Did she or didn't she? Course she did, you stud. Multiple or singular?'

John pushed hard and body-swerved Clive against the wall, but with desperate agility an arm grabbed him round his neck.

'Clive, for Christ's sake, this is sick, you're sick. I'm in deep shit and you've turned into Willy Wanker.'

They staggered round the room. John tripped heavily and Clive flopped after him and sat on his chest, his face pink and sweaty, his eyes and lips slick.

'Did she sit on your face and drag her fragrant, fringed, barnacled bits over your mouth till you thought you'd drown in lust? Did—?'

'Ahhhh. Help.'

'Did, did she swallow? Course she swallowed. Going, "Mmmmm, mmmmm, hot man juice." Did a little bit dribble out of the corner of her mouth? Did it? And did she grab you in the shower and, soaping her loins, say, shyly, "Why don't you bugger me, John? I want you to have all of me. Every hole is your playground."

'Did she stuff her warm, white, moist panties in your mouth and tie you to a chair with her stockings and put a cock ring made out of an old garter round your old man, and lie in front of you, teasing herself with an electric toothbrush?'

'What on earth are you doing?' Mrs Patience stood in the doorway.

'Just discussing the Booker Prize shortlist.' Clive reluctantly let go.

'Well, could we have you in the shop? There are customers. John, there's a man who wants something by a Frenchman called Bellamy, says it's a classic. I've looked him up; we haven't got it. Will you try to sell him something else.'

John, feeling ridiculous, picked a slim paperback off the shelf and trooped into the shop.

Mrs P. spoke to a pasty student at the counter. 'This is John, he'll try and help you.' It was said without much hope.

'Is this what you're looking for? De Maupassant?'

The student smiled and said, 'Ta.'

'Well,' Mrs P. huffed, as she watched him leave. 'He never mentioned Maupassant; he said Bellamy. You know, the longer I work in this business the more I think books are actually bad for you; they rot your brains. All you heavy readers are half witted, in a world of your own, with your Maupassants and Bellamys.'

The door opened and Dorothy, back from her break, strode across the shop. Without a word she came and hit John hard across the face, as hard as she could, with the flat of her hand.

'You bastard. You utter bastard. How could you? You contemptible shit.'

'You're all mad, all stark, staring, hardback mad,' Mrs P. exclaimed unsympathetically.

John stumbled against the counter.

'What have you gone and done now, John?'

Dorothy thrust the *Evening Standard* into her hand.

'What's this? Oh, John, that's you in the paper. And that's that Montana woman, who was here. Oh my dear, poor Petra. John, what could possibly have induced you?'

Behind her back, Clive ran through a mime of six or seven sexual practices and positions, grinning maniacally.

'Petra wants to see you in the coffee shop after work. I told her not to.' Dorothy was close to tears. 'I told her you weren't worth it, but she wants to talk to you. You hurt her any more and I'll kick your balls through your spleen, so you'd better practise your abject apologies. God, I hope she dumps you. You're a bastard.'

John said nothing. What was there to say? He just stared up at the two implacably furious women, their faces knitted together in disapproval.

The rest of the day was pretty miserable. He kept to the outer corners and culs-de-sac of the travel guides, business manuals and New-Age philosophy books. Mrs P. was truly angry. All her bitterness and humiliation about the absent Mr P. with his Saturday assistant leached back and haunted the shop. Dorothy was haughty, and Clive winked and nudged and sniggered, which was worse.

*

Petra was sitting at one of the three tables in the little takeaway coffee bar that they all used for the rounds of cappuccino that mark out a shop worker's day. She looked more smudgily dark and drawn and dangerously slight than usual. Her black eyes hooded under tented brows, a hard little self-protective smile. A cigarette tapped after every shallow puff was the only sign of nerves.

'Hello.' John sat down opposite her, met her eyes for a moment and then looked away. 'Look, I'm sorry. I'm really, really sorry.'

'Shove it, John,' she said with a trembling voice. 'Just shut up.' Tap, tap. A two-drag silence and then a calmer, 'Do you love me?'

'Yes, yes, of course.' He jumped at the question like an exhausted fox down a drainage pipe, without wondering where it led or whether it was actually a trap. He'd imagined loads of scenarios for this meeting; none of them had mentioned love. 'You know I do. Look, this thing, the photograph, it's not what it seems.'

'You fucked her.'

'It wasn't like that.'

'You fucked her.'

'Yes.'

'How many times?'

'What?'

'How many times? How many times did you fuck her, John?'

'Once.'

'Once?'

'Well, twice, sort of one and a half.'

'So it was just a one-night stand?'

'Yes. That's what I was going to tell you. It was just a sort of mindless one-night thing.'

'All right. Shut up. I don't want your excuses or apologies. You've made a fool of yourself, a public fool of yourself.'

'I've made a fool?' John was honestly amazed.

'Yes, of course, you idiot. You've been used. Picked up like some little tart in a disco, humped and dumped. You're a bit old to be a groupie, and, as my boyfriend, that reflects badly on me, and yes I'm hurt, but I'm more angry that you're such a weak, gullible idiot. What do you think she saw in you?'

Anxious not to contradict. 'Oh, I think she must have been lonely, bored. We didn't talk much really.'

'I ought to dump you, really. But you love me and I'm used to you. Dorothy says I should dump you, but that's because she fancies you.'

'Me? Dorothy? But she's your best friend.'

'So? She still fancies you, because I've got you; that's what best friends do. She trusts my taste and judgement. Anyway, it's beside the point.'

John was looking at Petra with a wide-eyed incredulity, almost admiration. Her tough little single-minded egotism was inspiring.

'Thank you for, well, seeing it this way. I promise it won't happen again.'

'Of course it won't happen again.' Petra raised her eyes to the ceiling and dropped a little laugh.

'So we can go back to how it was? Forget it?'

'Oh, no, no.' Petra snarled and grinned at the same time, and lit a cigarette with a theatrical gesture that didn't quite work. 'Oh no, John, you're not getting off. You've broken trust. It's going to be different. There are some new rules.'

'Rules?'

'For a start, you're never to talk about this to anyone, ever. No boasting, no boyish bragging.'

'Of course, I wouldn't dream—'

'No, *you* probably wouldn't, but Clive and Dom and Pete will. I'm not going to be pitied. Do you understand? I'm not jealous, not of some plastic, insecure, media bimbo. I'm not going to be made the victim of this. You're the fucking victim and I'm going to make damn sure everyone understands that. And, second, I want to know where you are all the time. No just checking out to make up poems. I don't trust you.'

'Yes, no, I understand.'

'And then there's your punishment – your medicine.'

John winced at the chilling dash between punishment and medicine.

'Petra, can't . . . This hasn't exactly been nice for me. Mrs P. hates me, Clive's being a complete prat and Dorothy hit me.'

'I knew she'd make a pass.'

'It wasn't a pass, it was a slap. It nearly broke my nose.'

'It was a pass. You don't know anything. Your punishment is that I'm allowed one away shag.'

'Darling?'

'That's the deal. If I fancy someone I'm just going to have them, and I'll tell you afterwards, and anyone else I choose, and you'll just have to lump it. So, you've got that to look forward to, John darling. The girl you love is going to sleep with someone else and it's your fault.' Petra was leaning across the table, her fists clenched, speaking through her teeth. 'It might be a friend of yours; it might be a big, black biker; it might be the Household Cavalry, and they might be better than you, which wouldn't be difficult, but it's going to happen and you're going to see how it feels. Right? Christ, look at the time. We've got to go.'

'Go? Where? I thought we might get a takeaway and watch telly, or I could just go home. I'm really knackered.'

'Oh no, John. We're going to the pub.'

'Petra, I really don't want to see anyone. It would be embarrassing.'

'I don't give a shit if you're embarrassed. You don't have any rights any more. I'm not hiding away, letting people think I'm crying into my pillow. We're going to the pub, I'm going to be the life and soul and you're going to be contrite. Come on.' She stood up. 'Give me a kiss, bad boy.'

John pushed open the door of Maggie's and the familiar noise and smell hugged him like a sloppy, smelly uncle. The half-dozen familiar faces at the bar turned to stare.

'Oooooh, would you look at who it isn't! I don't believe it,' Sean, the barman, shouted. 'I don't fucking believe it. It's Shepherd's Bush's American gigolo, our very own Hollywood gerbil, been up all the right places.'

The men at the bar made that noise in the back of their throats that men keep for erections and free kicks. Petra waited two beats and then, like a conjuror's assistant, appeared from behind John's shoulder. It was a good entrance. She pointed her sharp little chin at the bar and swept the room with hot, napalm eyes. The noise curdled.

'Hello, Petra love. Didn't expect to see you. Well, not both of you. Thought you might have killed him.'

'No, Sean. I'm just using his balls as fabric softener. If I traded him in, I'd just have to train another one, and you're all much of a muchness. At least I know where he's been. Get the drinks in, bastard.' And she stalked off to the table, where Pete and Dom and Clive were already sitting.

John sidled up to the bar.

'So what'll it be, stud? Slow, comfortable screw for you and a pint of arsenic for the little lady?'

The bar sniggered.

'Two pints, thanks, Sean.'

'Two pints. Straight glass for you, or are you drinking yours out of Petra's jackboot?'

'Oh, leave it out, Sean.'

''Ere. Later, you and I is going to have a little chat. Know what I mean, you little rascal. It's always the quiet ones. Isn't that right, Bill? Always the quiet ones. If your Marge copped a picture of you snogging Michelle Pfeiffer in the paper, what would she do, eh? What would she do? She'd stop taking the LSD, that's what she'd do. Am I right?'

Petra was huddled with the three boys. When John got to the table they all sat back and shuffled. Clive put an arm round both their shoulders.

'I'm really glad you two decided to be so grown-up about this.'

'I hope you know how lucky you are,' Dom said.

'To have Petra as a girlfriend, not the other thing,' clarified Pete.

'Do you mind if we don't talk about it. It's between Petra and me; we've sorted it out.'

'OK. Let's talk about something else.'

There was a quiet moment whilst everyone tried not to think of John kissing Lee, and then, brightly, Petra asked, 'So, Clive. Who shall I go and have my affair with?'

By closing time the drink, the ordinariness and familiarity of the place and the company had brought back an easy sense of normality. As the first bell rang, a studious, attractive girl, with a short, expensive, no-nonsense haircut, wearing spectacles and carrying a heavy shoulder bag, came up to their table.

She smiled. 'Aren't you John? John Dart, isn't it?' She took a ring-bound notepad from her bag. 'Can I buy you a drink? Juliet Blundon, *Daily Mail*.' She held out her hand. The table gawped.

'I really haven't got anything to say. Look, I'm not very interesting.'

'Well, that's not what my editor thinks. I've been sent all the way down here to find you. The photograph – it's a story, I'm afraid. I'm sorry, I know it's an imposition, and if it were just me . . . but then it's not. Look, off the record, John, all of Fleet Street's going to want to know who you are. Lee Montana is a big name. I shouldn't be telling you this, but if you give me just a couple of quotes, anything, that'll be the end of it. It'll kill the story for everyone. It doesn't have to be dirt, really.'

John looked desperately at the others. They'd never seen news before it was printed. They felt like insiders, fascinated to see how it was done. Petra smiled her humourless little smile.

The journalist went on with an easy, confiding voice. 'You can have complete control. I'll write down exactly what you say. You can check it. I'm not here to stitch you up, honestly. I've got to file something and it might as well be what you want. It can be as flattering as you like. And then there's an end to it. Help me out, John? Look, have a think. I'll go and get some drinks in. Pints, is it?'

'And a chaser,' said Clive.

'Fine.'

'Whiskey. Large ones.'

'Christ, what am I supposed to do?'

'Hold out, of course.' Clive was really excited. 'She hasn't brought the cheque book out yet. Ask her for an opening bid, or we'll go the *Express*. She said they were all after the story, well, we'll go to the *Express*. Let me handle it for you. Twenty per cent. I'll get you a really good deal.'

'No, Clive.'

'OK, ten.'

'Shut up, Clive.'

Petra lit a cigarette. 'Remember you promised, John.' She blew smoke, which was supposed to be full of menace, towards the ceiling.

'Could you mention our performance?' said Pete.

'Just in passing,' Dom chipped in.

Juliet Blundon came back. 'Here you are, pints and chasers. Barman says you're a poet, John. Had anything published?'

'Yes. *The Failed Stone*.'

'Love poems?'

'No. Well, a couple of them. They're more observations, really, some are about love.'

'And you work in a bookshop.'

'Yes. Look, please, I really don't want to talk about this. I understand what you said, but—'

'How much?' Clive blurted. 'How much are you willing to pay? Let's cut the crap, we could go to the *Express*, couldn't we. Sell them an exclusive.'

'And you are?'

'Clive. I'm John's friend, and agent, sort of.'

'Well, Clive, you're right to ask, but you know, selling a story is a tricky business. If you just tell me something, then it's up to you what's said and printed. If you want to make money out of it, then it's a contract, and the paper has to make sure it gets its money's worth. It's the readers' money. They'll want kisses for the cash, intimate descriptions, pillow talk. Now, if that's what you want, well, I can make a call. But look, John,' she leaned forward and put a hand on his arm; her voice was well modulated, Oxbridge, liberal, reasonable, confiding, 'again, off the record – I'm really putting my neck on the line telling you this, my editor would fire me – but in my experience no-one ever walks away happy after selling a story. You always look mercenary, and it isn't as much as you think. Don't believe what you read in the papers.' She laughed conspiratorially. 'Maybe a couple of hundred; not exactly a lottery win. How did you meet Lee?'

John stared into his tabloid whiskey. In wine is truth. 'I have no comment.' The expression sounded stupid and grandiose, like he was pretending to be a cabinet minister or a libel lawyer, not just a nicked philanderer in a pub.

Juliet nodded with a kindly, professional understanding. 'You must be Petra. You're John's girlfriend, aren't you?'

'He's my boyfriend, yeah.' Petra raised an arched girl-to-girl eyebrow.

Juliet took her cue and put her notebook on her lap. 'May I?' she said, taking one of Petra's cigarettes. 'Aren't you a bit pissed off? I mean, I'd kill him.'

'Yeah, well, I still might, but he's come back with his tail between his legs, so he's on probation.'

'That's very big of you.'

'Well, he dumped her and asked me to take him back. I've got a soft spot for him.'

'He dumped Lee Montana?'

'Yeah. Said she was a bit of a dog under all that make-up and the liposuction, and really self-obsessed, in a sort of Californian Oprah Winfrey way.'

'Is that true, John?'

Petra kicked him under the table. 'You remember what you said, darling.'

He put his head in his hands. 'I'm having nothing to do with this.'

Sean called time.

'He made a mistake and the best woman has won. He's a naughty boy and I'll spank him later.'

The two girls laughed, only Petra meant it.

'Fine. I think that's everything. Can you just give me ages and spelling and stuff.'

'We're Dom and Pete,' said Dom and Pete. 'We do performances. Perhaps you could mention it, in passing, you know.'

'Sure thing. Oh, Petra, by the way, is he a good poet?'

'Who cares?' Petra drained John's glass.

Juliet got up to leave and walked over to a long-haired, scruffy-looking man leaning on the bar and said something to him. They both came back to the table.

'Just a couple of pictures, if that's all right.'

'No, absolutely not.' John got up. His chair fell heavily.

There were three flashes. 'It's up to you, mate. Posed or unposed, it's no skin off my nose if they choose the one with your eyes half closed and your mouth open.' The photographer fired another shot.

'Look. You haven't said anything,' said Juliet. '"No comment" is all I've got written down. Your honour's intact.'

'It's OK, lover.' Petra took his arm.

'By the bar OK?'

The pub stood and laughed, shouting encouragement.

'OK, one of John just looking natural. Bit of a smile. Little bit more, lover boy. OK, now the two of you.' The photographer worked fast, knowing their attention span and tempers were short. 'OK, that's good. A bit closer. Look at me. Smile. How about a kiss? Just one more. A bit more passion. Why don't you put your hand round the back of her head and, love, you put that hand on his chest. A little closer.'

'Just do it,' hissed Petra and covered his mouth. Her flat, sour tongue pushed open his teeth. He thought he was going to suffocate. Not even Judas used tongues.

In Petra's chilly, rag-and-bone bedroom John undressed without enthusiasm. They'd walked back from the pub in silence. He was sulking. Sulking was his preferred form of attrition. Passive aggression. He hoped it looked restrained, manly, monumental. Actually it was just sulking. Petra was already naked, she lay on top of the counterpane, one hand behind her head. She was an advertisement. It was a brand-recognition look. This is what you nearly lost, this thin, grey body: the xylophone ribs; the concave tummy; the goose-pimpled thighs; the snack-pack breasts perched on a quail's chest; the dark tangle of armpit; the luscious, dense, game-crop of pubic set-aside; the angular, brutalist, minimal piece of spartan arse, built for post-ironic, post-feminist, post-modern, post-haste coupling. Petra regarded herself. She lived in a body that was the perfect synthesis of who she was and she was supremely satisfied with all its appurtenances.

'Come on, John, I'll die of cold. Come and justify your existence.'

He tried to get under the covers.

'No, lie here, next to me. I want to look at you.'

'I'm freezing.'

'Well, we'll warm up in a minute.' She laid a hand on his penis and gave it a squeeze. 'Now, tell me all about it. I want to know everything. What you did? What she did? How it was?'

'Petra, I've really had enough. You made me look ridiculous; you've had your pound of flesh.'

'Not yet I haven't. You owe me. What did she say? How did you first kiss? Did you undress her? God, what did those horrible, old-woman's plastic tits feel like?'

'Please, for the love of God, you sound like Clive.'

She grabbed the sides of his mouth and pinched them hard together. 'You fucking owe me, John. Now you tell me everything, from the start. You're in her hotel room. It was in a hotel room, wasn't it? She kissed you, right? Now show me. And then she got your sad little cock out. What did she say? Talk to me, arsehole.' Petra's other hand was between her legs.

John closed his eyes. He saw Lee lying on the bed in the hotel, her rounded hips, the curve of her breast, the beautiful blue eyes, the little smile. He remembered the warmth and the softness, the smell of flowers and amber and musk. He started to talk. In the pit of shame, in a whispered monotone, he described making love without adjectives or embellishments, just the facts, leaving out nothing, adding nothing – a love reporter. In his head Lee moved over his body; he felt her breath on his cheek, tasted the peppermint mouth, heard the rippling laughter and the stuttered breath, but that wasn't what he talked about. He described Petra and the last time they'd made love, a little act of rebellion. It made a perfect circle. Petra listening to an erotic fantasy about Petra. She scratched and rubbed herself against his body, transported, like an itchy bear on a stump.

'That was great, John. No really, the dog's bollocks. I really got off on that. We're going to do that again. I'd never have thought it would be such a turn-on to listen to your infidelities. I wonder if you'll be as thrilled with mine.'

John pulled the cover over himself and switched off the light. 'I've been wondering, how do you think that reporter knew where to find us?'

Petra sniggered. 'John, your naivety never ceases to amaze. I rang her, of course.'

'You did! I don't believe it. You didn't. Why?'

'It might lead to something.'

'Lead to what?'

'Oh, I don't know. Fame, success, celebrity, the rest of my life. It's got to start somewhere.'

And indeed a small, emetic, lukewarm drizzle of fame did descend on them, though without the added beneficence of success and celebrity.

The piece in the *Mail* wasn't quite everything Petra had planned it to be. The picture of John and Lee was set beside the similarly posed one of John and Petra. 'Naughty weekend with superstar Lee Montana. Roving love poet John Dart shows his girlfriend how it's done.' Even to Petra's self-obsessed eye the juxtaposition wasn't flattering.

The next day the *Sun* picked up the theme and ran a little box – 'Would you swap this for this?' – beside a picture of Petra looking furious and Lee looking sumptuous. After a wearing burst of puns, doggerel, limericks, scandal, better or verse, rhyme and reason, it invited its readers to phone in and vote about who they'd like to compose a lay with. The results were predictable.

The *Guardian* wrote a piece on the history of sexy poets – Catullus, Marvell, Lord Rochester and Byron – printing a side bar of poems, including one by John. He stared at the page for a long time. Seeing his words in print, he remembered exactly where he was when he'd written it. The first line had come to him in a cinema watching a boring, late-night, new-wave, French film in Oxford. He'd been stood up and had gone on his own. It was the only occasion he'd ever worn a college scarf. In the middle of the film there was a shot of a girl in flat shoes and a headscarf, running down a long flight of steps, and the first stanza had popped into his head, and, now, there it was on the page with Catullus and Marvell, rubbing rhymes with the great. His poem laid out with the works of stellar celebrities. The poem didn't look too bad, not too terribly bad, but it was imposing under false pretences.

A men's magazine included a photograph of him kissing Lee in their regular 'lucky bastards' list and a late-night radio show asked him to discuss celebrity sex with a psychologist, a cabinet minister's shuffled mistress and a stand-up comedian, and that was it. The news moved on, depositing him in the farthest corner of celebrity's green room.

His address, care of the bookshop, was on a dozen harassed researchers' Psions and Rollodexes and Filofaxes, filed under either poet, celebrity, sex or just totty – male.

Felix, his publisher, called at the shop.

'John, how are you bearing up? I thought I should just see that everything was, you know. God, the press are ghastly. When one looks at the state of mass culture in this country one could weep, one really could. God, is this the tilth that nurtured Carlyle and Hobbe, is this the language of Pope and Dryden, how can a grammar that's so elevated be, in the next breath, so mired in filth? We need poets as we've never needed them before. Which brings me to my good news. There's been a trickle of interest in *The Failed Stone*. You know it's been rather quiet. Well, we've had some orders. Don't buy the vicarage in Porlock yet, but it's gratifying. I was wondering how the next collection's going? Have you been writing? One's been thinking in terms of a blast at the crapulous media, perhaps, if the muse strikes you, and some love poetry maybe. Just a thought. Might as well use the filthy publicity to some purpose, grow diamonds in the shit. It's a possible title that, *Diamonds in the Shit*. Have a think. And could you possibly let me have something for a little anthology we're compiling, *Inside Outsiders*, something urban and contemporary. Do come up and have lunch soon, a loaf and a tasse of wine.'

John had the sweet pleasure of, for the first time, selling one of his own books. He'd always wondered who read his poems, who read poems at all. He'd never thought it would be a Betty. A Betty with a lazy eye and immaculate false teeth, somewhere in her mid-sixties, white shingled hair, collapsible umbrella, a coat that looked like it was made out of bus seats and an empty plastic bag. She'd come in out of the rain to browse through travel books, and she'd watched John with her wandering eye and after a time had approached him.

'You're that young man in the paper, aren't you? The poet? Do you have any of your poems?'

John had pointed her at *The Failed Stone* on its unguarded shelf and then watched her as she'd leafed slowly through the pages, silently running through the poems. Was there any meeting of minds? Any door opened? Was there any recognition, revelation, a sudden flattening of the ellipse, an analogy that drew aside the veil on the soul of things? She looked up and they fumbled with each other's glances.

'I'll take this, love. It's a bit over my head, but now I can put a face to them I'd like to try them. I can always come and ask, can't I.'

She laughed, that frail, purposeless laugh of old, lonely people, that really means, Don't take offence; don't hurt me; I don't understand anything any more and if I make this noise that sounds like laughter you'll think I'm still one of us.

The gush of pity, love, remorse and gratitude almost overwhelmed him. He wanted to say, Look, I'll come and read them to you in bed and make you milky tea, and look through your old photographs and listen and smile while you witter on about Arthur and the Morris Oxford. And I'll mend the lino in the hall and glue the china poodle and watch the news with you, and buy flowers on your birthday and cash your pension and get your prescriptions, and fill in the hole that your son left, but he didn't. He just said, 'Would you like me to sign it?'

'Oh I don't want to cause a fuss, you won't get into trouble.' And she laughed again.

He was also asked to sign a few copies of Lee's photography book by smirking girls who looked at his bottom and nudged each other.

Initially Mrs P. had wanted to send Lee's book back – 'I won't have that woman flaunting her tits in the shop' – out of consideration for poor Petra. But Clive had practically lain across the door, so finally she'd said they could put it at the back of the shop, between current affairs and history.

Berryman had called from the *Literary Review*.

'Would you review a biography of Sarah Bernhardt – *Love on a Wooden Leg* – John?'

Then there were the invitations, the friendless party shop-openings, galleries, charities, jewellery, photographs of 'It' girls. John had never been invited to anything by anyone he didn't know before, but now he'd been added to the addendum of PR party lists. If there was a room to fill with more than 500 people John Dart plus one was sent for. He was a spear-carrier, or rather a cocktail-stick carrier. There was, he realized, a whole parallel make-believe social life which only happened between six and ten, Tuesdays to Thursdays. It had nothing to do with hospitality or friendship or conversation or flirtation or even fun, in any conventional sense. It was an elaborate crowd scene, directed by ponytailed bouncers and girls with clipboards, performed for the benefit of magazines and newspapers and 'in-town-tonight' television shows. A rococo and wasteful trick of the eye to fill space and time.

Petra loved them. Well, she loved loathing them. She insisted they go so that she could sneer at people who had what she so desperately wanted. This was her perk, part of John's endless reparations, his Versailles treaty of accommodation. Sometimes they'd take Dorothy and the two girls would stand in a corner scowling and, tearing the underwear off the cast, hold them up to be ridiculed as they so richly deserved. John would walk in slow circles saying, 'Excuse me.' He began to recognize people and half smile at them, but he never knew whether he recognized them from last week's do or from the photographs of some other party he hadn't been to. It didn't seem to matter; no-one appeared to recognize him. Occasionally he saw the photographer who'd caught him and Lee outside the hotel and nearly said something, but didn't.

After three months that was the sum total of John's brush with stardom. Not much, no lasting damage, a slight change of perspective, a cheap lesson.

The men in the pub grew bored with growling at him. Mrs P.'s disapproval became too awkward to carry round all day, so she left it in the stockroom. John's mother left him a message at his digs, but he didn't call back.

But that wasn't all.

*

95

JOHN DIDN'T REALIZE QUITE HOW MUCH OF A HOLE THERE WAS beneath his waterline until one afternoon when he was walking in the park with Clive. They never walked in the park, but this Sunday afternoon they did. They were broke and bored, so they went and walked in Kensington Gardens.

It was grey and windy, the paths were sticky with leaves, dirty geese swam on the Round Pond and swans were blown into its eaves like discarded plastic bags. Dogs shivered under the dripping plane trees, their owners stamped and waited for them to shit and tried not to think what a monumentally stupid thing it was to take another species' bowel for a walk. The only other people in the parks were tourists, who'd rather get flu than spend any more time with their Bayswater hotel wallpaper; fathers, exercising their visiting rights, with crusty noses and wobbly wheels and itinerant youths. The park on wet weekends was sordidly depressing, a place of wasted time and zero options.

Clive and John sat with their hands buried in their armpits on a wet bench, looking into space. John's brief affair with Lee had affected Clive more than anyone, even more than Petra. It bothered him like a chipped tooth. The knowledge that it had happened, but not knowing what had happened, was a constant irritation he couldn't help running his tongue over it.

'John, you might be able to help,' he said, looking into the bleached distance. 'I've got this plot problem. McTavish, right, is with the princess, and that's all fine. They've sorted out the problem with breathing in her bedroom and he's beaten the scales out of her ex-boyfriend and the pearl business is coming on nicely. It's all going swimmingly, so to speak. She's thinking about starting a family.'

'Or a school.'

'No, not a school. She wants a baby.'

'Or caviar.'

'Look, John, we've been through all this before. She's a mammal, warm-blooded, and she lactates. Otherwise, as you so rightly pointed out, what would be the point of those fabulous knockers?'

'Ah yes. But the presence of gills implies piscine obstetrics, and her swim bladder would be awkward with a conventional mammalian pregnancy. For instance, she might float upside down and—'

'Look, John. She's a fucking mermaid. It's a fantasy. Her swim bladder, whatever that is, is self-righting. OK? It's not important; not my problem. My problem is that just as everything is paddling swimmingly—'

'It can't paddle swimmingly.'

'He goes and falls for this other mermaid, only she's not an ordinary mermaid, she's this mega-famous, babe-amaid, the most famous mermaid in the sea. Drop-dead, bollock-exploding, arse-rupturingly fantastic, and anyway, McTavish meets her by chance and they go and have this tidal wave of sex. The problem is I can't quite get it to live. I've got the big picture, I just need some detail. Do you think you could put your mind to it?'

'Clive, I'm not going to talk about Lee.'

Clive slumped forward and held his head with both hands. 'Oh, John, that was my best shot. I need to have live flesh and blood. I've looked at the book till I've got more print on my palm than on the page. I've tried until I'm purple and raw. I know every inch of her body better than my own mother's. Well of course better than my own mother's; I don't know my own mother's at all. The pictures sort of make it worse. They're dots and ink and mechanical shadows; you lust after them, fantasize over them, but I can't get to the other side, I can't make it live. All my life I'm going to see pictures of film stars and TV and videos and famous people; amazing bodies and lips and smiles and bits and everything, and I'll be alone with them, just me and them and the eye contact and the big come-on, and I'm going to say, 'Phaw, I could give her one,' but I can't. I won't ever; I don't know how they do it. I know they do it, I just don't know how. You're the only chance I'll ever get to be there, to smell it, to feel it, because we need to be told. Whoever said a picture is worth a thousand words was talking through their arsehole, pictures just imply a thousand other pictures. It's the words, the first-person-to-person words that make it breathe, so you can taste the sweat. John, are you listening to me? John?'

John sat, not looking at Clive, chin up, his long dark hair framing his pale face, and he stared out across the pond, over the dead princess's palace, over the church steeple, across Kensington, over Shepherd's Bush and Petra's flat and the Maggie O'Doone, across the M25 and the Cotswolds and theatricals playing Pyramus and Thisbe on the lawn, over Wales and the Bristol Channel and Ireland, and on and on, over the ocean, over the Atlantic, over New York and the Statue of Liberty, over the Appalachians and the flat prairies, the Rockies and on to the warmth and smog of California and Hollywood. He looked all the way, but he couldn't see. Tears filled his eyes, blinding him at the last moment.

'Are you crying? You are, you're crying. Shit. Why are you crying? You're crying, what's the matter? What did I say?'

John pinched his nose and blinked. 'Nothing. It was nothing you said. I don't know why, I've no idea why.' And it was the truth. He had no idea. A bloke plays away, gets caught and naturally imagines that all the shit's going to come head-on from the girl-friend and her mates. So that's the bit he defends and worries about, but that wasn't where it came from. That was just a feint, a decoy, full of fire and fury and photographers' flashes, and the papers and the little wounding humiliations, but that wasn't the real attack, the real damage. Silently, diligently, sappers had worked under cover of darkness, unobserved. Just now, when it was irreparable, John had finally smelled the faintly charred air and felt the draught on his back. It was dawning on him that his life was collapsing. There are moments for us all when we can't bear to walk the ramparts of our own lives for fear of what we might find.

'What's the matter, mate? Look, I'm sorry. Forget it. The sex. I'll stick to the pictures; the ones that aren't stuck to each other. Sorry. Is it something else? Is it Petra? Do you want to talk about it?'

'No, no, Clive, really. I'm fine, I'm just sort of depressed. A nameless cafard.'

'OK. If you're sure. If it's nameless, why's it called cafard?'

'Let's get out of this God-awful place. I'm freezing.'

They got up and walked down the wide, gusting avenue. Clive patted his friend's back and squeezed his shoulder in an uncomfortable gesture of something or other. They walked past a naked bronze man on a horse on a stone plinth. The horse looked as if it were considering jumping to the ground and galloping away in a scream of metal muscle; the man restrained it with one sawing, flimsy rein, his other hand shading his brow. The eyes cast a long parabola, as if looking for something over the rim of the horizon.

'She laughed when she had an orgasm.' John spoke quietly, his hands deep in his pockets. 'Really, thick, low, gasping chuckles. A sound of real joy from deep down. When I was inside her I could feel it, hot and hugging, a rhythm of happiness.'

'Bloody hell, John, bloody hell. That's amazing, that's, er, thanks, man, that's amazing.'

'I've never done that for anyone before, made them laugh like that. That's something, isn't it?'

That night John sat alone in his attic trying to get drunk. He'd borrowed a bottle of whiskey from Des and was already halfway through it. Downstairs he could hear the faint television cackle, the smell of frying chicken and tomato purée. Up here, in the eaves, it added to the quiet and melancholy. He realized what a fragile shanty his life had been until his affair with Lee. The beauty, the lusciousness, the pleasure had ruined it. It wasn't that he yearned for fame and four-star-quality lavatory paper and the precious, plastic, privilege-consuming experience, or the lush, exquisite, soft, luxuriant, effortless slither of that big, big comfort and that shiny, shiny, easy, trite, international hotel adjective of a life. It was having been given it and allowed to use it for a moment, it was ruined. His little life. He'd imagined his life was a puritan enamel aesthetic, an understated, noble, breeze-block, spartan, honest life, but it was just gimcrack and cheap and boring. These stacks and shelves and piles of books weren't cultural double-glazing, they were just other people's success, more fame and celebrity. They were written in comfy dens and leather studies for big cars and longer holidays and de-luxe, curvier mistresses and bespoke pockets with pudgy pig-skin wallets. They didn't say anything about him, about John. They didn't belong to him, they belonged to their authors.

John saw his life for what it was: a series of compromises, a grotty collection of accommodations, nods and winks and passed bucks. The job in the bookshop wasn't honest toil, mining in the caverns of literature, freeing his spirit for composing more lyric nuggets, but simply giving up before the contest had started. Failure insurance that removed all risk by stifling any probability of achievement. And his friends, what about his friends? His evenings in the pub, not the easy, solid, wholesome pleasure of working folk, but the lazy, low-definition monotone of just watching what came on. He hadn't chosen his friends because they were exciting or interesting or clever or naughty or attractive or thoughtful or wise or anything at all, they were just bods who happened to sit next to him and not hate him. The blurred bus queue of people who brought other people, who became friends in turn and then left to be replaced by someone else. If he'd sat and smiled in any dole office or dentist's waiting room in the country he would have found a random circle of similar friends. The pub was a petting zoo, lubricated with a mild analgesic, and he knew they felt the same about him. He elicited no passion, no excitement, no expectation, just a mild, anecdotal self-interest in others. And Petra, what about Petra? He put off thinking about her, poured some more whiskey and walked unsteadily to the window.

Outside the shabby street glowed in the pissy yellow light. He looked across the road at the warmth splintering out of other people's houses. He imagined the front rooms, the silent, accommodating couples, the disjointed conversations.

'Do you want to watch this?'

'Is cheese on toast all right?'

'That Malcolm's still giving me hell at work.'

The walking in little circles like toy trains; the back and forth, cup and spoon, paper and lists; and in the bedrooms the separate nightly rituals. The pecks and pats, tokens of a long-forgotten passion. Perhaps it wasn't like that; perhaps it was Puccini passion every night, men with wailing wives clutching their ankles, the smell of sweat and liniment, the thwack of belly on buttock, couples who couldn't keep their hands off each other, their eyes wild with lust, mouths gaping for genital contact, even after all these years. Driven mad by fierce jealousies. People who'd die for each other every Friday night.

He turned away. Frankly, either way, he didn't give a shit. He

100

wasn't interested in them, not remotely, not at all. And he didn't love Petra.

What's that?

You don't love Petra?

Don't love Petra? Don't love Petra? The thought, once it got its knees under a lobe, wouldn't let up.

I can't deal with this now.

What's to deal with; you don't love Petra. It's not like you've fallen out of love, you never loved Petra. What you don't want to deal with, pal, is not having a girlfriend. That's what you don't want to deal with. You would rather have Petra than nothing, because nothing is nothing, is where you started; no, it's less than you started with. Now we're here, now I've got your attention, how about considering that not only do you not love Petra, you don't like her. You don't even fancy her; you don't like sleeping with her, but you will, out of pity. Pity for yourself, because how pitiful would you be without a girlfriend. Petra is the hook on which everything else hangs: your shabby, shitty job; your stupid, shabby, shitty friends; your stupid, shabby, shitty, spartan life; and, seeing as we're doing home truths now, how about this?

John screwed his eyes and drained the glass.

Enough. Enough.

Oh, he says, 'Enough.' No, we're saving the best for last. Look at this. Lee, naked in the back of the car; Lee singing 'Miss Otis Regrets', Lee's head on your velvet shoulder in the mirror. You miss her, that's what all this is really about. That's what provoked the tears in the park, the bottle in the gloaming. You miss Lee, but how can you miss a film star? A fantasy goddess? You won the erotic lottery once, by luck. You made it with Lee Montana. It'll never come again. Nobody does it twice. Nobody gets the bonus ball from Fantasy Island twice, but still you miss her, and she's spoiled everything else. The price of getting into the most yearned-for knickers in the world is everything. Your life is matchwood, pal.

John pressed his eyeballs with the heels of his hands. Not quite everything. It's in the nature of mythological couplings that after the deity has departed the mortal is left with something; it might be a golden ram, a herd of white cows, a cave with a bed of gold coins,

101

or, if you're very unlucky, it might be being pregnant with a couple of swan's eggs. John looked at the irreparable trash of his existence, and there, in the rubble, he found it. Poetry. John Dart, Poet.

The next morning he woke with a head like a knife grinder's wheel. He had that ghastly sense of something being terribly wrong, and depression descended with a dull, damp thud, like a creaking lift. He tried to steam away the hangover in a bath, then shaved and dressed in his only suit, with a clean shirt and tie. Wearing a suit was his personal hangover cure: you make the outside look clean and sober and the inside will follow. Gingerly he went downstairs to the warm kitchen; Des was making coffee.

'Hey, boy. You look very sharp. Clean shirt and polished shoes. You going somewhere?'

'No, I've got a hangover. I feel hellish. Thank you for the bottle, by the way.'

'Don't mention it.'

Mrs Comfort came in, yawning. She was wearing an extraordinary pink nightie-and-dressing-gown combo which had ribbons and a marabou trim. Her large breasts swung like a pair of sandbags, slung on a rope round her neck. 'Hello, stranger. You look nice.' She went and kissed Des on the lips. 'Morning, lover.'

A large black hand gently patted her bottom.

'You joining us for breakfast, John?' Mrs Comfort yawned and went to kiss him on the cheek. One breast escaped and landed with a soft heavy plop on his arm. 'Oh, excuse my tit.'

'He's got a hangover. Drowning his sorrows.'

'What's he got to be sorrowful about? A nice fry-up's what you need. Soak up the blues.'

'No really, Mrs Comfort, I ought to go to work.'

'Oh, forget it for today. Phone in sick. Stay and have breakfast. I never get an excuse to cook a good fry-up. You'll stay, won't you, Des?'

So they sat around the Formica table, surrounded by china cats and plastic clowns and postcards from Jamaica and little boxes made out of shells and coconuts carved like dolphins and Radio 1, and ate eggs and bacon and sausage and beans and black pudding and fried bread and tomatoes and mushrooms and pancakes and syrup, and Des poured chilli sauce onto everything, and they drank concentrated-mango-juice cocktails and coffee. John started to talk about Lee.

'Oh you poor boy, you must miss her. Well, of course, we saw the papers and stuff, and we saw her when you went to the country.'

'I know just what it's like,' said Des. 'Exactly the same thing happened to me.'

'Like when?' laughed Mrs Comfort, pouring some more coffee. 'In your dreams.'

'Course it did. With you. She was a star, man.'

'Get away, I was a chorus girl.'

'She was a massive star.' Des was emphatic. 'Compared to me, a guy off the boat. I first saw her at the Brixton Theatre. It was really miserable; it was wet and cold and I got a ticket for the back. It was beautiful, magic, a fairy story.'

'Panto, love. *Aladdin.* We were the genie's helpers. Harem pants and an ostrich-feather hat. The kicks were murder.'

'I noticed her immediately; there was no-one else on stage, man.'

'Just Charlie Drake and Bernard Bresslaw. Oh, they were terrors.'

'Anyway, I went every night. Begged and borrowed the money for the tickets.'

'It was funny. We used to look out for him. This one big black guy in a navy-blue suit in the stalls, surrounded by screaming kids. He was very solemn.'

'Then it was the last night and they were going and I'd never spoken to her. I'd be left in the cold in this big city, so I went to the stage door afterwards and asked if I could see Karen du Prés.'

'My stage name.'

'And the geezer on the door asked if I was family, and gave me a nasty grin.'

'He wasn't bad. We weren't supposed to see johnnies, but Sid called up on the tannoy, "There's a negro for Miss du Prés," and all the girls laughed.'

'I went up to their dressing room. It was communal, you know, and my heart was in my mouth. I've never been so nervous – a black man with all those white girls. I thought, sure thing, they're going to beat me and lock me up. But I got to see her, and I walked in and, oh man, I didn't know where to look. It was all titties and bums in this little room.'

'They did it on purpose, you know, the girls. They were terrible. Took off all their clothes and just sat there as if butter wouldn't melt, teasing him. Oh, they could be wicked. You should have seen him, a picture, staring at his shoes, with a bunch of violets, trying not to touch anything. He was so handsome and grave. He asked me for a drink and I said yes. We went to the pub. He was sweet and gentle, and had beautiful manners. I had this suit – very nice, expensive, from Fenwicks. Fashion wasn't like today, there weren't a lot of nice things, and the hem had gone, hanging down, so he says, "I'll fix that. I'm a tailor. Only live round the corner." And I thought, Ooh, nice-looking, good manners and he sews.'

'I never had a girl in my room, certainly no white girl. I prayed the landlady wouldn't come out.'

'It was just a little walk-up; very neat, bed made, everything folded away, sewing machine and a gas fire.' She leaned across and held Des's hand.

'I made some tea with a jigger.'

'Yes. With rum. Delicious. And he said, "Slip your skirt off." Just like that, slip your skirt off. Well, he was a tailor and I wasn't exactly shy about walking around in my knickers, but I thought, Lord, here I am in a black man's room with my skirt off, and I've only known him a couple of ticks. Oh, you're getting too easy, my girl.' She laughed and patted his face. 'I didn't put it back on for thirty-six hours.'

'No you didn't.' Des chuckled.

'We lay in that tiny bed and drank sweet black tea with rum and listened to the fire hiss.'

'And we made love.'

'Oh, shush. He doesn't want to know about that. That was when I found out all that stuff they say about his lot is wishful thinking.'

She got up and started clearing dishes.

'Which bit is wishful thinking, man? The first six inches or the last?'

'Silly boy.'

'So that was it?' John asked. 'How you two got together?'

'No, I had to leave at seven o'clock Monday morning. We were opening in Cardiff and I was married, sort of, and wanted to give the bastard a last go, and then I was on the road, abroad: Dubai, Singapore, the cruise ships. We didn't meet again for, what, ten years.'

'I wrote.'

'Oh yeah, he wrote. Terrible, formal letters. "I hope this finds you as it leaves me." By then time had washed away a lot of the debris: my husband, another husband, two miscarriages, my bum. Des got his shop, had a daughter, went grey, got sciatica. The Beatles came and went, cabaret went, chorus lines went, and I was with the Great Toldini doing magician stuff – getting stuffed into a box with a lot of pigeons twice a night. Working men's clubs. I've worked with feathers all my life, but not with the bloody birds still in them. I thought it was time I retired, and I was in Brixton one day and I looked him up. There he was in that little shop, surrounded by his cronies in pork pie hats. I saw him and, it's funny, it all came back. It was the silliest thing, my heart stopped, really, not like me at all. Not after the life I'd had. I remembered that little bed and the gas fire, and I just knew that this was him: what I wanted.'

'She was just the same, man, just the same. A star, the most beautiful thing. So I do know what you're going through, man. I had to wait ten years, but it's worth it.'

'Yes, it's all right for you, cooked breakfasts and a hot bum to put your feet on. Are you feeling better, John?' She ruffled his hair and her bosom brushed his cheek.

'Yes, much, thanks.'

'Good lad. Why don't you take it easy today? Read some of those books.'

Back in his room, sitting at the desk, John didn't feel better. He felt ghastly in a different way. The depression of the night before was still hanging on his shoulders like an autumn rookery, but depression's funny stuff, there's a hint of grim pleasure in it. Des and Mrs Comfort's romance, their happy ending, didn't make him feel hopeful, it made him feel excluded, locked out, watching the golden glow from outside in the bitter cold, but it had added a gypsy violin to the song of self-pity and turned the grim torpor into a maudlin yearning.

He started writing. The lines, words and rhythms came with a desperate ease. There were few doubts. The poetry queued up and laid itself on the page, queued and pushed and shoved and squealed to be let out, frightened it might be forgotten. Writing had always been difficult for him; squeezing the end of the tube. It had been a vocation, not an innate ability. Today he felt possessed by it; it rained poetry. Not finished and perfect, not 'Kubla Khan', but rough, untidy, chunky lumps; beginnings, middles, couplets, quatrains, views and visions. The stuff that could be chipped and polished later, but it was real and it came from somewhere John hadn't looked before. And it gave him no pleasure.

When John finally looked at his watch it was six in the evening and the room was a dreary gloom; the desk was swagged in paper, but the bin was empty. He went to the cinema and watched an adventure movie, ate a kebab, bought a couple of cans of beer, went to bed, had half a wank and woke up in the morning in tears.

Life doesn't get any better than this, he thought bitterly, a week later, as he walked into work. It still took every ounce of will-power to get out of bed in the morning. He hated the shop, resented the boredom and drudgery of shelf-stacking, stock-taking, bag-filling and till-ringing, the days measured in coffee cups and Twixes, the chat and the bloody Three Tenors. Clive's fat, spaniel bonhomie, Dorothy's swaying from nice cop to nasty cop on her friend's behalf. The stupid customers; the indecisive present-buyers; the phoney intellectuals; the cultural weather girls, buying Booker Prize nominations to be interesting and lovable despite their saggy tits; the lonely escapists who could only rise to a paper-and-print life; the holidaying couples who only read twice a year and buy armfuls of paperbacks like bikinis, the less substance the better; the nosy biography neighbours, peering through revelatory keyholes; the angry, cookery-book larder-surfers, buying love and warmth and hospitality to read in bed instead of doing it for real; the self-help bores, avid for writers with more letters after their names than in them, who'll tell them they are addicted to absent men or aggressive women or food or love or masturbation or Persian cats or crazy paving or dollars and yuan or soft furnishings or competing, when actually they're addicted to books that promise to talk about me, me and me; the art-book peerers, too snotty and repressed to go and buy a *Shaved Pussy* monthly. He despised them all, but not as much as he despised himself for serving them, for being a clerk in this cultural hardware store.

John sat behind the till and flicked through the paper. A pretty woman, just back from dropping the glue that held her flimsy marriage together off at the nursery, plopped this week's contentious hardback on the counter.

'Excuse me, have you read this?'

'Yes,' John replied.

It was a policy that they always said yes when asked if they'd read anything, seeing as it was highly unlikely that any of the customers would either read them or remember what they'd said.

'Is it as good as the reviews say it is?'

The reviews had been universally bad. 'Gratuitously nasty', 'impenetrably pretentious', 'arse-paralysingly boring', and 'written with a piping bag full of syrup and semen' were a few of the epithets the publisher had plastered on the paperback, but it had been reviewed comprehensively, with a lot of photographs of the nearly attractive author, and that counted as good notices.

'I think the reviews were pretty fair,' he said.

'So you'd recommend it?'

'Well, it depends.' John picked up the ghastly tome and turned it over. 'Do you like thoughtful evocations of the solitary yearnings of women caught in loveless marriages on the Norfolk Broads, written with a raw urgency and a fine eye for detail?'

'I don't know.' She looked doubtful and mumbled apologetically, 'Is it very sexy?'

'Well, I'd say more powerfully erotic than very sexy.' John glanced at the dust jacket again. 'And there's always the slow build up to the terrifying and tragically inevitable denouement, of course.'

'Is that good?'

'Well, it depends if you like your tragedy as denouement or as a preface.'

'Denouement, I think.'

'Yes, I think so. Especially if it's inevitable.'

'I'll take it. Thank you. You were a great help.'

'Don't mention it. That'll be seventeen pounds and ninety-five pence. Tell me what you think.'

She gave him a sideways look. 'Would you like me to?'

'Yes, I would. Really.'

'See you next week then.'

He handed her the change and went back to his paper.

'Fuck, you're a slimy toad.'

'Morning, love,' he said, without looking up. The great thing about this depression business was that he was too busy being miserable to give a shit. The only social gambits that sprang easily to hand were irony for strangers and sarcasm for friends.

'I thought I was going to be sick.' Petra irritatingly prodded the paper. 'Do you talk to all your punters like that?'

'No, only the female ones.'

'Jesus. I thought you were going to lean across and suck her gusset.'

'Just trying to be helpful.' He folded up the paper. 'Customers come first. How's the photography business?'

'Now, you know it's Dorothy's birthday,' she whispered.

'Yes, I've remembered. We've all had a whip-round. It was a bit short, so I took a tenner from the till.'

'A tenner?'

'It's all right, I only put five in the pot, and Clive's got her something. A book, I expect. And there's a card – not from stock, but just as unfunnily dirty as the ones we sell, an orangutan saying, "Seeing as you're thirty, I'm going to stuff a banana up your arse," or something like that. We've all signed it, and there's going to be a short but emotional service of thanksgiving in the coffee break with a cake. Carrot, I think. Clive finally settled on this being most in keeping with the texture and colour of the birthday girl's thighs.'

'Christ, I'll be happy when you're over whatever it is you've got to get over. You haven't forgotten dinner this evening?'

'No, try as I might, I can't seem to shake off the premonition of slime sandwiches called bruschetta; pink putty salmon with cold boiled potatoes, and no beans because they never get to me; flagons of renal-failure wine and yet more cake. Brown, I would expect this time, either chocolate or coffee. Who'll be able to tell? Covered in a fine glaze of wax and spit after birthday girl has drunkenly sprayed out the candles. All of this couched in the unique discomfort of a Third-World, third-class, pseudo railway carriage miles away in Notting Hill-sodding-Gate, where we won't be able to get a cab and will have to walk home, pissed and starving, and, in Dorothy's case, probably in tears. No, I hadn't forgotten.'

'Right. Are you going to change?'

'Into what, or to whom, perhaps?'

'Forget it. I haven't got time. I wanted to show you the present we got her, that's all.' Petra scanned the shop and then, with a rhapsodic smirk, produced a box from her bag. Carefully she slid back the lid, and John leaned forward to find himself staring at a disembodied penis, very large and pink, which would be an insurmountable inconvenience to tailors.

'Well, at least it's something she hasn't got.'

'Isn't it a scream?'

'I'd have thought the first inch would be a scream, the rest is probably a yell, a howl, a wail, descending into a moan, a whimper and then a gibber. You're not seriously going to give her that? Leaving aside the tastelessness, it's disgusting and it's dangerous. Doesn't it have a big sign saying, "Not for internal use"?'

'It's not that big! It wasn't the biggest.'

'Sweetheart, the other ones were probably coffins for small dogs, or amusing prosthetics for limbless people, or floats for Mardi Gras. Petra, would you put that thing inside you?'

'I don't know. Yes, probably. Perhaps, given the right circumstances. It's got five speeds.'

'Well, that's four more than me. She'll hate it.'

'She'll love it. She's my friend, I know.' She put the penis back in its box. 'Anyway, I got her something else. A surprise.'

'What?'

'Wait and see. And try to be nice. Dorothy's had a terrible time; she's really unhappy.' Petra stressed the really, to differentiate her friend's unhappiness from the ersatz male version he was suffering.

Dorothy had indeed had a horrible time. She'd been dumped by the psychopathic plasterer at the same time John had been caught with Lee, so her loss had gone generally unremarked and she'd bled quietly in the corner whilst Petra had taken all the attention.

The departure of the chronic, frightening Slim had been a relief for everyone but Dorothy, although she'd disliked him and, indeed, had been alternately petrified and stultified by him, at least he was a boyfriend, and losing him to a cab driver had shredded her delicate self-confidence, at the same time as increasing her appetite.

She'd always felt inferior to Petra, which is why Petra had her as a best friend, but now, boyfriendless, she was relegated a whole division, almost a whole species. She became semi-mythical, one of those almost-invisible wraith-like girls who blow dowdily round late-night supermarkets buying tubs of taramasalata and baby pitta breads, a bottle of Pinot Grigio and the *Evening Standard*. They are transparent fairy folk, creatures bearing no weight or substance, smelling faintly of Christmas cologne. Pale, taupe creatures with downturned mouths and haunted eyes which leave no impression. They grow fainter and fainter until they hit thirty, and then they disappear altogether, leaving behind just a cheap Warehouse coat with a missing button and a pile of laddered tights. They spend eternity sobbing invisibly at bus stops and in the exits of multiplex cinemas.

This was Dorothy's twenty-ninth birthday, and it didn't look good. The knell of this penultimate anniversary had sent her to the single girls' gondola at Marks & Spencer, where she'd gannet-gulped boxes of Yum-yums. Food of the devil, snack of the antichrist, Lucifer's elevenses. It's impossible – physically, psychiatrically, spiritually, impossible – not to eat a whole packet of Yum-yums. They aren't made by human hand. Dorothy knew they had some hellish ingredient, that the E numbers hid a necromancer's potion. Yum-yums are cunning hunters, symbiotic parasites. It's their biological imperative to be swallowed by sad girls who aren't getting their bits felt regularly. Yum-yums lay their young in the host's thighs and buttocks and add fleshy bits behind their armpits, and they grow and grow more Yum-yums.

Well, if Dorothy was going to join the legion of the damned, of the Yum-yum unfucked, she wasn't going to go lightly, she was going to go stoutly. She'd managed to pile on a remarkable amount of weight. It hung in great folds, not evenly, not spread with love and care, but dumped in congealing dollops in crags and slopes and shelves, awaiting distribution.

But when all's said and done a birthday is a birthday. The childhood expectation is difficult to throw off completely so, risking the whole of her dwindling fund of optimism on the dinner tonight, she'd taken the afternoon off to buy a new plunging top, which made the most of the Yum-yums that clung to her chest, and to have her hair cut. This hadn't altogether been a success, and the pudding-bowl, geometric effect made you think more of spotted dick than retro-chic lust-kitten.

CLIVE AND JOHN HAD A PINT AT THE PUB BEFORE MAKING THEIR way up to Notting Hill.

Dorothy was already well into a bottle of near-champagne. Petra hovered beside her, patting and preening.

'It's your day, love. You're going to have the best time.'

They walked in, and Dorothy clutched at them with a manic joy.

'Oh, you've come. So nice to see you. God, you look great.'

Clive gave John a portentous, 'call the orderlies' look.

An hour later they sat down at the long, cramped, basement table, set for twenty. There were twelve of them, all girls, except for Dom and Pete, Clive and John. Dorothy's sister, another girl who worked with Petra, a silent Polish nanny, two friends from school and the waitress from the coffee bar, who didn't know anyone but whom Petra had invited on the off chance.

The date, who had been lined up with such care and cunning, and his mate and the boys who played football at the pub, didn't appear.

'Never mind.'

'Fuck 'em, eh?'

'Yeah, fuck 'em.' Dorothy's eyes shone with a fading hope that this evening would change her life.

Petra put John on one side of Dorothy and Pete on the other.

Dinner was hell. The food was as grizzly as anything he'd imagined, the service was patronizing and rude. This was a cheap, cash table, to be got in and out as quickly as possible. It was full of shop drones and tourists, looking for a bit of Notting-Hill smart; embarrassing to be found with them on the premises. They'd have been better off with Pizza Hut. The conversation flowed like a camel with prostate problems, in that it kept wanting to go but couldn't, so there was nothing to do but get drunk, none drunker than Dorothy.

After the cake, chocolate, coffee, whatever, Petra shouted, 'Presents,' which was a bit more embarrassing because there were only three. Clive produced a CD called *Great Mood Songs for Lovers*, music you'll listen to over and over while you sit on your Ikea sofa alone at night, going through the media jobs section of last Monday's *Guardian* and making positive lifestyle lists. One of the schoolfriends shyly handed over a Post-it holder in the shape of a spotted piggy-wiggy, with a spring tail which could cleverly hold a biro – just the thing for those do-it-now! lifestyle lists. And then there was John and Petra's present.

John groaned. Petra's face had the smug, I-know-what-it-is brightness of a wise king, who has not only bought the myrrh but a wholly unexpected mug tree as well. Dorothy unwrapped the ribbon, tore the paper, wrestled with the box and stared, and for a moment her face was perfectly calm. And then her lip trembled, her eyes widened and then closed. Two tears scudded from their corners and became one on the tip of her nose.

'Oh, thank you, Petra. Thanks a fucking million.'

'Joke, joke. Real present's coming later.'

Dorothy held the great medical thing in the air, like the Flame of Liberty, and plunged it into the middle of the cake, pressing or pushing or twisting something on the way. The penis rumbled like Frankenstein into life, sounding like a chainsaw on a wet sofa, and the cake shuddered, the candles vibrated, and there was a horrifying silence and then a peal of laughter. Dorothy, gratefully, joined in giggling and sat down, leaning on John. She put her hand on his lap to steady herself.

'Thank you, John. Although I know it wasn't you, but thanks for being here and thinking of me.' She had a whining little voice, like Tinkerbell thanking children for believing in her. 'Give me a kiss.'

He went to peck her damp cheek, but she put her head back and caught his mouth with hers, inverted lips sucking on his, her cold, sticky little tongue pushing at his teeth. Firmly, John disengaged, and they both looked over at Petra. This had been for her benefit. She smiled a hard little smile and winked. Dorothy kept her hand on John's lap, forgetfully.

And that pretty much was that, except for the bill. The sordidness of the bill took forty minutes of crumpled fivers and strolling ten-pence pieces and bits of paper and people reciting their eight times tables and rows and starting again. And then they trooped out into the cold night and went their separate ways.

'Happy birthday.'

'Happy birthday.'

Because you've got to shout 'Happy birthday' in the street when it's a birthday. It's a special-dispensation thing; it's a common law. And there were no taxis, so they walked back.

'Ta-ra! Here we are!' Petra pulled a bottle of supermarket vodka from the fridge. 'Knew we'd need a nightcap.'

Dorothy's eyes were already glassy and unfocused.

'Great,' she said, without enthusiasm. Her new haircut was sticking up at the back and there was chocolate/coffee slime on her new bodice. Her life was over, so she might as well have a drink.

'Look,' John clenched a yawn, 'I think I'll just get off to bed.'

'Oh, come on, it's my birthday.' The fairy voice whined. 'Have a drink.'

'OK. One. Is there any orange juice?' There wasn't. He topped up the glass with water. Cheap vodka and London tap water, the filthiest drink in the world, the late-night tipple of the poor, the single, the *Time Out*-reading classes, the bedsit cocktail. They drank in silence. John felt sick.

'Happy birthday, Dorothy.'

'Yeah, happy birthday. Wasn't it great?'

'Yeah, it was great.'

'Look, I really am going to bed. Thanks awfully.'

He brushed his teeth, undressed and slid between the bobbled nylon sheets. The room rocked gently. He listened to the girls' voices next door, and he was just drifting off when the door banged open.

'Da, da, da, da. Da, da, da.'

They stood at the end of the bed, slurring and naked, or rather, nude, both of them swaying slightly from side to side. Dorothy had her knickers on – her high-cut, birthday, cream silky knickers with a damp stain on the crotch. They struck a pose and giggled.

John just stared. It was a tableau that made you want to burn every bed in the world. Petra's idea, of course. You could tell immediately that she'd thought Dorothy's body would set hers off nicely. In truth, they looked like a distaff Laurel and Hardy. Petra, sexless, emaciated. Dorothy, lumpen, self-loathing, fleshy and grey; small, drooping breasts; roly, distended tummy sagging over her elasticated waistband; flaring, flying-buttress thighs, textured like raindrops in wet cement; and chubby sausage-roll knees. Her extremities were dabbed with a florid glow: blotchy face and hands, red stumpy toes, russet elbows. It was unfanciable, unpitiable, unloved and unlovable. A rented bed-and-breakfast body.

Petra jumped onto the bed, falling heavily on John. She kissed him and whispered, 'This is her surprise birthday present. She's going to sleep with us.' She rolled over. 'Come on, Dorothy, get in.'

Dorothy was very, very drunk, but still her bravado was leaching away. She was cold and embarrassed.

'All right, John?' she asked.

What could he say? What do you say? Your girlfriend brings her best friend to bed and says we're going to cosy up the slippery bits. What can you say? It's your fantasy, isn't it? Isn't it what all men want? Get stuck in there. Time to unwrap your present.

Petra pulled back the sheet.

'There you are. Oh, a bit sad. Come on.' She pulled at John's cock.

'Petra, for Christ's sake.'

'Come on. Dorothy, get those knickers off.'

She pulled them down. They stuck on her avocado hocks, revealing a dun mat of hamster-bed pubic hair. Dorothy half hopped, half fell on top of them.

'Why don't you give it a nibble?' She offered John's penis like a canapé.

'Maybe in a minute.' The voice was querulous, tiny, like a child's.

'OK. Just watch. Join in when you feel like it.' Petra kissed him theatrically, but with her eyes open, fixed on his. She rubbed herself up and down his leg and moaned, then moved down his body, biting painfully. She got to his cock and stuck it between her teeth like a cigar, and then dropped it.

'Here. Come here, come here.' She pulled the fat girl round. 'Here, sit on his face. You've been dying to. I told you he was ace with his tongue.'

'Petra, I don't know,' she croaked.

'Come on, this is your present. This is your night. Do whatever you like. You know you've always fancied him.'

'Petra.' Pleading.

'You have. You've told me often enough.'

'You promised.'

'Oh, he knows. They always know. Go on.'

'She doesn't have to; she really doesn't have to.' John very badly wanted this to stop.

'You shut up. What's it got to do with you? Come on.' Petra manhandled Dorothy until she was kneeling beside his head.

She lifted a knee and settled like a hen on a hard-boiled egg.

Poor Dorothy. What could he do? What could he say that wouldn't make it worse? She smelled musty and sour and tasted of acid wine, pee and damp talcum powder. The rash-rubbed thighs clamped his cheeks, bits of liverish flesh draped across his nose and coarse hair scraped his chin. There seemed to be such a lot of her. The flaps and filigrees of privacy, the delicate gristle, curled and folded like fleshy seaweed, swaying back and forth over his mouth.

John gulped for breath and got a mouthful of curly pelt and globular bits. He tried to lift the lardy bolster of bottom to get some air, but couldn't. He knew he couldn't fuck this; he couldn't fuck anyone, possibly ever again.

Petra was beside his ear. 'Go on, tongue her. She's never had an orgasm, have you, Dorothy? Never managed.'

There was a gurgling moan above them.

'Come on, John. An orgasm's her present from me.' She tugged his limp cock. 'You're useless.'

He felt her get off the bed, and a moment later the room was cut with the whine of a furious electric motor. It ran hysterically through the gears. Suddenly there was air and light, and John gasped and wiped his slimy face with the back of his hand. Dorothy was on her back and Petra was lifting her heavy legs. With her other hand she held, low, vicious, a domestic blunt object; the blackjack of lust; Cupid's cudgel; the monstrous vibrator.

'This'll do it; you'll come off in a moment.' She stabbed it between Dorothy's red thighs at the delicately cut mess of her sex. Leaning forward she pushed.

John saw the muscles tense on her shoulders and arms, the teeth bared, eyes slitted beneath a thunderous brow.

'Come on, come on.'

The engine dropped a tone and butted its blind Korean head.

'Ow, ow, ow!' Dorothy's hands went to protect herself. 'Petra, stop it.'

'Petra, stop it. Stop it. This is just cruel.'

'Fuck off.' She pushed John hard in the chest. 'Stay out of this until you can get a stiffy. Come on, love, this will do it. You can have one, really you can. And be normal. It'll be fine; it'll be sorted when you've had an orgasm.'

'Petra, for the love of God.'

Dorothy was sobbing, great, wet gobbled noises. She grabbed the plastic knob and wrenched it from Petra's hand, but instead of flinging the hellish thing at the wall she jabbed it at herself, pushing and rubbing, knees splayed, head thrown back.

'Yes, yes. I can. I will. Come on. Oh, please, please, please.'

John sat on the side of the bed and hugged his knees, disgusted

116

and riveted. Petra crouched beside her best friend, palms flat, banging the bed like a referee waiting for a submission.

'Yes, yes. Come on, come on, come on. Come on. Yes.'

Dorothy puffed and yelled and cried, raged for breath, threw her head from side to side, arched her back, twisted, knees pressed together, flung apart. She climbed the wall, thrumming with her scaly heels across the paper, bucking the howling vibrator, white-knuckled, breasts slick with tears and snot and sweat. She jerked and bobbed.

'Pleeeease, pleeeease.'

John buried his head in his arms. Then suddenly the epileptic dry-shag noise stopped. Dorothy, in her desperation to screw herself, had succeeded only in unscrewing the batteries, which slid with colonic plops from between her legs. She continued stabbing at her vagina for a few moments more.

Panting, 'Nearly, nearly, nearly.' And then slowly she ceased. The tragic fantasy slipping through her fingers. She was just a fat, nearly-thirty girl with a ridiculous fistful of cheap, plastic ventriloquist's penis. Slowly, silently, she curled into a ball, her back heaving with tears and exhaustion.

'Quick, quick. Get them back.' Petra scrabbled on the rucked sheets for the batteries. 'Hold on, you're so close. Fuck, which way up do they go?'

Dorothy slid off the bed, sat and then stood up. And in a calm, quiet voice said, 'I think I'll go to my own bed now.'

'Dorothy, don't give up. Dorothy. John, tell her to stay.'

'Petra, shut up. Night, Dorothy; it's OK. It's late and it's not your birthday any more.'

The door shut with a neat click.

'She's drunk.' Petra chucked the vibrator onto a pile of clothes. 'She was really close, but you know, she needs to relax a bit and lose some weight. That was quite horny.' She lay back and reached an arm towards John. 'Come on, let's have a quick fuck before sleep.'

He looked at her in amazement, almost awe. 'No.'

'You can't be that tired. Come on, just quick.'

He got back into bed and turned his back on her. 'No, Petra. Just no.'

The next morning John got up early and dressed quietly. He wanted to get out of the flat. Petra had the day off, so she stayed in bed. As he boiled the kettle he heard Dorothy's door open. She padded shyly into the kitchen, wearing a baggy Winnie-the-Pooh T-shirt and holding an armful of sheets.

'Hi, John. Morning. I didn't think you'd be up.'

They stared at each other. John thought she might start crying.

'How are you?'

'Fine. Well, no, not fine actually. I've got a terrible hangover. Awful. I can't remember anything from last night. Well, after we left the restaurant anyway. I've never done that before, ever.' Her eyes beseeched. 'Did I behave badly?'

'No, no, not at all.'

'Really? I didn't do anything stupid or embarrassing or . . .'

'No. You drank quite a lot of vodka.'

'Yes, I'm paying for it. Just as long as I didn't, you know, make a fool.'

'Of course not. There was only me and Petra here. What could it matter.' John wanted to reassure without breaking the illusion. He looked at the sheets.

'No. Well. Oh these; I must have spilt something on the bed or wet myself. I haven't done that since I was six. Is Petra awake?'

'I think so.'

'I'll take her a cup of tea then. She's not angry with me, is she?'

'Angry with you?' He was shocked. He wanted to say, Aren't you furious with her? How can you ever speak to her again? Why don't you go in and toss the kettle at her? 'No. What reason could she have to be angry? It was your birthday. We all got whingingly drunk, that's all.'

'Yes. Good. Look, will you tell Mrs P. I'll be a bit late?' She got mugs and teabags and sniffed the milk.

There was a calm about her, a sense of detachment. It was, John imagined, how condemned people must be when they get over the raving and tears and make their peace with whatever it is they need to make peace with, and they understand, finally, irrevocably, that there will be no reprieve, no late cavalry, no miraculous happy ending.

He'd never liked Dorothy terribly, but he didn't dislike her either. She was part of the baggage that comes with girlfriends, along with a terrible favourite song, a cuddly toy, a cack-handed make-up bag, an ex-boyfriend who had a bigger cock than yours, the best friend. Now, watching her carefully measure the sugar, exactly the way Petra likes it, he is moved by a great wave of fondness and an aching something. Something between pity and respect.

'Bye then.'

'Bye,' she replied without looking round.

THE SHOP WAS ANNOYINGLY BUSY. JOHN TRIED TO HIDE IN CORNERS. Customers were nagging at him, and Mrs P. kept up a constant stream of questions.

It, this thing, his life, all of it, was barely tolerable. He wondered if it would always be like this. Just tolerable. Maybe that was what the really intolerable thing was. He would tolerate everything; he would sink lower and lower but never touch the bottom.

'What about last night?' Clive dumped a box of books beside him.

He'd been carrying the box all day to avoid working. It didn't occur to him that carrying a box of books that didn't need to be carried wasn't intrinsically any different from carrying a box of books that did. That's what working in a shop does for you.

'Pretty grim, eh? Twenty-five pounds, twenty-five pounds. Petra said it would only be fifteen. That's really fucked me, I can tell you. Dorothy's not in yet. Bit worse for wear, wasn't she, last night? It was embarrassing. She was all excited and then that bloke didn't turn up. Well, none of those blokes turned up. God, she was looking rough. That haircut; it was sort of Rosa Klebb meets Henry V, and she's put on a bit of weight. Did you see the arse on her?'

'I thought she looked very nice.'

'You didn't. You said she looked like Miss Gonkland.'

'Well, you wouldn't be out of place in a soft-toy department yourself.'

'No. Granted, granted. And I'm not saying I wouldn't give her

119

one, if she begged, as a favour, but I wouldn't take my socks off for it any more.'

'We should be nice to Dorothy. I don't think she's very happy at the moment.'

'Are you getting the milk of human kindness delivered now? Who's happy? If you want to be nice to someone be nice to me. I'm an ugly, red-haired Scotsman. At least Dorothy's got a twat, she can get fed and laid whenever she wants. They can, you know. It doesn't matter how fat they are or how stupid their hair is. I wish I had a twat.'

'Or fins.'

'Oh, funny you should mention that. I wanted your input on a scene where the princess's best friend, Laguna – you remember the blonde with big tits . . .'

'They're all blonde with big tits.'

'This one's bigger, a sort of sub-aqua Pamela Anderson. Well, I'm thinking of giving her this thing with dolphins, you know, gang bangs at fifty knots, leaping in and out of the surf, the ultimate roller-coaster shag, with a flexible phallus in black PVC.'

'You know, there's some circumstantial evidence that dolphins are actually attracted to divers in a sexual way. I mean, they may mistake men in rubber suits for potential mates. There was a particular bottlenose in Falmouth that used to come up behind the divers and try to give them one. I remember reading about it somewhere. Dolphins, like most animals that live in schools, are competitive and highly sexed, and then, of course, there's the distinctly erotic sub-plot of all those Californian matrons who pay fortunes to go and swim with them, or give birth with them.'

Clive prodded him in the chest and stretched his eyes.

'No, it's real. Of course, if you think about it symbolically it all makes perfect sense. Dolphins are, as you pointed out, patently phallic, and water and waves have always been a metaphor for female sexuality, so a shiny black penis-shaped thing cutting through the surf with flecks of semen-like spume, etc.'

Clive nudged him again and hissed, 'Behind you.'

'Behind me? Oh, Flipper with a hard-on, of course. Hard-ons are a problem. Dolphins have rather larger penises than humans, with bones in them.'

Clive stared over his shoulder, his mouth open in pantomimic astonishment.

'If a human woman really did try to have intercourse with a dolphin there would be pretty unpleasant internal injuries, possibly fatal, and anyway, you're dealing with mermaids and you've made everything else up.'

'For fuck's sake, look.'

John turned, and there she was, standing in the middle of the shop, in a pool of surreptitious admiration. Lee – beautiful, stunning, surprising, transfixing and very, very famous. Even in dark glasses with her hair tied back she was instantly recognizable, unforgettable. John's vital organs all turned metaphorically, allegorically, symbolically and Freudianly into dolphins. She was looking for something. For an instant he was clutched by the fear that it wasn't him, but of course it was. She caught sight of him, waved and walked over and stood very close. The closeness of people who have already invaded each other's personal space.

'Hello, John Dart, Poet,' and she kissed him, a movie kiss. Slow, close-up, head tilted, lips between his lips. An infantile, suckling hello. 'How are you?'

'Lee. How nice.'

'Nice?'

'Sorry. It's such a surprise to see you.'

'But nice?'

'Very nice.'

'Miss me?'

'Yes. A little, a lot.' John saw his idiot grin reflected in her glasses. She smiled with just the corners of her mouth. Something prodded John in the back. He ignored it.

'Look, I know it's short notice, but how would you like to be my boyfriend again for a week or so, in France?'

'I've got work.'

There was a thump in his kidneys.

'Oh, I'll fix that, if you'd like to. Would you? You look rough. Beautiful, of course, but pale and tired. You could do with some sun.'

'Yes, yes, of course. I'd love to.'

'Love to? Goodness! Where's your boss?'

'She's over there.'

Clive squirmed between them. 'I'm Clive. We work together, John and I.'

'Hello, Clive.' She shook his hand. 'Now, what's her name?'

'Mrs Patience.'

'Mrs Patience. Right. You think he should come and be my boyfriend, don't you, Clive? You'd come, wouldn't you, Clive?' and she laughed and walked over to the till.

'Mrs Patience. Hello. You probably don't remember me.' She took off her glasses with a neat gesture.

It was the most improbable thing anyone had said in the shop that week.

'I'm Lee Montana.' She beamed. 'You were kind enough to carry my book. Could I ask you a huge favour? Can I borrow John for a week, ten days at the most? Would you mind? Please?'

Mrs Patience had said, in the not too distant past, that not only was Lee patently a vacuous bimbo with a body designed by juvenile delinquents, and built in Braille by a blind mammary-obsessed panel-beater, but if she ever saw her face to face again she'd pass on a few home truths.

So she looked Lee squarely in the eye and said, 'Oh, Miss Montana; wonderful to have you in the shop. We simply love your book; we're such big fans. We just love everything you do. Sorry, everyone must say that. John? Oh Lord, yes, take him for as long as you want; he's all yours.'

It's stardom; there's nothing you can do about it. From popes to bog-cleaners no-one's immune to stardom, but it's not quite true that no-one ever says no to them. There are some people with moral bottom who understand that they're really just the same as the rest of us and wipe their bums with the same hand and that occasionally you have to say no, and they do. They say, 'No, of course it won't be any trouble. No, you go ahead. No, no, I insist, take as many as you want. No, no, nothing is too much trouble.' There are rare people who can do that.

'I don't believe it. I don't believe it.' Clive sat on his box of books. 'Why does it happen to you? Who said lightning doesn't strike

122

twice. You bastard. You weren't even going to introduce me.'

'Sorry.'

'Sorry? That'll be written on my tombstone. France, sun, shagging Lee Montana. I'm just going to have to kill myself. Have you got a camera?' He leaped up and grabbed John's lapels.

'No.'

'Get one – a video camera – at the airport. I'll pay. Intimate shots, close up, candid, you know what I mean. Do it for me, please. And try not to get in the frame too much. Hey, what are you going to tell Petra?'

'Shit. Will you talk to her for me?'

'Oh, no, no, no, no. I'd do many things for you, but that's a bridge too far.'

'Please tell her. Tell her the truth. I'll get a Polaroid.'

'OK. Deal.'

'Let's go, kiddo.' Lee was standing beside them. 'All fixed. We'll pick your passport up on the way.'

'We're going now?'

'Plane leaves in a couple of hours.'

'But I've got to pack.'

'Yeah, more grungy jeans and T-shirts. We'll buy you a new wardrobe. He needs some clothes, doesn't he, Clive? Come on. It was nice to meet you.'

Hamed stood outside by the car. 'Hello, John.'

As they pulled away from the curious faces in the shop, he didn't notice Dorothy sidling along in the shadows, a cloche hat pulled over her new hair, carrying a laundry bag full of soiled sheets.

Fthe first time, and this was the first time for John – both the coast and the helicopter. They headed away from Nice airport out to sea and then hummed parallel to the land 200 feet above the little white sails of the yachts, skimming down to St Tropez. If you hadn't been told where this was, it wouldn't have been that exceptional a view – ordinary sea, meagre beaches, masses of cheaply hurried, low sprawl reaching up the crumbling grey hills, an occasional spot of green, some palm trees, a moment of beautiful stucco – but when you do know, when you know that over there is Monte Carlo and Cap Ferrat, Antibes, Beaulieu, Juan-les-Pins, Villefranche, then this is as grand and splendid a view as you could ever wish for. The names roll off the tongue like the battle honours of sophistication and hedonism. Picasso and Matisse, Léger and Cocteau, Hemingway, Fitzgerald, Henry James, Bardot, Belmondo, Niven. Impressionism, futurism, existentialism, hedonism, commercialism, naturism. This is Sophistication Grand Central, a great outdoor café of chic. Fame was invented here. This is where it all began. The rift valley, the cradle of stardom.

Lee didn't like helicopters. She held John's hand and stared at the greasy crop of the pilot's head. John stored it all, not wanting to miss a metre, and couldn't believe that he was here, with the sun pricking the little waves, the tiny cars zig-zagging down the Corniche, the little Dufy flags, the dashes of powdery colour. The melancholy and self-pity of the last month spun away, left on the tarmac in London, left on the shelf between Cowper and Day-Lewis, left in Petra's grisly bed. The joy and excitement, the pleasure and anticipation, the libido, the appetite, the future, all twinkled and glittered with tried-and-tested, confident élan beneath him.

They landed on a lawn with an 'H' painted on it, beside a tennis court on a hill above St Tropez.

'Thank God that's over.' Lee got out, holding her hair against the rotors' draught. They were met by a young man wearing a shirt with 'All right Already' written in gold letters on the front.

'Welcome, Miss Montana and Mr Dart. I'm Casper, the maître d'. I hope you had a good trip. I'll take you to your room.'

The house was long and low and timeless, in the sense that architecturally every bit of it was from a different time and overall it looked as if it had been built in the last ten minutes. It was not so much a design as a who done it, or who could possibly have conceived of doing it. Presumably out of embarrassment and belated modesty, the house had pulled the garden over itself like a duvet. Plants crept and climbed in a profusion up its Ionic, Doric,

Corinthian, Arabic and Hindu pillars, across its Italianate cupolas and Islamic minarets.

'Ah doll. Oh my God, oh my God, you're here. It's so great to see you. You look, godamn it, you look like a star. You are a star. Oh, that body, that butt, what a waste that God gave it to a woman.'

'Leo, you crock of shit.' Lee draped herself on the neck of one of the most terrifyingly hideous human beings John had ever seen.

He was 300 pounds minimum; three cows, a pig and a bottle bank minimum; and hospital-white, under-a-stone white, covered in a moulting matt of dark curly hair. His head was large and held forward on a vast, wobbling neck. He had pendulous lips and a nose of no particular shape or definition, a nose that looked as if it had been dabbed onto his face that morning with the thoughtlessness of a man who might put on a familiar hat without thinking. There were no eyes, just creases in his cheeks where eyes might have been expected to lurk, and on the memorial pate, above the single brow, a pair of sunglasses and a smattering of age spots perched, and at the rough juncture where his head and neck met at the back there was a short, black, greasy ponytail. This creature had huge floppy hands with nails bitten to nothing, and huge floppy feet with great yellow talons, like an ancient bear's. The man was naked apart from a nodular hint of white Speedo trunks, which peeped from beneath a drum-tight belly. A huge cigar, sodden and frayed for four inches from one end and dead at the other, was waved like a wand. Lee buried her head between his tousled breasts and rubbed his tummy.

'Now who's this? My, you must be John Dart, the poet. Thrilled you could make it. God, Lee, you told me he was cute, but he's positively Byronic. Oh, I can't wait to see you both in the pool, oiled and glowing, post-coitally. Sorry, John, to talk about you as a sex object, but I guess that's what you are, and I talk about everyone as sex objects. I only really like sex and objects. See you on a recliner in half an hour for lunch.'

Their room was a guest house, a little way from the main building. It was Jamaican Swiss with Mexican details and was the most sumptuous room John had ever been in. Sumptuous was not a word he'd ever felt comfortable using before, but it was the only one that would do here.

'Casper,' Lee called the maître d' as he left, 'Mr Dart doesn't have any luggage. We'll go into town this afternoon, but could you find a pair of swim shorts for him for now?'

John opened the French-Spanish-Italian windows and went out onto the little patio. He looked out over olive and oleander. Lee came and stood behind him, put her arms around his waist and kissed his neck.

'Quite something.'

'Yes, staggering.'

'Wait till you see the main house, but don't be fooled by appearances. Leo may be the Emperor of the Philistines, but that doesn't make him a bad person. Don't be put off by the way he looks.'

'It's difficult not to be put off, there's such a lot to look at.'

'I love him. He's been the best friend to me all my life. He helped my mum when she was into pills and serial suicide attempts, and when I was young and wild and angry he smoothed things out, and not just for me. Everybody has stories about Leo; he's legendary. God knows how many kids he's put through college, how many operations he's paid for. Generosity is his passion. He's given enough money to Israel to buy them Switzerland. He asked me to marry him once and I nearly did. Really, that close.'

'No. But he's . . .'

'Hideous? Yeah, but only on the outside.'

'I was going to say gay.'

'Oh yeah, he's gay too, but who wants a straight husband?'

'What does he do?'

'He produces things: films, music, theatre deals, treaties, agreements, rabbits out of hats. He produced my tours. He came from Brooklyn – Jewish immigrant parents – went to med school, qualified and then went on and did law. He says you know how Jewish mothers all want their sons to be "my son the doctor" or "my son the lawyer", well he was so big and fat and ugly, even by Kosher standards, he had to be "my son the doctor and the lawyer" before they allowed him home. He made his money, his big money, in videos. He was one of the first people to see the real potential of video. He made a fortune through pornography. Something like one in five porno movies sold in the States is made by him. And you know the great thing about porn: it doesn't date. Sex never dates.'

'Well I never.'

'No, you never.'

Casper brought a pair of swimming trunks.

'I can't wear this; it's outrageous.' John held up an orange posing pouch. 'There's no back to it. This only ever happens when I'm with you. Maître d's give me hideous things to wear.'

'Doesn't look like you've got much choice, chum.' Lee laughed. 'Come on, let's do the lunch thing.'

They walked through the garden, John wearing a towelling robe and feeling foolish and de trop until he saw the pool, which blew any self-consciousness clean away. It was huge and curved and swam to the edge of a cliff. Beneath were the roofs of St Tropez, and then the bay full of yachts, and then Provence and the sky and the little clouds. It was 180 degrees of fuck-off vista.

They'd only seen the back of the house. Out front it was the Alhambra copulating with Le Petit Trianon, lubricated with the High Chaparral, framed all about with royal palms, and around it eddied Lee's voice, singing from half a dozen cleverly hidden speakers.

'Welcome to the office.' Under an umbrella, on a thickly cushioned reclining day bed, Leo basked like a hot Jewish walrus in the detritus of work: papers, faxes and mobile phones. 'You like the music? Remember this number in Rio? I can't hear it without thinking of all those bodies. What do you want to drink? I'm having a Sea Breeze. Hey, have a swim. Did you get the shorts, John?'

'Thanks.'

'I chose them specially from my collection.' He laughed.

John shrugged off the dressing gown and dived in. He swam underwater, and still Lee's voice echoed eerily around him. Lee stood at the end of the pool laughing. She unwrapped her sarong and posed naked, and then stepped into the water, swimming carefully, not getting her hair wet. She hung on to his shoulder, her nipples cold and hard on his chest. They kissed. John trod water for both of them. It was the first time he'd been able to do anything for her. He looked and listened and tasted and smelled and thought and waited and just couldn't find a damn thing wrong with any of it.

'Here, take these horrible things off.' She reached down and pulled off his trunks. 'Don't be embarrassed. Leo's seen worse, or better, and anyway he likes to watch.'

'Lunch. No need to change, beautiful people.'

Afterwards, John lay in the hot and thought what a fabulous indulgence the sun was if you were rich. How it just poured down like God's custard and made everything sweet and silky. Here he was basking, smelling of coconut and bergamot, like an exotic pudding, and from the tips of his toes to the top of his head he felt the benefit of a rich man's sun. Nothing you could wear was as luxurious, as soft and comforting, as beautiful, as elegant as a multi-millionaire's hot daylight. It isn't as if the sun was the same for everyone. A hundred yards down the road there were men laying drainage pipes and a driver baking in his cab and a maid struggling with a box of baby aubergines. It was an altogether different sun for them. Harsh and stinging, unrelenting, blinding, sapping, a mass-produced nylon sun, with health warnings they couldn't afford to heed. It's not the rich that are different, it's the elements they inhabit; the sun is kinder, the water cooler, the air sweeter, the earth softer. Wealth bought you an altogether better, improved, bespoke world.

Having leveraged a timeshare on the sun, Leo wouldn't use it, wouldn't be seen dead in it. It was like the pair of Rolls Royces that gathered dust in the garage or the Monet that was unregarded in the hall. The pleasure was in discarding them and letting the guests use them. Leo was no different from all very rich men. In the end, when you'd bought everything twice the pleasure was in watching.

Lee wouldn't use the sun either. She travelled round the world to be with it, complained if it wasn't switched on first thing in the morning, but colour was for servants and gigolos and daytime soap bimbos. A tan was uncool, it showed that you didn't have work, that you didn't care that your skin was going to be an alligator hold-all in five years, but John wasn't rich and he didn't want to be famous. John just lay and loved it; he wanted to be a handbag for the rest of his life.

That afternoon Lee and John went to St Tropez and bought clothes: Euro-chic slacks and cornflower-blue shirts, slip-on loafers, a cashmere jumper and a patent belt. All the things he would never have bought or dreamed of wearing in a million years. He studied himself in the mirror before dinner – the jersey knotted at his shoulder, the thin cotton trousers, the shirt with the cuffs turned up just so, and he thought, I'd hate and despise this person if I met him. I've seen this man and he's a git. This bloke can make the perfect Bloody Mary, he knows how much cars cost, his favourite film is *The Godfather*, his favourite painter is Salvador Dali, his favourite book is his address book. He listens to Blondie in the car and can do the Macarama. The best sex he's ever had was with a girl who was really a boy above a bar in Thailand. He's a good guest and a bad host, good company but a bad friend. He has the manners of a Californian undertaker and the soul of a centrefold staple.

'Hey, my kinda guy.' Lee came out of the bathroom. 'What a transformation.' She patted his bottom. 'Mmm, blue's your colour. Do you think we should get your hair cut? Now stop hogging the mirror.'

Dinner was six matched queens winkled out of rented houses in the area: an antiques dealer, a record executive and a man who sold aeroplanes, and their silent, sphincter-mouthed boyfriends – lean dark boys, rented long term or just for the summer. They picked things up to look at their bottoms with arched brows, unaware that that's exactly what had been done to them. They all wore neat cotton slacks, slip-on deck shoes, cornflower-blue shirts and patent belts. John noticed but couldn't muster the ire to care. The conversation was sub-cranial anecdotage and gay mood cooing, and the high point of the evening was a tour of the house.

Leo, ugly and unco-ordinated, waved and showed them what you could do with serious money. The outside of the house had only been a hint at the miasma inside. The single interior-design rule had been that whatever it was it had to cost more than a million, and it had to be made by someone called Louis. Everything had been made by Louis. John thought this was probably so that Leo only had to remember one name. He slopped past the gilt and the marble, the marquetry and the dimpled cherubs going, 'Louis XIV, Louis XV, Louis X, Louis the fuck something.'

They ate grilled chicken and salad and sat in the library and drank decaff from Louis' little cups. The library was a big fuck-off Louis room, taken from a French chateau.

'I had to knock the fucking place down to get it out.'

There were thousands of volumes, all in identical, tooled-leather bindings. With a professional interest John took one down. It wasn't a book, it was a box. A video box. He laughed.

'We sold over a hundred thousand of that one.'

'Is it all adult entertainment? Is it all porn?' He thought of the bookshop and his own little room, with its stacks of culture, and he laughed some more.

Leo watched. 'I reckon approximately three fluid ounces a whack. At three whacks a movie, there's enough jism in this room to fill the pool. Ain't that disgusting? That's why they call it the money shot. You're sitting in a palace of solid fucking jism, from Louis the ten inches.'

At exactly twenty-past eleven all the rich queens took their glossy doll boys home and Leo splayed out on the sofa. 'Ah, thank God that's over. That's the fags done for this season. You know it's got to be genetic, being queer. I couldn't be one of them by choice. I'm going to bed. You do what the hell you like.'

'Who's Petra?' Lee lay on her back, still out of breath, her breasts rising and falling, sweat and semen splashed across her thighs. The sex had been different from how he remembered it, not cosy and touchy and funny. They'd got into the room and just done it, ravenously, aggressively, selfishly, silently, while the cicadas whirred mechanically outside. The room was full of the smell of stock and oleander. They'd grunted and snorted and gasped over each other, gnawed and gripped and bit like thin dogs, pelvic punching blow

130

for blow, slap for slap. Lee came with her mouth gaping, the sound turned down, tearing at the sheets and his back. He lay half on her, dazed and astonished, and out of the blue she just said, 'Who's Petra?'

'My girlfriend.'

'You love her?'

'No. Why do you ask?'

'I heard you tell that guy you work with. I was curious.'

'You know that's the first thing you've ever asked about my life.'

'Sorry. Do you want to talk about it?'

'No, not really. Yes, we ought to talk about it.'

Lee pushed him off and went to the bathroom. 'Talk away.'

'Well, I don't know. I'm a bit confused. We had an affair, a weekend, and that was fine, and you went back to your life and I went back to mine and that was that. Then out of the blue you turn up and we're in a bed in this Louis Wonderland in France.'

'You complaining?' She came back to the bed and kissed his chest.

'No, no. It's just that that wasn't it.'

'What wasn't what?'

'Well, you went back to your life, but I didn't go back to mine. I tried to, but it wasn't there any more. What was there didn't feel the same; it had been rubbished. I can't go on living the way I was, but you can.'

'I can.'

'Your having an affair with me is one thing – diverting and fun, I don't know – but my having an affair with you is devastating.'

Lee ran her hand over his forehead and said nothing.

'I'm not complaining, I do want to be with you, but I want to know what it is I've got instead of my old life. I want you to tell me why you came back.'

'I came back because I was in Europe and because we had a great time, and you're easy to be with and I thought this would be fun. John, what do you want me to say?' She got up, lit a cigarette and stood at the window. He noticed the little gap at the top of her thighs.

'You're a poet who works in a bookshop, I'm a film star. I'm one

131

of the most famous people in the world, John. That's not even, that doesn't balance equally. All my life I've had this – my friends at school, guys at college, boyfriends, it's never equal. However much you pretend, however familiar you become. Why do you think famous people marry each other? It's not always a coincidence that they just happen to find the one person in the world they can spend the rest of their lives with is another film star, they're trying to find equality. But, you know, it's worse, because there's always one of you who's heavier, bigger, hotter, and it's the little differences that annoy you most. If you're both in the same business then there's the jealousy, the smiling competition, the over-compensating, the guilt, the walking on egg-shells; it becomes intolerable. You know I nearly married Carlos. His father was a president, he'd grow up to be a president. Down home, it was the one place I'd been where there were more pictures of my boyfriend in the drug stores than me. I thought, He's got an army, he rubs people out, that's pretty heavy, that balances. But it didn't. Outside of El Pineapple Cannery he was still just my appendage, and anyway, he was a lousy, low-life cretin. You know, I'll just have to marry the Pope. This isn't the answer you want, John, but I can't insure your life against falling stars.'

'Did you think about me after you left? Look, I'm sorry, I don't want to sound needy, but if this were a film then there's a page of the script missing.'

'Yeah, I thought about you.' She flicked the cigarette into the night and came and lay on top of him, leaning on her elbows, their faces very close. 'I thought about you, I missed you, I wondered why you didn't call.'

'I didn't have your number and, you know, men in shops just don't call film stars.'

'I know what you want, John. You want a statement of intent, a commitment.' She kissed him. 'I can't give you one, and anyway mine are worthless, but I will take two things from my side of the scale and put them in yours and see if that makes a bit of a differ-ence, lightens the load. One, there are very, very few people I can go with. I know that sounds phoney, I'm Rear of the Year in four-teen countries, the biggest box-office draw. But it's true, whoever they are, most men are unfuckable. If you're me, then the few who are are either after your money or your fame or they're just padding their egos. I don't think you want any of that. I could be wrong, but I don't think so. So I may be famous, but you're rare, and rarity is a sort of stardom. OK?'

'And the other thing?'

'The other thing. I think that was the most exciting sex I've had for a very long time. It was definitely one of my top-ten big orgasms and I want you more than it would be healthy to tell you, and that's rare too.'

'Me too.'

'Of course you too. That's common as shit. Show me a man who doesn't rate me.'

'No. They fancy the film star. I lust after you, this you, the real you.'

'That's Hollywood syrup. There isn't another Lee Montana. Don't look for a hidden me, a quiet, home-loving, knitting, washing-up me, there ain't one. She's a myth put out by my publicity people. Close your eyes.' She kissed him twice. 'OK. Which one was the movie star? Which one was the simple down-home girl?'

'Easy. You close your eyes.' He kissed her twice. 'Which one was the poet? Which one was the shop assistant?'

'Would your poet like to fuck my film star again please?'

John woke up with a start. Where the hell was he? Christ, he was late for work. And then he saw the sun flooding through the open window and he shivered with the bliss of remembering that he was in the South of France with a film star and a brand-new pair of swimming trunks. Quietly he got up and went down to bathe. The day was fresh and clear and warm. He lay on his back and thought that whatever pile of flotsam his life turned into he must etch this moment on his memory, because this was worth it. He walked back through the garden, picked a hibiscus and went in to breakfast.

'Good morning, Mr Dart.' Casper, neat and ironed and 'All right Already', gave him a tour of the buffet. 'Fresh juice – orange, grape-fruit, mango; selection of cereals; fruit – guava, papaya, melon;

toast; brioche; croissants; Danish pastry; coffee cake; bagels; cream cheese; jams – strawberry, apricot, raspberry; marmalade; honey; coffee and tea; infusions.'

'"Stop, stop," said Moley.'

'What?'

'Sorry. It's a joke. *The Wind in the Willows*. Ratty describing a picnic.'

'I remind you of a Ratty?'

'No, no, not at all. Just forget it.' But, of course, having said it, that's exactly what he did remind John of.

'Would you like anything cooked?'

'Er, no. This will be just heaven.'

'Some crispy bacon perhaps?'

'Oh well, yes, perhaps.'

'An egg? An omelette perhaps?'

'Perhaps.'

Twenty papers from around the globe were laid out on a side table. He picked up *The Times* and poured some coffee. He never read *The Times* at home, but when you're abroad you feel you sort of should. Lee came in yawning.

'Morning. You weren't there when I woke up. I thought I'd been dumped.'

'Good morning, Miss Montana. I hope you slept well. On the buffet we have fresh juice – orange, grapefruit, mango; a selection of cereals; fresh fruit – guava, papaya . . .'

'Can it, Casper. I don't need a cast list.'

'Of course, madam. Would you like anything from the kitchen?'

'Yes. A knife. I think I'm going to stab you. Give me some coffee.'

'Your Federal Express, madam.'

Lee sipped in silence with her eyes closed and then ripped open the envelope. There were a lot of other envelopes and faxes and a small parcel with a ribbon.

'Oh good. This is for you. A present.' She slipped it across to John.

'A present? For me?'

'It's too early for the Shirley Temple impersonations. Just open it.'

Inside was a wallet – crocodile, so dark brown it was almost black; the neat scales shone like French polish.

'Lee, it's wonderful. God, how kind and thoughtful.'

Inside was a card from a shop in the Via Monte Napoleone in Milan and a Platinum American Express card. John pulled it out of its pocket. 'John Dart, Esq.'

'I don't understand.' He ran his fingers across the embossed letters. 'Look, this is embarrassing. I can't, I won't.'

'John, please. I want you to have it. It's nothing. You're not being bought. It's easier if you can pay for things. It's just nicer for you. Restaurants and shit. Look, it's no big deal, really. I'm always losing mine. If you've got it I don't have to think. Please don't take it the wrong way.'

'Lee, I really can't.'

'John, it's only money. Whatever happens between you and me, this affair is going to cost you a lot more than it's going to cost me. There's something else.'

He felt in the pocket. At the back was a black-and-white photograph of him and Lee kissing, caught in a flash, his hand on the back of her neck, hers on his chest.

'Outside the hotel. The paparazzi. You saw it in the paper.'

'Sure. I've got a cutting service. It's the best pap shot of me kissing anyone.'

'Have there been a lot?'

'Does the Pope shit in the woods?'

'Hold on. If you saw the papers, then you must have known who Petra is?'

'Hideous little troll bitch. "He dumped silicon bimbo to be with me." I almost flew back just to poke her rodent eyes out.'

'So you did think of me.'

'I told you I did.'

'And you do mind about Petra.'

'Of course I mind. She's a scheming dog.'

'Oh, who are we talking about? Have her over. She sounds like my kind of people.' Leo was the sort of vision that would put a refugee camp off its breakfast – wet and apparently sticky, wearing a Versace kaftan that clung and gaped over his many, many

135

folds and crevices. He looked like a Louis XXXI laundry bag.

'John's girlfriend.'

'He has a girlfriend as well? A penniless poet with a girlfriend, and Lee Montana on the side. You must be doing something right.'

The one thing John had brought from London, along with his passport, was a sheaf of poems. In the mornings, after breakfast, he would sit on the little verandah in his new linen shorts and lawn cotton shirt with a bottle of water and a bowl of peaches and gingerly polish the bleak jet certainties, the desperate élan of unhappiness. The feelings had gone, and now he stroked and edited with a querulous dither, reading the hard, hot-pressed words and the dry-spit syllables. He couldn't recreate the mood. He looked at the blistered lines and saw they had been written by someone else; they came from a cavernous dark that was closed to him now. He was amazed at the black, crabbed words from another hand and at the fact that he couldn't reach back. The sun he basked in cast no shadow and blinded him. So he tidied the lines like a solicitor amending a will, treading lightly on the misery, fearful that he might smudge the emotion, that this shallow happiness would corrode the iron. There is only slight art in contentment. He didn't want to rewrite in suntan cream what had been conceived in tears.

Poetry is the most ephemeral act of creation. Who knows how it lives or how it's born, what it eats, what its natural habitat is. It exists in a semi-mythical place of its own invention, where the road peters out and only a few can bear to visit – solitary hunters or the hunted. You can't be taught to recognize poetry or to produce it. No-one goes to poetry school for three years to get a degree in verse, and yet it exists at the very scalpel edge of culture, a perfect, bright, gleaming thing. Poems have ancient lineage, ancient and rare; a poem was there long before the recorded word of prose. It belongs with dance and rhythm and memory, the unique imperative of a barely new creature with a fearsome brain and opposable thumbs who has been given the peerless gift of imagining beyond the horizon and the dusk, who needs to remember and pass on the essence of things, the kernel under the husk. Poems are the patterns in things that can only be seen with the tracker's internal eye, poems are the spore of memory and John the poet couldn't remember.

He realized that these few spare pages were the diary of a journey he would never make again. That he had worked at being a poet, at making poetry, for so long, but only in these few weeks had he stepped off the well-worn lyrical track into the forest and found poetry growing wild in the roots and rotted sphagnum of his life. He might never find this place again and, he thought ruefully, he didn't want to go and look.

John picked up a peach and considered it. Dare I eat a peach? Nothing could crack the sugar coating of his day. Depression and despair were like pain or hunger or cold, feelings it was impossible to recreate out of happiness and warmth. That then was the poetic justice.

He walked down to the pool. Lee was lying naked on her tummy in the shade. He kissed her shoulder.

'Had a good morning, sweet? Full of rhyme and reason? Up there in bed, meeting the beat?'

He ran a hand over her glossy bottom. 'I think I'm going to compose a sonnet to your bum.'

'Only a sonnet? I expect a saga. You want to swim?'

'In a minute.'

Lee walked over to the pool, slid into the water and swam lengths with a slow breast stroke, her head high, as if she were balancing an invisible tray.

Over the other side of the pool, Leo, one hand down the front of his trunks, shouted into a mobile phone. 'I don't care! I don't fucking give a shit! You can fuck yourself! I said fuck yourself! Yourself! Speak English, you fuck! Fuck yourself and your sister and your mother! *Votre mère*, fucker! What! What! Fuck yourself in the arsehole with AIDS on! Shit, the man's a fucking fuck. Hey, John, what's the French for may wild donkeys piss in your daughter's cunt?'

'Eh, *le potage du jour est rognon, mon brave.*'

'Hold on, hold on, you shit sucker, get this. *Le potage du jour est* fucking *rognon, mon brave* fucker. Yeah, yeah. Fuck on that, you fuck. Hey, I think he's crying.' He tossed the phone down. 'What a country. What a fucking country. Their cheese smells like cunt and their cunts smell like roses.'

The phone rang. 'Yeah, Maurrie. No, this fucking country. Their cheese smells of cunt and their cunts smell of roses. Yeah, I just made it up. Yeah, I know. How's my money?'

John sat and watched Lee's neat pudenda open and close as she frog-kicked. The rest of her mail was strewn beside the seat. He picked up a letter, written on lined exercise paper.

'Dear Miss Montana. I love you. I have seen everything you've done. I expect you get lots of letters like this, but I really want to be like you. I'm seventeen. I'm in hospital at the moment. I have cancer and all my hair has fallen out. I asked for a wig like your hair. I can feel you fighting the tumour. It's late, I am having another operation tomorrow. I know it will be OK because you are with me. I love you and I know you love me.'

It was signed Susan.

Another hand had written LP and put a tick at the end.

He picked up another letter, written with an old manual typewriter. The 'O's and 'P's and full stops had punched little holes in the thin paper.

'Dear Miss Montana, your book is really great. I got it from a shop. You are some piece-of-arse lady. I mean that respectfully, but looking at it I can see that you're a lady who likes it, but I guess you don't get it much in Hollywood with those AIDS fags. You look like you could do with some down-home all-American cock. I'm the man. I know we would make beautiful music together, as they say. I'm twenty-five, six foot two, with blond hair. I was in the military. I work out regular, my dimensions are chest 50", pumped biceps 26", neck 20". The bit you're interested in is 13½" at attention and 7" round, prime American meat. I shave all my body hair. I am smooth and lean from my balls to my eyebrows. A typical date with me would be, I'd pick you up and we'd plan to go and have steak and a pitcher in some fancy joint but you'd say, "Why don't we eat in?" Then you'd grab my old man and we'd go to it, on the leather sofa, and you'd eat my meat till you choked, and then you'd fix some beer and potato chips and we'd watch blue movies and you'd say, "Will you do those things to me, honey?" and I'd say, "Sure," and whack it up your butt hole, because that's what you really want, and then I'd kiss you goodnight 'cos I know you're not used to being treated like a lady. Yours in anticipation, Andy Miskow, Marines (Honourable Discharge), 1356 Neil Armstrong Road, Coolidge, Indiana, 4580. Phone 234 7850 (Ask for Andy, the spray guy). P.S. There's no need for to wear a rubber 'cos I'm real clean and never had anal with a guy.'

There was an LP and a tick added to the bottom.

A third one.

'Bitch, great whore, etc. You think you can get away with it and laugh at God and me and make sex all in the street (posters, TV aerials, etc.), but you'll pay in hell for eternity, etc. You and the Yid bankers and politicians and Imran Hussein and all doctors, etc. I will be the instrument of vengeance. God will cut out your womb with a knife, dipped in dog shit, by my hand, and you will not breed more filth but die. Bitch. Whore of unclean uncircumcised things. I saw you outside 436 Hollywood Boulevard, 11 o'clock, 12 June. I followed you. I know where you live in sin. No-one can see me because the Lord hides me in his wing, but I can see you. I'm coming for you. I can see you right now.'

'Fans. Aren't they wonderful?' Lee dried herself.

'Sorry. Do you mind my reading this?'

'God no. There's plenty more. I don't get sent most of it. My office deals with them. They just pass on the ones they think I should be aware of, or which will make me laugh.'

'This one's really frightening.'

'The one who wants to gut me with a shitty knife? Yeah, he's a regular. We're passing him on to the police.'

'Doesn't it depress you?'

'Sometimes, but I've had it all my life. You get used to it.'

'But they're mad. That sex fantasist. The girl who thinks you're going to cure her of cancer.'

'Yeah, well, maybe I will.'

'Lee.'

'You're right. Sick and mad. Terrifying. And there are thousands of them. I'm just one film star. Think of Hollywood. Think of what the mail in California is like every day. Thousands and thousands of sweaty threats and sticky fantasies, the pleading and the begging and the revelations. A whole book of revelations every day, with illustrations – the drawings, the defaced photographs, the biro cocks in your mouth, the daggers and cleavers and needles, the Polaroids of their bodies – and the stuff that's packed up, sealed, stamped and sent. My secretary has to wear body armour and surgical gloves to do the mail. The world is awash with psychosis, it's a joke. Tampering with the mail is a federal offence, but the mail's a sewer, it's a moral offence.'

'Don't you feel responsible?'

'What, John? Like this is my fault?' She picked up the threatening letter. 'The victim teases the stalker? Oh sure!'

'No, I don't mean that. I mean, well, this whole thing of stars and fame. It acts like a magnet, a funnel for all the delusions, anger, fears and frustrations; it inflames them, makes it worse.'

'God knows. You mean if there was no-one to stalk, there'd be no stalkers, and if there were no cars there'd be no drunk drivers. But there'd still be drunks. I don't ask for this, I just want to sing, do my act.'

'Perhaps that's what they're doing, the letter-writers; it's just their act. Chanting and make-believe.'

'Either way it's pretty Tony Perkins. You know someone interviewed me once and said, "Who do you think of when you do your thing?" I made up some shit, my mum or someone, but the fact is that I try not to think about any of them. I don't want to look at them in the concerts and the crowds outside the movie theatres. They all seem so normal, so ordinary. But these people, they know everything about me, more than I remember about myself. They keep scrapbooks and paper their attics with my picture. They go home and take a tampon out of their body, put it in a Jiffy bag and send it to me, and then they get on with their day, watching the TV, phoning a friend, making tea for the kids. That's so weird. The guys who jack off onto photographs, well that's sort of understandable. That's normal compared with some guy who squats over a sandwich box in his bathroom, with the door locked, to send a shit parcel to a girl in a soap opera who's just read an autocue that says, "Brad, I'm pregnant with an alien." Or like the man who finds a dead rat in his garbage and thinks, Oh, I'll send that to Lee Montana; she sings a song my wife likes. The one thing no-one ever said about fame is how frightening it is. Outside, they're all there; the ones who love you are as scary as the ones who hate you. Their adoration gives them squatters' rights on your life. If I change my hair a thousand women wish me dead from cancer because I've let them down, they wanted to be me. Let me tell you, only famous people know what a fucking free-range lunatic asylum the world is. You all think it's full of pretty regular guys and just a few sad bunnies, but I know that under the surface they're all raving berserk, emotional loony tunes, perverts, monomaniacs, copraphiliac exhibitionists. I know that sounds paranoid, but you haven't stood on the edge in the spotlight.'

John did think it sounded paranoid. 'What's this LP and a tick at the bottom of the letters?'

'Oh, that means they've been sent a letter and a photograph. Standard "Thank you for writing. It means so much. Hope you enjoy the new film/album, whatever".'

John imagined the discarded Marine in Indiana getting his and said nothing.

'You know what really gets me? It's when stars say how much they love their fans. That "I just love you all" bullshit. We're terrified, terrified and disgusted by them. Being a performer is like being employed by a board of mutant, cretin savants, half of whom hate you and half of whom want to fuck you in the ear; and they pay my wages. This is the damnedest job in the world, but nobody wants to know about that bit of it.'

'Lunch,' shouted Leo. 'It's Lobster Maurice Chevalier, or some damned thing.'

And so it went. The sun rose and set. The lobsters and the labial cheese and the cold wine came and went. John turned from parchment to brown paper. A tan suited him. His blue eyes looked icy, his black hair fell in glossy ringlets, his shoulders relaxed. He stopped looking like a bent coat-hanger and walked with a lazy nonchalance; he learned to lounge. In fact, he'd never felt better. Food and sleep and sun and sex. He and Lee fell into an easy rhythm of morning fuck, then swim, then breakfast. John would work on his poems, then lunch, then a siesta and a little restful, dry sex, then a trip to town for a drink, amusement shopping and evening swim, dinner and bed.

His head drained, the tinnitus of worry and evaluation was turned down, leaving the low hum of smiley synapses. Through lazy eyes, he watched Lee, without the stomach-churning anxiety and disbelief, and he noticed that she didn't have a natural muscle in her body, every move she made was choreographed. There was a way to light a cigarette, a way to smoke a cigarette, a way to get up, sit down and walk into a room. She had two laughs, one with her head back, one slightly bowed. A way to look over her shoulder. There was a way she took a shower, as if she were advertising soap. She sat on the loo and made it look like a Porsche in a motor show. She was a strict classical ballet without music. She knew exactly how she looked all the time. There was a personal radar in her head, keeping track of her profile and limbs, eyebrows, the angle of her bosom. Even, no especially, when they made love. She performed for the cameras. She would start with the establishing shot, then track and zoom and finish with a lingering close-up. He wasn't complaining. John wasn't complaining about anything. He had a mauve cashmere sweater over his shoulders, no socks and a big smile.

Celebrities live in a different space, a parallel Alice universe, a one-way looking-glass world, where the great anonymous can peer in, but the objects only see their own reflection. John learned this on their trips into town. It was amazing, people would stare without embarrassment, without concern, as if they were staring at a screen or a page. They would come up close and glare, go off and get their husbands and bring them back. Lee would look right through them, smiling at her reflection. John also found there was a whole new etiquette to be learned when you were out with a celebrity. You didn't open doors for them, you went in first, alone, to take the brunt of flashbulbs or dead rats or tampons. When you'd secured the area, the object would enter and stand in the door for two beats. Lee walked very close to him with her arm through his. On the first morning he understood that they couldn't wander like other couples in meandering patterns. If he wasn't there beside her all the time there was a real panic. His job was to be a tug on a short rope, piloting this great liner through the shoals. Lee couldn't be on her own, not for a second. She was just too vulnerable, like a white seal pup wearing a Rolex. He had to carry everything. Well, that was all right, he expected that – bags, flowers – but she couldn't have anything in her hands at all. She needed them free at all times to protect her face, her breasts, her crotch, in case the man with the shitty knife was just round the corner. Just in case. John didn't mind, and after a bit he didn't notice; this seemed natural in an unnatural way. Lee shouldn't have to live by the normal laws of social physics. It was as natural as the everyday life of fairy tales. St Tropez was her natural habitat.

They walked, arms round each other, down the quay, past the absurd boats, which looked like giant bathroom fittings with crapulent overflows, rocking in their own bilge. The anonymous stared and were pleased. If you go to Africa you want to see lions; in London, Beefeaters. In St Tropez you want to see celebrities; they are part of the wildlife.

Lee stopped at a news stand.

'Do you want to send a postcard to anyone?'

There was a rack of bare-breasted girls sitting in the sand or a selection of four bottoms, 'Views of St Tropez', and he thought about the bookshop. 'Glad you're not here. Having a lovely time. Give my regards to the Penguin Classics, especially F. Scott Fitzgerald.' Or Petra. 'Darling, sorry to leave without saying good-bye. Getting a tan and fucking Lee Montana (you remember). Tell you all about it when I get back.' His parents. 'Dear Mum and Dad. A bit different from our two weeks in Worthing, but enjoying myself, without being a nuisance. Love Johnny.'

'No,' he said. 'I can't be bothered.'

'Will you send me postcards when we're apart?' Lee hugged his arm.

'If you give me your address.'

She laughed. John imagined the girl in body armour holding up a picture of Byron with rubber gloves and scribbling LP with a tick, saying, 'Oh it's him again, the nuisance.'

'I'll send you cards thanking you for curing my cancer and that I

143

really want to fuck you like a dog and that God has told me to follow you and that I really, really love you.'

It hung in the air.

'Oh, this is such a great shop. I was here before. There's something I want to get you.' She pulled him in.

'Bonjour madame, m'sieur.'

Lee took a pair of sunglasses off a rack and fitted them over his ears. Sunglasses. He'd always known sooner or later it would come to shades. Sunglasses were a problem for John, and they were a bigger problem when they were called shades. Shades were his line in the sand. He didn't do shades. He'd never owned a pair. He wouldn't wear sunglasses on principle. The only people who were allowed shades were blind men and celebrities. Everyone else was a ponce or a poseur. Sunglasses had nothing to do with sun, you didn't see Indian peasants in shades or African tribesmen or Aborigines or Bedouin – all the people who live in a megawatt glare. Sunglasses came with a ghetto blaster, a Kalashnikov, a Mercedes and a UNICEF bank account. Sunglasses were for stupid, insecure wannabes, who thought that enigma was an anagram of interest, people who thought that if you couldn't see their eyes you might mistake the rest of them for someone attractive. Shades were for human ostriches. Except in Lee's case, because the normal rules didn't apply to her. She fitted a pair over his ears. The label hung down across his nose.

'No. No, you look like a fag biker.' She pulled glasses out of the rack and handed them to him. 'No, too severe. No, too small. No. No.' Finally, 'These. What do you think?'

He looked in the little mirror, and there was his face, tanned, big mouth, high cheeks, strong jaw, framed in dark hair, with these wire aviator shades.

'They make you look sort of sexy, sort of international, sort of cool in a hot way, sort of enigmatic. Sort of "catch you later". We'll take them.'

He stepped over the line. It was no big deal.

'Thank you, darling. Really sweet.'

They kissed.

His black orbits reflected in hers, back and forth infinitely.

The Peek-a-boo was a restaurant. Really it was just a collection of huts and clapped-out garden furniture on the beach. You got to it by driving through the grey dunes and then walking up rickety duckboards between wooden fences. There was a cabin that did for the kitchen and loos and another one that had a little shop selling expensive bikinis, sarongs and silverish jewellery. The dining room was a collection of pink-clothed tables which stood hugger-mugger on an uneven floor under stained umbrellas and a plastic awning. It was dotted with sickly, potted castor-oil plants. The bar wailed with loud, distorted pop music and the Mediterranean shifted sullenly in the background. It smelled of rancid fat, rotting salty rubbish and fried onions. Anywhere else in the world The Peek-a-boo would have been closed down as an eyesore, a health risk, a squatter camp. Here it was the most, the best, the smartest place to eat lunch. They got out of the Rolls.

'You know this meeting is important, and it's really why we came here,' said Lee.

'Oh yeah. I thought it was to eat all my food, drink all my drink and stain my sheets,' laughed Leo.

'That as well. Remember everyone?'

'Yes,' said John. 'So you really are going to do *Antigone*?'

'Ninety per cent. You think it's a good idea?'

'No. I think it's a great idea. It'll be a challenge.'

'Yuh. I can do it once and then tell those doublet-and-hose geeks to fuck off.'

'I think it's a fucking dreadful idea,' said Leo. 'You need your head examined. Who gives a midget's prick for some Greek bitch who insists on burying her brother; it's so depressing. No-one gets fucked and there's a miserable ending. If I were the king, what's his name? Creon? Yeah, Creon. If I were Creon, I'd just say, Do what you like, bitch, I should care. And that's an end to it. I'd send her to the Betty Ford to get her straightened out.'

'You're so full of shit. Why do you go on pretending to be such a philistine? I remember you lost a fortune putting on *Oedipus and the Bacchae* on Broadway.'

'That's different. A guy who schtups his mother and a bunch of sex-mad chicks who tear men to bits, that's entertainment, and anyway, I was mad for Damian. You remember that lousy actor. God, it cost me a million dollars to give that prick a blow. You know how bad an actor he was, he couldn't even act grateful.'

The place was packed; the bar was covered in fat, Middle-Eastern men, wearing baseball caps and watches like gold loo seats, feeling up spindly girls in string bikinis, who jigged and shimmied to the music. There was a regular pop of corks and little shrieks of faked glee. At another table John noticed Joan Collins sitting with Roger Moore and an elegant boy he recognized from the Sunday-paper photographs. George Michael was a little further off, silent in the middle of a jabbering group of Brazilian boys. Oliver Hood and Stewart Tabouleh were huddled together at a big table.

Oliver, uncomfortable and hot in a striped shirt and an insufferably jaunty Panama hat, half got up and stretched his arms in benison. 'Lee, Lee. Well met, my dear, in this fool's paradise. And, John, how nice.'

'Do you know Leo?'

'No, I don't think so. By reputation, of course.'

'Yeah, we met in LA. You wanted me to put money into *A Winter's Tale* or something.'

'Oh, of course. Forgive me. Unfortunately, it never got off the ground. I still have the script if you're interested.'

They both laughed.

'Like I'm interested in frostbite.'

'Let me introduce Stu Tabouleh.'

Stewart nodded, raised a delicate hand and looked very gay in prim, ironed khaki.

'I'll just go and get the girls.' Oliver squeezed through the tables to a line of sunloungers and returned with Betsy, dark and drawn, her arms and legs muscled and scrawny, her skin tight and dead, and Skye, grotesquely fat. She must have put on a stone since John had last seen her at the mill pond. Her breasts shuddered in a tiny cut-off T-shirt, her corrugated bottom wobbled and sagged over a lime-green thong, she was bright, blotchy red and greasy, and wore a huge pair of mirrored shades which made her face look like a bad special effect from a science-fiction movie.

'Hi, people,' she shouted at the table.

John caught Lee's look of revulsion, and behind her shoulder Joan Collins turned in her seat, said something and laughed.

Skye sat down heavily beside John. 'Hello, have we met?' she said archly.

'Yes. Gloucestershire. You showed me your pond.'

'Oh, right. You meet so many people. Is this your first time here?'

'Yes.'

'Isn't it great? This is the coolest place, in Europe anyway. Not counting America. We've always come. It's quiet this year, but still it's the place, isn't it?'

'Yes.'

'So, you and Lee, you're still an item.'

'Yes.'

'Good for you. I thought after that stuff in the paper you'd be out in the cold, but you obviously handled it. Good for you.'

There are few things more titanically annoying than being patronized by an ugly teenager. John just smiled and sipped his water.

Lee sat between Oliver and Stewart, who took it in turns to talk intensely to her. Lee concentrated, staring at the tablecloth.

Leo made one-lump-or-two small talk with Betsy, who watched Lee like a whippet watches a Mars bar.

'How's school?' John tried to keep the malice out of his voice.

Skye made a bored face. 'Oh, one goes through the motions.' She was obviously having a Merchant-Ivory phase. 'I'm leaving next term. Dad says I can go to stage school until I'm sixteen, and then go back to LA. So, John, tell me about your sex life.'

'No.'

A photographer did the rounds of the tables. 'Would you like a picture all together?'

'That would be nice,' said Oliver.

'Not really,' said Lee simultaneously.

'No, no.' Oliver changed tack in mid-sentence.

Behind Lee's shoulder a girl appeared at the table; she was pale, with spiky, gamine hair, freckles and slanting green eyes. 'Miss Montana? I know this is really impertinent, I'm sorry.' She spoke with a Scottish accent and a lot of charm. 'But please could I have a picture with you?'

Lee moved sideways to get a better look at her. 'Honey, it's a bit . . . oh well, sure.' She smiled at the camera.

The girl bent down.

Now the photographer saw his chance. 'Or one of all of you? It'll only take a moment together.'

They squeezed up; Skye put her arm round John's shoulder and squished her bosom into his side.

'Thank you so much,' the girl said. 'I'm such a huge fan. I just love all your songs; you're a great influence.'

'Thank you, dear.' Lee turned back to the table.

'And we have the same record label.'

The interest of the group turned from mild embarrassment to curiosity.

'You sing?' asked Stu.

'Well, yes, I'm in a group. Sorry, I should have introduced myself. I'm Isis, my group's called Up Late.'

Everyone looked blank except Skye, who said, 'Oh my God, oh my God. You're Isis from Up Late.'

'Yeah. Hi.'

'I'm Skye Hood. Oliver Hood's daughter. That's my dad.' Skye's voice was squeaky with excitement.

'Hi.'

This was becoming deeply awkward. Did they introduce the whole table, because that would elevate this person from self-confessed fan to peer, and how famous was she exactly? Skye knowing her was hardly a recommendation, but then pop and the youth market were huge, really huge. And you never knew. They racked their memories. Was this Isis someone they should know? Was this about to be a *faux pas*? Perhaps she was *someone* and not just *anyone*. The table shuffled.

Finally Leo took a punt. 'Look, why don't you join us for a drink, Isis. Are you with people?'

'No, no. Just my manager and a journalist, over there. They're drunk and looking for sex and drugs. I'm here doing a promo shoot.'

'You're in the charts, aren't you?' Skye beamed. Suddenly she was the expert.

'Yuh, in seven countries, but one of them's Luxemburg, so six and a half really. I've just heard the album's gone gold, that's why we're drunk. They're playing it now.'

That settled it. She was one of them. Welcome to celebrity.

'I'm sorry. Were you talking about something important?'

'No, no,' said Oliver, 'we've finished. In fact, let's have a toast. I think we can make an announcement, can't we, Lee? Glasses, everyone. Here's to Antigone and Lee Montana, two formidable, timeless heroines. Antigone and Lee.'

'You're going to play Antigone?'

'It looks like it,' Lee smiled.

'Oh, that's great. I love that play. Oh, you'll be perfect. Are you doing Anouilh's translation?'

Lee looked blank.

'Yes. Basically, we are. You know it?' Stu broke in.

'I was in it at school, I was Antigone.'

'That's funny, I was the chorus,' said John.

Lee shot him a look he didn't understand but didn't think was nice.

'Why don't we all go down to the house and hang out round the pool? This place is getting like a petting zoo,' said Leo.

'Yes, come back and have a swim,' Lee smiled frostily.

The bill came and John grabbed it. 'Let me.' He'd never paid for so many people before, the satisfaction value was remarkably high, even if it wasn't his money. The figure was histrionic, disgusting, laughable. He added a 15 per cent tip to the service charge and signed with a flourish. No-one was watching, no-one was impressed.

They all lay in the hot afternoon sun. Oliver and Stu cornered Lee to talk serious greasepaint. John could tell she was bored and annoyed. Her attention span was short. They had a lot to say and didn't they just have the longest way of saying it. Lee was not a good listener.

'Honey, I don't do audience.'

John thought about rescuing her, but then didn't. If she wanted to do theatre then she could suffer the grease of the producer and the roar of the director, and anyway he was intrigued by Isis. He couldn't stop looking at her – rangy and supple, her long fingers and air of lazy confidence and an utterly winning smile. She was very, very sexy. The sort of girl that Petra should have been if Petra hadn't been, well, hadn't been Petra. John put the thought out of his mind.

'Look what I've got.' Leo trotted down from the house. 'It's Isis's album, Casper had it.' The music pumped out of the speakers; the voice was growling and husky, with thrilling, clear, high notes and an electrically augmented power. John realized he knew it, that it had tumbled out of pub jukeboxes, jeans shops, delivery vans and passing televisions. It was the great democratic thing about pop music, it was the people's culture whether you wanted it to be or not. Lord or labourer, everyone was doused in it. He watched Isis lie in the shallow end of the pool, her long arms stretched out across the handrail. Lee was now lying on her back, her arm cocked over her eyes. Either side of her the ardent theatricals sat, talking, a long rally, as if she were the net.

'So who are you?' Isis came and sat beside him.

'John Dart.'

'You're Lee's boyfriend. God, listen to me, calling her Lee.'

'Yes, I suppose. Yes, I am.'

'And you're in this business?'

'Films? No, I'm a poet.'

'Really? A real poet? That's fabulous. How great.'

'And I work in a bookshop.'

'Nooo. I worked in a bookshop, well, it sold records as well. In Forfar. It was hell. Oh heavens, the boredom.'

'I know. I'm not sure I can go back.'

'It spoils you, doesn't it? All this.' She gestured to the pool and the house and the view and the cloudless blue sky. 'Well, not you. It spoils everything else.'

'Yes. I've just been thinking that lately.'

'But this, it isn't an alternative, is it? It isn't for every day. It hasn't got, you know, a mission statement.'

'A mission statement?'

'Yeah, I mean, look at us here around this pool. We're such a weird collection. You and Lee and then Oliver Hood and that director, and that poor, fucked-up wean turning herself into a mixed grill, and that strip of angry-rawhide stepmother with piles, and Leo. What's he when he's at home? I presume this is home, and not the most expensive bad-taste joke in the world.'

'A billionaire pornographer, a Zionist philanthropist.'

'Oh. Why didn't I guess? I mean, what are we doing here altogether? It's friendly, but it's not like we're friends, as I understand it. At home, if someone came to have a few drinks round my house with a few mates, well, it was different. You'd have a sort of homogeneity, you know; there'd be a mission statement. It's not just to do with money.'

'No, it's celebrity,' said John.

'You think that's it. Well, that's me fucked then.' Isis laughed.

'Don't you like being a celebrity?'

'Aye, it's great. It's what I've prayed for day and night for seventeen years, but I'm not used to it. I've only been famous for about five minutes. Last year I wasn't in *Who's Who* in Angus, now, well, I have to check my shoes for fans in the morning.'

'You'll get blasé about it.'

'You reckon? You're an expert?'

'No. But it doesn't take long to just take it all for granted, does it?'

'Like signing the bill this afternoon?'

'You noticed?'

'I do that look. That fuck-look-at-all-the-noughts look, and then, fuck, who cares? I'm glad I'm not so blasé that I'm still impressed by Lee Montana, though. Now she's what I mean by stardom. Really, I've loved her for years. You know, really loved her. Been passionate about her, tears-on-the-pillow, wet-knickers loved her. I'd hate to get blasé about that.'

'You gay?'

'Noo,' Isis laughed. 'If I had any time I'd shag boys. Oh, but I want to snog the mouth off her. I suppose I'm bisexual – men and goddesses. It's only Lee and Marilyn Monroe, Patti Smith and St

Teresa of Avila, oh, and Betty Boop, that I fancy.'

John looked at her laughing, and laughed.

'Don't you think that those stars, real supernova stars, are just so great? They've become omnisexual, they're bigger than gender. Oh, I mean, couldn't you just melt into the arms of Cary Grant? Couldn't you sleep with, I don't know, Paul Robeson or Keats?'

'Not Keats,' said John. 'He'd keep you up all night with that coughing.'

'But you know what I mean. The normal rules don't apply when you're a fan; it's worship. That's got to be about sex too. What are your poems like?'

'Poetry, slight observations. Old-fashioned really, gloomy.'

'My sort of stuff. Have you got any here? Can I see them?'

'You don't really want to; they're all rather rough stuff I'm working on. I really don't know if they're any good.'

But of course he wanted to show her. Run, don't walk. He wanted her to see them. He wanted to show off. In this seal colony of show-offs, he wanted to show off. It annoyed him that Lee had never asked about his poems; he worked every day and she never said, 'Read me one.' His poems were his hobby, his matchstick model of Big Ben. So he led Isis to their room and she sat on the bed.

'I'd better read them; they're not really legible yet.'

He sat beside her and quietly recited.

The first time a poem gets a voice is a precious, eerie occasion. Few people ever hear it. Like a rare bird leaving the nest, this awkward, beady bundle of feathers and beak joins an invisible element and becomes. A poem's premiere occurs in a minimal *sotto* splendour. Imagine being the first person to hear the opening of *The Iliad*, or *Paradise Lost*, or having someone say, 'What do you think of this? "In Xanadu did Kubla Khan . . ."' The wing beat that changes the climate of a civilization. Well, this wasn't 'Elegy Written in a Country Church-Yard' or 'Anthem for Doomed Youth', but, as John heard his own lines take to the air, he knew they were good, better than anything he'd ever written. After the third he looked up.

'Sorry, are you bored? Shall I stop?'

'No, they're fabulous. They're really great. The last one about love, I loved it. Could I have it, could I have a copy?'

'I don't know that it's quite done yet; it needs some work, polishing.'

'No it doesn't, it's finished. Leave it. Will you give it to me?'

John beamed and blushed. 'Yes, if you like it.' And he copied the three short verses.

They talked about poetry and writing. Isis wasn't as well read as he, but she was more passionately read. She went to the ramparts with an evangelical fury for her books, grabbed his arms, puffed her cheeks and hooted. They talked abut *Antigone* and school and teachers and being provincial and the sweets they'd bought when they were little and wanting to escape and about shops and customers, and they didn't notice the dying of the light.

Suddenly Lee was standing in the door. 'Here you are, giggling in the dark. Right. Well, they've gone. They sent their goodbyes to both of you. If you'll excuse me I'm going to have a shower.'

Isis jumped up. 'Sorry.' She looked desperate, like a girl who'd been caught smoking by her favourite prefect. 'I'll leave you.' She ran outside.

Lee slammed the bathroom door. John tried to follow but it was locked. After ten minutes she emerged, swagged in a dressing gown with a turban towel piled on her head, looking unnervingly like Norma Desmond in a towering rage.

'I'm sorry,' John started, to get his white flag in first.

'Let's get something straight. You're here because I asked you here with me.'

'Lee.'

'Your job is to be supportive, to look after me, not some spindly little bitch.' She was shouting; her trained lungs heaved and she didn't care who heard.

'Lee, I'm sorry. But I'm not an employee.'

'No, but that doesn't mean you can't be fired. Look, John, maybe this is all a mistake, maybe you're just another selfish little hustler on the make.'

'That's not fair.'

'Fair?' She jutted her chin at him. 'Fair? Tell me about fair. You left me with those two towering bores to be lectured about the fucking altar of the stage that I'm about to be sacrificed on, and shit, did you care? Did you come and look after me? Did you think about me at all? No, you were sitting in the dark, in my fucking bedroom, trying to get to first base with some little do-wop doll. Well, John, I'm not about to be humiliated by some shop boy and a devious bimbo who thinks she can give her sorry little career a boost by being associated with me, humping my boyfriend behind my back, because it'll get her photograph in the *National Enquirer*. I know why she was here, but boy, I didn't expect it from you. OK, let's just call it quits. I'm disappointed, but frankly I'm not surprised. I've told Casper to book us on a plane tomorrow. I'm going back to London; you can do what the fuck you like.'

'Lee, let me . . .'

'Just leave it. It's over, done.'

John sat on the bed while she took the rest of her anger out on her *maquillage*. London. He'd known, of course, that they were going back, that they'd been here ten days already, but the thought of going back was as bad as breaking up. Miserably, he shuffled and picked up his scattered poems and didn't notice Lee's hand tremble as she held her lipstick or her eyes fill with tears.

'I've got to say something.'

'There's nothing left to say, John.' Her voice was husky.

'Perhaps. But I've got to say it. You can think what you like, but I've got to say I left you with Oliver and Stu because that's part of your work; I didn't want to interfere. I don't know anything about it, but that's not important. Isis just wanted to hear my poems, that's all. There was nothing else; she was just interested. I'm sorry it looked bad, but you're wrong about her. She's terrifically nice, and it's unfair, she adores you really.'

'John, she's just another fan. They're all the same.'

'No, she's not a sad loony. She's very successful in her own right and she truly admires you. Don't be ungenerous, it's beneath you. Are you sure this isn't all about your being jealous?'

'Me? Jealous? Me? Do you think I'm jealous? Of her?' Lee's mouth opened and closed and opened again, but she said nothing more and turned away. A tear hung on her lash. 'You bastard, you bastard. Why do you make me feel like this?' Her voice was quiet and small. 'Yes, I'm jealous. She's young and she's beautiful and you were laughing.'

John got up and awkwardly went to hug her, but stepped on her foot instead. 'Sorry, sorry. Oh Lord.' He knelt down and held her foot and kissed it. Lee laid a hand on his head.

'John, what am I going to do with you? I can't be made to feel like this. I haven't got space for this.' She looked down with a long face, her intense blue eyes stroking his cheek. 'I'm getting too damn attached to you. You're very lovable.'

They kissed.

'Come on, get showered. Leo's asked Sy Baum for dinner. Heard of him?'

'No.'

'Nobody has. He wrote "New Jersey Moon".' She hummed a couple of bars. 'Sung by everybody who thinks they're Tony Bennett in every cheap lounge that thinks it's Las Vegas. He's a shit-eating name-dropper and snob, a huge fan of mine, naturally, and we're bound to get a medley of his hit, and I'll have to sing it.'

Washed and changed, John took Lee's arm. They walked through the cricket hum of the garden.

'Really, you're wrong about Isis. It was you she fancied. She's really attracted to you. Nothing to do with me. "Snog the lips off you" was how she put it.'

'She said that? Christ, is she a dyke?'

'Apparently not. Hero worship transcends gender, according to her.'

'Fans. I told you, they're sick fucks.'

John was suddenly wrapped in a shroud of depression. He was sad that they'd argued, sad that he was leaving this place, sad that Isis had already gone and hadn't said goodbye, and sad that he hadn't kissed her after all.

But Isis hadn't gone. She was in the library with Leo, watching a simply huge black man bugger a very small blonde girl. Their gross obscenity was as nought compared to the horrendous soft furnishings they were both getting a grip of.

'Oh, no. Not in her bum now. I can't believe it. What is she like?' Isis shrieked.

'She was a Biology major from Sarah Lawrence and has a bonsai shop in Michigan somewhere now. I still get Christmas cards.' Leo sucked on a huge cigar.

Isis turned, saw John and Lee and flashed them a huge grin. 'Have you seen this stuff? It's amazing. I had no idea. What a sheltered life; it's amazing. We've watched three. There's a man with a thing that's so grotesque you wouldn't feel safe knowing it was in the house. Oh, I can see how people get addicted to this stuff. It's fantastic. They say rock 'n' roll's raunchy but why does anyone bother going to a concert when they can watch this?'

Lee ignored her. 'I need a drink.'

'I've asked Isis to stay to dinner. She'll impress the shit out of Sy.' Leo fast-forwarded to the money shot.

'Great.'

Dinner was difficult. Sy was a dapper little man with tiny feet, pressed into thin, coffee-coloured crocodile shoes. He had a cucumber-green blazer, white trousers, a mustard-coloured face and a prawn-cocktail-coloured wig. He wore a diamond the size of a cherry pip on his neat pinkie. His conversation was as relentless as it was insipid. He had, through the years, developed a tried-and-tested formula for placing names on the table. It was like watching someone play celebrity dominoes.

His monologue was directed solely at Lee.

'Hey, I've got a message to pass on to you. I was staying with Barbra. She's thinking of doing a *My Favourite Songs* album with Jackie. Anyway, she sends you a whole bundle of love. We went and saw Bob. He's frail, but, God willing, he's still all there. Anyway, he said to pass on his best to you and asked when you were going to come and sing for him. New York's just impossible at the moment. I was going to dinner with Lord Lloyd – he said hi, by the way. It took an hour to get up-town, so we were stuck in traffic when I saw this awning. Guess whose playing at the Plaza? Liza. Yeah, I know. She's clean and she's beautiful and the voice, I'd swear it was her mother. You know we were just like that. Jesus, I loved that dame.

Anyway. We go the next day and Liza does the whole spotlight schtick, "Gee folks, guess who we've got in tonight, the man who gifted the world with 'New Jersey Moon', etc., etc.", and I take a bow and, would you believe it, sitting on the table right over in the corner is Perry, large as life and twice as beautiful. Lee, the man's desperate to meet you, said he's got this project and he wants to cut some studio time, just the two of you. I said I'd pass it on. Solly gave a little dinner for me at Minsky's, just a few of the old Tin-Pan-Alley boys, Danny, Graham, and Lee, your ears should have been burning. They were talking, just kvetching about getting old and their illnesses and someone, Englebert I think, says, "Who do you want to sing at your funeral?" They want Barbra, Shirley, Gloria, Whitney, you know, everyone's got names, and then Tony says, "There's only one voice going to get me into heaven: Lee," and they all slapped their foreheads and went, "Lee, of course, yeah, Lee. We've got to have Lee." So you've got a lot of bookings for the next ten years, though, God willing, not too soon.'

'I'd be happy to sing at all your funerals, Sy, you know that.'

Isis choked on her wine.

And so the dinner crawled on, like an Emmy awards ceremony in a Yiddish retirement home. Everyone drank too much except Sy, whose mouth was a one-way street. They got up and went through for coffee. He waddled straight to the baby grand piano and started trilling a run with his left hand, playing snippets of classic ballads from *Lifts You Have Loved*, with all the curlicues and decorations his right hand could manage. The style was happy-hour baroque. After dinner, white baby grands were Sy's life. He travelled the celebrity world with a skin like a burnt-umber elephant and hands like fairy bratwurst, turning music into plastic daisy chains.

'Come on, Lee,' he said over his shoulder. 'Sing it for me.'

'Oh, Sy. I've just got my coffee. You add fat to the Gershwins for a bit.'

'Hey, hey,' he cupped his ear. 'What's that they're playing? Oh no, oh no. It's your intro. Oh, come on, Lee, no-one does it like you. Make an old Jew happy.'

Lee rolled her eyes and, without getting up, ran through his 'New Jersey Moon', with its banal sentiment and ear-searing rhymes. She added an Irish vibrato and aspirant vowels, and when the diamond pinkie was finally made to jump off the end of the keyboard, Sy, with his head bowed, wiggled his shoulders as if coming out of a trance, and with all the gravitas at his disposal said, 'Nobody sings like that. That song was written for you, Lee. I know I wrote it, but it's yours. You owe it to posterity to record it, really you do, Lee.'

'Yeah, sure, Sy. Sure.'

'OK. What do you want for an encore?'

'Why don't you play something we like?' said Leo. 'We've got the great pop sensation of the year here. Isis, you sing something.'

'No I can't. I'm shy. Not in front of Lee.'

Lee gave her an icy smile. 'Come on, honey. Please. I'd love to hear you. So would John.'

'Oh God, it's like auditions at school. Do you know anything that was written since I was born?'

They laughed. Sy laughed loudest.

'He can play anything, or maybe you can only play one thing and make it sound like anything.' Leo poured out Armagnac.

'Do you know "Delta Lady"? That's my mum's favourite.'

Out of an improbable candyfloss opening a recognizable tune shyly emerged. Isis grabbed it with both hands and ran. Her voice was huge and raw and intense. It buried the piano. Sy pressed his foot to the pedal and hammered. She finished two bars ahead of him. The room echoed. She waited a beat and, putting a restraining hand on Sy's arm, she sang 'Blackbird' a cappella, sweet and clear and yearningly sad.

It swung John back to university: his digs in the evening, working in the summer with the window open, the sound of the high street drifting in. Only popular music and the smell of cabbage and floor polish can do this for you. It has the unique power to trap a moment in your life, like a fly in amber. He could see the books on his desk, his unmade bed, the worn patch of carpet by the door. How miserable he had been, and how happily he could remember that misery.

Isis stopped, they clapped and she sat down and looked at Lee. Lee got up and walked slowly to the piano. This wasn't business, this was personal.

'"The Man I Love" and cut out the schmaltz, Sy.'

If this was a duel somebody had turned up with a rapier and somebody else had turned up with a nuclear bomb. It was a firestorm. Lee evaporated the room, atomized it. She had the capability, she had the button and she pushed it. Lee had been doing this all her life, she was born for it; she was the finest body of light entertainment on earth and she turned it all on full beam. 'The Man I Love' isn't just a song, it isn't just a beat-the-intro, happy-memories number, it's lethal and dirty and she aimed it at John. The most powerful song known to man. She gave it to him point-blank. It was a thoroughly professional hit. Later John would realize there was no defence in the face of this sort of thing, not even deafness protects you. If you're involved with someone who can just call up George and Ira Gershwin or pole-axe you with Cole Porter as easy as drawing breath, there's nothing you can do. These are professional hit men, they don't fool around. Lee had a presence that could elevate sports stadiums into Nuremberg rallies. She could reduce half a million people to a syrupy mush just by making noises at them. One neo-romantic poet, prone to melancholy, sitting four feet away, hadn't a prayer. Not a hope. Forget it. He was history. And Isis. Isis was collateral damage; she got blown away in the flash. Nobody applauded, they just gaped. It was magnificent; it was scary.

'Honey, do you know any show tunes?'

Isis sang 'Loch Lomond' – a clever choice. Sweet, childish, non-competitive – a white flag. Lee did 'I'm Gonna Wash That Man Right Outta My Hair' just to show there were no hard feelings, and so turn and turn about they sang, rummaging emotions, playing fast and loose with memories, hopes and loves, just because they could, just showing off.

Through the open French windows in the heady garden, the staff sat silently and drank beer. The lights of St Tropez twinkled, the yachts bobbed. The great big moon just did its clichéd thing, happy it wasn't over New Jersey.

The women leaned against the piano, relaxed, sappy, confident, and then Isis started, '"After one whole quart of brandy, like a daisy I'm awake, with no bromo-saltza handy."' She shouldn't have. Under normal circumstances she wouldn't have, this was rustling. This song was branded as Lee's, but it was late, and she was a bit stewed, not thinking, not looking. ' "Bewitched, bothered and bewildered." ' Lee smiled, a narrow-eyed feline smile and held her fire. Then she pounced, light as a feather, sure as a switchblade, picking up on the downbeat, ' "He's a fool and don't I know it, but a fool can have his charms." ' They did it together, their voices a perfect match, rough and smooth, high and low, nature and nurture.

' "Worship the trousers that cling to him." '

Face to face, sharing the breath and the beat. On the last note Lee bent her head slowly forward and kissed Isis full on the mouth, an open, scorching, lingering kiss.

' "Vexed again, perplexed again, thank God I can be oversexed again." '

The helicopter lifted off from the lawn. Leo, Isis, the olive trees, the magnolia and the palms all waved frantically. Lee squeezed John's hand.

'I hate this bit.'

John hated this bit worse. He hated the ground dropping away. The absurd palace and the little guest bungalow spun out of sight. He thought of their bed, with the twisted, damp sheets and the lingering scent of the night, and the packing and the wandering round looking for the other half of things. The last swim, the last peach, the last coupling. Tipping the staff, signing the visitor's book, the thank-yous, the unfamiliar weight of a new bag full of new clothes. He squeezed Lee's hand and watched the coast run away like the credits.

They flew back to London in silence. She read magazines and dozed. Questions and exclamations stuck in his throat, blue sky turned white. London was cold and wet, naturally. It wouldn't have seemed like home any other way. They were whisked through passports. Lee already seemed as distant as the Mediterranean, her concentration was somewhere else. This holiday romance had always been her gift, and the scales tipped further in her favour. John wheeled the luggage through customs.

'Put on your glasses.'

'What?'

'Just do it.'

Walking through the electric doors was a bit like walking onto a stage. The audience of assorted Indian families worried that a mother wouldn't make it through immigration; drivers with their lost-businessmen cards; wives with excited children, waiting for fathers; nervous girlfriends in short skirts and welcome-home knickers, distant relatives looking for long-lost Christmas-card senders; nuns and pimps picking up novices; seedy hookers procuring lost boys; stoic policemen trysting with bashful burglars. This twenty feet of catwalk must be the most narrative-rich strand of pent-up emotion anywhere in the world. Small explosions of joy and tears going off like pro-personnel mines.

'Lee, Lee. Over here Lee. Lee, over here. Give us a smile. John, a bit closer, mate, give her a kiss.' Four photographers thudded and elbowed through the crowd, scuffling, tripping over trolleys and bags.

'Had a nice time, Lee? Just pose for one, love.'

The cast waiting for their cue at the rails swivelled and craned, hungry for celebrity. Lee Montana. Hey, hey, it's Lee Montana. Small-time love, longing, lust and duty could loiter with its bags, this was more important. A man took hold of the trolley handles; it was Hamed.

The big Mercedes joined the crawl into London. John needed to say something, rescue something. He leaned across to kiss her; she turned her face a fraction and pressed him away.

'Do you want to be dropped off at home?'

'Lee.'

'I've got to have dinner with some film people. They've come from LA. Call me in the week. I'm at the Connaught. Hamed, can we drop John off at home first?'

'Fine.'

They each looked out of their respective windows.

Hamed dropped the bags on the pavement.

'Lee, I just wanted to say—'

'Don't. I hate goodbyes.' She kissed him neatly. 'Call me at the

Connaught. Really, let's have dinner. Go on, John, don't look like that; it was fun. We'll do it again. Take care.'

DES WAS IN THE HALL.
'Well, boy. Look at this, sweet pea. Look who's returned, brown as a berry. You have a good time? She's not coming in for a cup of tea? Well, there's a few messages for you. Your mum called three times, says she hasn't heard from you for nearly three months. The shop called once, that Clive, and Mrs Patience and your publisher. You want to come down for some supper? It ain't Provençal, bubble-and-squeak but we can put garlic in it.'

John opened the door to his room and flicked on the light. It stared back at him, like a blanket-gagged and cloth-bound hostage, just as he'd left it, the atmosphere unchanged, like breathing the same air twice. The solitary desperation, the crumpled life, the small-change loneliness. Slowly he unpacked, laid the motley of happiness on the bed: linen trousers with a small spot on the knee and five bright shirts. He put his hand on them to feel the faint ghost of warmth, the smell of cigarettes and Lee's perfume. Tears had waited for him here, confident that he would return for them. You can go to the ends of the earth, sonny, but we're here to be shed. We knew you'd come back for us. We're bought and paid for. He dribbled despair and pity into the rough wool of the cold attic, then lay on his bed. He'd come full circle; he was back. There was nowhere to go, no-one to be.

A knock at the door. 'John. You awake? There's a call for you.'

He stood up and there was a rush of dizziness. He rubbed his prickling eyes.

'Yeah, yeah. What time is it?'

It was late: eleven. He ran downstairs, two at a time, stumbling in the hall.

The receiver was lying on its side. The most heart-stoppingly romantic image of the late twentieth century: a reclining, nude telephone. He snatched it up, held it tight and leaned against the wall.

'Hello.'

'You're back.' Clive.

It took ages to find the hospital entrance. He followed the signs, but they forgot themselves and had no sense of direction. They rambled and lost their point and became something else. Hornchurch became Webster, Webster had a change of heart and decided to become Cardiology, which turned out to be a chapel, which in turn led him to Sullivan, and Sullivan was caught short in Urinary and Gynaecology, which were the long cut to Obstetrics and finally Day Care, which led back to the carpark. Finally he followed a wheel-chair into Accident and Emergency.

There was a smell of beer and sick and disinfectant. A tramp lay across a bench, his head lolling. A child screamed, a single, repeated, incessant note. Its mother's face was white with terror. She held another child, mute and limp. Around the walls silent people tenderly held bits of themselves – a foot, an elbow, an eye, blood coagulated. A teenage girl with ripped stockings wept and was hugged by a friend, who shivered in a little silver T-shirt and said, 'It'll be fine, it'll be all right.' It wasn't. A small red-haired girl was curled up, wheezing like a ruptured pressure cooker, sucking weakly on a plastic asthma inhaler. Another drunk bellowed and spat, a security guard lounged against a wall, a coffee machine dripped dark mucus.

John joined the queue. A man in a dinner jacket, holding his son tight to his chest, stood in front of him. The little boy stared at John with big eyes, glittering with fear and fever.

'He's got a temperature of a hundred and three and a quarter. It just happened,' he said to the receptionist. The man looked astonished, as if this were one of those dreams where you're in-appropriately dressed in an inappropriate place. 'It just happened, so suddenly. It might be meningitis, mightn't it?' His voice was ragged with terror. Meningitis. He could hardly bear to say it. Please, please. A nurse took the boy's name.

'Timmy. Tim. His mother calls him Timmy. Timothy.'

And age, address, allergies. The terror hissed. The man held his boy and tried to be the father he'd always promised to be, tried to fix it.

163

John watched the curve of his back, and the weight, the agonizing weight in the nape of his neck. John could sense the keening, desperate prayer.

My son, my son. Please take anything, take anything, but not my son. I remember when he was born. I remember when I loved his mother, when I could put my arms around my whole life, and I swore, I swore on the generations that had brought us to this boy, that I would be a daddy for ever and ever, that I would fix it, until I died. You must understand that this is my moment. All the rows and the unkindnesses and the infidelity and the arrogance and the sneering and ignoring were paid for with this moment, because now I must protect this child, our child, against anything. I promised to stand in the door, to defend the bridge. It would be my hand that caught him when he fell, I would face the dark and, with my fists and my power and my skill and my money and my connections and my position, I would vanquish what would harm him. That was the deal. That was the deal for being a dad. And then this came in the dusk and crept past me, while I shaved, to his bed, and it's taken him and, you don't understand, I should have been there, with my loud voice and my pen and my lawyers and my credit cards. I should have protected my son.

The nurse looked up for the first time. 'Take a seat. Someone will come soon.' She reached out and touched the small dangling hand. 'Brave boy, Timmy.' She used his mother's name. 'We'll make you better.'

The man sat like a man who has gambled everything and lost.

'Yes?' said the nurse. John started to talk. 'No, you're in the wrong place. You want Sullivan. Follow the signs.'

The small ward was six neat beds. At the end, under the window, Petra and Clive sat side by side.

'Sorry, I got lost. What's happened?'

Petra stood up; she was tired, with purple rings under her eyes. 'An overdose.'

Dorothy lay in the bed, eyes closed, sickly glow and greasy hair. Her mouth was open. She looked dead. Only the drip in her arm implied life.

'Hi, John.' Clive smiled. 'What a great tan.'

'Why? I mean, what happened? What happened?'

'We don't know.' Petra sat down again. 'I came home and just did some stuff, and then I went to her room, by chance, and there she was on the bed. She nearly died. It was just luck.'

'She's going to be all right?'

'Yes,' Clive said emphatically.

'Probably. They got her in time; they're just checking to see what she took. Headache pills mostly; she didn't have sleeping pills or stronger stuff.'

'How terrible. I'm so sorry. Have you spoken to her?'

'No, she's been sedated. We've been here all day.'

'I thought you'd want to know.' Clive looked awkward.

'Yes.'

'Where have you been, John?'

'I've been in St Tropez.'

The name sounded ridiculous, insulting around this bed.

'St Tropez,' Petra repeated. 'Why didn't you tell me? How could you?'

'Look, I told Clive to tell you. This isn't the place to . . .'

'John, I needed you. We needed you.' She rested her head on the bed.

'I'm going to shoot off.' Clive got up. 'You'll take Petra home, won't you? Look, I need to tell you,' he put his arm round John's shoulder in a man-to-man way, 'I'm your mate and everything, but you've been a real bastard. You know, a real, fucking bastard. OK. That's enough said. Won't mention it again. So, cheerio then. Petra, see you in the shop tomorrow.'

John sat on an empty seat opposite Petra and looked across Dorothy's body.

'OK, OK.' She wiped her eyes. 'How could you? How could you just go off like that?'

'Petra, we need to talk about this, but not now, not here.'

'Yes, now. I need to talk about it now. I didn't even know you'd come back. I've been calling. And would you have even bothered to see me if Dorothy hadn't been here?'

'Yes, but . . .'

'But what, John? All right, just let me say something. Don't interrupt. Look, I forgave you the last time you went off with her; I thought you were an idiot, but we were bigger, stronger than that. This time it really hurt; really, really hurt. You've no idea what it's been like, how much pain, how desperate I've been, and now this.' She stretched her hand across the bed. 'Hold my hand. Christ, at least you can hold my bloody hand.'

He held her hand; it was clammy, cold and needy.

'Petra, there's—'

'Don't interrupt.' The tears swam. 'Listen to me. I've been thinking about it, and I'll have you back. I'm not going to make a scene about it or punish you. It happened, and now I love you, and I know you love me.'

The statement lay between them, said over Dorothy's miserable, comatose, chemically barbed stomach.

'I love you, and I know you love me, right. Right? That's right, isn't it, John?' It came out as a pleading whine.

'Yes, I love you.' The coward's answer. 'But . . .' with the coward's caveat.

'No, no buts. You said you loved me, John, and I *know* you love me. I love enough for both of us; I'll make it all right. I don't know what it was that made you go away, but I'll make it better.'

'I don't think you can. It wasn't to do with you. It wasn't anything you did. I think we need to be . . . I don't know.'

This was a Petra he didn't know; this wasn't what she was like. She never begged; she sulked, she brazened. He was the malleable plastic one; she was stainless steel, unbreakable, no moving parts.

'I know, I know. Trust me, John, please. Don't go.'

She squeezed his hand and pressed it down on Dorothy's stomach. The drip shook.

'Please.'

A nurse came in. 'I'm sorry, you'll have to leave now. The hospital's been closed to visitors for half an hour. You can come back in the morning. She'll sleep tonight.'

'You'll take me home? You promised Clive.'

'Yes.'

They walked down the glossy chipped corridors; coughs and snores slipped out of dark rooms. Petra held his arm tightly, as if he might dash off into the night. Leaning against the wall was the man in the dinner jacket, holding an unlit cigarette.

John went up to him. 'How's Timmy? I saw you in Casualty.'

The man rubbed his eyes. 'OK, I think. They say it's not meningitis, thank God. A bug or something. They don't know; they're keeping him in overnight.'

'Good. That's good news.'

'Yeah. Do you two have kids?' He looked at Petra.

'No, not yet.'

'Don't. They're not worth it.'

Outside, in the cold, damp street, they started to walk. There were no cabs.

'Have you eaten?' Petra asked.

John realized he was famished. 'No. I'll get something later.'

'Let's get a takeaway.'

They waited silently in the stinking, garish jollity of Petra's local Mohti Mohal. She beamed bravely and hopefully at John. He paid with Lee's credit card.

'How did you get that?' Petra picked it up. 'And that's a new wallet. She's just bought you, hasn't she? Credit cards, wallets, clothes. OK, I'm not making a deal about it, but if I'd known we could have gone and got something better than this.'

She picked up the plastic bag.

They sat at the kitchen table. Petra poured acid wine and made bright, one-lump-or-two conversation and touched him whenever she passed. She didn't mention Dorothy or Lee. They ate. It was oily, hot and nasty. John wasn't hungry for this. He noticed how quickly your tastes change, your expectations. He got up to go.

'Don't you want a bath? I'll run it.'

'No, I think I should go.'

'You can't go. You said you'd stay. You said . . .'

'Petra, I didn't, and I don't think it's a good idea. I don't think this is going to work.'

'It will, it will work. You said you'd stay. You said you loved me, you did. It'll be all right. You said it would be all right.'

'No. You said it.'

'You agreed, you agreed. It's a fact.'

'Look, Petra, for Christ's sake, I've been sleeping with someone else. This isn't right. We're not right. I don't make you happy.'

'You do. I love you.'

'We're neither of us happy, we were just convenient, and it was too much trouble to get out. Well, something happened and it gave us a way out, and I think we should take it.'

'No, no, no,' hands over her ears, head shaking.

'Look, just for a bit. Have some time apart. Find out what's there. Maybe you're right, but I think it's better for both of us if we separate for a bit.'

She was sobbing. 'Please stay. Just tonight, just tonight. I can't be on my own. What with Dorothy and everything. Just tonight. It's not fair. She's had you for two weeks, give me a night.' She wrapped her arms around him and clung to him. 'Kiss me. You haven't kissed me once. Let's go to bed.'

'No, Petra.'

'You bastard, you owe me. You made me so miserable. All I want is one fucking night. One.'

She pushed him through the door onto the bed. His feet snagged on the reef of clothes. She tried to kiss him, but butted his eyebrow. Her pickled tongue licked his nose.

'Let's make love. Please, please. My best friend's in hospital dying, you've been away. Love me, make love to me,' she sobbed and panted, her hands pulling at his trousers. She had the strength of despair. 'You can do anything, anything you want. Do what you want. What did she do for you? What did she do? I'll do it better. Her blow jobs better than mine? Teach me, show me, I'll do it. Is her cunt tighter than mine? Was it hotter? Wetter? You can bugger me, John. Is that what you want? Tie me up. You want to hit me, beat me, do it. Nothing you can do can make me feel worse than not having you do it at all, just please don't leave me. Please, John, I'm begging. I'm begging you, don't leave me.' Petra was raving, howling, spitting.

Spit and tears sprayed his face. It was repulsive and sordid, and he felt strangely cold, disgusted and disengaged.

He struggled to get up and shouted in her face as hard as he could, 'Petra, I'm going. It's over.'

'I'll kill myself, I'll be like Dorothy. You can kill both of us. I will, you know, John. I will, you know. I will, I'll die for love of you.'

'Petra, Petra, please. For Christ's sake, just stop it, stop it. Look, I'll stay for a bit, but I'm not going to sleep with you. We're breaking up, I'm leaving, for a bit. I don't know. But I don't love you, I can't love you the way you want me to. Do you understand?'

She knelt on the floor at his feet and ran her hands up his thighs. 'You'll stay.'

It was as if someone had changed her half of the air in the room, made it lighter. She bounced onto the bed, lit a cigarette and patted the mattress.

'Here, lie down. So was it fun in the South of France?'

'Yes, it was great.'

'You really look beautiful. You were always beautiful, but you look amazing, you know, with a tan. All over?'

She put her hand on his shirt. He moved it away.

'Good food?'

'Yes. Salad and fish and stuff. Lovely.'

'Luxury hotel?'

She kicked her shoes off.

'No, we were in a house.'

'Oh. With friends? Parties round the pool?'

She undid her shirt.

'No. Well, you know, sometimes.'

'Anyone famous?'

Her jeans slid off.

'No, not particularly.'

She was naked now, one hand on her small bosom.

'Petra, look, I told you.'

'No, you told me.' She laughed. 'But, darling,' her voice was honey and gall, 'it's late and we're a little drunk. Come on, what's the matter? I'm too tired to argue, we might as well fuck, it doesn't mean anything.'

She pressed her hard little body against his and pushed her tongue in his ear.

She was right, it was late. He was a little drunk and sadness pressed in on him. Her familiar fingers busied themselves at his waistband.

She undressed him, cooing and chuckling. 'Oh, I've missed you. You look great. It's almost worth letting you go if she sends you back in this condition.'

He tried not to listen.

She nuzzled his penis. 'Hello, big boy, we've missed you. Where have you been? Naughty! Tell me, what was she like? What was it like? Was it like this?' Her eyes wide and mad, she looked up at him from his groin. Gently, then less gently, she bit. 'Only teasing, you bad boy.'

She sucked and bobbed and ran her nails up and down his legs.

'Now fuck me. You choose, any way. You tell me, make me. Make me do things.'

He pushed her on her back and scrabbled molishly between her legs.

'Yes, yes. Oh, it's big, it's big, it's huge.'

Petra never spoke like this; this was an act of fantasy. It was someone else, a homunculus made up for him, a witch's familiar.

'Fill me up, fill me up. Thrust it in my honey hole.' She was sucking air. 'Yes, yes. Push, push.'

She was groaning with an American accent; she was being Lee.

'You remember the first time, baby; this is like the first time. It's so hot for you. Oh wow, pussy missed you. Oh, so good, I'm so hot. Yes, yes. Oh boy, aaah.' She panted and bit his shoulder. 'Give it me, boy, stick it in me. Yes, yes, aaah.'

She rolled her head and arched her back.

'I'm going to come, I'm going to come. It's so huge. I can feel it coming, coming. Yes, yes, ooh.'

Petra's multiple orgasm wouldn't have fooled a medieval hermit. She bucked and rolled her eyes and gasped and flung her limbs about. Her face contorted in a grimace of unspeakable agony that slid into a contemplation of Nirvana.

'Come on, lover. Faster, faster. Hammer me. Spurt in me. No, come on my tits, come in my mouth.'

Silently, thankfully, John finished and rolled off her onto his side. She hugged his back. After a moment there was a deep silence which was supposed to be bonding but was as phoney as her ecstasy.

She spoke in a Shirley sex-kitten voice, 'That was the best, your best ever. You're mine, aren't you? No-one will take you away from me now, will they? You love me, you're in love with me. Really and truly, for ever and ever, aren't you?'

'Petra, please.'

It was just grammar now, the pathetic, meaningless language of breaking up.

'You are mine, aren't you? You wouldn't have done it to me unless you loved me? Now sleep, baby. We'll do it again in the morning, and tomorrow night, and the night after, and the night after, for ever.'

But they both knew they wouldn't.

John woke with a start. His hand was still asleep. He looked up. Petra was sitting at the end of the bed, naked, cold, shivering, her arms folded across her chest, her brow knitted, watching him. It was unnerving.

'What time is it?'

'Nine.'

'Shit, I'm late for work.'

'You're leaving, aren't you?'

'Petra, I've got to go to the shop.'

He searched for his trousers.

'No, I mean you're leaving, you really are going to dump me.'

'Yes. I think it's for the best, for both of us.'

'For her.'

'This is nothing to do with her.'

Petra smirked. 'That's not what your credit card says.'

'Petra, I'm not going to argue with you any more.'

She got up, half turned away, then swung and hit him hard across the face.

'Cunt. You made love to me last night. How dare you?'

He touched his cheek. 'You're mad. Neither of us made love. You threatened to kill yourself if I didn't stay. It was the most humiliating night of either of our lives, Petra. Just leave it.'

171

She sat down again and hugged her shoulders. 'Aren't you going to ask about Dorothy?'

'What about Dorothy?'

'I called the hospital.'

'And . . .'

'They asked if I was a relative. I said I was her sister. It's serious, the pills she took were paracetamol.'

'Is that bad?'

John looked under the bed for his other shoe.

'Apparently. She came round and had some breakfast, but there might be liver damage.'

'But she's not going to die. Not if she's eating breakfast.'

'The nurse said they were hoping for the best. They've got to do transfusions and things.' Petra started to cry. 'John, I'm so frightened.'

He put his hand on her shoulder.

'Don't touch me if you don't mean it.'

'I've got to go. Look, Petra, I don't want to leave like this.'

The finality of it was sadder than he was prepared for. He wanted to leave, but he wanted to leave something behind as well, something soft, something to stop the door slamming, something to keep their relationship ajar.

'I'm sorry, I don't want to walk out like this, but we need to, you know, have some time, and I'll see you. I'll . . . I'll go to the hospital after work. Perhaps I'll see you then. We can be, you know, friendly, friends. We've shared such a lot. It's a shame.'

Petra picked her toenail.

'Yeah, whatever. I fucked Clive, you know.'

'What?'

'Yeah, I fucked your mate, Clive. Here. You know, he's quite good at it. Now that's a funny thing. You wouldn't think so to look at him, but you never can tell. Terribly eager, which is nice, and hung like a Jamaican mule, which was a change. He did it all night; couldn't keep him off me. And so grateful. That's nice too.' She looked up, a little blank face. 'So, there you are.'

'Why?'

'Why? Because I felt like it, because I could, because my

boyfriend had fucked off with some ancient slag.'

'Why are you telling me?'

'Why do you think, Mr Fucking Poet? Because it's fucking poetic, that's why. And I want you to know so that you can make it rhyme.'

He turned away and let himself out. The door slammed.

It was chilly and damp, his clothes were thin. Petra leaned out of the window above him.

'Here, bastard.'

The wallet splattered into the gutter.

'Let me tell you something else, bastard. Clive, your friend, he hates you. While we were doing it he said it wasn't just screwing me that turned him on, it was screwing *your* girlfriend, *you*, Mister Fucking Bastard.'

At the corner of the street there was a phone box. John looked at the working girls' cards; they teased him with their honesty and their decent presbyterian simplicity. Why did anyone think of using anything else, just to save twenty quid? Love was a false economy. He phoned the Connaught, swallowed hard on the lump in his throat.

'I'm sorry, Miss Montana isn't taking any calls. Would you like to leave a phone number?'

'Just say John called.'

'John who, sir?'

Clive was sitting behind the till, chewing a pastry, reading the paper.

'Hi, how did it go last night?'

'Not great.'

'Sorry. Seen the paper? Great picture of Lee; shame about the dork she's with.'

'Ah, John. You've decided to come back.' Mrs Patience bustled out of the stockroom.

'Hello, Mrs Patience. Yes. Sorry to be so long.'

'Right. Well, we need to have a talk. I'm not best pleased with you, but it'll have to wait. You've heard about poor Dorothy. Go and sort out the children's section. There are a lot of boxes just come in.

More books,' she added, as if she'd been hoping for petunias.

John worked solidly, the time crept. He looked at the clock every couple of hours, but it had only moved five minutes. He felt sick, his stomach knotted, stupid with worry, guilt and despair. He couldn't concentrate – a dozen times he stared at the book in his hand and tried to remember what he was doing with it. He sat in the stockroom, remembering lying on his back in the swimming pool, looking at the sky, the sun on his chest, Lee's cool nakedness resting against him, but he couldn't recreate the benefit of it. The picture slipped and broke up. You can't remember pain and you can't recreate contentment. Finally it was lunch.

'Will you just take half an hour, John, what with us being so short today.'

He scooted round the corner to the pub and waited for a fat plasterer to get off the phone.

'No, it was there when I left. It was there. It was in the what's-its-name. I seen it. He's a lyin' slag and I'll fuckin' do the tosser. On my life, it was in the what's-its-name.'

The man put his hand in his pocket and pulled out a small painting. It was a miniature of a man holding a rose, painted on ivory. It shone like a jewel. It was by Nicholas Hilliard. The plasterer looked at it, bemused.

''Old on, it's in me bleedin' pocket. No, I just got it. Yeah, as you were, OK. See ya. 'E's still a fuckin' slag, the cunt.'

He put the receiver down and pushed his way to the bar.

There was no answer from Lee's room.

'I'm sorry, there's no answer from Miss Montana's room. Would you like to leave your name and number?'

John drank a pint of fetid, thin beer quickly and ate a packet of crisps, then went back to the shop. The afternoon was a test of passive attrition.

Half an hour before they closed Mrs P. called him into the storeroom.

'Right, John, close the door please. I've got one or two things I want to say. I'm disappointed; no, I'm upset and angry.'

Why, he thought, do women never get upset without being angry at the same time?

'You've let me down pretty badly. It was very selfish just running off like that. Selfish. And it shows you don't really have any consideration for any of us.'

'Mrs P.—'

'Let me finish. This isn't a discussion.' She was working herself up, steeling herself for unpleasantness. 'Now, your private life is, of course, your own affair, and I've never taken a moral line with any of my staff, but I can say that your behaviour hasn't been anything to be proud of. We all have to work together, and if your private life impinges on the shop then I'm afraid it becomes my business and I must make decisions. This isn't fair, John. The atmosphere has been really uncomfortable since you went with that Montana person. You're taking advantage of Clive and poor Dorothy, not to mention me. John, I think the time has come for you to ask yourself if you wouldn't be better off somewhere else.'

'You want me to leave?'

'I think, all things considered, it would be best if we let you go.'

'You're firing me? Because of my sex life?'

'That's exactly the sort of attitude I'm talking about. Did you ever think about us? The rest of us. With the publicity and the unpleasantness.'

'But you can't sack me because I'm sleeping with someone famous.' He was incredulous, too shocked to be angry.

'I'm not sacking you, I just don't want you to work here any more. I just don't want to work with you any more.'

'But what will you do, with Dorothy in hospital? Neither you or Clive knows a thing about books.'

She smiled a hard little smile. 'This shop managed before you, and I expect we'll get along after you. The customers will still be able to read. It's all on the dust jacket, you know, and as it happens Petra has said she would like to work here, to be with poor Dorothy.'

'You're going to give my job to Petra?' John realized his voice was squeaky.

'Not *your* job, John, *a* job. It would hardly be fair to expect her to work alongside you after the way you've treated her. Now, you get a week's notice, which I think we can take as last week's time off, so we're square.' She held out her hand. 'Thank you for the time you've spent here, John. I'm sorry it had to end this way. Of course we'll give you a reference if you need one, but a bright lad like you should be doing more with your life than working in shops and being a gigolo.'

Clive carried two pints to the corner table.

'I'm really sorry, mate, it's a bummer. I tried to talk her out of it, but she's got herself into a real state. You know how she is. What'll you do?'

'Christ knows. Look for another job. Sign on, I suppose.'

'Well, something will turn up. Maybe your poems or something, you never know.'

'No, you never know.'

'So, anyway, Mrs Lincoln, what happened last night?'

'I broke up with Petra.'

'No. I mean, I'm really sorry.' Clive tried to sound solicitous but couldn't. 'So she dumped you. God, what a day. Well, hardly a surprise, what with Lee.'

'She told me, Clive.'

'Told you what, mate?'

'She told me you'd slept with her.'

'Oh, she told you that.' Clive paused. 'I rather thought she might. I was going to tell you. I didn't think you'd mind terribly if I rooted in your leavings. You know, pity to let it go to waste.'

'You're an arsehole, Clive. You're supposed to be my friend.'

'No, listen here.' Clive leaned across the table and pointed a finger. 'You're in no position to call anyone an arsehole, you were a prize cunt. Petra was gutted; it was more sympathy and a dick to cry on than anything.'

'Oh yeah, right. Tell me, how did it actually happen?'

'You don't want to know; it just happened.'

'No, tell me.'

'You want to know?'

'I want to know.'

'Well, I went and had a drink with poor Dorothy. Actually, she

176

was a bit low. We had a bit too much, I took her home, put her to bed and Petra was in the kitchen. She practically raped me on the table. I make no bones, it was a revenge fuck for her. I'm sure she was thinking of you, but it would have been rude to refuse.'

'Hold on, let me get this straight. You asked Dorothy for a date?'

'It wasn't a date exactly.'

'An evening out is a date. You took her home, both of you a little pissed. Did you make a move on her?'

'On Dorothy, of course not.'

'Clive, I know you. You were sniffing her knickers in your lunch hour. You did, didn't you?'

'We kissed, just a friendly, jokey snog, nothing serious, not what you'd call a pass.'

'And then you took her home and went up for coffee, know what I mean. You get upstairs and hump her best friend, so she goes next door to her solitary bed and listens. That's what happened, isn't it?'

'It wasn't like that, John.' Clive was breathing hard.

'When was this?'

'I'm not talking about it any more. Leave it.'

'When, Clive? I need to know.'

'Thursday. What's it matter?'

There was a pause. They both knew why it mattered.

'You mean the day before Dorothy's overdose?'

'That's nothing to do with it. Nothing. I'm not responsible, not at all. Neither's Petra, for that matter. But you can't talk. Have you considered that you might be responsible? This wouldn't have happened if you hadn't fucked off with Lee Montana. I don't blame you, but it ruined everything. We were fine before that, all of us: you and Petra, the shop, the pub with our mates, Dorothy. It was all great, but you got all superior and special.'

'You're talking bollocks, Clive.'

'Yeah, and you're not the same. Look at you. Look at that. You look like some prat out of *Hello!*, all linen and tan and fucking shades in an airport. Who the fuck do you want to be, John? You need a lesson in reality, mate. You're just the same as the rest of us, and I'm saying that as your mate.'

'You didn't try and talk Mrs P. out of firing me, did you? In fact,

177

I bet you suggested it. No, hold on. Not you, Petra. She lay in bed with your fat cock in her hand and said, "Why don't I work in the shop with you? Then I can give you blow jobs in the storeroom." That was going to be my punishment, wasn't it? You've been used; you've been had.'

'You're way off line, John. You're mad, raving.' Clive stared at his empty glass.

'But neither of you had second thoughts about poor Dorothy, did you? You notice how she's become "poor Dorothy"? How she's become hyphenated, poor-Dorothy. Everyone calls her poor-Dorothy. She's had so much disappointment, she's so used to misery, she'll never notice a little bit more. She might even appreciate it. A bit of new misery might take her mind off the old misery.'

Clive shrugged. 'Yeah, well, fingers crossed. Your round.'

And John went to get the drinks with his last fiver. Because it's branded on the frontal lobes of all men that whatever else happens you always get in your round, your shout.

They drank in uncomfortable, manly silence.

'We're still mates, though, aren't we?' Clive shifted and looked at the door. 'I mean, despite all this. Friendship's deeper, you know, blokes, and fuck it, they're only birds.'

'Of course, Clive. Still mates.'

'Shake?'

He looked relieved, unconvinced but relieved.

John felt the fifty pence in his pocket. He thought of asking Clive for a loan but couldn't. I know you fucked my girlfriend behind my back, but could you lend me a fiver till pay day? What pay day?

Lee's card.

He should really send it back, but he took it to a bureau de change, where a little Indian sat behind half a dozen panes of glass watching television.

'Can I get some cash with this?'

'Yes.'

'What's the limit?'

'Whatever your card provider stipulates.'

'Right. Can I have fifty pounds?'

'Fifty. There's a two-pound service charge.'

178

'Oh, OK, make it a hundred.'

'OK.'

John thought about no more pay days and his rent. 'No, hold on, make it two, no, five hundred.'

'Five hundred pounds. That it, sir?'

'Yes.'

The man swiped the card and waited, then gave John the docket. He signed.

'I'm sorry, sir, I can't accept this.'

'Why?'

The man smiled and pushed the card through the window. 'Sorry, sir.' He settled back to the TV.

John picked it up and looked. Across his signature, written in thick black felt tip, was 'Whore'. There was no answer to that. Thank you, Petra. Where do you start with an explanation? He walked towards the river. It began to rain.

A N HOUR LATER, SOAKED AND FREEZING, HE LET HIMSELF INTO HIS lodgings. He stood in the warm hall; downstairs a radio chirped, his trousers clung like cellophane to his legs, his feet squelched and his long hair dripped down the back of his neck. John looked at the phone in its cradle in the hall – nothing, no bright-yellow Post-it, no calls. He picked up the receiver.

Des shouted up the stairs, 'Is that you, John? Will you come down here? I've got something for you.'

He replaced the phone and walked gingerly down the stairs to the basement. Lee was leaning against the sink, smoking a cigarette, beautiful, cool, dry.

'God, you look like a stunt man. What have you been doing?'

'Lee, you're here. I had to walk back. I've been trying to call you. I thought you were avoiding me.'

She turned to Des. 'I told you. He never kisses me hello. Kiss me. Look like you're pleased to see me. Oh, you're freezing. I was try-ing to avoid you, but then, here I am. And Des here has been really sweet and made me tea with rum in it, so I'm smashed, and he's been telling me about his love life. Don't you think it would make a great film? I'm going to buy your rights, Des. Get Wesley Snipes to play you and I'll play Mrs Comfort.'

'Can't I play me?'

'You can stand in.' Lee was flirting fit to burst. 'So, how's your day been, John?'

He sighed and sat down, making a noise like a squashed frog. 'I lost my job, my best friend cuckolded me, another friend took an overdose and is in hospital, I'm broke and I had to walk home in the rain.'

'Oh well. Now you see, I've had the most terrible day. I really need to talk to you.'

They stood in the door of John's room. 'Not big on creature comforts are you? What do you call this? Minimalist early spartan?' Lee sat on the edge of the bed. 'You know, this is the sort of room I imagine my fan letters come from. Weird little guys telling me about the favours they could do me.'

John started taking off his wet clothes. 'Sorry, I don't entertain much; it's all I need.'

'Well, you're certainly the least-demanding boyfriend I've ever had.'

John stood, shivering, shrivelled and naked, searching for some clean clothes that weren't ones that she'd bought him. He was angry and frightened by the fleetness of foot that events could take when they set their mind to it. How dare she dip in and out of his life, leaving a trail of destruction, and then poke fun at him because his room wasn't soignée or some other damned eurotrash chic, bella thing.

'Look, let's just drop this boyfriend thing. I'm not your boyfriend.' He hopped up and down with one foot stuck in the Y bend of his underpants, his willy jiggling like a Punch-and-Judy sausage. 'I don't know what I am. I'm an accessory, a divertissement. I was called a gigolo before I was fired today. A gigolo! What sort of raggedy-arsed, useless amateur gigolo would I be? You just took me on holiday like a new hat. I know no-one twisted my arm, I wasn't forced and I was happy to be there.' He found a pair of jeans and an old baggy jersey. 'I was more than happy. It was fantastic; you were fantastic. Do you know how much I've missed you? How disappointed I was not to speak to you? How sad not to wake up with you? And of all of the shitty things that happened to me today that was the shittiest. That's all I could think about, even with Dorothy lying there in the hospital, for Christ's sake. I've got no job and all I can think about is that a film star won't take my calls. Well, of course she won't, why should she? Why should a film star take my calls?'

'John, calm down. Why do you think I'm here?'

'Actually, that's a good question. Why are you here?'

'Well, for much the same reason you're shouting at me.'

'Because you've been sacked?'

'I'm sorry you lost your job, John.'

'Really?'

'No, not really. I don't want a boyfriend who's a shop clerk. I like you being just a poet.'

'I'm not your boyfriend.'

'So you keep saying. I didn't take your calls today because I was upset.'

'You were upset? What have you got to be upset about? I thought you were entertaining important film producers from LA.'

'Oh God, John, that was just code – I'm in a meeting. No, I spent today in bed watching chat shows. Jesus, they do dreadful chat shows in this country. I was thinking about us, you know. I fall for this young guy, a lot younger than me actually, and we go away together and it's great. And then we come back and does he say, Hey, let's go to the theatre or dinner or I've got some people I'd like you to meet, even just a movie? – you know, John, you've never asked me out – I thought it was because he was embarrassed about not having any money, so what do I do, I give him a credit card and now he can ask me out. But to add to that he's already got a girl-friend, who he's in all the papers with saying he prefers her to me. So I get back and I think, Lee, you don't need this; there's no fool like an above-the-title fool. Cut your losses. It was a great week but that's all. Why would he want you? He's a young guy, he does what young guys do.'

181

'Hold on, hold on, I'm confused. What did you say right at the beginning?'

'I don't know. I'm not good at retakes. What did I say?'

'"You fell for this young guy."'

'Yeah, I fell for this young guy.'

'You fell for me?'

'I fell for you. What is this, John? Have we got a communication problem? Is this the divided-by-a-common-language shit? I've seen *Brief Encounter*, I know how you speak.'

'You fell for me? Really?'

'Really already.'

'Fell for me, as in love? Falling in love?'

'Hold on, John, don't turn over two pages at once. Of course I fell for you. What do you think? I only have to trip over guys to sleep with them?'

'No. Well, I just didn't think. Well, it never occurred to me that someone like you would be, you know, serious about me.'

'John, I'm a film star, I'm not another species. I'm a female; I fall for men, like other girls do. And you didn't think that I might need some girlie-type encouragement. You know, to be flattered and courted, flowers and what-the-hell. Didn't you fall for me?'

'I did. Can't you tell?'

'As in love? Falling in love?'

'You've seen *Brief Encounter*, you know. We don't talk about that until right at the end.'

'But you've still got a girlfriend.'

'Ex-girlfriend.'

'Ex-girlfriend? She dumped you?'

'No actually, I dumped her because I'd fallen for you, and despite the fact that I thought you'd dumped me.'

'I have – dumped you. Because you hadn't fallen for me.'

'I'm confused. I don't know who's fallen and who's dumping.'

'John, let's cut to the chase.' Lee got up and stood in front of him. Taking two great handfuls of jersey, she pulled him so they were nose to nose and, very slowly, as if talking to a naughty dog, she said, 'Why don't you ask me out?'

'On a date? Like for dinner?'

'On a date. Dinner would be perfect.'

'Right. Are you, um, er, what are you doing, say, tomorrow evening? If you've got nothing planned, would you like, you know, to have dinner?'

'John.'

'What? You're busy? Well, some other time perhaps.'

'I'm hungry, I'm starving. Now.'

'Oh, well. Do you want to go and eat?'

'Yes.'

'Right then. We can talk about the date another time.'

'You're doing this on purpose, aren't you?'

'I'm happy now.'

'You'll have to change. I'll go on a date with you, but I'm not having dinner with that jersey.'

'Oh, I just remembered, we can't. I haven't got any money.'

'You've got a credit card.'

'Not exactly. I'll explain when you're sitting down.'

'I'll pay.'

'Good.'

They got to the bottom of the stairs.

'Can we clear something up? Am I your boyfriend or not?'

'John, haven't you been listening? You tell me. Are you my boyfriend?'

He pushed her against the wall, put a hand behind her head and kissed her. 'Yes, yes please. Yes. Yes, if that's all right with you.'

'Christ. Smug and humble is a really bad mixture. I'm glad we settled that, but just remember, you're my boyfriend, I'm not your girlfriend.'

'You're not my girlfriend?'

'No. I'm too old to be a girlfriend, it's not dignified.'

'So what are you?'

'I'm Lee Montana and I'm the biggest star in the world.'

'You tell 'im, doll.' Des's throaty laugh rolled up from the basement.

John pulled the door on his raised-and-salted life and walked Lee over to the big Mercedes; like Bilbo Baggins he stepped out into the big adventure across the Styx through the looking glass down the Yellow Brick Road and into celebrity Shangri-La. The fabled, semi-mythical place of valet-smirking, queue-dodging, clipboard friends. The land of waving palms, girded all about with velvet ropes, where a man's shadow is rarely his own. Life on a dimmer switch, where the big can-I-help never sleeps, where everybody's happy to see you and even small inanimate things in hygienic, stay-fresh plastic bags are complimentary.

As is the nature of adventures, he didn't look back. He wasn't to know that in the years to come he would think of this place often, this nowhere street, this dreary little attic, and he would remember it with a foggy fondness. He would picture his desk and the piles of books and the sexless bed as a golden aesthetic place, set in a time of intellectual struggle and angst. The loneliness, worked through the miracle of a wavy-screen flashback, becomes wrestling with creativity. His short stay here would transmute into the coin passed to Charon to place him on the farther shore. It was his due, so that he would be able to say, 'I once wrestled with the abstract and with simile. Once I inhabited that rare and wonderful place, the aesthetic garret.' In time and remembrance this would evolve into a mahogany-brown grandeur and he'd miss it like a lost childhood, but that's a long way ahead. Now he just sits in the back of the car with Lee's hand on his thigh and a mobile phone in his hand.

'Where do you want to go?'

'Lordy, John. You decide. You're taking me on a date. You do it. The only thing you ever make decisions about are positions in bed?'

'The Ivy?'

'The Ivy would be sensational.'

He dialled information, then the restaurant.

'Er, hello. Look, um, do you have a table for two tonight? Well, now? Right, well thanks anyway.' He clicked the phone shut. 'Not till June, I'm afraid.'

Hamed laughed. 'Here, give it to me. Hello, is that Ferdinando? I've got Lee Montana. Just crossing the river. Can you do her two? Cheers, mate.' He put the phone down, smiled in the mirror and shook his head.

'Oh, don't look so crestfallen, you'll learn. I think innocence is endearing, just as long as you are not naive about it.' Lee laughed.

They sat at a side wall where the most tables could get the benefit of their view. They ignored the room pointedly ignoring them.

'It's nice to be here with you. Sort of official.' Lee kissed him and ran her fingers through his hair. Blobs of glup slid off a dozen dangling forks.

'My coming-out dinner,' said John.

'You're coming out? You're going gay on me?'

'No. Like debs.'

'Who the fuck's Debs? Another girlfriend?'

'No. Curtsying in front of a cake, tiaras, ostrich feathers, balls, the Queen.'

'You are a faggot, I can't bear it.'

'I'm pleased we're out together.'

'Out together? I'm a faggot too?'

'There's Joan Collins again. She was in the South of France. She's waving.'

'Wave back.'

'I can't. I can't just wave at Joan Collins.'

'Sure you can. Practise. You're with me, kid. You'll be waving at all and sundry. It's a celebrity perk, waving. We all do it. Look, there's the *Death Wish* guy.'

'Michael Winner?'

'Yeah, wave at him.'

'I couldn't.'

'Go on, trust me. You can do it. Just a little wave, just a raised palm. He hasn't had a hit for ages.'

'You really think I should?'

'Go for it.'

John raised his hand and smiled.

A waiter trotted over. 'Yes, sir?'

'Oh, no, sorry, nothing. Thanks. Actually, while you're here, a Gibson, no, two Gibsons. Thanks.'

'It'll come,' said Lee, 'don't worry, easy mistake. Now let's talk business. Where are we going to live?'

'Live? You live in Beverly Hills and I exist in Wandsworth.'

'Well, John, I'm not commuting to London from LA five times a week and matinées, but I'd rather do that than spend a single night

185

in your cell. I'm sick to death of the hotel, so we've got to live somewhere.'

'Together?'

'You don't want to live with me?'

'I don't know. I've never lived with anyone except my parents, and that didn't set a great precedent. And isn't it rushing things, you know? Shouldn't we work up to it?'

'Fine. You don't want to live with me.' Lee mashed a potato with the back of her fork and pretended not to see Trevor Nunn wave at her. 'Look, neither of us snore, we don't have habits, you don't play the euphonium, I don't have cats, and tell me, which nights of the week don't you want to sleep with me?'

'Lee, living together is a big decision. A wistfully wished-for junction, surrounded with trepidation and hope, arrived at by cold feet. There's an accepted procedure set by precedent. You start with a toothbrush and a bra, and then a spare shirt and some earrings, then a bedside book – nothing too threatening, Martin Amis or Jilly Cooper – and then some shy joint purchases: a favourite CD, some Turkish coffee, but nothing that needs a hammer or costs more than ten pounds, and then you slowly work through the living-together list. You put a tick when you've made up a major row without having to resort to sex, when you've shared a foreign holiday, when you've spent a weekend with each other's parents, when you've seen your partner take a crap, when you've been able to take a crap whilst being watched, when you've had a Christmas and a New Year and a birthday each, when you've both had at least one minor illness involving simple nursing skills, when you can share a bath without the urge to light candles and then, and only then, can you, by tradition, live together. Generally, it's the person with the nicest curtains who says, "You know, we waste a lot of money keeping two flats, why don't you move in?" And the other one says, "Well we practically live together, don't we?" And then you have the other key cut, the one for the deadlock, that you only use for holidays, because they've already got the Yale one for convenience, and your mother gives you both a casserole dish and makes a veiled reference to the bounty of a wedding list and their father comes and checks the window locks. Then you start giving dinner parties

186

like it's the end of rationing. That's how you live together.'

Lee looked at him with a wild surmise. 'What are you on? What are you talking about? I feel like Captain Kirk. Look, I don't want to interfere with your ancient tribal customs, but shit, I'm talking about sharing a bed and a fridge, not bone marrow. We live together, we like it, we go on; we don't, we live somewhere else. What's so complicated? I want to live in the same house as my shoes, why not my boyfriend?'

'You're right. I'm mad. It's mad. What was I thinking about. Do I want to live with Lee Montana or on my own in an attic in Wandsworth? It's no contest. I apologize.'

'Right. So, as I was saying, where shall we live? Why don't you go and buy us somewhere tomorrow?'

'Buy somewhere? Tomorrow? What about renting?'

'I don't rent. I buy.'

'Well, how much do you want to spend?'

'Who cares?'

Later, back in her suite at the hotel, John got out of the shower. Lee was sitting on the loo reading *Vanity Fair*.

'See, here I am ticking off your ancient customs as quickly as possible. I'm having a crap and you're watching and there's not a candle in the room.' John brushed his teeth.

'Don't we score double for sharing a toothbrush? I'm sorry, that's as close to blind infatuation as I get. Are you going to tell me about those?'

'What?'

'On your back?'

John turned and looked over his shoulder. In the mirror there were long livid fingernail stripes across his back and bottom. 'Christ, I never noticed. They don't hurt.'

'I wasn't asking if they hurt. How did you get them? If you got them the way I think you got them I hope they hurt like hell.'

'Oh, it doesn't matter.'

'Fuck you. Fuck you it matters.' She threw the magazine hard at his head. 'You went straight from my bed to hers, you bastard.'

'She's my ex-girlfriend. We broke up. We did, we really broke up.'

'You dumped her, then you fucked her, or you fucked her then dumped her?'

'Lee, listen. There's no nice or creditable way of describing what happened last night, there just isn't. I didn't behave well, I don't even want to think about it, but please believe me, I hated it more than I've hated anything I've ever done. It was humiliating and cowardly and sad. Please trust me. It was utterly without pleasure; it was just sordid and dysfunctional. It was the end.'

'Oh bullshitters. Men, you're all bullshitters. Do you know how many times I've heard this? "Lee, it was nothing; it was just a physical thing. I hated myself, Lee baby, trust me." Trust you, for Christ's sake! Why do I pick Aboriginal pricks? Maybe it's my father. He had a yo-yo zipper. Every time I catch them with their pants down, doing secretaries or hookers or groupies or journalists or maids or the old, the underage, the ugly, how do you think that feels, John? How do you think it feels? Well, fuck it. Expecting it doesn't stop it hurting like a blunt knife. Why aren't I ever enough?'

'You are. More than enough.'

'Yeah, well I'm not going to take the rap for it any more. It's not my history, childhood or subconscious. If you can't control your hormones you're to blame. Fuck, why should I be made to feel guilty and inadequate.' She blew her nose. 'We start with a clean slate from tonight, but so help me, you slip it into the help or some groupie just once and that's it. If I even find you jerking off over *Playboy*, it's over. No explanations, no excuses. You're with me one hundred per cent or not at all. It's not open to discussion, and let me tell you there'll be a lot of opportunities – people: sluts who want to make a buck, who want to tango with the guy who tangos with Lee Montana; chancers who want their name in the tabloids; models who want to get into the movies; and the plain curious. Fame is the one great immoral aphrodisiac, John. You will be as close as a lot of people ever get, and you're beautiful and sweet. Do you understand me, John? I don't rent out boyfriends.'

'Yeah, Lee. I understand. But, well . . .'

'Now get out. I've gone off the idea of wiping my butt in front of you.'

John went and sat on the bed and listened to the shower. Finally she came out glossy and hot, and stood in front of him, hands on hips, pearls of water sliding along her throat, across her stomach and into her pubic hair.

'I'm still angry.'

'Sorry.'

'No tick on the list for this one, I'm afraid. This isn't going to be one of those arguments that we can make up without fucking.'

'Oh dear.'

THE NEXT DAY JOHN BOUGHT A HOUSE.

He and Lee were sitting in their white towelling robes around the little table in the room, buttering up brioche and each other, watching the news, reading the papers, being perky and bright, and there was a knock at the door. Hamed ploughed into the room, with his TV presenter's suit with the gold lining and the silk polo neck. His body always seemed to be saying, We can do this the nice way or the other way.

'Morning to you.' He pulled up a chair and poured himself some coffee, and slipped John an unsullied American Express card.

'Can you take John and buy a house, Hamed. I won't need you. I'm going to hang out here and go to the gym, have a facial.'

'Sure. Anything in particular?'

'Don't know. He can choose. I trust you, darling.'

They sat together in the front of the Merc. Hamed punched the radio, looking for some particular type of pop music that was unlike the other particular types of pop music he seemed to be getting.

'We'll go and see Judith,' he said. 'You'll like Judith.'

'Right,' said John. 'I thought we might be looking in estate agents' windows.'

Hamed laughed.

'Hamed, sorry to be inquisitive, but what is it that you actually do?'

'Do? What would you like me to do?'

'You're not just a chauffeur, are you?'

'No, mate. I'm freelance. I'm an MIA.'

'MIA?'

'Make It 'Appen. I make it 'appen on a freelance basis. When Lee's in town, I make it 'appen for 'er.'

'Make what happen?'

'Anything. I am the special-forces all-purpose servant. All that upstairs downstairs; yes sir, no sir; silver-salver shit – butlers and footmen and maids and housekeepers and bodyguards and watch-men – all that's for rich pricks who are wannabes with social whore wives, with nothing better to do than waste time and make servants' lives a misery. If you're a player, a real player, a real body, you get me. I make it 'appen. Tables, tickets, drugs, boys, girls, gerbils, houseboats, planes, Picassos, a blackened Cajun squab, an underage Faroe Islander at four thirty in the morning, flowers, videos, phones, meetings. I can make it 'appen. Lighter, warmer, colder, safer, and sometimes I make it not 'appen. Nerds, geeks, chancers, liggers, crashers, loonies, jobsworths, journos, ex-exes, coppers, customs, narcs, nags, dogs, mosquitoes, *Big Issue* sellers, lawyers, drunks. I'm the janitor of a perfect world. Now I'm about to make Judith 'appen.'

John didn't like Judith. He didn't like her on sight and almost on principle. Hamed wasn't going to make that 'appen. She was neat, within four or five teeth of forty; she had twenty-year-old blond hair and a nose like a Swiss-Army-knife bottle opener and a lot of cold, gold things dangling from her wrists, fingers and ears. Altogether she looked as if she'd been made out of the bits of chicken that nobody else wanted to eat.

'Hello, John. Nice to meet you.'

They were in a bijou little Kensington front room which doubled as her office. Every available surface, of which there were a lot, was crammed with silver framed photographs of people on skis. It was like being watched by a gay penguin colony.

'Do you know what you want?'

'Well, um, something unobtrusive, small, there's only two of us, um, bedroom, living room, big kitchen I suppose, a bathroom, no basement.'

Judith laughed. Hamed laughed. They savoured his innocence.

''Ere, John, I've done this before. Judith finds houses for players, trust us. You've got to have five bedrooms, minimum, big entertaining room, fuck the kitchen. Lee ain't going to start baking. You're going to be catered for. Four baths, possible staff flat, double off-street parking, garden.'

Judith looked at him with something approaching lust, but it might just have been avarice, and spread a sheaf of particulars on the coffee table.

'These are all available. Most of them aren't on the market yet.'

John picked one up. A photograph of a white stucco, Victorian, four-storey town house.

'That one's just around the corner, a quiet street in Kensington.'

'It's huge,' said John. 'And there doesn't seem to be a price.'

'Don't worry about that.' Hamed looked over his shoulder. 'Vacant? We need it pronto.'

'Of course. And cash in Zurich, OK?'

'Anywhere you want, doll. Let's go see.'

It was a big empty house. John walked through the rooms, listening to the echo, ridiculously flicking light switches and pointlessly opening cupboards to see if they had cupboard inside. He knew he should be asking a million questions, but he couldn't think of a single one except, How much? Finally he said, 'Where's the fuse box?'

'Do you like it?' Hamed asked.

'Yes, I suppose. It's big.'

'Right, doll. We'll take it. Will you do the biz? Get us the papers by this afternoon, and we need Susie.'

'She's on her way.'

Susie was an interior designer. She'd been pressed from the same Sunday lunch as Judith – another forty-something, long blond hair, utensil nose and clunky jewellery. The two were friends and plainly hated each other.

'Oh, John, wonderful house. What sort of thing would you like?'

'Well, I don't know. A sofa, some chairs. I'd like a desk. I've no idea.'

'It's OK. What's your star sign?'

'Cancer. Why?'

'And Miss Montana's?'

'I've no idea.'

'Scorpio,' said Hamed. 'Her favourite colour's cream.'

'Good.' Susie made a note. 'Old or modern?'

John tossed a mental coin. 'Modern.'

'Fine. Have you got any things you want incorporated, furniture, family portraits, silver?'

John thought about his room, his family. 'No, but bookshelves, please.'

'Oh, right.' Susie raised her eyebrows as if this was rather an outré request, like his-and-her Turkish bugger stools or a lobster tank. 'What sort of books?'

'What do you mean, what sort of books?'

'I mean, mixed, or would you like all leather sets. I've got a chap who sells them by the yard.'

'No, no. That's fine,' said John, 'I can manage the books.'

She made another note and looked as if he'd just said he would supply his own lobsters.

'Is that it?' John belted himself back into the car.

'That's it.'

'But shouldn't we at least have looked at a few others?'

'Why?'

'Well, I don't know.'

'Trust your instincts, John mate. If you don't like it in a month, change it. Get another one. It's no big deal; it's only a house.'

'But isn't this supposed to be the most stressful thing you can do after divorce and burying a loved one?'

'No, mate. The most stressful thing you can do, in my experience, is have a facelift. A facelift and byline envy. That's pretty stressful.'

'Look, Hamed. Would you like to have lunch with me? I think we ought to have a talk.'

'Sure, John. I can make that 'appen. Let's go to my club.'

'OK. What does money get you?' Hamed sat back in the booth and pushed away his plate with an expansive gesture. The club was a discreetly unmarked, thin Georgian house in Soho, with a bar and a warren of little sitting rooms. They were sitting in the light dining room and were served chichi food. It was half full of young men, who John thought were probably in or of the film industry. They all seemed to know Hamed.

'What does money get you?'

'Everything. Anything,' replied John.

'So does burglary.' Hamed lit a big cigar. 'When you've got all the knick-knacks, the stuff, enough equipment and clobber to last ten lifetimes, there's only two things left. Money buys you two things: time and space. Look what we did this morning, bought a fuck-off house before elevenses. Well, that's the space. You'll be moved in by the end of next week. That's time. How long do you think it would take an average punter to arrange that? Six months, nine months? How long do you think it would take your dad to earn the mill-and-a-half to pay for it? A hundred years? A hundred and fifty? That's a lot of time. You see, money buys other people's lives, other people's time, and adds it to yours. Rich people live longer than everyone else. Things happen quicker for them. At this moment twenty, thirty, forty people are adding little bits of their lifetime to yours in exchange for cash. Hundreds and hundreds of people all over the world are giving their time to Lee. You know, animals live according to their metabolism: a mayfly races through its mortal coil in a day, a tortoise in two hundred years. One's frenetic and packs it in, the other's sedentary and ekes it out. The rich live like mayflies, but they live as long as tortoises.'

'It's an interesting idea, but I'm not sure I'm quite with you.'

'You know what annoys them more than anything?'

'What? Tortoises?'

'Yeah, rich people. We're talking seriously rich. It's waiting for things – jams, queues, crowds, delays, cancellations – they all drive them bonkers. You see, they're not getting their money's worth. They're suddenly having to live at the pace of everyone else. You want to sell anything to a rich man, tell him it's fast, that he can have it last Friday. It gets to be a mania with them. Executive lounges, limos, jets, nippier computers, faxes; the rich employ people to read for them. I work for a geezer who has every bestseller sent to him and just reads the last four pages. He can't stand waiting to see how they finish. He can only watch movies on a video, so he can fast-forward them. The very rich, the most privileged, and the underclass have one thing in common: tiny attention spans. You listen to them, John, their conversations grow shorter and shorter. They lose patience with anything that isn't a synopsis. I used to drive one of the richest men in the world. He'd see a bit of totty and say, "Hi, you're pretty. I'm worth four bill, suck my cock." Flirting was a waste of time. That's all you need to know about the rich, mate. They consume time, vast, vast quantities of it, and they need the space to put it all in.'

'Well, that's fascinating, but I don't really see that Lee fits into all that; she's not like that at all.'

'Ah. Now Lee's a star. Stars are altogether different. There's rich, and then there's famous. Fame trumps rich. Although to be rich and famous is to inhabit the starriest place this side of the Bible. What you need to know about stars is that they don't deserve it, not really. The fans might think they deserve it, every drop of it, but they don't. And in the bottom of their hearts they know they don't. They know there are prettier, more talented people who never make it. And what's a celebrity done to deserve all that attention and adoration compared to, say, a doctor or a teacher? Fame's a fraud, a con. Stardom's a con on all sorts of levels. It's artifice, it's one-dimensional, it's manipulation and it's transient. They know it, and they're constantly frightened that they're going to be exposed, that *it's* going to be exposed, that it's going to be taken away. They don't know why they got it in the first place, and they don't know how to hold on to it. So your star is constantly beset by two equally powerful and contradictory feelings. One is the need to be reassured that their stardom is the truth, and on the other hand the absolute knowledge that it's all lies. Remember, fame, by definition, only exists in the eyes of the viewer, not the viewed.'

'That's all extraordinarily profound, Hamed, but tell me, how did you arrive at all this?'

'I read Sociology at Princeton.'

'You were at Princeton?'

194

'Yeah. I majored in business. My parents are from Bombay, but they live in Michigan.'

'But your voice, it's so indigenously South London.'

'Yeah, right. Your voice is your uniform. You sound like a bleedin' poet, Lee sounds like a star, I sound like a bloke who knows what's what.'

'I'm still not sure how I fit into all of this. I feel like I'm floating, like I've just chucked the oars overboard to go faster.'

'You think too much, John. Just go with it. A word of advice: go and shop, go and do some serious shopping. You've got to get beyond this money stuff. Understand the price-and-value equation. Price and value aren't the same thing; the price is what it costs, the value is what it's worth. What you need is a new idea of value. Go and buy Lee a present. They all love a present, even if they've paid for it themselves and they've already got fifteen in every colour under the sun.'

John wandered around Soho, looking in windows. Did he fancy a leather coat? A suit? A lifetime's supply of poppers? A case of South African wine? A Georgian travelling clock? A pocket ashtray? A Turkish carpet? A three-tier wedding cake? A set of pornographic playing cards? A can of Coke? A get-well card? An *Evening Standard*? A copy of Chatsworth made in platinum? He could have any of them; he could have all of them, if he wanted them. He walked, looking, willing something to shout, to jump up at him and say, Have me, eat me, buy me, wear me, use me. He stood for a long time in front of a shoe shop – brown brogues with buckles? Boots with soles like rubber teeth? Patent-leather loafers? A girl with large, floppy bosoms, a beehive haircut and a pronounced pudenda which looked like a camel's foot inserted down the front of her pink, plastic hot pants, asked if he fancied it. Did he fancy it? Any of it? He didn't.

He walked on and finally came to an antiquarian bookshop, with framed ornithological prints and maps of the world in the window. Right, you're not leaving until you've bought something. Inside it was dark and cool; he scanned the shelves without appetite. A complete set of Somerset Maugham, a paperback of *Summoned by Bells*, the memoirs of Glubb Pasha, signed Glubb.

A young man sidled up. 'Can I help you? Looking for anything in particular or just browsing?'

He was tall and rather stooped, with a long chin and an intelligent, apologetic look.

'Hello. No, well, yes. I'm looking for a present for someone, but I'm not sure what.'

The boy smiled. He had crooked teeth.

'Well, what are they interested in?'

What was Lee interested in? Lee. Movies. Sex. Lee. Theatre.

'Do you have a theatre section?'

'We've got some plays, a nice set of Barrie, and some criticism.'

'No, something lighter, a bit more fun.'

'Ah.' The boy thought.

John saw himself, helpful, reticent, dismissive. They were about the same age.

'I work in a bookshop. Well, used to.'

'Oh.' The assistant smiled politely, without interest.

I know that look, thought John. That's what I did just a couple of days ago.

'Well, we have some fashion books, photography, Cecil Beaton – that's got photographs of film stars.'

The boy was going through the motions. John had been marked down as a time-waster. He'd wander around the shop for five minutes and edge towards the door. He'd look at the last shelf, Victorian topography, and then make a break for it, saying thank you apologetically. John wanted to laugh, to pat the boy on the arm and say, Look, I know what you're thinking, really I do. I'm like you, I'm not one of them, I'm one of us, but he wasn't any more.

'Do you have a poetry section?'

'Yes,' the boy pointed. 'There are some first editions in the cabinet.'

Little prick, thought John, judging me, making assumptions, being dismissive. He felt an irked righteousness. It came to him with a sparkly newness, like lavender cashmere and a snakeskin wallet. It was a completely original feeling for him; it was a celebrity feeling, irked righteousness, a knobbly, user-friendly, matt-black little feeling, and he rather liked it. It was pleasantly comfortable, a sort of fake-fur anger. He searched the shelf – Edwardian-calf and cloth-bound, gold-embossed parlour poetry. He had most of them in paperback and nothing would make him own the complete works of Southey or Hood.

He ambled over to the cabinet and said, 'Can I see that?' pressing a finger to the glass.

The Four Quartets, a first edition, mint and inscribed.

The boy opened the case and gingerly, reverently, handed him the slim volume. The tea-colour paper was warm and crumbly. A smell, as fugitive as dust but as powerful as thunder, swam out of the covers, like a genie from a bottle. It was the smell of lonely rooms, damp tweed, warm mahogany and of sighs through yellow teeth, of concentration and sadness, of lost words and one syllable too many. It was the smell of the slow gears of genius, and John's stomach melted with memory and reverence. The scent of a first-born volume of poetry is civilization's aftershave.

He turned back to the flyleaf. There was the crabbed little signature, legible and introverted, the antithesis of the celebrity autograph, with its swagger and hollow, profligate love and gush. This thin cardboard and cellulose yellow book, how much greater was it than all the hysterical encores, standing ovations and scrawled programmes? John wanted it so much it made the blood in his head sing.

'I'll take it.'

'Oh, right. Well it's . . .' The boy was rather taken aback. He mentioned a price.

'Thank you. And I'll take that.' He pointed at a gaudy, over-decorated, vellum-bound copy of *The Rubáiyát of Omar Khayyám* illustrated by Arthur Rackham.

'Oh good.'

He signed the docket with an impatient, inarticulate flourish.

'Where was the bookshop you worked in?' The assistant handed him the bag, wanting to make small amends.

'Oh, it was a long time ago,' said John.

'Did you get one?' Lee was lying on the bed, watching television, surrounded by her usual attendant junk: magazines, faxes, fruit, make-up and bottled water.

197

'Get what?' asked John, guiltily.

'A house, of course. You didn't forget?'

'Oh yes, we got one.'

'Well, what's it like? Where is it?'

He thought for a moment. 'Do you know, I don't know. I've forgotten the address.'

'You mean we've bought a house, but you don't know where it is? Are we going to have to get the police to go and find it?'

'Yes, it's a worry. It might get taken in by the Salvation Army and be adopted, and then come and find us when it's eighteen, full of anger and resentment, wanting to know why we abandoned it.'

'I expect Hamed knows.'

'I expect he does. Hamed seems to know everything.'

'What does it look like?'

'Big and empty, but I'm assured it will be full of creature comforts by next week.'

'Next week. I can't wait till next week, this hotel's driving me crazy, the gym's a medieval armaments bazaar.'

'Ancient or modern? Furniture? Do you like old or new?'

'Modern.'

'Good. That's what I said. It's such a relief that we share a taste in light fittings. I bought you a present.'

'You did!' Lee sat up and clapped. 'What? Oh, I got you one as well.'

He handed her the plastic bag, and received a small, professionally gift-wrapped box plucked from the litter.

'A book. You gave me a book. No-one's ever given me a book before.'

'Lee, that's not clever or funny.'

'It's true, we don't do books, unless we're going to option them. It's old. How beautiful. *Omayer K-ham*. How do you pronounce it?'

'*Omar Khayyám*. It's a poem, a love poem. One of the greatest ever written.'

'You are sweet, that's so romantic. Now, darling, open yours.'

He pulled the ribbon. There was a box, and in the box there was a watch. A vast platinum thing with dials and nuts and bolts on a great, complicated bracelet.

'It's amazing.'

'Do you like it? Everyone was wearing them in St Barts last year. They look great with a tan. You need a watch.'

John looked at his wrist and heard, distantly, from out of the past, his father's knock on his bedroom door. 'You still awake, John?'

It was the night before he went up to Oxford. His father came in and sat uncomfortably on the end of John's childhood bed under the poster of Jack Kerouac.

'You know we're very proud of you, your mother and I. I don't know where you get it from, really. Not me, anyway. We know you'll do your best, and, well . . .' he rubbed his flannel thighs, as if drying his palms, 'I've always been proud of you. There's something we wanted you to have. Think of your mother and your thick old dad sometimes when you're mixing with all your new intellectual friends.' His face had been in deep shadow, but John knew there were tears in his eyes and he was embarrassed. 'Anyway.' He put his hand into his pocket and brought out a watch. 'It's an Omega. Won't let you down, so no excuses for being late for classes. It's got a guarantee and a date and, er, anyway, we wanted you to have it. Well, there you are. Oh, and it's waterproof and shock-resistant, and, er, dust and stuff. Early start in the morning. Get some sleep.'

John looked down at the plain functional thing, with its ugly numbers and sensible worn strap. He knew it must have cost his father a lot; he also knew, but didn't want to think about, what it had really cost, what it represented. Eighteen years of worry and small sacrifices, of doubt and frustration, of holding on and making do. His father had never missed a minute, never done anything unexpected, just quietly counted the hours, put in his time, done his job. Neatly these two watches ticked out the distance between price and value. He undid the worn, cracked, soap-supple strap and clipped on the great new thing. It felt like his arm had been put in plaster. He pushed a button and the second hand sprinted. Other, lesser dials shot after it. The rich live like mayflies for as long as tortoises.

'It's great. I just love it. No-one's ever given me a watch like this before.'

'You're so handsome. Come and read me some of this. It needs a Limey accent.'

'I should warn you, this is not a poem to be aimed indiscriminately. It's a proven aphrodisiac; it'll melt knickers at five stanzas. In fact, I've never known it to fail.'

'Oh. So you've used it before?'

'Hundreds of times. "Come fill the cup, and in the Fire of Spring the Winter Garment of Repentance fling: the Bird of Time has but a little way to fly – and Lo! the Bird is on the Wing."'

'Oh, oh. Oh my. Oh my.' Lee ripped off the bed covers, depositing half a ton of rubbish on the floor. 'Take me now, take me this instant, you troubadour stud.'

And then the phone rang.

Lee leaned over, laughing. 'Whoever you are, your timing's lousy. Oh, it's for you.' She handed the receiver to John.

'Hello?'

'John, it's Clive. What are you doing?'

'Slipping Lee Montana a length of *Omar Khayyám*. Do you want to listen?'

'Yeah, very funny. Look, I thought you should know, Dorothy's not going to make it.'

THE FUNERAL WAS HELD IN A GLOOMY, FIFTIES CREMATORIUM IN West London. Gloomy is, of course, what crematoria are supposed to be. You wouldn't build a jolly, ironic, exuberant crematorium. But it was the wrong sort of gloom; a post-rationing, make-the-best-of-it gloom. It had a sort of serviceable, shy taste. The red brick and white stone was a reasonable shell-shocked excuse-me. It was municipal planning from a time that never wanted to hear a raised voice again or people crying, a time that built crematoria like supermarkets and town halls and blocks of flats with exactly the same querulous emphasis, a Festival-of-Britain dancing-in-the-ashes fatality. Buildings that said, We hope the searchlights will never fret the sky again, but when the bombs return, as surely they must, it won't matter much if this building is reduced to rubble. The architecture of the Fifties lacked the one asset all architecture should have, a sense of its own permanence. The crematorium looked temporary because death isn't. But perhaps, as a reminder of the vanity of life, and Dorothy's sad little existence in particular, it was appropriate after all.

Hamed parked outside and John, wearing one of his now numerous new suits, walked through an instantly forgettable garden of remembrance. The congregation was a *Reader's Digest* précis of Dorothy's birthday party. They stood outside in a little knot, waiting for a master butcher who'd succumbed under the knife to be roasted. Dorothy's widowed mother, a hair-pin lady, with red eyes, a turned-down mouth and a bobbly tweed coat, was talking to Petra, who stared at John from beneath hard, beetled brows, her eyes dark and manic.

'You made it.' Clive looked uncomfortable in a grey jacket and trousers that nearly matched and a riotous tie.

'Like the tie.'

'I thought she'd appreciate it. Got it from Oxfam. It's a shame you didn't manage to get to the hospital.'

John had meant to go and see Dorothy, but Lee had needed him at an awards dinner; she simply couldn't go alone. And then there was a cocktail party, a film, a dinner with money people. She'd pulled a face and then sulked. It must be said that John hadn't needed a lot of convincing. Dorothy, he said, didn't need his solemn, lying platitudes to take to the next life, but he still felt guilty.

'She was in a coma, wasn't she?'

'At the end, yes. They found a donor. It looked hopeful for a bit, but, anyway . . . Isn't this ghastly? Look John, I know this really isn't the place, but could you do something for me. Be cool with Petra. She . . . we're . . . well, she and I, well, we're sort of an item. Nothing official, but, well, early days, and she's still pretty cut up. I know it's the rebound and stuff, but I really like her. Please don't wind her up.'

'No, of course. I'm glad for you; it's a relief.'

But it wasn't. The heart is a contrary bleeder, John noted, with a violently sharp tug of jealousy. He didn't want Petra, he didn't fancy her and he was deeply into something or other with Lee; he liked Clive, and yet, and yet.

The service was too thin even to be ghastly. A few words from a vicar who knew no-one in the room, living or dead. A hymn no-one sang and an all-purpose new translation of St Paul's fax to the Corinthians, read by Mrs Patience, and then the vibrating whirr of the conveyor belt as the coffin shuffled without solemnity behind the Pollock's theatrical curtain to the oven. In the front row Petra sobbed, great inhaled wails of misery, and John saw Dorothy's fat, unloved, pent-up body squirming on his bed. 'Please, please, please.'

Afterwards they sucked heavily on cigarettes outside in the garden, looking at the five sorry bunches of forecourt flowers laid on the gravel.

'Are you coming for a drink?' asked Clive.

'Yes, OK.'

'Good. We should get a bus.'

'Well, I've got a car. I'll give you a lift.'

Clive, Dom and Pete slid into the Mercedes, giving Hamed surly looks. They drove in silence. The resentment was palpable. A limo and a chauffeur were solid manifestations of the distance John had already travelled from their collective life.

'Mind if I smoke?' Dom asked the back of Hamed's head.

'Of course not,' said John.

It was late afternoon and Maggie's was empty. They'd closed off the little back room for the wake. A tray of sandwiches lay on the pool table. They all tried to say jolly, nostalgic things about Dorothy, but, sucking on their beer and staring at their feet, they couldn't think of anything, so they lied instead.

'She'd have appreciated the service,' Clive kicked off. 'Quite laid-back, you know.'

'Yeah,' said Dom. 'She had such a great sense of humour.'

'Yeah, really dry,' added Pete.

'Real life and soul,' said Clive.

The inappropriateness of the expression fell to a deaf floor.

'And sexy,' Pete punted hopefully.

'I'd say so.' Dom caught the expression. 'You remember that number she wore at her birthday. What a body, dead sexy.'

The carpet ignored that too.

'She'll be missed by everyone. Us, of course, but loads of people who never really knew her were touched. You know, I was in the newsagent and that geezer said, "Where's your friend? I haven't seen her for ages." There'll be lots like that.'

'Here's to Dorothy,' cut in John, raising his glass. 'Sexy, funny, unforgettable.' He tried to remember her face, but it had already passed over. He could only focus on an image of her back, standing in the kitchen stirring Petra's tea.

A pair of large boys blocked the door, hoping for a game.

'Fuck. Looks like someone died.'

'Someone did.' Clive took an aggressive step forward. 'Dorothy. Used to drink here.'

The boys looked at each other and shrugged. 'Can't place her. You going to be long?'

One of them had been the date that had been so carefully lined up for the birthday party. Dorothy's last, best hope.

After a bit the wake moved back to their regular table in the pub. The room began to fill up with late-afternoon drinkers coming 'for the one'. Petra arrived, having taken Dorothy's mother to the station.

'Hello, John.' She kissed him on the cheek. 'So you managed to find the time.'

'What do you want to drink? It's my round.'

'They don't take credit cards here. Whiskey.'

She followed him to the bar.

'There were one or two things I wanted to say to you.'

John saw Clive's nervous, imploring face over her shoulder.

'Can't it wait? I'll call you in the week.'

'No. We need to sort this out now. First, your things. Will you come and get them?'

'Keep them. It's nothing, some clothes, books. Keep them, throw them away.'

'How can you say that, John? That was our life together.'

'I'm sorry, I didn't mean it like that. I just don't want them.'

'No. You've got better things.'

'Yes.' A better life.

'You know, I really hate you.'

The directness of the statement connected and stung.

'I really, really hate you.' Her eyes filled with tears. 'You walked off without a second thought. So cruel. You never cared. You didn't. You can't have done.' Her voice rose. 'You didn't even come to see Dorothy when you knew she was dying.'

The pub hushed and listened.

'You didn't give a fuck about her, or me, or any of us.' She waved at the tables. 'You came to cremate all of us, your mates, to make sure we really were dead. You bastard. I hope you get AIDS and cancer and die on your own of loneliness and guilt. I hope you take an overdose and your liver turns to mush.'

She summoned a great wave of unhappiness, her little body as taut as a steel hawser, indomitable, with a poor dignity. She was full of sober Brechtian righteousness.

'I will never cease to loathe and despise you.'

She jerked her head back and spat in John's face.

She might have been going to hit him, but a hand grabbed her arm and spun her away. She tripped and fell to her knees. Hamed stood in front of John.

'Fuck,' said Clive, lurching across the table at him.

There was a hollow smack. The palm of Hamed's hand caught Clive's face as if it were a rugby ball and pushed him back into and then over his chair.

'Right, you two,' pointing at Dom and Pete, 'forget it.'

Sean came round the bar, threatening. Hamed turned and stared at him. 'We're just going, unless you want to make this ugly.'

John moved to help Petra.

Hamed held his shoulder. 'She's fine. Get in the car. In the car.'

John sat in the back. The car seemed very big and he felt very small.

'A word of advice,' Hamed said after a bit.

'I don't want any advice, Hamed.'

'Yeah, whatever. You're sitting there thinking, How can I make this better? Will it calm down? Can I send flowers? Take them out to dinner? Buy a present? It was just the funeral, naturally everyone was upset. But it wasn't just the funeral, and they won't get over it and you can't make it better. Move on.'

'They're my friends, I can't just move on.'

'No, they're not. They were. They're not now. They don't like you. I can't tell you how many rock gods and movie stars I've taken back to their roots because they've suddenly got an itch to scratch the past. Back to nowhere – little terraces and grubby little boozers. The excitement, "Ooh, that's where I went to school, Hamed. That was my auntie's shop. I had my first shag in that bus shelter." It's always the same: ends in tears. I've got a scar on my arm this long given to me by a miner who was the best mate of a guitarist. We drove up to Nottingham, and in the back it was Trev this and Trev that, the best mate a bloke could ever have, all the stuff they'd done, the girls they'd pulled, proper little rascals. Trev was his one true mate, all the rest were because he was a star, but he'd die for Trev. He didn't have to, I bloody nearly did. Went for him with a screwdriver and a lifetime's resentment. The thing is, it's not jealousy, although everyone thinks it is. They're not all venal; they know what money is, what it buys and what it doesn't, and what it costs. It's that your success, your getting out, takes away their excuses. They can't look at you and say, Oh well, if I'd had his breaks or his education or background, I could have done that, because they've had everything you had and they didn't. They were just like you. You're the constant reminder for the never wases. You see, you can always go back, but they can't go forward. They'll never forgive you for that. Forget it, forget them.'

'Is there no end to your fucking wisdom, Hamed?'

Hamed laughed without joy and put on a tape of Lee. Her naked, hot voice slunk through the car.

THE NEW HOUSE WAS WHITE, WHITE ON THE OUTSIDE AND WHITE ON the inside. John looked at it and saw that it was white. Susie, the designer, corrected him. It wasn't white, it was raw yoghurt, starched linen and Highland steam. John and Lee walked through the rooms. The place made John feel dirty. It was like living in a cloud, heaven's departure lounge. The impracticality of everything was awe-inspiring.

'It's like moving into a sanitary towel,' he said. 'Don't you have the terrible urge to flick ink over everything?'

Lee nuzzled his ear. 'Come on, let's put a stain on the sofa.'

And so they began the complex gavotte of cohabiting.

John soon got used to the dozen small white conveniences he'd never considered before: a fridge that spat ice cubes; a ceramic plate for his watch, wallet and keys; coasters; bidets; dimmers; suit bags; lemon-pip strainers; security cameras; asparagus steamers. His grasp of the rich world grew to match his reach. He had his own small study, a pristine room with a view of a fully matured all-flowering, all-dancing white garden. A pile of intimidatingly lustrous paper stood on a blond desk. He would go there in the morning after breakfast and think about writing, but his eyes slid and skidded off the blankness of the room and his concentration elided over subjects and words. There were no edges, there was no roughness to snag his concentration, no grit in this mother-of-pearl shell. His mind would meander and he would follow. He wandered through the house, making coffee, taking baths, and he'd look in the cupboards at the neat piles of laundered sheets and napkins and shirts.

But it didn't matter, he didn't feel unhappy about not writing; the muse had slipped away without a whisper. In fact, it was a relief, like waking up to find you don't have a familiar ache. John had a formless, pointless contentment. He smiled and chewed his nails and watched videos with the sound turned down. He ate light lunches, drank light soda, had light conversations, all sweetness and light; and there was Lee. The house suited her, a silk and cottonwool gift box. She nestled into it like a fabulous jewel and he was childishly entranced by her. The beauty, the sparkle never wore off, never dimmed or became blasé. His eye never got enough of her; the rods and cones vibrated with her, the aperture widening, taking in as much of her reflected light as possible, and Lee liked to be watched. She would wander in and out of his peripheral vision, posing and revealing. They were the happy dovetail of exhibitionist and voyeur, narcissist and epicure, star and audience.

And of course there was the sex. Lee craved the applause, the standing ovation, the ejaculated bouquet, the smell of loins and the roar of blood. They would fuck for hours, anywhere, everywhere, crawling over each other like junkie paraplegics. She'd pull him to the floor in the hall, kneel over a table, lie opposite him in the big armchair and slowly masturbate. He'd watch, impaled with an endless fascination. She was always touching herself. On the telephone she'd brush her nipples; watching television or reading the newspapers she'd tease her pubic hair; just staring at the sunlight her hands would wander across her body, and John would watch until she reached over, wordless, and pushed his fingers between her liquid thighs and they'd fold together to spin, glistening.

They caught a truth that is generally only known to solitary men addicted to pornography, that feeding an appetite doesn't satiate or dull or devalue the hunger, it elevates, magnifies, hones and ravens it. Exploration and examination don't lead to familiarity, but to further, deeper mystery and craving, that fucking, hump-backed, Siamese-muscled bulging and aching. Bodies tingled and shivered, the nerves hyper-sensitized to touch, orgasms became classier and rounder, swooping glissandos. John grew imbecilic with lust. A pussy-walloped, cunt-stuck, groin-drunk snatch junkie. And Lee. Lee glowed, wallowed, took evangelic encores and deep bows, fanned by John's adoration. It showed.

In the evenings they'd entertain movie people or music people, news people, fashion people, now people, people people.

A man of reptilian hideosity watched Lee with glistening, scrotal eyes and pinched the back of John's neck between a finger and thumb.

'I don't know what the fuck you've done to her, but Christ she looks great. I've known Lee for years. She's never been so fucking gorgeous. Just watching her's giving me a hernia. She should be in LA with that look. That's worth an extra two mill above the line. Why's she doing this crazy nickel-and-dime theatre thing? Talk to her, John, talk to her. If it's some contractual thing, I'll wipe my arse with it.'

'Have you talked to her?' Stewart caught John in the kitchen.

All the original alfresco players from Gloucestershire were here.

'Have you talked to her about the play?'

'No, why?'

'Well, you know we're starting rehearsals soon. I was wondering if she'd shown any interest in the text or anything.'

'Oh, I think she's been reading it,' said John, loyally.

'Good. It's just that I've been leaving tentative messages and she never calls back. You know it's going to be quite a steep learning curve, or whatever they call it. Perhaps I'm just being nannyish.' He picked up a canapé and popped it in his mouth like a particularly scrumptious choir boy. 'Could we perhaps have a longer chat? A cosy lunch or something. I'd really like your advice on a few things, you know, a poet's eye. And it would just be nice to have lunch?'

He removed an imaginary bit of fluff from John's lapel. 'She's looking utterly pampered, your Lee. I expect you're spending all day in bed, cosseting her all over. Seeing to her every whim.' He giggled. 'Well, stop it. She's far too luxuriant for Antigone. I want her to look haunted and drained, not like a *Playboy* harvest festival. Ravaged not ravishing.'

Oliver Hood stood in a corner of the big living room, glowering at the richer, more successful, urbane and less well-read denizens of California. He looked like Hereward the Wake at a Battle of Hastings regimental reunion.

'You're angelic to put up with all this, you know. These philistines at the hearth, dear boy.' He patted John on the back. 'Blow them away with a great triumph. I expect Lee's deep into Sophocles by now. God I envy her. Can you imagine the rapture of coming across the Thebans for the first time? What wouldn't you give to be able to read it now with all the experience and knowledge of a grown-up life behind you? Oh the joy, the excitement. That's the problem with the liberal classic education we've had, you consume everything in great draughts too young and inexperienced to savour it fully. I'm a great believer in keeping the classics back from the young. I've just been to see the education minister, you know. Nice enough chap, but essentially a red-brick low-brow. "Dave," I said, "Dave, darling, you must take the tragedies off the syllabus, and the sonnets. By all means allow them the treat of the comedies, *Twelfth Night*, *Gentlemen of Verona*, tease their appetites with a romance and perhaps the easier histories, but for the love of God, lock up the Dane, restrict Prospero, and then, when they're older, they'll fall upon them with awe. They'll thank you, invest statues to you, as the man who understood that education, like everything else worth having in this crapulous world, is all about timing.'

John nodded.

'I don't expect he'll do anything about it. He asked if I could recommend a musical to take the Angolan president's wife to.'

John raised his eyebrow and made that bobbing, tutting noise that is the one thing Englishmen share with meerkats.

'You know, I've always assiduously protected Skye from dabbling in great literature. "You may by all means experiment with the lightweight," I've told her. "Go and have fun with Colette and Hemingway, but please, not the hard stuff, not till you've shed some grown-up tears." Sometimes I think it's all you can do for your children. I mean, can you imagine reading Dostoevsky before you've fornicated, John? Absurd.'

John had an image of Oliver reading *The Brothers Karamazov* after fornicating.

'By the way, if you see Skye anywhere can you tell her we need to go. I don't think I can stand these cultural dung-beetles any more, present company excepted, of course.'

By chance, John did find Skye.

'She was in the loo.' He pointed at the bathroom.

'No.'

John and Lee were lying on their bed, sharing a last bottle of champagne and eating popcorn after the party.

'She was with that thin man with the sleazy smile and the floral waistcoat.'

'Bo Devereux! Here! That sleazebag. The publicist from the studio. What was she doing with him?'

'You can guess. She was on her knees and there was a rolled-up fifty-pound note on the sink.'

209

'Euuch. She was giving him a blow job? I don't believe it; he's so disgusting, and he's fifty.'

'Yes, she was pumping away with a look of utter concentration on her face and her shirt pulled up over her bosom.'

'Oh, this is so gross. What was he doing?'

'Well, getting a blow job. And looking at himself in the mirror, inspecting the crease of his nose for blackheads.'

'I love it. He's got herpes, you know.'

'How do you know?'

'Must have. All publicists have herpes. What did they do when you walked in?'

'Well, she uncoupled and smiled, as if she were trying to get the sleeve onto a collapsible umbrella. "Hi, John," she said. "Great party. You don't mind us using your bathroom?"'

'She's an animal. What did he do?'

'Well, that's the funny part. He started and stopped. He ejaculated all over her head. Well, basically into her ear.'

'Oh my God, oh my God, oh my God. How could she?'

'Well, I expect she was eager to get to grips with Dostoevsky.'

'What?'

'Oh, it doesn't matter. Both her father and Stu asked how you were getting on with their play?'

'Oh, come on. We don't start rehearsing for ages.' Lee poured more champagne. 'And that goes on for weeks.'

'Well, perhaps you should read it. I just happen to have a copy here.'

'John. I'll read my part tomorrow. Come here.'

'No. Why don't we read it together, all of it, now?'

'Oh, John, it's work. And this is bedtime. Don't make me work.' She reached over to him. 'Come in my ear.'

'Lee.' He held her hand.

'Oh, all right. Just tell me what happens, a synopsis. One side.'

'Antigone is Oedipus's daughter.'

'The guy who fucked his mother that we hear so much about?'

'The same. She wants to bury her brother, but her uncle, Creon, says that if anyone tries to bury him they'll be executed.'

'Nice. Where's the brother?'

'Outside the city wall.'

'He's not on stage? We don't have to act with a rotting corpse?'

'No, you never see him.'

'Good.'

'Antigone is betrothed to Haemon, Creon's son.'

'They sure like to keep it in the family, don't they?'

'She argues with Creon, and goes ahead and buries Polynices.'

'Right. Then the son comes in at the last minute and does the father-son huggy thing and rescues her and they ride off on the Trojan Horse into the sunset.'

'Not exactly. Creon has her bricked up in a tomb.'

'Nice.'

'Haemon kills himself and so does Eurydice, Creon's wife. Creon is forced to live.'

'Oh great. So there's someone left to turn off the house lights at the end. Is that it?'

'No, but that's the bones.'

'Sure is. So why can't anyone bury the brother?'

'He's tried to invade the city and he's killed his other brother, the king.'

'OK. An everyday story of pre-talkie incest victims. So from the audience's point of view it's all a will-she-get-the-guy-in-the-box-and-then-get-the-guy-or-is-she-going-to-get-buried sort of Hitchcock meets Zorba type of thing?'

'No, you're told right at the start by the Chorus – he's the MC – that she's going to die, everyone's going to die.'

'Hold on, the audience knows how it's going to end?'

'Yes.'

'Let me get this straight. This is a play about an in-bred girl who has a thing about a corpse and gets her uncle to brick her up in a tomb, and there's no money or sex or drugs or power thing going on that you haven't told me about, and everyone knows the ending, right, and this is the oldest play in the world. How did it ever get to play a week, let alone a thousand years?'

'Two thousand five hundred actually.' John laughed. 'No. It's really about destiny. It's Antigone's destiny to die. She doesn't want to; she has no choice. Creon doesn't want to kill her; he has no choice. They are set on paths that will lead to both their destructions. Creon tries everything to stop it happening, even when Antigone finds out that her brother was a real low life and doesn't deserve a burial. It makes no difference, it's fate. It's about our inability to escape fate.'

'But despite everything, Mrs Lincoln, it's a good play?'

'It's great. It's perfect. It has the germ of all drama in it. It's the template for everything, for all theatre, TV, movies, everything that came after.'

'Oh, come on, John. This would make one lousy film. Who'd buy all that destiny crap? Films are all about choice and free will and will she or won't she.'

'No, no, they're not. You know from the opening titles how it will end. You know the destiny of the characters. It's set out right at the start. You know the hero will win, you know the policeman who shows his family photographs is going to get killed and you know there's a maniac in the house when she starts to run the bath. The music, which is the modern equivalent of the chorus, tells you. Films are all on courses they can't avoid, one act leads inexorably to the next. You can do the dialogue in your head. You know the entire plot before you've seen it. We may not believe in the same gods, or any gods, but the rules of drama are exactly the same, and they were invented here with the Theban plays.'

'Do you think I'm up to this, John?' Lee drained her glass and looked at him seriously.

'You know who played Antigone first in London? Vivien Leigh.'

'Oh, I loved her. Fabulous. You know I was offered a remake of *Gone With the Wind*. I turned it down. "Tomorrow is another day." How could you follow that? She's my hero, I always wanted to be Vivien Leigh. It's fate.'

'Actually, *Gone With the Wind* is quite a good example of what we've just been talking about. Scarlett O'Hara is a heroine who's directly descended from Antigone. You tell me that it's no madder to throw away everything for a burned-out house than for the body of your brother.'

'Oh, you're so clever. I'm amazed you don't keep yourself awake at night just listening to yourself think. Enough stories now, please.

Let's do some extemporary movement. This is one Antigone who's dying to bury a stiff. Come and seal my fate.'

Next morning John came out of his study after an hour of reading the paper and looking out of the window to find Lee in the big blond sitting room, wearing her old ripped jeans and a T-shirt. She had the play and a pencil.

'Hi. What are you doing?'

'Reading this fucking text.'

'And making notes. I'm impressed.'

'Sort of. I'm editing.'

'Editing?'

'Yeah, you know. Taking out some of the dead wood, making it easier to say, putting it into my own words.'

John looked over her shoulder. The page was a mass of scorings out. She'd added 'You don't say' in front of one of Antigone's speeches.

'You can't do that.'

'Of course I can. I've got script approval. I always have script approval; it's in all my contracts.'

'This isn't a script, it's a play. You can't change the lines.'

'I'm only doing my part, I'm not touching the others. Well, only when they're really ridiculous.'

'Lee, if it needs cutting the director will do it, that's his job.'

'The director's job is to make sure I get lit properly and make sure the producer gets laid.'

'I don't think you're approaching this in quite the right way.'

'No, John. What you're saying is that you don't think I can do it.'

'I think you can do it, but it's not like a film. You've never acted before. Perhaps you should look at some of the conventions.'

'Never acted before! Fuck you, fuck conventions. I've been acting all my life, I learned my first line when I was four. I've got fucking Oscars.' She got up and paced around the room.

'This is different, Lee. It's theatre; there are different disciplines.'

'Don't give me that snotty English yellow-teeth discipline crap. I know what you mean by discipline, you mean spanking. You don't think I can do it because I'm a philistine, gum-chewing, blond, Yankee bimbo with more tits than IQ. Oh, God, you're supposed to support me, you shit. You're supposed to be on my side.'

'Darling, I am. But it's like when you do something new, you should treat it with some humility.'

'Humility? Oh, that's what this is about.' She stood with her hands on her hips and her chin pointing furiously at him. 'Tell me, what have I got to be humble about? I'm a fucking star, John, a fucking huge fucking star. They can spell my name in Karachi and they can't even pronounce Sophocles. I don't do humility. It's a contradiction to my terms. It's not in my contract.' And she made an exit that would have had them gasping in Covent Garden.

John went out and walked and thought. He walked up Charing Cross Road and hung around the second-hand bookshops. More and more he found himself drawn back to old books. The dark corridors of polite words, with shabby torn jackets and serious, clenched-pipe hubris, forgotten authors with their eulogistic quotes from long-gone critics in dead papers. He thought of Ozymandias, 'Look on my works, ye Mighty, and despair!' Great feet of paper, standing trunkless, slowly turning to desert dust.

He rescued an overpriced first edition of a Siegfried Sassoon. He was fast building a small, eclectic nest of modern poets. Nest wasn't the right word. What would be the right collective noun for modern poets? A blank perhaps? A remainder of poets? A howl?

Back out in the street the sunlight blinded him. He stood on the pavement, wondering whether to go on or to go home, when he heard his name shouted.

'John.'

A car stopped in the middle of the road and a head poked out of the window. He squinted.

'John, get in. I'll give you a lift.'

A lift was just what he was in the market for. It was Isis. She shuffled over, and her version of Hamed checked John out in the mirror. She kissed him.

'You look pensive, lurking in bookshops. It's nice to see you.'

She was handsome and willowy and gave off a nervy energy.

'I've been meaning to call you, but everything's so hectic. You know we've gone double platinum?'

'No, I didn't.'

'Here, have you got time for tea?'

They sat in a small tea shop in Soho, which had once been famously frequented by kitchen-sink authors and splashy painters. They had cake and hot chocolate. The young art-school customers watched her through spiky fringes and metallic shades.

'So, how have you been?'

'Well, good. Lee and I are living together now.'

'Great.'

'Yeah. Well, we've just had a bit of a row, actually. The play. I think she's nervous.'

'She'll be fantastic. I've thought about you both a lot. It was great in the South of France. That evening, singing with her, was the most amazing thing I've ever done. Oh, when she kissed me. God, what she's like, I thought I'd pass out and go to dyke heaven. It was love. I'm besotted. When I die and my life flashes past, that'll stick in the shutter. How's the poetry going?'

'Oh, you know.'

'Look, that's what I was going to call you about. You remember that poem you gave me? Well, I set it to music. I want to sing it on the next album. Do you mind?'

'No, of course not. I'm thrilled.'

'Well, who's your agent? I'll get my people to do you a contract.'

'I haven't got an agent. Don't bother, it's yours. I gave it to you.'

'Don't be a divvy. You might as well take the record company's money, they don't need it.'

They sat and gossiped for an hour and he realized how much he'd missed talking to someone his own age, who'd grown up in his country, who shared his references. Or perhaps it was just Isis. They exchanged numbers and said a long goodbye on the pavement. She kissed him on the corner of his mouth, a kiss that was neither an invitation nor entirely chaste.

*

Over on the shady side of the street Ronnie Fox checked his motor drive and thought this was his lucky day.

Lee was lying on the bed with her security mess, watching one of her old movies on the video, fast-forwarding through everyone else's lines, replaying her own. He went and lay beside her.

On the small screen she was also lying on a bed, shouting at a man out of shot. The real Lee said nothing.

The man walked over to the bed. He had a bronzed lumpy body. You couldn't see his face, just a bristly neck. He was wearing a short towel. Lee leaned forward and pulled it off, her face a mask of ecstasy. She leaned her head forward to his groin. There was a slow mix of Lee lying on her back, a man between her steepled knees, a close-up of her nipple and a tongue, her straddling him, soft light, pumping music.

John felt sick. She wasn't acting. He knew every look on her face, every move of her body. This was Lee making love – the concentration, the parted lips.

As if reading his mind she said, 'Best love scene I ever made. We really did it, you know. Just the director and the cameraman. No cuts. You can tell, can't you?'

'Yes,' John replied in a whisper, and watched as her fingers twisted the sheets, the tendons straining in her neck.

Lee, his Lee, reached over and took his hand. After a long moment she said, 'It isn't real, you know. We're not really fucking. I'd never do that in front of a camera. He was a dingbat with halitosis, and anyway, he's gay. He was fucking a make-up guy.'

She pushed the fast-forward button. The actor's bottom jerked ridiculously, Lee's head rocked frantically from side to side. It was absurd.

'I'm sorry, that was cruel, but you couldn't tell, could you? You thought it was real, didn't you? And you were jealous. You see, John, I can act. I do know how to do it.' She laid her head on his chest. 'I'm still mad at you, I guess. I thought about what you said this morning and I called Stewart.'

'Good.'

'He wants me to go to an actors' workshop. Go to school, take acting classes, for Christ's sake.'

'Marilyn Monroe did it.'

'Marilyn Monroe did everyone and then killed herself. He's picking me up tomorrow morning. John, you do think I can do this, really, don't you? I'm sorry to go on about it, but I really need you to be one hundred per cent.'

'Of course you can. If Vivien Leigh can do it, Lee Montana can. You're a star, you can do anything.'

It was, he knew, a ridiculous thing to say, a line from a bad film. If John had had script approval over his own thoughts, he'd have drawn a line through it.

The atmosphere in the house had changed. The confidence leaked away and there was something else, a presence lurking in the sweaty, binary whiteness. Just out of sight, leaning in the shadows of the corridor, running her hands along the tables in the kitchen, lying restlessly, biting her nails on the big sofa downstairs. Antigone. Nursing her two and half millennia of destiny, furious and righteous, casting her pall over this tenuous new life built on duck-down and cashmere.

John and Lee were reaching a final act. Their path grew narrower. There were no more crossroads, no more forks, just the straight and narrow. Unsmiling and unblinking a princess stole through their lives, closing the doors, blocking the exits and turning off the lights. They both lay in the gloaming, lit by the cathode flicker, holding hands and sharing the premonition without speaking. Lee, who'd grown up with free will and can-do and life's-what-you-make-it and make-your-dreams-come-true, the world of thirty-day diets and rolling frontiers, your money back if not completely satisfied, 101 toppings and self-help determinism, the cash and carry of endless choice and boundless hope, Lee heard an older, harsher truth from a clearer age, the ancient, muted tramp-tramp rhythm of nemesis, still wordless but there. John too felt it and he could put a name to it, but he chose not to. He lay in the rudderless whiteness and was pulled along in Lee's phosphorescent wake.

*

217

The next morning Oliver announced that Lee Montana would play Antigone in Jean Anouilh's classic adaptation of Sophocles' tragedy in a small, but artistically prestigious, West End theatre, directed by Stu Tabouleh and humbly produced by his own good self. The evening paper carried the news with a large photograph of Isis and John kissing in the street and a smaller one of Lee in sweat pants and dark glasses, with her hair tied back, going to the actors' studio.

The apple hit John just behind the ear with a satisfying, squelchy thud. It was the shock more than the pain that made him drop the milk bottle. Lee had come into the kitchen and picked up the first thing, the first thing ever thrown by a woman at a man. She pitched the apple with a low curving trajectory which is technically called a spit ball, learned in a dozen family summer photo opportunities.

'Eeek,' John squealed pathetically.

'Out,' bellowed Lee. 'Get out now. Fuck off. Don't say a word. I told you. I warned you. No explanations. That's it. You can't keep it dry for an afternoon, you fucker. "A bit of humility, Lee,"' she imitated. 'I'll supply the humiliation. Well, get the fuck out.'

'What? What have I done?'

'What? You fucker! This!' She flung the paper on the floor; milk seeped through the photograph.

'Oh, good Lord. I didn't even see a photographer. Look at that girl staring at Isis. How can you go out in a dress like that?'

'Fuck the fucking girl's dress. Look at fucking you and what you're doing with her. No, don't bother. I don't believe you.'

John laughed, relieved. 'I met her by chance on Charing Cross Road. We had tea.'

'Tea. How jolly English of you. Tea, before or after? You bastard.'

'Neither. Instead. Lee, I've not slept with Isis or anyone else for that matter. How could I have found the time, let alone the energy?'

'Promise?'

'Of course I promise.'

'Why didn't you tell me you'd seen her? Your timing's perfectly crapola, as ever.'

'I forgot. She's singing one of my poems on her album.'

'Oh.' Lee sank into a chair. 'I just had a shitty day.'

'How was the acting class?'

'No wonder the fucking theatre's going down the tube and it needs to be subsidized with grants like some Third-World country. It *is* a fucking Third-World country. There's the real world, the world of entertainment, and then there's the fucking theatre. I've just spent all day in one of its refugee camps. God I need a drink.'

John mixed some Gibsons. Lee slugged two and lay on the floor.

'You know, if I were a stand-up comic I'd have enough material for a thirty-state tour. I get there, and it's some freezing-cold basement with neon lights and plastic chairs. The teacher's this big dyke with an orange crop and teeth like a taxidermist's oddments box, and she doesn't speak any known language, but she bellows Kurt Weill backwards. I later discover she's something called a Geordie, which I imagine is some sort of disability speech-impediment thing, so I can't understand a word she says, and have to keep saying, "What?" But the rest of the class all speak it fluently. Oh God, I can't tell you, John, this profession. You have never seen such a collection. I mean, I didn't exactly go glamorous, but this lot, it was like skin diseases grown on lard, and the worst collection of bodies you have ever seen. There were eighteen-year-olds who looked like ninety-year-old chickens. I wanted to go the front and say, Forget it, really, all of you, trust me, I know. Even if they remake every Alfred Hitchcock film and bring back *The Twilight Zone* and Stephen King buys Universal Studios, you're never going to work. They've got special effects that can make people like you. Save yourself the time, don't do anything that involves bright lights.

'So anyway, we start with warm-up exercises that involve being epileptic a bit at a time, and then we do stretching, which frankly isn't going to do this lot any good unless they bring in weights and pulleys, and then voice exercises, which is just asking for the sugar in Geordie, and then the dyke says, "Today, we're going to do power and confrontation. We're going to explore the projection of power and how you take it and direct it." Then we have to get into pairs, and I'm killed in the rush, so I choose this tiny guy, this munchkin with greasy hair and bandy legs and a nice line in battery-farm blackheads. Big mistake. A little guy, big mistake. And the Geordie says something I can't understand, and he looks up at me and he starts shouting, "I know you've been with another man, you slut, you whore. I'm going to teach you." He's got this voice that goes all squeaky, so I stand there and I think I've got to, like, act. So I look interested and he goes on and on, stamping his little feet and frothing and rolling his eyes, and my embarrassment meter is getting critical, but I nod and smile and, like, humour him, and the dyke says, "Very good, Trevor, but invade her space, claim the stage." And he lunges and grabs my tits, and I'm so surprised I burst out laughing and just look at this little geek hanging on my chest like a hungry monkey, and I lose it completely, and he lets go and looks all hurt and the rest of them stop. The dyke comes over all smiling anger and says, "You've got to try to make this work, Lee. You should concentrate and try to get back the power from Trevor." And I say, "Honey, I just did, and, you know, I didn't even have to act."

'So then we do some other damn fool thing and then we have lunch in a coffee shop, which is inedible, and I have to sign a million autographs, and one of the little bitches sneers and says, "Isn't it very humiliating?" And I say, "Nothing like as humiliating as having Trevor grope you." And frankly, if she doesn't want to sign autographs, why the fuck does she want to be in this business. She says she wants to be a proper actress, anonymous and blank in real life, and then reveal a character on stage that so moves the audience they remember it for ever but don't recognize her in the foyer. And I say, "In your dreams. That's a crock."

'Then in the afternoon we do working from the text in a circle, which is from a thing called a miracle play, that's written in more Geordie, which I can't even pronounce, let alone speak. Have you ever heard of this thing? It's five fucking hours long and is so boring, but they're really into it and I just say, "The only miracle is that this ever gets put on. They wouldn't even watch this on death row if it counted as time off for good behaviour."

'Then we get into this row about Hollywood and the dyke says, "Stop. We should turn this into an extempory piece of drama," like she's fucking Mickey Lesbo Rooney. And I end up gagged, on the table, with Trevor simulating sex with my bottom half, and all the others shouting, "Schwarzenegger, Schwarzenegger, Schwarzenegger," around me. Then it's time for our mothers to collect us. What am I going to do, John? Don't tell me to go back. Nobody can want to act that badly.'

She held out her empty glass.

'Let's get drunk and watch *Breakfast at Tiffany's.*'

'John, what ho. Oliver here. Look, I understand Lee's sojourn at the actors' workshop wasn't a huge success. I saw the diary piece in the *Mail*, spiteful little shit. And Stu called. He was very apologetic and said it was all his fault, he should never have suggested it, and I think, on balance, he's probably right, but, you know, we do need to do something with Lee. The theatre is a foreign language for her, and while I'm sure she'll be fluent in it in no time she needs the basic grammar. I was thinking, why don't I come over and give her a sort of linguaphone masterclass on the basics, to get her conversational with the boards. Do you think that's, er, a possibility?'

'No, no, no, absolutely not.' Lee pulled a pillow over her head. The bed was now so replete with rubbish it looked like a Tate Gallery installation. 'I'm not having that pompous has-been come and patronize me with more anecdotes about Larry and Dickie and Johnnie and Sneezy and Bashful and Doc. I refuse. Tell him I'm in bed with Stanislavsky; tell him I'm working on the Theatre of Hate; tell him I've gone shopping with six characters in search of pharmaceuticals; tell him to go and fuck himself for a curtain callgirl.'

'I told him you'd be thrilled and honoured. He's on his way.'

Oliver stood in the middle of the room, his legs apart, arms spread wide, claiming the stage, imposing his presence. His famed smile played over his weak little lips. Lee and John sat side by side on the sofa, Lee radiating a passive hostility that would have swept him through any proscenium arch in the world, but being the true professional he was Oliver mistook it for rapt attention and a thirst for learning.

'Mother Theatre,' he declaimed, paused and repeated, 'Mother Theatre. Father Theatre, Brother, Sister, Friend, Lover, Mistress

Theatre. Our family is about to welcome a new child to the ragged orphanage which is our noble calling.' He paused again.

Lee opened her mouth. John squeezed her knee.

'Lee, welcome. You know, people often talk about theatres as being haunted, haunted by the actors and playwrights. Well, I don't believe in ghosts, but I do believe theatres are invested with spirits, the shades of performances. Unlike TV or film we work in the moment, the line is delivered and then it's gone, but it's not gone. Film rots and dies, embalmed with a mechanical literacy, but a performance, a theatre performance, lives on in the audience and the actor and the air. On the hallowed mystical space of the stage it grows and changes in the mind's eye and ear, transient but eternal. We represent the last true priests in a godless age, called to the communion of truth, real truth. The truth between facts, the truth of make-believe. We don't perform before an audience, we perform with an audience. It's the joining together of priest and congregation that is the unique divine honesty of theatre, a shared communion, a moment of truth. To be part of it, just to carry a spear or stand in the wings, is the greatest privilege civilization can bestow. All other mediums are just entertainment, joke-telling, titillation, childish divertissement. Only theatre has that golden moment.'

John felt Lee vibrate beside him. He slipped a restraining arm around her shoulder.

'Now, the nuts and bolts, the work. One word, one word only. Veracity. Lee, talented, brilliant, bright-star Lee, you must, imperatively must, unlearn, dislearn, delearn everything you know about performance. We are the brotherhood of the wooden 'O'. We don't perform, we reveal. It is an amateur mistake to imagine that acting is about taking on a role as if it were a costume, adding things to your character, like prosthetic noses or funny voices. The stage is a confessional, the act of revelation is stripping away, peeling yourself—'

'Like a foreskin?' said Lee.

'Like an onion,' corrected Oliver. 'You pull away the layers and reveal the truth of a character, a situation, a line, and that is the naked veracity.' He finished with a slow, showy gesture that was bona fide bogus.

He continued in much the same way for ten minutes or so, warming his backside on the radiated heat of his own crackling brilliance. Finally, in a flurry of curtain calls, ovations and reprises, he was dragged off his own stage with a deep bow and exited pursued by Lee's vaunting irritation.

'Fuck,' she said as the door closed fast on him. 'Fuck that patronizing fucker. Explain to me, how is it that theatre people can spend so much time and energy getting the motivation to pick up a cup of tea and devote their entire beings to understanding the crappy human dynamics of every little shitty thing and still be so arrogantly blind to what arseholes they are when they're not speaking someone else's lines?'

'Insecurity,' said John.

'Insecurity? Did that look like insecurity? That man could walk on his own water.'

'Still,' said John. 'Still, it's insecurity. Any art that has to spend so much time dissecting itself and explaining to you why it's so good is very unsure of its real value.'

Lee kissed him. 'When we talk about films, all we talk about is money and audiences. No-one ever talks about acting. I mean, that's just what we do.'

'Yes, but understand, theatre doesn't have either money or audiences. They can't judge their value against popularity or a market. If they did they'd have to kill themselves. There isn't even fame. Television and films make actors famous, theatre has to generate its own worth out of something else, out of thin air, out of ghosts and "the moment". But look, Lee, what I don't truly understand is why you want to do it.'

'Oh, don't think I haven't asked myself. It's like I said, it has a lot to do with my dad, and him, you know, always wanting to act in the theatre, and wanting him to be proud of me up there. I suppose I bought into all that magic-moment stuff. It's like belonging to this church and being told there's a secret chapel that only the very good get to go to. It's an elite; they have their knowing, holier-than-thou smirk, I've done it and you haven't. You always want to be let into the club that won't have you as a member. Fuck it, it's only a play. There's no money and no-one's going to see it. Why should I worry?

I'm not going to think about it, rehearsals aren't for two weeks. Let's go on a bender.'

John laughed. 'OK, but perhaps we should go and see some theatre.'

'What? Real live plays? Must we?'

'Might be a good idea.'

Hamed stopped the car in an underground carpark.

'Is this it?' Lee peered out of the window at the pee-stained concrete walls, the oily pools and the rubbish. 'This is the Royal Shakespeare Company? Royal, as in regal? Shakespeare, as in the greatest genius ever and pride of jolly olde England?'

'This is it. Welcome to the Barbican.'

Stu got out of the car and stood in a puddle of viscous, evil-smelling soup. 'Mind the step.'

He'd agreed to chaperone Lee and John to a very respectfully received production of a rarely produced Restoration tragedy, which had a boy in it he thought might be perfect for Antigone's lover.

'I've heard of English reserve, but don't you think putting the Royal Shakespeare Company in an underground lavatory in the middle of nowhere might be overdoing it? Oh, Christ, Stewart, is this going to be our audience too?' said Lee. 'It's a pity we didn't bring any drugs with us, they could really do with some.'

'Would you like a drink?' asked John.

'Yup. Can I have it in the South of France?' Lee glared at the station buffet bar. 'Oh, a Scotch, a big one.'

John sidled off.

Stu and Lee stood in awkward silence in the middle of the room. An ageing couple approached them with the supplicating grins of fans. Lee arranged her face.

'Oh, we so loved your last work,' the lady said, in a breathy, high-pitched voice. 'Would you be so kind as to sign my programme; it's for my daughter.'

She held it towards Stewart.

Lee folded up her smile.

'We thought *The Entertainer* was splendid,' added the old man.

224

'We try to get to everything now we're retired.'

'You're welcome,' said Stu. 'I'm so pleased you liked it. This is Lee Montana, she's going to be starring in my next production.'

The old lady patted her hand. 'You're a very lucky girl.'

Lee's eyes crinkled. 'Aren't I just? Do you ever go to the movies?'

'Oh no,' said the ancient gent. 'They're all so, well, ignorant, aren't they?'

'Uncultured,' said the woman. 'Like the television. We don't have one. Who'd want to watch all that when you can have all this?'

She waved her hand at the Stygian concrete walls as if they were halls of Xanadu.

'A radio?' Lee ventured.

'Oh yes, for the news. You've got to keep up, haven't you? We won't take up any more of your time. It's been a privilege talking to you, Mr Tabouleh.'

And they shuffled off.

'I'm sorry,' Stu blustered.

'Oh, heavens, don't be sorry. Fans is fans, and it's interesting to see your public.' She couldn't quite keep the cattiness out of her voice.

A bell rang and they all trooped into the small black theatre. The seats were uncomfortable benches; Lee slid in and flicked through the programme.

'Three and a half hours,' she said, in a voice that carried to the back of the foyer. 'They've got to be joking.'

And then the lights went down.

There was a moment for the ancient magic of luvvy revelation to adjust its codpiece and cough. The audience waited blindly, like the endlessly hopeful participants in a suckers' seance, for the spirit to appear and deliver a life-changing message from beyond the grave.

Three men ran onto the stage backwards, as if watching something in the wings. They arranged themselves all akimbo, claiming the space.

'Hush, he comes, something, something, he comes. Friends, deport yourselves, if something as if nothing. Aye, something something.'

The men laughed uproariously, throwing their heads back and then jogging in little circles, slapping each other on the back.

A fat bald man in a cape walked on. 'How now, what do you here, my Lords? Something something.'

And so it went.

Young men jogged on, jogged around and then jogged off. They spoke interminable, convoluted junket at each other, standing very close, then slapping their leather shoulders before jogging somewhere else. Each took it in turn to put his feet up on a stool, which together with an urn and a bed were the only props on the set. They all spoke with the same emphatic, dumpty-dumpty cadence, giving the lines a numbing sense of being a tandem ridden over corrugated iron. A girl appeared – a very small girl with a voice that was strained and hoarse. She didn't jog, she swayed, back and forth and on and off. The only time the cast weren't jogging or swaying was when they were supposed to be listening. They listened with their pelvises, as if seventeenth-century men had hearing aids in their knickers. They swivelled their groins to face the perambulating speaker, shifting from one hip to the other until he'd finished speaking, and then they'd all have a bit of a jog, a slap and a sway, and then it was someone else's turn. By way of acting, there was a lot of dagger-pommel-fondling, ruff-straightening, hair-tossing and masses of cod-grabbing. Each note and scrambled line was accompanied by a semaphore of limb business, so it all looked like a deaf-and-dumb signing of *The Joy of Sex*.

The audience, a numb-bum static congregation, expectantly waited for the flicker of the Holy Spirit to ignite amongst them. Finally, eventually, the men jogged off, the girl swayed an exit and the house lights came on.

Lee elbowed her way to the bar, shouting over the heads of the scattered, stumbling crumblies that she needed five large Scotches, now.

She turned to John and Stu. 'Never in my entire life . . . I can't believe it . . . I have just sat through . . . It was without doubt. No, I'm at a loss.'

'Rather wonderful, isn't it?' beamed Stu. 'Remarkable. What do you think of the duke, John?' He swivelled his groin to listen to the answer, and stroked John's shoulder.

'Oh, wonderful. Really compelling. I haven't read it for ages, but they've got the spirit so well, the darkness and the sense of rising hysteria. It's very powerful.'

'Isn't it just,' nodded Stu.

Lee looked from one to the other with her own powerfully rising hysteria.

'It's extraordinary how relevant it all seems, how aggressively current,' said John.

'Oh, quite,' agreed Stu. 'The use of the power and vulnerability of lust, the fist crushing the rose.'

'OK, OK, enough already.' Lee gulped her second drink. 'I get the joke.'

Both Stu and John looked at her blankly.

'Oh, come on, come on. You have got to be joking. You can't be serious. This is fucking ghastly, I've never been so bored in my life.'

'Really?' said John, truly surprised.

'Oh,' said Stu, 'I'm sorry. I thought it was, well, very Hollywood actually. Tons of sex and violence.'

'And spitting. Do you think spitting is Hollywood?'

'What spitting?'

'We sat through the same show, didn't we? How can you say, "What spitting?" All they do is spit at each other. That little girl, who didn't quite get it, got covered in it. That's all they do: spit. How can you not have noticed?'

'No, it's funny, I don't think I really did. Of course, there is some aspiration when they speak, but it doesn't seem very important,' said Stu.

'You don't think it's important? Personal hygiene isn't important? Fine. Right, you've both read this? You know how it ends, so we can go. I mean, let's go and have dinner, because I don't care – no, more than I don't care, I actively don't want to see those high-velocity dribble bores ever again.'

'Lee,' John was honestly shocked, 'you can't walk out in the middle of a play.'

'Why not?' she whined. 'Please. We paid for the ticket. Why can't I have dinner?'

'Because you can't be so rude. I couldn't.'

'Actually, Lee, they'd notice. It would be very difficult. It might get into the papers, and you're about to join these people. It might be political to have them on your side,' added Stu.

'Oh, I can't bear it.'

The bell went.

'One more drink. Put a bag over my head if I start snoring.'

Finally, when the stage was a pile of corpses, each of whom had spluttered a valedictory speech, Lee was released from purgatory. She clapped slowly as if slapping an annoying face.

'Thank God.'

'Come on.' Stu took her arm and ushered her through the crowd. 'We'd better go back.'

'Go back where?'

'Go back and say hello to the cast.'

'Oh no, no, no, I can't. I can't. Don't make me, John. Tell him I don't have to.'

'It's only polite, just for a moment. They all know you're here.'

'What can I say? I hated it, I hated them, I hated every inch of all of it.'

'Oh come on, Lee, what do you say in films?'

'Er, it'll gross fifty million and open in two hundred multiplexes. Well done.'

'Not really appropriate,' John smiled.

'I always find "Get you" said with emphasis and open palms catches most performances,' offered Stu, helpfully. 'Or you could always do the old Noël Coward line, "No-one has ever" – stress the ever – "played Lady Macbeth like that."'

The dressing rooms were tiny, white-washed neon cells that smelled of sweat and nicotine. The actors, all with bright greasy faces and lank hair, appeared in beaming pairs and all kissed Stewart, who made expansive mewing noises at them. They looked expectantly at Lee, who hung silently behind John. Finally, the large man who'd taken the loudest applause, said the most things and expectorated the most saliva offered her his hand.

'Lee, this is Gregor.'

Gregor beamed. The cast beamed and waited.

'Get you!' exclaimed Lee, waving her palms like Al Jolson. 'No-one has ever played Lady Macbeth like that.'

There was a confused silence and Lee stared deadpan. Gregor gave a great guffaw and the cast held their sides and chortled. How funny, how smart, how touching that this newcomer to their Elysian Fields of excellence had bothered to learn their little in-jokes, like learning how to say, 'Ich bin ein stage-door johnnie.' How touching, how darling. Welcome to the motley.

'Spit on me.'

'No.'

'Go on, dammit, spit on me.'

John was lying between Lee's thighs, inserted in the go, go, go position of love.

'Why do you want me to spit on you?'

'Practice. If I'm going to be a proper actress I've got to learn to be spat on. Spit, damn you.'

'I can't, my mouth's dry.'

'Oh, just do it, do a bit of method spitting. Think of lemons. Spit, damn you, because that's what's going to happen to me in two weeks. I'm going to be spat on and then fucked, well and truly fucked.'

'You spit.'

'Yeah, I'd better learn how to spit.' She spat.

A bobbly white gob hung on John's chin.

'Yuck.' He stuck his tongue out and blew a farting wet raspberry.

'Oh gross, gross.' Lee shook her head and laughed and tried to spit back, but just dribbled down her cheek.

John hawked fruitily.

'No, no, not big ones. They don't do lung cookies, that's only for Shakespeare.'

'They might. Creon might,' John said, like a ventriloquist through clenched teeth.

Lee laughed and laughed. Her groin clenched peristaltically at him.

Afterwards, John lay and listened to Lee breathing, her face rest-ing in the crook of his arm, her hand draped over his chest, and in the dark he heard, or perhaps just thought he heard, the echo of laughter, humourless this time, mocking, down the hall in the dark. Antigone bided her time. John lay awake and listened to the shuffling in the dark, the little clicks and chunters of their life rolling down the track, imperceptibly gaining momentum, picking up speed, unseen hands pulling the levers, clicking the switches, turning the lights to green.

LEE GOT UP IN THE MORNINGS AND POWERED INTO HER DAYS LIKE A Montessori outing. She took great gulps of air and beamed and talked too loudly and was vivacious. She went out and spent thousands of pounds on nothing, and sat in the living room in a bunker of boxes. She made love to John, snatching at him, sucking the warmth and solidity out of his body. She would sleep, curled and clinging, like a child. John realized she was bleeding to death; the confidence oozed out of her and lay in sticky pools. Cold fear crept in, sapping her strength, her resolve and her attention. She never mentioned the play or picked up the script, she was just too plain terrified.

At the end of the week John was seriously worried about her. There was a hint of mania in her desperate happiness.

'Darling, I think you should . . .'

'Don't, John.' She put her hand over his mouth and held him tight. 'Don't say anything. Just be happy. Pretend it's all happy. Please. I know what I'm doing.'

But she didn't. She was just doing what she knew.

Their days passed. She grew pale and haunted and spent hours in front of the mirror arranging her make-up, taking it off, putting it on and just staring, trying to read something in her own face.

The sex became ever more urgent. She did away with foreplay and kissing and intimacy, simply pulling aside the clothes that were necessary, fucking like speeded-up, dull pornography, skipping to the money shot, to the climax. The rush of taking applause.

IT WAS THE NIGHT BEFORE REHEARSALS STARTED. THEY WENT OUT FOR dinner. Lee smiled and waved across tables at people. People came over, she drank a lot, they chatted, and the words became uncoupled and slurred and finally they sat saying nothing.

'Take me home.' She got up and didn't look at him.

She sat in the car, eyes shut, a fretful drizzle beating on the windows. She walked ahead of him into the dark house, poured a glass of vodka, kicked off her shoes and went upstairs to the bedroom. John followed.

'Look at me. Do you remember when you first saw me?'

'Yes, of course.' He moved to hold her.

'No, stay there. Stand over there by the wall. Tell me.'

'Tell you what?'

'Tell me what you thought.'

'I thought, There's Lee Montana.'

'And?'

'And she's very beautiful.'

'And?'

'And?'

'And you wondered what she looked like naked? You wanted to fuck her.'

'Yes, I suppose.'

'You suppose? And?'

'And?'

'And how was it? Lee Montana naked? Was it what you expected? Were her breasts what you wanted? Were her legs as long as you needed? Was her sex pouty and wet enough, her hair soft and shiny enough? The crease of her bottom, the nape of her neck, was it what you wanted for your fuck?'

'Lee, darling, you know it . . .'

Lee swayed and held her forehead, as if trying to remember. 'And is it still?'

'Yes, more, better. You know—'

'I don't mean me, I mean this.' She stepped out of her dress and slapped her stomach, leaving a red hand print. She hit her thigh, her shoulder, slapped her face. 'Is this? Is this, still?'

'Lee, stop it.'

'Don't move. Stay there. Then why can't I feel it? Why don't I feel wanted and lusted after and adored and fuckable? Why do I feel so inadequate, and why don't you look at me the way you used to look at me?'

'You're frightened.'

'I'm worried about this, this fucking play. I'm frightened of Antigone.'

'I know, but you won't talk about it. Why don't you—'

'Sssh, don't say it, I know. Just watch.'

She drained her glass; she was very drunk.

'Just watch. Stay there. Don't say anything. Watch.'

She slipped to the floor and the glass rolled away. She lay on her back, knees in the air, sucked two of her fingers and then started to masturbate.

'Lee, please.'

'No, you look. Watch me, watch. How would Antigone do it? Does Antigone do it? That tight-assed bitch. Yeah. She goes upstairs to her cold little bed and finger-fucks herself, thinking about that old uncle of hers, that hard old man. Do you suppose she lies there curled up like a baby, a hand between her thighs, kneading, kneading the little button? Because she wants, what she really, secretly wants is for that old uncle man to come up to her room and slap her contrary little tight ass and say, You need to be taught a lesson, Antigone. Don't give me that fate shit, I'm the king. I'm the king, the destiny man, all the fate you're going to get. I know what you need, you want a length of cock. You want a seeing to, rough. Is that what does it for you, little holier-than-all-the-fucking-world Antigone? She wants her dirty uncle to come and hit on her and grab her wrist and force her head down and go, Scream girl, holler all you want, I'm king here. Who's going to stop me?'

Lee rubbed herself, her knees spatchcocked apart. 'I've got little Antigone's number. She shoves her bitten fingers into her wet little virgin cunt and feels guilty because she fancies that wicked uncle. Antigone's, ha, she's just chat-show trailer trash.'

'You're drunk. Come to bed.' John knelt beside her and pulled her hand away. Lee didn't resist. 'I told you to stand there.'

'Come to bed.'

'I'm frightened. Fate, my ass. It's not fate, it's guilt and frustration, that's what makes Antigone a bitch.'

'Well at least you've been thinking about it.' John undressed and got into bed beside her.

'She's here, isn't she?'

'Who?'

'You know.'

JOHN WOKE TO THE SOUND OF RETCHING. LEE WAS THROWING UP. IT was six o'clock. She came back into the bedroom.

'What shall I wear? Jeans, a sweatshirt?'

'Yes.'

They sat in silence in the kitchen drinking coffee, watching the grey dawn.

'Well, this is it.' Lee held his hand.

'What time's Hamed coming?'

'Nine o'clock.'

'How do you feel?'

She shrugged.

'Look, last night—'

'I'm sorry, I was drunk.'

'Yes, a bit, but actually you said some good things.'

'I was just drunk. I don't remember.' And then, looking into her cup, 'I'd give everything not to have to do this, you know.'

'Well, Lee, you don't have to do it. If you really, really don't want to.'

'Yes I do.'

'If it's contracts and stuff I'm sure your lawyers can fix it.'

'No. It's just I have to do it, go through with it. It's not just my dad, it's me. It's like boxers, you know, they always get into the ring and you think, Why? You've made all this money, you're never going to be any more famous than you are now, why go back in and risk it all, having your brain pulped and the dribbling blood on the canvas. Why risk losing it all? But they still do it. I've got to get into the ring with this thing and risk it. I've got to know where the fame and the stardom stop, where the edges are. I have no idea where I go on to, where I finish. It's a weird thing, if you've got power you want to know where your reach ends. Does that make any sense?'

'Well, not entirely. It's only a play.'

'Have you heard of Ty Gettin?'

'No, I don't think so.'

'You've heard of *The Sophomore*?'

'Yeah, of course.'

'Well, he wrote it, the biggest Broadway show of the early Sixties. The film took a million, made Clara a star, won Tonys and Oscars, made Ty a bit of a fortune and a reputation as the most promising début playwright of his generation; the new Tennessee Williams, all that shit. I met him once, you know, in New York, a couple of years ago. He lives in a dark apartment on the Upper West Side with two dachshunds. He never wrote another thing. He sits in his studio with a typewriter and all this blank paper, surrounded by framed posters and awards and reviews and the cartoons for *The Sophomore*. He can't do it. It's not writer's block. It's fame block, star block, fear block. He just couldn't find out if his talent went any further than that play, where the edges were, and now he knows. His fame goes no further than the doorman. His friends say, "Why bother? You wrote *The Sophomore*, that's enough. That's more than most people do in a lifetime." But, you know, it's like he's got cancer. It's turned into a tumour, a hard, malignant thing that's eaten his life away. That's why I've got to do this. I've got to know.'

'You'll be great.'

'You think so? Really?'

'Really.'

The doorbell. Hamed.

Lee checked her bag, script, gum, lipsalve, handkerchief and cigarettes.

'OK, I'm set. God, I feel like I'm twelve. It will be all right, won't it?'

'Of course. You don't want to be late on your first day. Here, take an apple for Stewart. And call me.'

Lee picked everything up and ran to the door, then turned and came back and hugged John hard. She held his face between her palms and stared at him with a furious, intense beauty.

'I love you.'

And she was gone.

John sat for a long moment. It was the first time she'd said it.

In bed they'd gasped and whispered, loved bits of each other, loved moves and looks and stuff, but not altogether, not with their clothes on. It had never been declared. Really, this should have been the beginning of something, but it felt like the end. The house was drained of the maudlin gloom. Lee had taken the premonition and the presence with her. Now there was just the ticking coldness. John felt unaccountably lonely. He went out, looking for his friends and the lost books.

'HELLO.'

'Hi. You look smooth. Yeah, definitely smooth, like you've been blended with Bond Street.' Clive sat down next to him. 'Is this mine?' He picked up the pint that had been waiting for ten minutes. 'Sorry, I'm late, couldn't get away. So, how's it going in Starsville?'

'Well, you know, starry.'

'I bet, I bet. We keep up, you know, through the gossip columns and the magazines. Lovely picture of you in, where was it, Cartier or Aspreys. Might have been Tescos, but you looked great. And that jacket? That is smart, isn't it?'

'Clive, look, stop it. I'm sorry.'

'Sorry? What about? Nothing to be sorry for.'

'After the funeral, the fight, and, you know, Petra.'

'Forget it.'

'You two still together?'

'Petra and me? Yeah, in a fashion. We do it at the weekends if there's nothing better on, but it's not official, we're free agents. Well, she's freer than I am, but it's something.'

'And the shop?'

'Oh, still full of books, much as you left it. Customers, Mrs P., not enough money.'

'Dom and Pete?'

'Same, fine.'

'And *Fins of Desire?*'

'*Fins of Desire* hasn't had much done on it recently, hit a bit of a wall.'

'Maggie's?'

'It's all the same, John. Everything's inexorably, remorselessly the same. Working lives just go on, mate. It takes the Luftwaffe or the Gordon Riots or the Magna Carta to make any difference to us. There are still thirty-six hours of ninety minutes each in the working day, a pint still costs forty pence more than you can afford, the milk still clots in the morning, the bus is still late, the sex is still cold and over too soon and the jokes are still the same. What did you expect? That we'd all say, He's gone, now let's have a rocking time? Sorry, it's nice to see you, I'm just a bit pissed off; it's not your fault. Anyway, how are things with you?'

'Well, fine on the surface. Actually, I'm feeling a bit pissed off too. Lee's doing this play and she's worried about it, really frightened. I don't know, I've got this terrible premonition, this sense of dread about the whole thing, a foreboding. I don't know, that's too literal, or too literary. I don't know what to do about it, how to turn down the anxiety; it's corrosive, it's eating away at us, sabotaging the good things.'

'Bummer. Yeah, well, I can see that. She's rich and famous and beautiful, you've got a fab house and millions of starry friends who don't have to work, I can see how that would get you down, you know, give you a bad dose of the forebodings, the runny dreads.'

'Oh come on, Clive, that's not fair. You know that having money doesn't take away your right to be unhappy or concerned or fearful.'

'No, fair point. But listen to yourself. It reeks a bit of "my other butler's got measles". So she's having a bad-script day, so what? Get real, John, wind your mind back, you know what it's like down here with the drones. What would you have said? If you want sympathy for problems take them to people who can identify with them. If you'd said I've broken my leg or she's got cancer I could be there for you, but, you know, being mates is sharing the same references, living in the same muck, and we don't any more. You're an elephant coming to a mouse and saying, I've got this really painful trunk. Oh yeah, what's a trunk?'

236

'Fuck off, Clive. Where do you get all this elephant and mice shit from? You spend a good deal of your life identifying with women who are half fish, what's that? Problems, depression are like algebra. They're like "X" and "Y". It doesn't matter what the specifics are, it's the dynamics.'

'Oi, oi, we're not on *Start the Week*. This is a pub, in my lunch hour, we don't have arguments about the abstract nature of stress. People like us, we get subs.' Clive patted John on the shoulder and smiled. 'Let's talk about something else.'

'Does Petra ask about me?' John means this to be unkind. He's shocked and hurt by the distance Clive has put between them.

Clive squirmed and rubbed his face. 'Yes, sometimes. She's still pretty angry. Not, like, it's a big thing,' he added, unconvincingly. 'And she misses Dorothy. That and her chucking you has sort of rolled together. If you're planning on seeing her I'd leave it for a bit, actually; it would be better for me if you didn't see her.'

'She giving you a rough time?'

There was a long pause.

'I wouldn't say a rough time. Yeah, it's not easy. It's just that I'm more in love with her than she is with me.' Clive looked away and talked to some point on the far wall. 'It wasn't a good time to get together, but what choice did I have? You take what fate chucks at you.'

'Do you believe in fate?' John jumped on the word. 'I don't fucking believe in mine.'

'Oh come on, I'm a shop assistant, we don't have fate, we get destiny's parings from people like Lee and you. Oxfam fate, second-hand.' He looked back at John with stony, wet eyes. 'I love her so much; she's been so badly hurt by you. I know you don't see it like that, but I see her. She's like a wounded animal and there's nothing I can do about it. Yeah, John, I do understand the algebra of your problems, but frankly I'm not that sympathetic. I've got problems of my own and my coat's thinner than yours and I've got to get back to work.'

They stood awkwardly in the street.

'I'll see you, give you a ring,' John said.

'Yeah, sure.' Clive looked at his watch and turned to walk away.

'Still mates?'

Clive grinned. 'Don't talk like a cunt, I always hated you. Course we're still mates.' He turned and, with an uncomfortable gesture, like a man underwater, hugged John the way Americans hug on daytime television, but it wasn't the same, bad timing. Nothing they could do, it was out of their hands, just bad timing.

'GET ME A DRINK.' LEE LEANED WITH HER BACK AGAINST THE DOOR. 'A Gibson?'

'Yeah. No, no I can't drink. Fuck. I'll have some tea.'

'So, how was it?'

'It was fine. It was a read-through. A get-to-know-you, like the first day at school. Stewart gave us a little speech, actually it was a very long, rambling speech and we shook hands and did some deep breathing, and then sat in a circle and read. Well, I read, they all know it.'

'They can't all know it.'

'That goody-goody who does the Chorus knows it all, the others look at their books occasionally just to stop me feeling like an idiot. Oh, God, John, they're really so good at it. They just read and it sounds like people talking. It's their goddamn accents. If you make a mistake in an English accent it sounds like you're being thoughtful. They say things like, "Stu, do you think I should breathe on that syllable or go on to the next?" Oh for God's sake, I don't even know how to breathe.'

'I'm sure it's not that bad, I'm sure you were fine.'

'I wasn't fucking fine, I sounded like a fucking American who can't do Royal Shakespeare Company breathing.'

'It was your first day. Do you want to go out somewhere tonight? See some people?'

'Are you insane? I've got to learn this. I'm having an apple in my room.'

And she did.

John watched television in the kitchen. At eleven he went upstairs. Lee was sitting up in bed with her text. John slid beside her and reached inside her dressing gown, kissing her neck.

238

Lee grabbed his wrist and pushed it away, shrugging with annoyance; her shoulder caught his chin with a clunk.

'Don't, John.' She was cold and emphatic. 'I haven't got time. I need to get on.'

'Sorry.'

'OK.'

He slid out of bed. 'Do you want anything?'

'No. Quiet.'

He started to get undressed. She looked up, as if watching something deeply annoying.

'Look, John, do you mind sleeping in the guest room tonight? Just, I must concentrate. Sorry.'

'I do mind.'

'Oh, for Christ's sake,' she shouted. 'Just fuck off next door. It's no big deal. Just leave me alone.'

John stood for a moment with his shirt tail out, foolish.

'Fine. I'll see you in the morning. We'll have breakfast.'

'Jesus.'

They didn't.

John heard her get up, heard her move about the room, talking to herself, repeating her lines, heard her walk down the corridor, pause outside his room and then move on. He heard the front door close and the car drive off. He got up and went to her bedroom; the floor was damp with her footprints and the room heavy with the bright smell of morning soap, toothpaste, deodorant, make-up and the musky odour of sleep. He got into her side of the bed; there was still a residual warmth, a hair on the pillow. His side was plump and smooth and cold.

He was woken by the telephone.

'Hello.'

'John, get out of bed, get in the shower and get down here. It's Isis, by the way.'

239

THE KRAKEN WAS MOORED AT CHARING CROSS AND IT WAS ABSURD. A thirty-foot Viking long ship bobbing beside Cleopatra's Needle. The dragon's-head prow rolled its wide eye over the granite Embankment 700 years too late. A dozen lorries and vans, generators humming, were parked beside it. Cables snaked and self-important young men in T-shirts and jeans with walkie-talkies talked and walked simultaneously. There was an air of frantic can-do and the smell of bacon fat. It could only be a film crew.

John stopped a walking, talking fellow and said, 'Isis' with a question mark.

The fellow stopped another walking, talking fellow and John was shown to a fat-sided Winnebago, the late twentieth century's take on a pirate galleon, a mobile pillager of cultures.

Isis was sitting in front of a mirror eating a cream bun with pink icing. A make-up girl with an expression bereft of cream or icing stood beside her, holding a wad of tissues.

'John, come in. Would you look at this? My own caravan. Isn't it great? It's got a shower and a fridge full of infant heavy-metal food, and there's a crate of Jack Daniels and . . . Oh, do you want one?' She held out the cake.

'No, thanks. But I'd love a cup of coffee.'

'We've got espresso.'

A silent Japanese man with cropped hair, who'd apparently been folded away in a cupboard, emerged to make coffee.

'My chef,' whispered Isis. 'Sit down. I've got something to tell you.'

John sat.

Isis was dressed like a pre-Raphaelite vision of a Viking princess, with circular breastplates and a chain-mail miniskirt. Her arms and legs were hung with runic bangles; she looked like Bede's illuminated page three.

'Your poem, the one I turned into a song, remember?'

'Yes.'

'Well, they loved it. Hollywood really loved it, and, this is so exciting, it's going to be the single, my single, the Christmas single.'

John realized he ought to feel something other than a mild discomfort at not having the right expression on hand when told that

240

your poem is going to be a Christmas single. He stood up and smiled and said how jolly nice and then awkwardly leaned forward to kiss her, collecting a small smudge of cream on his cheek.

'Jolly nice? Is that it, John? Aren't you impressed at all?'

'Of course, I'm just not very up on pop records; this has never happened to me before.'

'We're shooting the video to go with it on that ridiculous boat; that's why I got you down here. Would you like to be in it? You could be a berserk oarsman. I've saved you a horned helmet.'

'It's awfully kind of you, but I'd rather just watch.'

The filming was terminally dull and as tedious as any cultural form can be with the possible exception of engraving the Lord's Prayer on grains of rice. Isis mimed to little bits of the record from the prow of *The Kraken* as it was towed up and down the Thames from St Paul's to Westminster. John sat behind the twelve-year-old director, Bod, and watched London drift back and forth.

He thought of Handel playing his *Water Music* for the first time here, with an orchestra on a boat, rowing like mad to catch up with German George. He imagined him standing in his damp wig and laddered hose trying to conduct as they wallowed and rolled through the stinking river. The sublime, clear, Corinthian music floating out over the side, through the streaming gunnels, cutting like spars of noise through the yellow fug of sewage and mucus, as dead dogs and cabbage stalks drifted past.

When you thought of it, no less ridiculous than listening to a rhyme about a sleeping girl in a flat in Shepherd's Bush on a Norse long ship at the end of the twentieth century.

'What did you think?'

They were back in the caravan. Isis was wearing a towelling dressing gown.

'Very impressive. I still don't understand why it's in a tenth-century boat when it's about a twentieth-century bed.'

'Oh, that's something Bod dreamed up. He's this week's genius. Who cares? But what do you think of the song?'

'Well, I didn't really hear it, just bits and pieces, over and over.'

'Oh, you should have asked. Here, Yoko, put the record on,

will you? And go and get me a hot dog from one of the stands.'

The chef put down a large plate of sushi and, scowling, did as he was told. Pop stars!

John composed his face to listen. There was a big orchestral build-up, then a big drum beat and then, soaring over it all like a military fly-past, Isis's supersonic voice, with its fiery growl: 'I watched you sleeping.'

And again, John didn't know what he was supposed to feel. It sounded big and glossy and cosmetically enhanced and moreish, in the way that expensively mass-produced things are. It was like the click of a bottle of scent or the rustle of tissue paper in the bag, the hum of an electric gate. It had the luxury noise of the yummy, must-have twentieth century. It was upwardly clever, but it wasn't his any more.

He tried to think of Petra's tight little face with its Gordian brows and the grey pillow. The smell of her cold bedroom. He conjured the sense of departing, the slow pulling away of their affair as she slept. He tried to remember the feeling of his sticky socks, the stiffness of his neck, his clamming fingers and the silence, but he realized that he was the only person in the world who would ever see that. No-one would ever know this particular set of images; they would see a Viking boat and Isis's face and long legs, or their own lovers in other beds at other times. This poem, all poems, were so intensely personal. The words opened a secret, heavy door, were the combinations to a safe. What the reader found inside was unique and personal, it wasn't what the author had put there in the first place. That, thought John, was a profound magic, a sad magic. He'd imagined he was sharing something of himself in his poems, but he wasn't.

He'd lain in bed and read Marvell's 'To His Coy Mistress' to Lee one night, when they'd just started their affair. 'Had we but world enough, and time, This coyness, lady, were no crime.' There had been no coyness, of course, their bodies were supermarkets for each other, open all hours, and yet this, the most powerful aid to seduction ever thought or spoken, washed over them both and peeled Lee like a fig. That poem would always be Lee for John, her breasts, her body; it was so inappropriate but so utterly identifying.

It was a total truth, skimming 300 years since it was first said, sliding out of his mouth as bright and fresh and new as a penny. But who had Marvell first said it to? A fat little girl with black teeth and a pocky skin, smelling of lavender and stale sweat, with a laugh like a creaking door and bitten fingernails that tugged at the linen? He couldn't know. There were hundreds of poems, thousands; in the verse an infinite number of coy mistresses were invented, fresh and panting every time it was spoken. That was magic, that was magic and poetic licence.

'What do you think?'

John's eyes were full of tears for Lee and Petra and the dust of a long-dead girl who had opened herself to a poem ten generations before.

'It's magic.' John finally found the appropriate response.

Isis leaned over and kissed him a little on the lips, like a tap on the window, and their tongues slid together and danced in the wet darkness.

'Thank you.' She kissed his eyes. 'Haven't we both come a long way?'

For no particular good reason John walked home. Perhaps it had been seeing the city from the river. The streets were full of strangers, people in badly fitting, worn clothes. John noticed how tired and bad-tempered everyone appeared, a sighing queue of frustration, bunions, bad backs and unpaid bills, seething, holding on to their tiny bubbles of space and solitude, endlessly crossing and criss-crossing each other, correcting small misjudgements, scuffing and bumping, swivelling shoulders, carving the air with their arms, silently desperate to be away, to be singular, out of this soup of plurality. John was in no hurry. He sauntered along Piccadilly, past the park, across to Hyde Park Corner and stopped beside the 'Machine-gunners' Memorial'. Camp, naked David, leaning on his sword, his pert bronze bottom mooning at the crawling traffic. So inappropriate a metaphor, John thought, for the squat, hunched, mechanical checkout of the machine-gun. Two of them were carved in stone on pedestals beside David, classical and culturally benign, like futurist cherubs. He wondered why he'd never noticed them before, never stopped to read the sickening inscription, 'Saul hath slain his thousands, and David his tens of thousands'. It was as if he'd come to the city again for the first time. He didn't belong to it in the way that he had; he wasn't one of the great masses any more, with their irritated, ticking imperatives. He wasn't part of the peristaltic throb, the guts of the city. This was a different place. He no longer automatically checked bus numbers or looked at the prices in the windows first, because it was a waste to hunt the impossibly expensive. This town was now beautiful and romantic and lyrical, historical and metaphorical in a way it had never been for him when he was scuffed and bumped and made to queue and push. This was now just a city among cities, a choice weighed against other choices. With one bound he'd been set free of it, no longer indentured. He wasn't blood of its sluggish blood, and it filled him with a sense of sweet loss, a maudlin sadness, which might have been a projection or a transference. The slowly seeping, gaseous realization that things were not right with him. He was reaching the final act: all drama must come to an end, and the fates were waiting in the wings to present a bill.

Lee and Stewart stood in the big white living room; the atmosphere was humid with temper.

'Where have you been?' Lee said, with her back to John. 'There's nothing to eat, nothing in the fucking fridge.'

John and Stu caught each other's eyes in the manner of reserved English gentlemen exchanging three pages of single-spaced information at a glance. They were both embarrassed by Lee's temper, but agreed to put it down to her being American and a star. It had been a bad day at the theatre and Stu wanted to talk about it, but later, in private.

'How were rehearsals?' John asked.

'Fucking awful.'

'Early days,' said Stu quietly.

Lee didn't come to kiss him hello and her radiating anger forbade him going to her. She picked up her bag. 'I'm going to have a shower, John. Do you think you can get something for us to eat, for Christ's sake?'

'What would you like? Sushi or something?'

'I just want something to eat. I don't want to make a fucking catering decision on top of everything else. I've been bloody working all day while you've been doing God knows what. Just get me some food. Not sushi,' she added.

Stu and John walked down the road to a pizza restaurant and, while they were waiting, drank a fizzy, thin beer at the bar.

'So, it's not going too well?'

'No. It's not.'

There was a silence. Stu was weighing up how much to say, considering whether John would be a help or an extra dimension of the problem. And then the need to talk, to tell all, was too strong and it came out like ticker tape.

'It's not that she doesn't know her lines, although she doesn't, so she's working from the text and everyone else is pretty much word perfect. It's not that she can't remember the block, though she can't. It's not that when she says her lines she switches off because it's not her close-up, although she does that. It's not that she hasn't the smallest consideration for the other actors, or the audience and what they might be seeing, or even where the fucking audience is, which she doesn't. It's not that the only way she can evoke emotion is to raise and lower her voice like a flag, and that she sounds like Annie Oakley herding cattle or Shirley Temple talking to puppies. It's not that she has no idea why her character is doing or saying what it is. It's not any of that, John, all that's fixable. It's just that she's Lee fucking Montana and you can't take your eyes off her. Whatever else is happening you look at her and go, "Oh shit, that's really Lee Montana." The rest of the cast do it; they try not to, but wherever she is on stage is magnetic north. They radiate from her, are pulled to her, and it highlights how God-awful she is. This is one of the most powerful plays ever written, it's fought for survival through two and a half thousand years, when most plays disappeared under the waves. Anouilh's version was written during the Second World War; it played in Paris against the Nazis and won, for Christ's sake. All that, and it can't compete with Lee. If this were the premier performance of *Antigone* no-one would ever produce it again. That's something, isn't it? To be such a huge force of collective nature that you can trash one of the greatest plays ever written, that really is something.'

'But apart from that, how's it going?'

Stu shook his head and swallowed his beer. 'You know the canon of theatre that is truly, timelessly first division isn't vast, it isn't infinite. Plays that can't date, that have something universal to say, are probably one bookcase full, and that's it, the real sum total, and they get a definitive outing, what, once a generation. The last one for *Antigone* was Olivier and Vivien Leigh fifty years ago, now it's time again, and this production may well kill it stone dead for another fifty years. Maybe we'll brick it up for ever.'

'Don't you think you're being a little dramatic about this?'

'I'm supposed to be dramatic, John. Being dramatic is my job. I know this sounds selfish, but look, and this is between you and me, *Antigone* is very important to me, to my career. I've done London theatre. I know that sounds arrogant and, of course, I could go on and on and, heavens, I love it and that would be fabulous, but, John, I want to do movies, films, and this production with Lee is it. This is the one that should get me to Hollywood, but unless something pretty extraordinary happens no-one's going to let me direct a soap opera after this. Please can you do something?' Stu leaned forward and gripped his arm. 'Please, anything. Talk to her, read it to her, give her multiple things. I'm desperate. Actually, I'm terrified. I'm so frightened because you only get one shot.'

'Well, you're not as frightened as Lee is. This is her shot too, her one go at theatre. And your collateral in this gamble is all promise, is all tick and credit, but she's putting up a real bright-lights reputation, all of it, a lifetime's work. You may have a lot to win, but she has everything to lose.'

They eat the pizza in the kitchen, Lee morose and hungry, Stu picking, trying to talk about the text, but every time he mentions a scene or a speech Lee grunts through the mulch in her mouth.

'He's a cock-sucker. You'd think he'd get his bag seen to.' Or, 'She's got hairy legs.'

She relentlessly shut down any attempt to discuss the play seriously. When she'd had enough to eat she pushed away the plate and fixed Stu with a python's eye.

'Right. I need the room to be warmer, and I want a separate rest room that's mine, with a bed, a fridge, a phone and some fruit. I'm not eating those disgusting sandwiches any more. And, Stewart, I've put up with this for long enough now because this is your thing and I'm new to it. But I've had it; you've got to direct this thing for me. Forget this ensemble shit, I need more support. I don't want other actors in my sight lines, in front of me or moving when I'm speaking. Do you understand?'

Stu opened his mouth to speak.

'No, listen to me. Remember who's selling the tickets for this, who's name is going to put jam on your bread. I'm the star; this is about me, OK?'

Stu slapped the table. 'Lee, I've never heard anything in my whole life in the theatre . . . No-one has ever . . .'

'No, Stu, no-one ever has. That's plainly obvious. You may know all there is to know about the boards, but frankly you know jack-shit about stars. You want to work in the real world, for real audiences and real money, then you need to grow up. You may think this is just towering ego and bad old Hollywood power behaviour, but let me tell you, you haven't seen anything yet. I'm your biggest asset and I'm the biggest asset you will ever have; you get the use of me for another two weeks and that's it. Make the most of it, Stewart, because at the moment you're treating me like just another spear-carrier, and I'm not. The rest of the cast know I'm not, the press know I'm not and the audience will know I'm not. Only you're in the dark about how important I am, Stewart, and it's pissing me off. Right, I'm going to bed. See you in the morning. Don't be long, John.'

'Well, that's me told.' Stu was white with rage. He stood up. 'Thank you, John, for supper.'

'I know she sounds fantastically arrogant, but we're not used to people like Lee. We don't produce them, stars like that. She may have a point.'

'And she may just be the egomaniac bitch from hell. Sorry. I'll see you.'

John went upstairs and stood outside Lee's bedroom.

'John, John, are you there?'

He waited a beat.

'Goodnight, Lee. Do you need anything?'

'Come in, John. We need to talk.'

We need to talk. The four most frightening words in the English language.

She was sitting on the bed, holding her thick address book, the phone beside her. 'John, this isn't working.'

He sat beside her. 'No.'

'We can't go on like this.'

'No.'

'I've made a decision.'

'Yes.'

'I need someone else.'

'Someone else?' John's stomach turned; he felt as light as helium.

'I'm just not getting the support.'

'Who?'

'Who? God, John, I've got people back home. I'm going to call them. Look, Stewart's not up to this, he hasn't got what it takes. I know you two go way back, but he's small-time.'

'Stewart! Oh, you mean Stewart.'

'Yes. I'm going to call some people in LA and get them over to fix this thing. What did you think I was talking about? You thought I meant you?' Lee smiled and then laughed. 'You thought I was calling someone else to replace you?' She rustled his hair and kissed his neck. 'You looked so frightened, silly boy. Baby.' Her head rested on his shoulder for a moment. 'Yeah, well I thought about that too. We're not singing from the same hymn sheet, are we? We're drifting.'

'Apart?'

'Yeah.' She searched his face with her pale eyes. 'John, do you love me?'

He felt her breath on his lip. 'Yes,' he whispered.

'Yes?'

'Yes.'

'Sure?'

'Yes.'

She kissed him again and nodded. 'Good. So, where were you today?'

'I saw Isis.'

'Oh. And how was your other star?'

'She's making a video for her new record. It was on a silly boat on the Thames.' He was going to say 'my song' but this was the first soft moment they'd had together for an age and he didn't want to cast a ripple.

'How's it sound?'

'I don't know; it's a pop song. Fine, I suppose; she's got a great voice, but it's not really my thing.'

'John, you're sweet.' She pinched his cheek. 'Of course it's your thing, you can tell me. It's your song, isn't it? Your poem?'

'Yes.'

'You thought I'd be jealous?'

'Well, you've got enough to think about.'

'John, it's great. I'm really proud of you. People sell their children to get a star like Isis to listen to their songs, and here's you, you've written the single. Sure, I wish you'd written it for me, but I'm pleased. Did you fuck her?'

'What?'

'John, I understand. You fancy her, it's a big moment, all that excitement and gratitude and energy flying around. Did you fuck her? In the caravan? God, I always have to fuck someone when I'm filming.'

'No, Lee, I didn't.'

'OK, don't get huffy. Just checking. Actually, I wouldn't have been that understanding, I'd have killed you both. Would you like to sleep with me? We haven't for some time, have we? Stay with me tonight. I've just got to make some phone calls first. Catch LA before they close up.'

John lay in bed and listened to Lee talk, taking control of her life.

He was aware of something else, someone else, just outside the door. Antigone, with her eye pressed to the keyhole, watching him, muttering her ancient, righteous fury. This wasn't a change of direction, this was just time-out on a predestined journey, a break, a warm sun through the cloud. No amount of smoothers and folders, massages and conditioners from over the water were going

249

to make any difference. He and Lee were dancing on the edge, laughing in the dusk.

JOHN WOKE TO FIND HIMSELF ALONE. IT WAS TEN. LEE MUST HAVE gone to rehearsal. He got up and went down to the kitchen. There were voices.

Hamed sat at the table with a cup of coffee and a little computer organizer. He raised a finger in greeting. Lee, in a dressing gown, was pacing with a mobile phone wedged between her shoulder and ear.

'Yeah, yeah, yeah. Absolutely, Midge. It's a relief to know you're on the case. See you.' She folded the phone and put it down. 'Morning, John. Coffee's in the pot.'

'Why aren't you rehearsing? Has something happened?'

'I phoned in sick. Midge is getting the midday BA from Frankfurt. Can you sort him out?'

'Sure thing, Lee.' Hamed tapped his keys.

'What's the matter?'

'Nothing's the matter. Well, I'm fixing what's the matter.'

Then her phone rang.

'How the hell are you? When do you get in? Three-thirty local.'

She waved at Hamed; he nodded and tapped his little box again. 'God, it'll be great to see you, I can't wait. Yeah, it's a crock, but, hey, we've done worse.' She laughed. 'OK, ciao. Do you know, I'm feeling better already.'

'Lee, I don't understand. Was Stu all right about your not turning up for rehearsal?' For John, being imbued with the am-dram belief that the show goes on even if the entire cast and audience are in comas, not turning up for rehearsal was unquestionably the eighth Deadly Sin, only omitted from the original list because it was too horrible to commit to stone.

'Stu has to learn to be grateful for what he gets. Who gives a shit whether he's happy, sad or sucking a gibbon with syphilis? They've got plenty to be getting on with. They can do their breathing or patronizing or competitive anecdotes.'

'OK, love,' said Hamed. 'I'd better be off, the first lot's getting in in half an hour. I'll bring them back here. The caterer will be over.'

The phone rang again.

'Hi. Oh hello,' Lee's voice dropped three degrees and an octave. 'Yeah, he told me, it's very exciting. Good luck. No, I haven't yet. Yeah, I'm sure I will. Here, I'll pass you over. Darling, it's Isis for you.' She gave him a brittle smile.

'Isis, hi.'

'Thank you for coming yesterday.'

'Oh, that's fine. No, it was fun.'

'No it wasn't. You thought it was tacky and juvenile and boring.'

'Only a bit. I think the song sounds good.'

'Yeah, it is good. Look, do you want to have lunch today?'

'Don't know. Can I call you back?'

Lee shouted at Hamed. 'Can you arrange for John to have another phone, we need his line.'

'Sorry,' said John.

THE FIRST OF THE AMERICANS ARRIVED EXACTLY AN HOUR LATER, A sweating, podgy man with a thick moustache and no chin, dressed in crumpled khaki.

'Lee, goddamn it, only you. I take that flight only for you. Am I the first?'

'T.P. Great to see you.' Lee bounded across the room and hugged him. 'I'm so glad you're here. We've got a problem.'

'Nothing we can't fix, Lee, nothing we can't fix. Here, where can I plug in? And coffee, I need coffee.'

'Oh, anywhere you can find a plug. Here, take John's office, it's down the hall.'

'Hello, I'm John,' said John.

'Oh, this is John. He's a poet.'

'John, pleased to meet you. Right. Lee, I made some calls on the way over, balls are rolling.' He huffed off to the study, shouting for coffee.

'I'll do it,' said John. 'Milk and sugar?'

'De-caff, low fat, Sweet and Low. Thank you.'

'You know he's the best tabloid man in the business.'

'He's your press agent?'

'T.P. is freelance, he's a crisis manager.'

'But we're not having a crisis.'

'We're not. And I want to keep it that way. OK, this is my business, I know what I'm doing. Just keep out of the way. Go upstairs and play your record.'

Sporadically, in ones and twos, Americans made entrances like secondary characters in situation comedies. Slumping in the door, shouting rhetorical questions to the room. Lee hugged and greeted each of them: managers, agents, speech coaches, movement coaches, a masseuse, flak catchers, technical directors, re-directors and a short-order cook. By teatime the house was like a cross between a fraternity club and a politician's re-election office. Every plug sprouted wires, modems and laptops. There was a constant babble of mobile phones. There were impromptu meetings and huddles in bedrooms and corridors and a steady stream of finger food from the kitchen.

'Hey, anyone promise an exclusive of Lee's wardrobe to the women's eighteen-to-thirty-five AB glossies?'

'What's the position on celebrity at-homes?'

'After newsprint and TV, but not this home, we're setting up in a hotel.'

'Fine.'

'Hey, what about love life?'

'Keep it vague; we're pushing singlish but happy.'

'OK, but you know George is in town. I thought we might do the rumour, photograph outside a restaurant or something.'

'I don't know. Is his divorce through yet?'

'His last picture bombed on opening weekend; he's contagious. It would do George a lot more good than us.'

'OK, anyone got a Royal?'

'We're working on it, but they're all so goddamn short. Anyone got a prince whose feet touch the carpet when he sits down?'

'Send out for one. France, Holland, Germany, somewhere.'

'Does France have them?'

'It will if I say it does.'

Lee spent the day on her bed, seeing the Americans one at a time or in pairs, being stroked and oiled and kneaded. Occasionally she made a morale-boosting progress round her praetorian guard, squeezing shoulders, patting heads, reading screens. Her mood was palpably lifted; she beamed and swaggered and accepted the steady stream of compliments and reassurance. Someone pinned up a small American flag.

John crept around the house saying excuse me and generally getting in the way. He went into the kitchen and stood behind two fat men in identical Armani suits who were rooting in the fridge for the right sort of soda, the sort with nothing in it at all.

'So, what's this play about then?'

'Play? Beats me. Theatre stuff, who cares?'

Feeling utterly de trop he went out into the garden; it was dark. He sniffed the white air; it smelled of cigars. There was a glow over by the far wall.

'Wotcha. Feeling a bit like a spare prick?'

Hamed.

'Yes, it's getting crowded in there.'

'Do you want to do some dinner?'

They went to a restaurant on the roof of a large, expensive West End hotel. The menu was international American, long on cocktails, and the only other customers were a table of Japanese who looked inscrutably baffled by quite how moribund this corner of swinging London was.

'I like it here,' said Hamed, after he'd ordered a complicated burger. 'It's anonymous, no fuss, I could sit here for a hundred years and never bump into anyone I knew. Madonna could be shafted by Princess Margaret with a strap-on dildo on the carpet here, and you'd never hear about it.'

'Somehow I doubt that.'

'No, well, it's discreet and the burgers aren't bad. So things aren't looking too good?'

'Aren't they?'

'Come on, John, it's me you're talking to, not one of those step-in fetch-its.'

'No, things aren't going too well. Antigone and Lee, me and Lee, Lee and Antigone. In fact me and Antigone are the only ones who do get on, and even I'm getting a bit pissed off with her. I don't know. It's as if there's nothing we can do to stop it ending badly. I don't want it to, and I'm sure Lee doesn't want it to, but it's as if we're predestined to come apart over this play. Every day I can feel the seams ripping.'

'Fate. You reckon it's fate.'

'Well, it seems like that. Despite our best intentions calamities happen.'

'It's appropriate for Sophocles then, isn't it?'

'Yes, I've been thinking that.'

'Very prone to fate, stars are. They love the idea of destiny; it's very neat for them. It stops them being just plain common-or garden lucky, makes their fortune sort of cosmic and important. Yeah, Lee would like the idea of kismet.'

'But it's so sad.'

'Yeah, well, time to move on. The Furies have arrived, that's always the beginning of the last act.'

'The Americans? You've seen them before?'

'Oh yeah, dozens of times. When things go wrong, when things get rocky or a little too real, they're there: ego bodyguards to make sure the precious confidence isn't damaged. They don't do much, just go, "Yes, yes," and, "Wonderful, wonderful, wonderful," filter the atmosphere. They're human pot-pourri.'

'Why? Why would anyone want that, all that paid-for, transparent sycophancy?'

'Bollocks. Who wouldn't want it? When life gets a bit thick, a dozen people telling you you're marvellous. Fuck, I'd love it. Famous people aren't stupid, they know what it means, but, shit, John, there are another million people out there who'd tell you you're a useless, talentless has-been who got lucky, and they'll do it for nothing. No, it's money well spent, but it means she's thinking of going. She's brought a bit of home here; they'll carry her back soon. Like the evacuation from Saigon. Anyway, it was always a stupid idea, Antigone. She hasn't got the eyes for it.'

'The eyes? For Antigone?'

'She can't see it, wrong tradition. Not that she's a bad actress, she's certainly no worse than Vivien Leigh, but Vivien came from a tradition that understood Antigone, and she was stark staring bonkers, which helps. But Lee, those Americans, it's not in there, it's not in their cultural paintbox. They can't appreciate it. When they see classic theatre it's like us looking at Balinese dancing, you see one thing, but they're doing something quite different.'

When John got back all the lights were on, but the house was quiet. A publicist lay snoring on the sofa, clutching a press release. He went upstairs to Lee's room. The door opened a crack and a strange eye peered out at him.

'Can I help you?'

'Er, I live here. I wanted to see Lee.'

'What for?'

'Well, I don't know. I wanted to say goodnight, I suppose.'

'She's meditating at the moment. I'll pass it on.'

The door closed, and then opened again.

'Who shall I say it was?'

'John.'

'John who?'

'She'll know.'

'OK. Goodnight.'

'Goodnight.'

The next morning he went down to the kitchen. There was the caterer with a pile of Danish pastries and bacon rolls and T.P., on his mobile phone, who waved at John.

'Trust me on this one. It'll be you and her, minimum an hour. Look, you're knocking on an open door. Lee's desperate to meet you, she was just saying you're the only journalist worth talking to; she loved your George Peppard. No really, yes. She's staying in town especially. OK, any photographer you like. Yeah, we're easy. Hey, a kid with a pinhole couldn't take a bad snap of Lee. But we want to see the contacts. OK, fine. Just for consultation. And you can ask just whatever you damn well like; this isn't *Vanity Fair*, right? You've got integrity, right? Deep as you like, but we can go off the record? OK, it's a cover? You're going to fax me the editor's letter? Of course I trust you, but I trust faxes more. Yeah, you too. We must. Have a good one.'

He put down the phone and smiled. 'Top of the morning, John. I trust you slept. I'm in this really dinky hotel round the corner, just like a town house from a departed age of elegance, so there's no fax, no bar, no-one can take a message or make a decent cup of coffee, but they have a lot of pot plants. Oh, by the way, Lee says, hi, sorry to have missed you, and she wanted me to pass on a kiss that you can take as passed on.'

'Where is she?'

'Gone to rehearsals, like the good little trooper she is.'

'And where's everyone else?'

'Oh, they've gone to rehearsals too. I drew the short straw and I'm minding the phones, and the Danish.'

'They've all gone to rehearsals? All together?'

'Sure, she needs them: speech coach, movement, personal director, lighting designer, publicist, manager, secretary, masseuse. We want this thing to be done proper.'

'Right. Did the papers arrive?' John poured some coffee and picked up a bacon roll.

'Papers. Which one do you want? We've got stuff in the *Express* and the *Mail*, the *Mirror*, *The Times* and the second edition of the *Telegraph*. Only squibs, but not bad for a first day.'

'I'll take the *Guardian*. Thanks.'

John was on his second cup and the obituaries when the phone rang. It rang quite insistently for a couple of paragraphs and, as T.P. seemed to have left his post, John answered it.

'John, hello. Oliver here. How are you bearing up? Look, I've just had a rather confused call from Stu. I can't really make head or tail of it. I'm on my way to Sandringham, a little informal committee I oversee for Charles. I was wondering if you could look in at the theatre; there seems to be something amiss, just nerves I expect but I would appreciate it. Would you mind, dear?'

'No, of course not.'

'Well, as soon as poss. Oh damn, here are those impossible guardsmen. Must speak later. Thanks.'

The rehearsal rooms were in a church off the Tottenham Court Road. John made his way past the advertisements for Indian tap-water and Colombian basket-weaving co-operatives to a door marked 'Hall. Please take your litter with you. Children play here'. Inside was a long, high room with plastic chairs arranged round the walls and a couple of tables covered in styrofoam cups. The floor was marked with tape. Standing on either side of a line were two gangs: on one side the Americans, on the other the English theatricals. Between them stood Stu, holding a rolled-up script like a club. If you hadn't known you'd have thought Stu was about to start, 'When you're a Jet, you're a Jet all the way,' and for the rest of them to click their fingers and do shoulder rolls. Everyone was talking at once.

Stu: 'Fuck off, fuck off all of you. Fuck off or, or, or . . .' The 'or' hung in the air, a bollockless threat.

The leader of the Americans stepped forward, armed with a flick telephone.

'Whatever, Stu, whatever. We have to work this out. No-one is undermining your authority here, just think of us as extra resources. Stu, we're here for you. Frankly, we don't think it's arrogant to say that no other Limey theatre could afford the resources you see ranged before you now.'

'Oh God give me strength, God give me strength. John! You're here.'

'Hello, yes. Hello. Oliver called and said you wanted to see me.'

'Yes. Take five, everyone.'

The English actors went to their side of the room and picked up crosswords and knitting, the Americans retired to theirs and played with their computers and phones.

'This is some kind of hell. It's my worst nightmare. No, it's worse than any nightmare. Thank you for coming. Let's go and talk in the pews.'

He led John into the church, which was cool and unexpectedly calm for an urban, Anglican church.

'What's the problem?' asked John, helpfully.

'The problem? Them. That ratpack, the cast of *Reservoir Dogs* in there. Do you know Lee has her own personal director? I direct and then he directs. He's bringing in someone else to organize Miss Montana's lighting. She doesn't even know the fucking lines yet, but I suppose that's why she's got a personal speech coach. "Louder, Lee; softer, Lee," ' he mimicked. 'It's intolerable. There's a man in there who says he's in charge of marketing. Marketing! Marketing Sophocles, for heaven's sake. And they want to bring journalists into rehearsals. Tabloid journalists. None of them has read the play; they've got no idea what it's about. The rest of the cast are livid, as you can imagine. I've got no work done and we start previews in a week.'

'Yes. I can see it's all very unusual.'

'Unusual, John? It's unprecedented. It's everything you've ever heard about bloody Americans, about Hollywood. And Lee. John, I'm sorry, I know she's your partner, but she's become a monster; she's Joan Crawford with PMT.'

'Well, hold on, Stewart. Have you thought that perhaps she's frightened?'

'Her? Frightened? She's too vain to be frightened.'

John bridled. 'Look, all you and Oliver have done is tell her how special and different English theatre is, what an elite little club it is, and how philistine and stupid everything she's been doing for her whole lifetime is. You haven't been putting her at ease, you've been trying to elevate yourself at her expense so you don't feel intimidated.'

'John, I thought at least you'd understand and be on my side. No, on Sophocles' side.'

'Oh, bullshit, Stu. Sophocles doesn't need my support, neither does the English stage. You want me to do a little bit of arm-twisting so that Lee comes to heel, because, let's not make bones about this, you want to go to Hollywood. You want Lee to invite you back to her place, and you're doing it in that peculiarly English way of asking a favour from someone by first of all making them feel like a stain on the Queen Mother's underpants.'

'John, what I want to do is direct this play, and I'm hardly going

to be intimidated by a Californian pop singer and her entourage.'
Stewart became very queeny; he pursed his lips and John suddenly
remembered how much he'd despised him at college. 'I don't like to
pull rank, but I do have some reputation in this business. I've
worked with actors who have more talent in their make-up boxes
than Lee has in her entire CV. That's not to belittle her potential, of
course.'

'Fuck it, Stewart. Is there no bottom to your patronage? Lee's a
star. We're not talking about talent or ability or any of those things
you nurture at RADA. Being a star is another dimension. It's genius
without substance, it's the pheromone that turns the most highly
intelligent species on earth into moths. Of course it's frightening,
and of course you're intimidated.' John's voice rose more than was
polite in a pew. The pent-up worry and lurking fear of the last
month rushed to put out the words. 'And what's worse, what's
most hypocritical, Stu, dear heart, is that you want to succeed on
the back of Lee's stardom, but actually you want her to fail. You
don't want some American chanteuse swanning into your precious
theatre and being able to do it, just like that. Lee asked for help and
you and Oliver just lectured and humiliated her, so she went for a
second opinion. Well, just try thinking that all those Californian
can-do merchants might be a help to you too. But that wouldn't suit
your ego, would it, Stu?'

Stu stuck his chin in the air and snorted. 'Now you're just being
absurd. I suppose loyalty to your meal ticket is admirable, but I had
hoped you'd take a more catholic and civilized view.'

'Yes, Stu. I'm sure you did. Where is Lee by the way?'

'In her embarrassing caravan, which appeared today beside the
vicar's Volvo.'

'No she isn't,' a husky voice said behind them.

Lee was sitting with Hamed. She smiled broadly, but without
humour.

'I heard everything. Hamed and I followed them into the church.'

Lee was sitting on the white sofa surrounded by her entourage.
They were having a team-bonding drink at the end of the
day. Crowded round like an infant school being read a story. John

stood apart by the fireplace, not yet a member of the gang.

'Oh, you should have seen Stu's face, it was a picture. Just perfect. He couldn't stop apologizing. He must have said sorry more times than a blind man in a lap dancing bar. I've got his balls in my pocket.'

'You're brilliant, Lee. You know, you're just something else. Actually, while you were out of the room delivering the *coup de grâce* to friend Stu, we had a pretty successful couple of rounds with the rest of the cast, didn't we, Susie?'

Susie jumped at her cue. 'Yeh, we promised Creon a trial for a sitcom; he can now be hand-fed. Haemon wants an American agent, so that was easy to fix. The little girls want to meet Stephen Spielberg and have an interview with *Vanity Fair*, and the rest rolled on their tummies for a new set of publicity shots, a couple of tickets to New York and a table at Balthazar. They come cheap, these Limeys.'

There was general, good-natured, inclusive laughter.

'Oh and,' another chipper little fellow added, 'we've got a new poster. "Lee Montana is Antigone". We need to do some shots, Lee. And the costumes, thank God we managed to get them in time. Lee, you were this close to appearing in early *Star Trek* meets *Ben Hur*. We've sorted that out I think. Valentino's really interested in doing something classic but sporty and sexy.'

'A pretty good day's work, team,' said T.P. 'I think that's just about everyone on side. What about Oliver?'

'I've seen to Oliver,' Lee said. 'It just so happens Leo is interested in his dreadful adaptation of *A Winter's Tale* again. Oliver's bought and paid for. Thank you, guys, it's a real pleasure working with professionals. Oh, but a special thanks to John,' she looked over to him, 'for being so loyal and saying such nice things. We couldn't have done it without you, love.' She blew him a kiss.

'Well done, John.' T.P. clapped, and the little huddle gave him a grinning round of applause. He was being included; a member of the team, an employee, a junior, a yes-man, another Limey quisling who'd been purchased with a stick and a carrot.

'Right,' said Lee, getting up, 'I'm going to bed. Up early in the morning.'

The team got up to leave, to go to their respective hotels, restaurants or bars, where they could brag and laugh at the badly served drinks, the inefficient service and the simply fabulous taxis.

Lee shimmied over to John and put her arms round his neck. 'OK?'

'Yes, if you are.'

'I'm OK.' She hesitated a little. 'Actually, I feel tired and bloated, but I'm much happier about this damn play.'

'Good.'

There was a silence as if each wanted the other to say something.

'I'm off to bed. See you in the morning.' She kissed him softly on the cheek. 'And thanks again for being so loyal and sweet about me. I really do appreciate it. Sleep well.'

John stayed up and watched television. Finally, as he went round the quiet house, turning the lights off, he felt that still, cold restlessness just out of sight, the now familiar sub-audible whistling laugh. Lee may have paid off the temporal players, the strutting princes and kings, but Antigone was still there, playing cat's cradle with the thread of their fate. Nothing had really changed. The drama was still black and white on the page, as stark and unrelenting as it had been two and a half thousand years before.

And so it went that last week. Lee and her team flung themselves at the play, pulling against the current, struggling as the text rose and fell between them. Occasionally she'd experience moments of calm, when she felt in control, but really the old story was just playing with her. And then the elements would rise up and buffet and howl at them until Lee didn't know which way was up, and she'd return home exhausted and wrung out. The drama was inarguable, inevitable, a force of human nature.

They got through the rehearsals and then the dress rehearsals and then started the too-short process of previews. The rhythm became regular and smooth. It was as if Lee were held in the curl of a whirlpool, circling, being drawn down, down. John watched, helpless. Helpless was what he did best.

He remembered a little yacht his godfather had sent him for his tenth birthday. Beautiful, a proper wooden boat, painted glossy red and white, with real cloth sails and rigging, called *The Swallow*. It had felt shiny and heavy and had smelled of varnish; it was far grander than anything else he had ever been given. It was a proper toy, something you could pass on to your children. He'd never had a potential heirloom before.

He took it to the little stream near his house, a miserable black stain of water, full of rotting things and thick stinking mud. There was a patch of gravel on the bank where kids would go to throw stones and break bottles. He took the boat and launched it. It sat perfectly low and fast in the water, rocking gently, sails feeling tentatively for the breeze. Rooks circled above the dripping elms on the opposite bank. He remembered their cawing. *The Swallow* tasted the first mouthful of a breeze and rippled its sail, then, taking hold, the jib slid beautifully to one side and, as if moved by an invisible hand, she cut the water, leaning elegantly to one side, skimming for the current.

Too late John had realized the truth, the stupid landlubber's obvious truth, that in his hand, on earth, on the soft billows of the counterpane of his bed, this boat was one thing, a static ornament, a beautiful object, a metaphor; but in its element, here in the water, it became alive, a live thing. It did what it was born to do, sail away, deaf to his gasp, alert only to the quickening air.

In his mind's eye, John saw it turn again in the stream and brilliantly take its maiden and valedictory voyage, but what he remembered most keenly was his own inertia, his hopeless watching.

He could have waded into the water; it wasn't too deep. His ruined shoes and stinking mud and the short walk with sticky, cold trousers would have been a small price for this miraculous, beautiful thing, but somehow he hadn't, couldn't. And he didn't search for a stick, or something to hold it or trap it with; he was transfixed, earthbound. Neither did he run after it as *The Swallow* disappeared past the overhanging brush. He could trace the stream in his mind; he knew the banks became steep and clagged with branches and brambles.

He imagined it travelling to the slow bend that was the frontier of his world, and from there it might have gone on for ever, out to sea, sliding its razor cuts through the mountainous waves of the

Atlantic, passing whales and icebergs, with the caw of rooks changed to the lonely, mad laughter of the albatross.

There was hell to pay at home, of course. He'd lost the boat, been parted from a gift, an expensive gift. There were post-mortems and inquisitions and anger and sorrow. Unable to let the misfortune alone, his father had made him go back to the bank to show him, made him miserably go through the motions. Why had he let it happen? Why hadn't he stepped in to stop it? Why? And John had morosely looked at the black mud and said nothing. He didn't know; he couldn't say that he was born to watch with regret.

The two of them had stood on the bank together, silently staring at the dark water as it shied away from them, and the worst thing was his father's unspoken despair that somehow he'd passed on to his son the genetic sickness, the family curse, of letting things slip through their fingers.

A ND NOW JOHN WATCHED LEE.
'Do you want a drink?'

'No. I don't want anything. I want it to be over. I want it to be half past ten and I want to hear the audience go, "Bravo." You have no idea, do you, about this? No idea what it feels like, waiting to perform.'

'I don't. No. Like going to sit your Finals I suppose. That's probably the closest I've come.'

'Finals. Yeah, there's something very final about this. Oh God, I can't sit or stand, I can't remember anything. Anything. What's my first line? Oh God, I can't remember my first line.'

'Nowhere . . .'

'That's right. Nowhere. "Nowhere. It was beautiful. The whole world was grey when I went out,"' she recited. 'Oh, this is impossible. Let's fuck.'

'What?'

'Fuck. I want to fuck. We haven't been in the same bed for a month. Perhaps it will relax me, take my mind off tonight and pass the time. Come on.'

It had never been difficult making love to Lee, not what you'd call a hardship. They'd always had a natural ease, slipped together with the confidence of a handmade box, even the first time, but now, as John undid his buttons in the day-bright bedroom, as they tentatively kissed, he caught the nerves. His fingers trembled and his throat felt dry. It was like a first time, or a last time. They lay on the bed and picked at each other's bodies like fastidious models. Slowly the urge crept through them and they made love with a polite, intense desperation, pressed belly to belly, tensing and letting go, eyes closed, both imagining the person they were with, but at another time.

Fucking for a reason, as inoculation, a sinecure, or for confidence; fucking to forget or regain or confirm is always a risky operation. Sex is best when it's self-contained, when it's its own motivation. But how often it comes trailing the barnacles of other expectations. This afternoon fuck tried to hump more baggage than it could carry and afterwards they lay together.

'Did you?'

'No, nearly though. It was nice.' Lee kissed his shoulder. 'I've missed you. It was nice. Oh God, I think I'm going to be sick again.' She slid off the bed and ran to the loo.

John sat on the edge of the bath and stroked her back in that pointless, mildly annoying way you do when a loved one's lunch is on the move. Lee showered and sat in front of her mirror, staring at her face.

The doorbell.

Hamed.

'I'm a bit early, but traffic's bad in the west and I thought you'd like to get to the theatre in good time. No rush.'

Lee checked herself again, picked up her bag, looked round the room and caught sight of John.

'OK, I'll see you after the show. Come back and get me; there's some sort of party.' She sounded just as if it were another appointment.

The worry and the fretting were gone. The clattering, nerve-jangling journey was nearly over; she'd found the equanimity to take the last few steps.

There were yards of things John wanted to say. He put his arm around her and she looked away.

'First, obviously, good luck. I know you're not supposed to wish that, but good luck anyway. I'm sure it will be wonderful; you've worked so hard. I know we've not had the best of times recently, you and I, but I just wanted to let you know . . . Well, I hope you never doubted . . .'

Lee gently pushed him away and pecked his cheek.

'John, I can't. Save it. I can't think about all that now. We'll talk later.'

'It's just, well, remember there's at least one person in the audience who loves you.' It sort of came out wrong, sounded odd.

The house was silent and empty for the first time in ages, the detritus of Lee's can-do caravan lodged on shelves. Coffee cups and scrolls of fax paper and ashtrays and plates of sushi. The household had an exhausted, mordant calm. Everyone had gone, including, John realized, their furious poltergeist. He couldn't feel her brooding presence. Antigone had left for her first night.

'I'll drop you here.' Hamed stopped the car. 'It'll be quicker if you walk.'

John turned into the crowded Soho streets. It was a warm evening; people lounged in the doors of cafés and shops, getting into character for the night ahead. As he got near the theatre they got thicker, until he was pushing his way through clammily warm bodies and late-lunch breath.

The theatre was small and ill-prepared for crowds or success. It had put up barriers, making a thin catwalk to the door, a gauntlet of scrutiny. John showed his ticket and walked the twenty feet between sullen crowds, their blank, vegetable faces mildly resenting his anonymity. If they were going to stand in this uncomfortable place the least he could do was be notable and not waste their time. A phalanx of photographers shouted at him and fired off a few shots just to be kind.

Inside, the small foyer was also packed with London's professional first-nighters: the critics, theatrical impresarios, television presenters, faces, arts journalists, a smattering of peers with

National Trust-restored wives. They all looked animatedly bored, wearing the privilege of their position in here, as opposed to out there with the hoi polloi, as casually as their expensively rumpled jackets. Oliver was standing in the corner, patting the shoulder of a man who was staring hard into his glass, and beside him Skye pouted with every roll of her ballooning post-pubescent figure.

She waved and came over.

'Hi, darling.' She kissed him messily on both cheeks. 'Didn't think you'd be here.'

'Why on earth not?'

'Oh, I heard that you and Lee had split.'

'No. Whoever told you that?'

'Oh God, one hears so much, I don't know. I thought you'd moved on to Isis.'

As if on cue, Isis appeared.

'Hi, John. What a crowd.' She kissed him.

Skye smirked. 'Yeah, I can see I was misinformed.'

'What?'

'Skye's just been telling me that you and I are having an affair.'

'Oh, that old thing. I heard that too, from loads of people, who all mentioned that Skye told them.'

'I didn't.'

'Generally before she went down on them.'

'I don't.'

'Skye love, you're a poisonous, unhappy little tart.' Isis smiled. 'And if you want to lead anything like a happy, productive life you should be a lot more careful about what goes in and comes out of that mean little gob of yours.'

A bell went.

'Come on, John, that's three minutes. We've just got time for a quickie in the Gents.'

John's seat was beside the critic from the *Sunday Times*, who folded a raincoat across his knees, placed a ring-bound notebook on top and wrote '*Antigone*' and underlined it three times. Then 'Lee Montana', and added an exclamation mark. The seats filled and the audience fussed and settled. Slowly patching into the collective antennae, they became a single conscious eye and ear, a connected tribe, the dark protecting them, allowing them to subsume the individual and become clan.

The lights slowly rose on the stage, revealing a circle of earth that formed a small hill, like a tumulus. It was rather good, dramatic. Looking back at the audience were the cast, waiting patiently, as they must, for the Chorus to set them off on their preordained path. The Chorus lit a cigarette, blew a cloud of smoke and began.

'Well, here we are.'

John felt his heart thump in his chest. The nerves were almost more than he could bear.

'These people are about to act out for you the story of Antigone.'

John felt a cold breeze on his cheek, as if someone had brushed past him.

'That thin little creature sitting by herself, staring straight ahead, seeing nothing, is Antigone.'

Lee hugged her knees on a corner of the stage. Her hair was tied back and she wore a simple, classic dress with a brooch at her breast. She looked so utterly beautiful, so finely sculpted compared to the other characters on the stage, with their off-the-peg human bodies. Lee was another genus. Her knuckles were white, a lock of hair trembled. John felt his eyes fill with tears; it was going to be awful and he couldn't bear it.

The Chorus went through his soliloquy.

He'd always known it was going to be awful, from the moment the name had been let out into the air in Oliver Hood's Gloucestershire garden. He stared at the curve of her neck and wanted so much to rescue her, to take her up, to hide her from what was to come, to bury her in this darkness with the clan. He looked at her and felt great waves of love, silent scree falls of tenderness. He felt something break, not snap like a bowstring, but a slow release of tension. The glittering thread that connected the two of them sagged, like a ship casting off, feeling the hawser's absence, like the end of a cotton reel spinning in the air. They were connected and then they weren't.

He watched with the clan's eye the tragedy of Antigone. It was Lee's alone. The rest of the cast were just incidental on the stage. Next to her they were rendered invisible. The room's concentration was focused solely on Lee; it couldn't drag its eyes from her. Whoever was talking there was only her. And she couldn't do it. Her movements were awkward and bogus and her voice was unnatural; she could only raise the volume to add emotion, but most of all she couldn't stop being Lee. You couldn't pretend otherwise, and the tribe never for a moment wished it to be otherwise. They wanted to see a star; they wanted Lee Montana not Antigone, some difficult little Greek bint. They wanted to be in a room with Lee Montana, to be with it, to have it, that stardom thing, and Lee couldn't, didn't, know how to be anyone else.

The swift, osmotic realization that this was going to be a truly, deliciously ghastly event made the air crackle. The tribe smelled rare, expensive failure. Lee had a long way to fall and they were going to enjoy every foot. They sighed and devoutly wished for it. Pricked ears and gimlet eyes drank in the humiliation. To be here, to be part of it, how fabulous, what luck. They could talk of this till their teeth rotted in their gums, the memory would never fade, that magic of the wooden 'O', that coming together of audience and player, joined through words and emotion in a transient but fixed moment, was happening. This was a far more galvanizing tragedy than Sophocles; this was modern and relevant and now, and the tribe shuddered as Lee shuddered with the cold, dreamy horror of it – the oldest theatre of all: human sacrifice.

You could have cut the atmosphere with a sharp tongue. They willed her to fail, to monumental star's martyrdom, and when she forgot her lines and had to be prompted the tribe could have sobbed with joy. She was such a beautiful corpse, such a fittingly, elegant, rare gift on the altar of their theatre.

The interval arrived. John stayed in his seat and listened to the excited hooting and disbelieving guffaws. The *Sunday Times* critic got up for his complimentary glass of red and John saw just one word on his pad: 'Unspeakable.'

The three bells, like cock crows, called them back. The tribe returned, oiled and nicotined, and settled for the final curve of drama.

On stage the cast looked as if they were swimming in mud. Sweating in their costumes, they gasped and pounded out their lines like dray horses pulling for home. Lee, her face drawn with misery, hacked and sawed at hers, wolfing great gobbets of speech like the torment of an inoperable sickness.

Finally Creon cried for the guards to take her away, to put Antigone out of her misery, and she replied, 'At last, Creon,' with unmistakable, desperate relief. Lee was standing centre stage, facing the audience. The two guards sauntered on, violent, confident, helmeted bouncers, and as they went to take her arms, she took a step and a half-turn. Her hand went to the gold clasp of her dress and she pulled with a ripping relief; it came away and fell to the floor.

Oh my God, oh my God. There was a collective gasp. Eyes bulged. Lee Montana, naked. There in front of us. Just so close you could almost reach out. Stark, butt naked. The shockwave bounced off the sweating walls and surged back across the stage. The actors froze, thunderstruck; this was not what they'd rehearsed. John gasped with the rest of them, and noticed a moment before everyone else that Lee had shaved off all her pubic hair. She had this big, sexual, omnipleasure, sophisticated, fuck-me dream body, with beads of sweat running down her stomach – the sublime bosoms, the deep rose cone nipples, begging for the palm of your hand; the rolling thighs, curving and glistening; the drift of taut stomach; and there, at the hot centre of it all, this little virgin's immature pudenda; the neat slit of innocence and the smutty, slut-shaven slot, the hide-under-the-mattress fuck fantasy.

The messages that flashed and semaphored and crackled round the room were as confused and complex and shamingly uncomfortable as you could wish for. The tribe reeled. The metaphors and similes, the symbols and nuances of that body were slippery smooth with implications. The audience was a sponge for nuance and metaphor; they could spot a symbol in almost complete darkness. Oh, they got it, they understood. They'd willed this martyrdom, the tragedy on top of a tragedy, and here, now, they'd ripped the dignity from this celebrity star thing, this strip fantasy. They'd even plucked the hair from her vagina for a dirtier, better look. She had, with one swift move, turned them from an audience into voyeurs, and they were suitably chastened, suitably shocked and suitably guilty. It was a true *coup de théâtre*. Lee faced the guards and led them off stage.

The rest of the play got through to the curtain, just. Lee came back, dressed in her frock, and mummed her last scene. Those that were predestined to die got on with it, but the tribe wasn't watching, they'd stared at the brightest light and the ghost image of it seared, swam and flickered on their retinas – the image of that pudgy mound, that secret fig of flesh, the crack where Antigone is walled up to die – and all they heard was the hissing of their own disbelief.

Finally the Chorus tidies up. Only the guards are left and none of this matters to them.

The stage went black and the actors came on to take their bows, exhausted and terrified, eyes trying to pick out expressions in the clan. The applause was ragged. And then Lee walked on with her easy, sinuous walk, stony-faced, angry even, eyes bright. The cast parted for her. She stood in the middle of the stage, chin up, sweeping the blackness with her famous face. The collective consciousness in the pews was lost for a response, the balance quivered and hung. The clapping died. And then, in that eerie way that crowds have, the scales shifted and tilted; they decided. This had been a good thing, no, a great thing, a fabulous thing. There was that short, barked exclamation of enthusiasm that you rarely hear in England, and then the cheering and the clapping rolled over Lee like ecstatic poison gas. The audience shot to its feet, yelling. Only then, only when everyone was standing, did she return them a stiff, formal bow. The other players watched in dumb awe. She was not one of them, never would be. Another species altogether. They were paint and wind, she was flint and steel and that ineffable spark. A star. What a star, what a consummate, consummate star.

The stage door was packed with reporters, fans, friends. John elbowed his way through. The doorman had given up on his clipboard.

'Upstairs. Follow the sound of kissing.'

Lee sat in front of her mirror, a white bandanna holding back her hair, her face glossy with cold cream, a silk kimono draped over one shoulder and a glass of Scotch and a cigarette in her hands. She was laughing. The room was full of her American servants. They were still at the exclamatory stage: 'Unbelievable, fucking unbelievable.'

'Oh my God, oh my God, oh my God,' a whip-thin publicist woman repeated, rising up the tonic scale.

'John, darling.' Lee held out her arms, stressing the 'darling' with an exaggerated English accent. 'How the hell was I?'

'I love you.' He hadn't meant to say that, but it blurted out.

The Americans nodded approvingly; semi-religious exclamations of devotion were appropriate at this moment in time.

He blushed and recovered. 'Darling, no-one has ever done Lady Macbeth quite like you.'

The yes-people bridled uncomfortably. Was this the famous Limey humour they'd all heard so much about?

Lee threw back her head. 'No, they damn well haven't, have they? Have a drink. Kiss me.'

More people pushed into the room, all shouting and laughing. John was edged to the wall and then elbowed out of the door.

'I'll see you in the car,' he mimed, pointing to himself and making steering wheel movements. Lee raised her hand and went back to swallowing plaudits whole.

Stu was standing on his own on the half-landing. He saw John and turned away, but there was no polite way of pretending they hadn't seen each other. Still carrying the excessive emotion of the dressing room, John offered both hands.

'Well, congratulations.' He added more exclamation marks than he would normally have felt comfortable with.

'Fuck off.' Stu waved him away with a very Greek gesture of despair.

'What's the matter? They're ecstatic. The audience, they were, you know, jolly appreciative. You should see Lee's dressing room.'

'That cow, that bitch. That was the worst two hours of my life. No, this is the worst moment of my life, here, now, having to know that I've got to live with being the man who brought that filthy travesty to the stage.'

'Oh, come on, Stu, it's only a play.'

'Only a play. How fucking dare you? It's my life; it's everything I believe in – text and drama, the moment of telling a story, a truth, being part of a tradition. It's my life and she trashed it. What she did was just philistine. It was evil. No, no, really, I mean it; it was sinful. Did you see her?' He was shouting now, bits of spit hung from his lip. He held John's arms hard. 'That cunt; that cheap, club-act cunt, stripping. That's the summit of her ability. Getting out her disgusting, fishy tart's twat for the boys. That's her party trick, that's all she has to offer. Drama, theatre, the ensemble of actors who perfect a craft, it all means nothing to her. And not forgetting me. That's how she repays my hours of careful work, the nursery hand-holding, the remedial explanations, the time and effort and goodwill to allow her to take the stage and be part of something great. What's her response? To get her kit off and invite the audience to fuck her. Oh so dramatic.' He was crying tears of fury and frustration. 'So cultivated, so grown-up. The civilization of the brothel.' He paused and drew a ragged, queeny breath.

John searched for an appropriate response, and then just burst out laughing. 'You ridiculous little queen. Until Lee stripped you'd only managed to produce one of the all-time most dreadful productions. Her fishy twat, as you so charmingly put it, was all that stood between your reputation and being a prize prat. It's an abysmal production, and of course Lee doesn't act like those tired, second-hand emotion pedlars; she's a star, something none of them will ever be. You wanted her to fail on your terms so you could feel better about yourself. It's pathetic, Stu; you're pathetic. Just standing here watching you now is one of the most gratifying reactions I've ever seen in an audience. You're moved to tears, a hard, cynical, queeny old professional like you is moved to tears by a performance by Lee Montana.'

'You know, John,' Stu wiped his nose with a little silk handkerchief and patted the back of his hair, 'I thought, for a moment, that you were one of us, but I was mistaken, wasn't I?'

'You know, Stu, I thought I was one too. Thank God I'm not.'

The guards, now changed into their civvies, pounded noisily down the stairs with their girlfriends and mothers and pushed between the two men. John turned on his heel and followed them.

*

The party was held in a large, Fascistically minimal restaurant, which would have comfortably held 200, uncomfortably 300 and was now packed with 500. There were another 500 baying at the door. Waiters of every sex, painted bronze and wearing short togas, squeezed through the press holding trays of wine, souvlaki and olives. There was very loud bazouki music playing. It was a pretty first-rate, PR-organized hell.

Hamed edged the big Mercedes through the streets. John and Lee sat in the back. Lee looked tired; her face was pale and sagged at the edges. She wore large dark glasses and her fingers fretted. She fidgeted with the exhausted, last sour traces of adrenalin, as if an electric current had been passed through her body. John rested his hand on her thigh and chatted about the audience and the play and Stu.

'We're not going to stay here long,' she interrupted. 'I hate these things. Just a turn for the photographers, no interviews. I expect there'll be TV. Hamed, are we nearly there? And did you organize a separate table?'

'Another couple of minutes, love. They said there was a roped-off area. I'll stick with you.'

They pulled up outside the restaurant and the crowd surged round the car, flashlights filling the interior like tracer.

'Oh, Jesus,' Lee muttered, 'there aren't any security guys.'

Indeed, there were only a couple of beefy men in dinner jackets trying to hold people away from the door.

Hamed got out and made them come over and form a tight little cordon. Lee stepped out and there was a noise, a cross between a shout and a hiss. Hamed pushed towards the door. A policeman appeared and, with cruciform arms, moved the crowd aside.

'You'll have to move that car,' he called.

'I've got to stay with Miss Montana, mate. I'll shift it when she's inside.'

'No, you won't, sir. You'll shift it now. You're blocking the street. They're backed up to Piccadilly. Move it. Don't argue with me, son.'

Hamed turned to John. 'Stay close to her. Right up with her. Keep moving until you're inside, find a corner and stand in front of her.

This is a nightmare. I'll dump the motor and come and get you. Don't leave hold of her for a moment. You got that?' He slid back behind the wheel.

'Hamed,' Lee shouted, but the car slid away and the crowd filled the space like the tide reclaiming the shore.

'Come along, don't push, stand back.'

John noticed the policeman was about eighteen. He looked surly and unsure of himself.

'Come along now. Let Miss Montana through, you'll all get a look.'

Lee clung to John, burying her face in his shoulder. He started to edge towards the door. It was only a matter of yards, but the weight of bodies was solid, immovable.

''Ere, stop shoving. Move back, move back. 'Ave some sense, 'ave some sense, 'ave some sense,' a voice behind him kept repeating like a demented bird.

They moved slowly, eddying one way and then the other with little hobbled steps, like two drunks in a three-legged race. The restaurant door vomited people coming out to see, drawn by the light and the noise. The policeman's helmet was tipped over his eyes and then fell into the crowd. He had tight, curly ginger hair. He reached an arm out to grab it, furious and indignant. The hat bobbed away across arms and shoulders, like a black cork. A bouncer, finding a small gap, pulled back his fist and punched a photographer in the side of the head. The blow rippled through the crowd setting up a rocking momentum. John turned and looked at Lee. Her glasses were skewed on her face, her mouth was open, as if she was saying something. She was terrified. John felt the fear shudder through her body into his. He shouted, 'Oi, oi,' but no sound came. The crowd reached into his mouth and pulled the voice out of him. The rocking, reeling motion slurred them along the pavement towards the restaurant. Above the rolling roar of the crowd there was a descant of shrieking, high-pitched noises. No words, just noises, like tearing cloth and grating rock.

The momentum swayed and buffeted, the noise grew, something jabbed him hard in the back, something sharp, something metal. He swivelled his head and saw just other heads, mouths gaping, chins up, trying to stay upright, stay afloat in this maelstrom. Beady eyes and flaring nostrils, teeth slimed with strings of saliva. A face pushed right up against his, rough chin scraped his neck. He stared into a dark eye, as round and blank as a shark's. The mouth was laughing. He smelled beer and vomit and it slid away into the eddies. He thought of the man with the shitty knife, the stalking killer – 'I know where you live, I know what you want.' Lee's body was rigid and jerked beside him. She struggled like a salmon in a net, her head pulled back, staring at the moon. Her white neck arched, the tendons straining. A rough hand was twined through her hair, jerking, another grasped her breast. John pulled his weight to the other side, frantic. The hands slipped away, like drowning men losing their grip.

The body of the crowd shuddered and strained and flexed its muscle. It was a single animal, a fluid, unco-ordinated, slow-motion epileptic fit, with a thousand straining heads and tens of thousands of grasping, probing fingers. Slippery and solid, it skiffed and screed. John felt as if it were all his own body – uncontrollable, flailing, a mad thing, thriving, trying to tear out its own vitals. He felt the resistance strain and sigh and then give.

The tension momentarily released, and above him the window of the restaurant shuddered and gave. Plate glass popped and snapped into thousands of shards, and through the ragged hole people fell. John saw a naked bronze statue with a pink mouth working syllables fall head first into the hydra and float for a moment above the waves and then sink. He felt the mass lurch and implode as feet snagged, legs buckled and heads disappeared beneath the dung quicksilver mass. The movement became faster, the tiny dancers' steps more frenetic, the body had chosen a direction: down. Down, down, pell-mell.

With a rush, panic enveloped him. He struggled to find his arms but couldn't. He bit at a face beside him and tore a mouthful of hair. Now, as if being washed out to sea, he couldn't touch the floor. His feet occasionally kicked something soft and fragile, heads butted at him. A woman with a look of astonishment disappeared directly in front of him. He heard a noise, like distant seagulls: 'Lee! Lee! Lee!' And then he felt himself turn and slide over and he let go.

To save himself he let go of Lee. His arm flew back and landed on a face, grabbing a cheek, his fingers sliding into a gaping wet mouth. He pulled himself upright, touched ground again, stood for a moment and then punched blindly. His fist connected with an arm and then a shoulder, punched and punched, noses and foreheads. There were other punching, flailing hands, punching and pushing and screaming with a desperate, petrified fury. 'Lee! Lee! Lee!' Pushing and jabbing away at the great hideous lump of unwashed smell, the breathing, stupid, bovine, dangerous, despised, un-comprehending, inquisitive, dribbling, foul, prurient sans-culottes. Punching and pushing at the public interest, he gulped for air, and fought for space in the slowly, blindly whirling, thoughtless carousel, staggering from footfall to stumbled footfall. Each in-distinguishable from his neighbour, an eliding grey blur of bodies and faces, wild eyes milling in a thick, grey, steaming, sweating, stew, beating itself with fear of itself.

In the cocking of an arm he saw Lee's face, clear in the stuttering light, surprised, frightened and disbelieving. Their eyes locked for a moment. He grabbed for her, but the crowd closed in and swallowed her. Howling and roaring, it had what it had come for. He'd let her go.

An elbow jabbed hard into his temple. He fell, skidding and slid-ing through the bodies, helter-skeltering down past breasts and bellies and acid groins, past the clubbing knees and stamping feet, into the glass-bright gutter. The foaming whirlpool moved over. He was no longer part of it. He was a dead cell, sloughed skin. It moved on, across the neon sparkle of the pavement that glittered around him. Over on the other side of the road he saw a figure standing in the blue light, a figure amongst other figures, watching. But this one he knew. With a cold certainty he knew the taut, wiry girl. He could just make out her pale face grinning. She hopped from foot to foot, clenching her fist, beating her thighs. Dizzy with pain, John knew, against reason, against knowing, that this was Antigone. Of course. Why had he imagined she would be defeated with one performance on a stage? How had he imagined that her righteous anger would dissipate with an ovation, that fate could be wiped off like make-up? These were her Furies, this crowd.

The girl darted into the slow traffic and scuttled round the steaming cars, their red brake lights dousing her limbs bloody. He watched her search for him, the dark head bobbing like a hawk. She saw him and, hunched over, ran through the ragged edges of her people. He screwed his eyes shut and pressed his face into the broken glass on the sticky pavement. He felt the breath on his neck.

He looked and stared into the beetling black face of Petra. Her lips were pulled back over her teeth, grinning. Her hair stuck damply to her cheekbones. She reached out, and with two bony fingers pressed the side of his head. It hurt and they came away bloody.

She hissed a sibilant little laugh. 'Bastard, bastard. I told you. I said I'd bury you.' And she turned on her heel and scuttled away into the river of traffic.

John let himself into the house. It was quiet. A single reading lamp flung deep-blue shadows over the white living room. It smelled of stale ashtrays and bourbon.

'You got back.' Hamed sat in an armchair at the far end of the room. He put down the first edition of *The Waste Land*.

John was on the verge of tears. He was shaking with fear and guilt and pain.

'I lost her in the crowd. I've lost Lee. I've been looking. I don't know what happened to her. Oh God, Hamed, she could be anywhere; anything could have happened. They might have . . .'

'She's upstairs in bed.'

John slumped onto the sofa and held his head.

'Is she . . .'

'She's OK, a bit shaken and she's got a bruise, but she's fine. I gave her a pill. She's worried about you.'

'Me? It was my fault. I lost her. I let go; I couldn't hold on. It was terrifying. She just slipped out of my arms.'

'Yeah, it's frightening if you're not used to it, but it's OK, I got her, straightened out a few people and brought her back here. It's OK. You look like shit. Here, go and wash up. I'll make you a drink.'

John went to the bathroom and turned on the shower. He peeled off his damp, filthy suit. There was blood down the front of his shirt and the sole had come away from one of his shoes. He looked in the mirror; there was a purple welt on his shoulder and his knuckles were skinned raw. His face was a shock, caked and scored, as if he'd been rubbed with a muddy cheese grater. His lip was split, and through the dark hair his eyes shone with a piercing, rose-rimmed, blue intensity. Carefully he washed away the blood, sweat and tears and doused himself with the comforting chemical fragrance of improbable flowers, lathered away the damp musky stink of the street, and then wrapped himself in the nappy softness of a dressing gown and went back into the white room.

Hamed handed him a whiskey and a cheese sandwich. The whiskey burned his lip.

'Did she say anything? No. Does she blame you? Probably. They always blame someone. A platinum blame card is one of the perks of stardom. More importantly, do you blame yourself?'

'Yes, I suppose so. Yes, I should have been more . . . I don't know, done something.'

'What? You did all right. What else could you do? You didn't wish Lee harm; you wanted to protect her. But the crowd, what could you do?' He paused.

John chewed slowly and sipped.

'You felt it though, didn't you, when you were in there? In the middle, pressed into all that humanity. It's awesome, the power. And that was small. Imagine thousands, hundreds of thousands. You lose yourself, become part of something huge, and you panic. You got the panic. That's when you realize who you really are, that really you're just part of what you've been part of all along. You see, we live our lives as individuals, solitary, making choices. We want to be like little billiard balls that only meet where they touch, so we can roll on, but really we're part of this great thing. And when you fit in, when you feel it, when you're there, when you meet the beat, that low throb, it's like fission, the energy, it's who we really are. That crowd, that society, that's what civilization feels like in the engine room. It's more than everything; it's bigger than fame, bigger than stardom, bigger than love. That crowd just washed it right out of your arms, and in the end it washes everything away. That, mate, was the march of humanity.'

'I don't know where you get it all from, Hamed, but if you ever want to start a religion I'll buy shares. I'd better go to bed.'

Hamed smiled. 'Yeah, it's late. I've got to go and get the first editions and see what humanity thinks of our performance last night. She was worried about you. She may blame you, but she loves you. She told me. Don't know why people tell me things.'

'Yeah, well she hasn't seen me looking like this.'

'You look fine. Like you've just seen a ghost.'

The bedroom was warm; the first bars of dawn seeped across the bed. Lee lay, foetally huddled. John lay on his back and watched the grey light on the ceiling. A hand slid across his chest and down his stomach.

'I'm not asleep.' Her voice was a whisper.

'I'm so sorry I let you go, that I lost you. I'm sorry.'

Lee turned over and coiled her arms around him. 'It's OK. It was fine. Hamed came to the rescue.'

'But it was scary.'

'Yeah, all of it. A big, red-letter scary day.'

'The play. You know, I'd almost forgotten.'

'Thanks. I hadn't. I've been lying here full of Valium, thinking about it. I've never been that frightened, ever, in my life. Shit, I've never, ever.'

'You were amazing.'

'Tell me the truth, John. Now, just here, just the two of us, tell me.'

'Really?'

'Really.'

'The play was terrible – the production, I mean. Wooden and mannered. You looked nervous, everyone was nervous, gummed up with nerves. The first half wasn't good, but then, oh, you were extraordinary.'

'You mean when I got naked?'

'Well, yeah. It wasn't just shocking or salacious, it was extraordinary. It was real theatre. It was as theatre should be. It was appropriate, but utterly unexpected. That's Antigone; she's naked,

279

she has been stripped. All that's left is her self-sacrifice. You were right, you had to do something to stop it being Lee Montana pretending to be Antigone. Stripping actually removed the artifice in a way. It wasn't denying that you were Lee, it was making Lee Antigone, a girl who has risked everything. There was nothing between you and the audience.'

'There certainly wasn't. Just getting my kit off said all that, did it? Well, I suppose I can claim it was appropriate to the role then.' She laughed. 'And I just thought it was going to give you boys a thrill and take your mind off the fact that I hadn't the slightest idea what I was doing on that goddamn stage.'

'When did you decide you were going to do it? Because the cast were obviously as thunderstruck as we were, and Stu was incandescent.'

'Oh yeah, he was, wasn't he? It was worth it just for that. That arse-wiped faggot. I got to the theatre, and in the dressing room I just knew it was terrible, that it was going to be terrible, that I was terrible, and that I was waiting to take the biggest almighty dive of my life. I knew they were going to crucify me and I thought of my dad, you know, how I was doing it for him in the first place, and I thought, You old bastard, what the fuck did you ever do for me? Nothing but leer and breathe whiskey fumes. But I did remember him saying that when he was doing burlesque, if an act died on stage, if they started throwing stuff and tearing up the place, then they'd send on the strippers. It worked every time, he said, nothing like tits and arse to calm the savage breast. So I thought I'd better bring on the strippers, and as it was either me or that misshapen, cellulite fat farm who plays my sister, it had better be me. So I stood in front of the mirror and thought, Can I do this? What does the old body look like? And you know, I'm not a little girl, so I thought, This bush has got to go. I stood in that freezing, pissy shower with a compact mirror, trying to trim twenty years off my pussy with a disposable razor, nervous as hell and with curtains in ten minutes.' Lee sat up and lit a cigarette. 'And I kept taking a bit off here and a bit off there and, you know, the thing looked like Groucho Marx with a stroke, so then, what the hell, I whipped the whole lot off.'

'It was really shocking.'

'You liked that, did you? Men. You're so easy.'

'No, I don't. I don't know. I liked it before.'

'I'm surprised you're not already down there having a look-see.' She pulled back the sheets.

'You've got to admit, it's a very neat one. I wouldn't have done it if I'd had all those fringy valance bits.'

John had a look-see. It was shocking and exciting, and men were so easy.

'Ouch.' He winced. 'I'm sorry. I've got a split lip.'

'Just my luck. I get the full Yul Brynner snatch and you get Bob Mitchum's mouth.' She gently pulled him up and kissed him. 'Remember the first time we did it?'

'Of course.'

'It seems like a long time ago, doesn't it? It was about this time in the morning. You tried to break my wrist.'

'Yes.'

'You remember what I said.'

'Er, straight sex, no foreplay and I'm going to sleep afterwards. Something like that.'

'You think you can manage it again?'

This time Lee didn't go to sleep afterwards.

'I can't sleep. You're losing your touch.'

'Let's go downstairs and see if the reviews are in.'

Hamed had laid out an American breakfast: bagels, lox, cream cheese, coffee cake, three varieties of Danish, juice, champagne, coffee and the papers, neatly folded to their appropriate pages.

'How did we do, Hamed? No, coffee first. Don't tell me. No, just tell me.'

'You're still a star, love.'

'How big a goddamn star?'

'Well, there are two overnight reviews. The *Mail* hates the play but loves you, adores you. It says, "This goes beyond acting; it's a moment of pure theatre. I was in the presence of a diva who, with one tug of her frock, revealed herself to be the embodiment of all women. I have never seen an audience so stunned, or made to

281

confront their own fears, sexuality and their relationship with the performer so dramatically." *The Times* is a little more circumspect, saying, "It's a flawed rendition, overpowered and up-staged by the blinding light of Montana, whose depilated nakedness, though dramatically brave, drove all thought of text and context not just from the minds of the audience, but apparently from the rest of the cast as well. An image in the night that will burn in my memory for as long as I live." He then goes on to have a pretty thorough go at Stu. Um, I seem to remember they had a scene. Anyway, he's another queer. You made the news pages of all the tabloids. This is my personal favourite.'

He held up the front page of the *Sun*; a banner headline read, A STAR IS PORN, with a topless photograph of Lee taken from her book.

'Oh, that's brilliant. I want that one framed.'

'I think the *Telegraph*'s getting something in the late editions, and that's about it. That's as good as it gets, Lee. Shall I open the bubbly?'

'Yes.' Lee threw back her head and hugged herself. 'Thank you, God. I'll never, ever do this again.'

'You've got to do it tonight,' said John.

'Shit. I've got to keep shaving my bits for a month. I'm never doing another play. Remember I said I wanted to see where the edges of my envelope were. Well, this is it. Inviting the audience to a gynaecologist's open day is as far as I go.'

'Miss Montana's not available,' said Hamed. 'I'll tell her you called. Yes, I will. Yes, I'm sure. She is. Yes, of course. Thank you.'

'Hamed, you'd better get the team over here, I think it's going to be a busy day. I'm going back to bed. Coming, John?'

THAT NIGHT IT WAS A DIFFERENT PLAY; NO BETTER, JUST DIFFERENT. John went again and sat in the house seats. The audience, he noted, were also quite different. No better, just different. The difference between a first- and second-night audience is the difference between Paris, France and Paris, Texas. The cast, too, were different, resentful of the reviews. They realized they were simply a backing group for Lee and wrung out their lines as fast as possible. The only emotion that came across the footlights was pique. It was just a long, slow build-up for that moment. Lee, by contrast, was much better, relaxed and at times almost dramatic. When finally Creon called for the guards the audience craned forward in their seats. Lee paused, teasing them, before ripping her frock off with a cheerleader's flourish. She stood for a moment, while the retinas clicked, and then stalked off.

Stu wasn't in the theatre, which caused more resentment among the cast, who thought they'd been abandoned to carry his can. Somebody wrote under the poster on the staff noticeboard, 'Transferring to Stringfellows'. Lee laughed when John explained what Stringfellows was.

Stu wasn't in but Oliver was. He blustered into the dressing room.

'Lee, darling, what can I say? What can I say? Unbelievable, unbelievable.'

'You could say, "No-one has ever played Antigone like that".'

'Well, dear heart, no-one ever has. Ever, ever. It's definitive. You're definitive. I wanted to tell you yesterday, but there was all that fuss at the party and I can't get past your askaris on the blower, but, heart, you should be very, very proud of yourself, and in my own small way I'm proud of myself. Grant me that. I saw it was there, the spark, the nascent possibility. Others pooh-poohed, but I persisted. Mark my words, mark my words, I said, and aren't they now.'

'Apparently not Stu. He's conspicuous by his absence,' added John quietly.

'Yes,' said Oliver, sitting heavily in a chair and putting on his serious face. 'Yes, I'm afraid I've had words with friend Stu. You know, of course, what his problem is? Well, I shan't bore you with Stu's problems.' He brightened up. 'Let's just say he's not the director I'd come to believe. He's no more than the sum of his rather limited parts, unlike you, who are far, far greater than your parts, as it were. The arrest scene, darling, was pure, pure theatrical brilliance. It ranks alongside Thorndike's Phèdre, Campbell's Ophelia,

Redgrave's what's-it. Brilliant. But you see, that's Stu's limitation. Set amongst cabochon talents, I grant, but a flaw nonetheless. Being of the Oscar Wilde persuasion, he can't see beyond his own proclivity. I can tell you now, but do you know who he first suggested for your role? This is strictly *entre nous*. Brad Pitt. No, I know. An all-boy *Antigone*. "Let's get back to basics," he said. It's just too funny. Now, darling, tell me, the naked thingy, when did you realize its rightness? Never mind, it was a stroke of genius.' He rested a hand on her thigh. 'It's a performance I want to see over and over. Now, would you mind terribly if we chew a little business?'

'Chew away.'

'Well, we're sold out, of course. In fact, we could sell out ten times over. The clamour for tickets is beyond anything. We have, as they say in Hollywood, a hit you can take to the bank. Now, unfortunately, we can't extend on the three-week run here, but, um, I've found – don't ask me how many strings I've tugged – but I've found another theatre: Her Majesty's. Less intimate but more seats, so we could slot you in there with just a week's break, and a run of at least three months. But now, here's the big news: Lee, don't thank me, it's all down to you, but I have a firm, I repeat firm, offer of an open run on Broadway. Broadway, Lee. Think of it, going home in triumph. Isn't that amazing?'

'Amazing?' Lee shouted at the top of her voice. 'Oliver, listen. Listen to me very carefully. If you think I'm getting butt naked and flashing my fanny in New York, where people know me for Christ's sake, in front of Americans, you are out of your tiny mind.' She laughed. 'Not in six months, not in six years, not ever. Ever. I am not going into another theatre, whichever Majesty's it is. I'm doing three weeks and that's it. If I could stop tomorrow, I would.'

John watched Oliver and savoured the moment. His was by far and away the more exotic and exciting strip. His face and body visibly sagged, deflated. He had the grail of a Broadway transfer held to his lips and then dashed away. Everything he believed in was being chucked in the bin as dross. He was a picture.

'I can't believe what I'm hearing. Broadway, Lee. Broadway. Apart from all the other considerations, don't you think you owe it to the cast? No? Well, to me? I've put a considerable amount of money – inconsiderable compared to your talent, of course – but still, darling, heart, we could make a fortune. The Tonys are a certainty. No, please, say no more. I shouldn't have brought it up here; you're still raw from the boards. Foolish of me, thoughtless. Please consider it. Don't make any decisions.' He got up and backed towards the door. 'Consider, dear, brilliant lady. I'm privileged. Adieu, adieu.'

John thought for a moment he would burst into tears, but he misjudged it and was through the door before he could summon up the necessary mucus.

Lee waited a beat, then burst into peals of laughter. 'God, it was worth it just for that, just to tell him to shove his fucking theatre.'

'But, have you thought . . .' John couldn't resist following with the question that itched at the back of his mind. 'Have you thought what you're going to do after the run?'

It hung in the air. Lee examined her perfect cheekbones in the mirror.

'Come on, take me to The Ivy for dinner. Let's party.'

As they were leaving the restaurant a fat balding man dressed twenty years too young approached them.

'Look, I'm sorry to disturb you, but I just had to say congratulations.'

'Well, thank you. Never be sorry about saying nice things.' Lee was expansive and slightly drunk. The restaurant had been fawning over her singly and in mute, adoring groups for the last two hours.

'Oh, Miss Montana, yes, of course, you too. But actually, I meant John. Hi, I'm Mike Dibbs.' He paused. 'Mike Dibbs, president of Two-Way.' He paused again. 'Two-Way Records?' Pause. 'Well, you're obviously new to the business. We put out Isis's music.'

'Ah.' The Tin-Pan penny dropped. 'The song I wrote. Thank you.'

'Has Isis told you?'

'No, I don't think so.'

'We released it this week, and it's gone straight to number five.'

'Oh, good,' said John, with insufficient enthusiasm, owing to ignorance.

'Good, darling?' Lee said. 'God, that's amazing.'

'Well, not too amazing. I decided it should be the single,' Mr Dibbs added, 'but it is very, very congratulation-worthy. It'll be number one next week, undoubtedly. There's nothing to touch it, and the vibe from America is excellent. I wouldn't be surprised if we have a worldwide thing here. A bona fide humungous hit. It's made Isis. She's going to be mega. Not quite in the league of present company, of course.'

Lee made a 'Who, little me?' face.

'She's no one-track wonder now. I understand this was your first lyric, John.'

'Yes.'

'Well, that's great. You know, people, talented people, work their whole lives to get a top-ten hit, and here's you, first shot a coconut. Look, I don't want to impose on you any more. Here's my card, please be in touch. Anything you've got I want to see. We'll have lunch and I'll make you a very rich boy, I mean it, and you can make me an even richer old Jew. OK? Tell him, Lee, I mean it.'

They got into the back of the car and, on cue, Isis's voice was there.

'Got it today,' said Hamed. 'You know it's gone to number five. Isis told her bloke to tell me to tell you, and will you call her. It's a great song.'

'Yes, John, it is a great song, and she sings it well.' Lee smiled.

John listened and couldn't somehow connect with it. He felt uncomfortable because he didn't have that great rush of pride or joy or amazement; nothing, just a lingering disbelief.

In the weeks, months, indeed in the years to come, he would hear it often, although he never played it himself. It would be there when he opened café doors, or over the television. Snatches, lines would be thrown out of car windows, like cigarette stubs at traffic lights. Once, in a queue, he stood behind a man who sang the first stanza over and over and got one word wrong. He should have tapped the bloke on the shoulder and said, 'I wrote that song and it goes like this.' It would have been an anecdote people would have smiled at, but he didn't because he didn't tap people on shoulders and because the song didn't feel like his. The tenuous connection of authorship had been worn away by the beat. He understood that this was the biggest thing that had ever happened to him, the biggest thing he'd achieved, but he'd missed it, and somewhere deep inside he realized this wasn't to do with the poem or the pop music – he didn't mind it being pop music, all poetry had started as pop songs – the missing connection was in him, a dud receptor, a small thing compared with all the things that could go wrong, but also somehow vital, a tiny malfunction that affected everything he did.

'What does it make you think of', asked Lee, 'when you hear your words? "I watched you sleeping",' she sang along.

'You, of course.'

She hugged his arm and purred.

The lie was easy because it didn't remind him of anything. He couldn't conjure the picture of Petra in her filthy room any more, or that last back squeak of tenderness and remorse he'd felt for her, and he couldn't revisit the anguish of his attic misery when writing it. And then suddenly an image did come, as clear as morning. Sitting on the bed in the dying light, Isis beside him, the touch of her bare arm on his, both of them bent over the sheaf of paper, the faint smell of her, the rise of her small breasts, the blond hair on the back of her arm, and his voice giving the words air. The first time it really became a poem, spoken out loud, that moment when the verse took wing, the moment when it was real and his, and then gone.

The biggest thing he'd ever done until the next morning.

'John, there's no easy way of putting this.' Lee walked into the bedroom.

He was reading the paper. There was a tortuous feature on post-feminist nudity pegged to Lee's performance.

'So I'm just going to say it. I've got blue piss.'

He looked blank.

'I'm pregnant.' She threw a small slip of litmus paper onto the bed. 'Shit. I've never said that before: I'm pregnant. Oh my God, I'm pregnant, I'm pregnant. Me, me. I'm having a fucking baby. Say something, dammit.'

John hysterically rummaged around his head for a feeling. Where was the damn feeling? There must be a feeling here somewhere. You can't not have packed a genetic response to becoming a father, for Christ's sake. What does it look like? Nothing. He found nothing. Make it up.

'Congratulations.'

'What? Is that the best you can do? Congratulations. Jesus. What do they do to you at school over here? Is it something in the water?'

'Sorry. That's wonderful. I really am, um . . . Is it . . . ? Um, I mean, do you want it? I mean to have babies?'

'Of course I want to have babies. I'm an American woman from Hollywood, aren't I? I just don't know whether I want to have this baby. Oh God, I'm in shock. Maybe it's a mistake. No, it's not a mistake. I've been sick every morning for a month.'

'I thought that was the play, nerves.'

'So did I. Then I thought I missed my period because of anxiety, but it's been eight weeks and, oh God, this isn't how it's supposed to happen; this is not a good time. I don't have a room that's painted peach; I haven't even got a crib with bears on it. I haven't interviewed a thousand Scots nannies. Oh God, John, do something. No, you've already done more than enough.'

'But I thought you always took precautions, that rubber pigeon thing.'

'Rubber pigeon thing? What are you talking about? Yeah, I do, always, but hell, nothing's one hundred per cent, except your little tadpoles, apparently.'

'Yes, clever little chaps.'

'Oh right, that's all I need, you getting a dose of the old genetic imperative. God, of all people, you're so woozy about everything else; you'd just have to have Schwarzenegger sperm, wouldn't you?'

'Thanks.'

'Sorry, I didn't mean that.' She flung herself on the bed, rolled across his arm and started to cry, then giggled. 'It's started already, the little bastard's knitting with my emotions.'

'Do you want to keep it?'

'An abortion you mean? I'm American, abortion's murder, worse than murder. Abortions are worse than sex. Do you know what an abortion would do to record sales? Do I want to keep it? Yes. No. Definitely no. I'm thirty-two. Yes, yes, of course I want it. Oh, I don't know, I don't know. No, look, I can't think about it. Pretend it never happened.'

'We can't just pretend it never happened, Lee. We've got to make a decision.'

'I've got to make a decision, and my decision is to pretend I never did the test. I don't want to talk about it. Don't mention it again. Swear.'

They lay together in silence for a long time.

'It will be beautiful,' Lee whispered. 'Would. Would be beautiful. I never said that.'

And so they never mentioned it.

John wondered who he could mention it to. Who was there left to tell? He had become completely detached from the semi-detached life he'd once had. There were no ties, no commitments, no obligations that held him to this place or that person, or the person he'd been, and what's more, he didn't care. It didn't bother him. He had Lee. By a process of elimination and omission there was now only Lee in the spotlight, and they shared a secret. It seemed to John that it drew them together after the distance and anguish of *Antigone*.

Lee brightened and lightened and, as doctors, midwives and text books devoted to such things will tell you, she blossomed. John saw that the pregnancy, their child, their future, pleased her. She laughed a lot. Her demeanour, if not her body, became rounded. For the three weeks of the play they had what John thought was a golden time.

True, Stu wrote an arch and bitter piece denouncing *Antigone* and Lee, before departing for a previous engagement in Morocco, but she just shrugged. Compared with the bouquets in the rest of the press, who cared?

'He's a silly boy,' said Oliver. 'After that act of betrayal he'll be lucky if anyone employs him to direct a nativity play in Merthyr Tydfil.'

Oliver called most days with the diminishing hope of a Broadway run.

Lee went to the theatre without complaint and actually grew into her part, became competent and then good, and finally almost revealing. It was as if she'd discovered something, a sympathy for the tough little girl, a compassion that placated her. There was a synchrony, and the audience stopped fidgeting through the first act and sat again, as audiences have sat, for 2,000 years, rapt and horrified.

Even that arresting moment changed subtly. Her defiant nudity became more voluptuous nakedness, and John found it harder to watch, as he did every night. He tried to close his eyes or turn away or stare at something else, but he couldn't. The uncompromising beauty of her was transfixing. He minded the other eyes, minded them seeing what was his, but moreover he minded not really knowing if what he saw was different from these anonymous stares. Was he just sitting in the dark, watching a film star? Just another fan with privileged access. He couldn't personalize the glamour, the fame of her body, and that smoothly juvenile vagina, which wasn't so much a dare or an accusation now, but a sordid lie, barely hiding their secret. It was a relief when the run drew to a close. He dared to look up, to glance covetously at the future and be fondly hopeful.

And so when it happened it was a shock. After the penultimate performance John went backstage, jogging along to the dressing room. Lee was sitting, as usual, in front of her bright mirror in her dressing gown, wiping sludge across her face. The telegrams and cards and bits of amusing tat that had looked so Mardi Gras at the beginning of the run now had a lacklustre ennui. He pecked her greasy cheek, poured himself a drink and noted the smoking cigarette. She'd been meaning to cut down, without much aptitude. He decided not to mention it.

'Good house today.'

'John,' she caught his eye in the mirror and looked away, 'when the run ends I'm going back to the States.'

There it was, like the flash before an explosion. He knew.

'I'm going back.'

He said nothing.

She ploughed on, 'Have you thought what you're going to do?'

'Um, no. I thought, well, I thought . . . I did really think . . . I suppose I imagined I'd be with you. Um, are you going for long?'

'I don't know, but that's not the point. I'm going.'

'Lee, are we breaking up?' This was beyond pain, beyond dignity, beyond, way beyond. This was worse than it ever got. John felt his body change shape and dissolve.

'Yes, sweetheart. I think that's what we're doing.'

'You're not sure, though, you're not . . .'

'John, I'm certain. I'm finishing this. Please, darling, don't make it worse. I hate this. I've thought about it; it isn't easy, but it's best for both of us, really.'

'No, no.' The tears flooded his eyes. He stared at his hands, which hung limply over his knees. 'What about the baby? That's our baby.'

'Yeah, that has something to do with it. John, it's my baby. You're not carrying it, you're not going to give birth to it.'

'You've decided to keep it then?' A small triumph.

'Yes, I'm going to have it, but I'm going to have it in America, on my own. Of course, you'll always be its father. I'm not cutting you out; you can see it, be its dad, but not with me.'

'But I love you.'

'I know.'

'Don't you love me?'

'John, I'm sorry. I don't know. I love bits of you, I love lots of you, probably most of you, but . . .'

'Why?'

'Why? Oh, John, what possible difference can it make? Just leave it alone. Don't make this any worse for either of us.'

'Lee, please,' he was sobbing, 'please,' sobbing and begging. There was a weightlessness, a sense of falling, a dizzying rush of air, nothing to hold on to, falling past this clichéd conversation, this ex-lovers' litany, this balance sheet without profit, only loss. 'You have to tell me, what did I do?'

'John, you didn't do anything. And look, if this were a movie I'd say, "And that was the problem," but it's not. There are things I like about you, love about you, but there are also the things that, in the end, make this relationship finite. We've always known that this was an interlude.'

'An interlude!'

'Listen. Yeah. You knew; we both knew. It started as a night, then a weekend, then a couple of weeks, then it got an extended run because you're too damn sweet and good and kind and funny and ironic and, oh, I put it off, and I didn't think about it because it was just too cosy and nice, but this time it's finished. I'm pregnant and I'm going to have this baby, and I thought, Can I do it with you? And the answer's no. I'm sorry, I'm really sorry. I'm pleased you're the father. If I had to choose any man I've ever known to be the father of my child it would be you. All your qualities – your cleverness and humour and observation and, you know, the questioning – all those things, I'm sure it ain't gonna get from me. I'm pleased about that, but it just wouldn't work, not on a permanent basis. I've tried to imagine you in California, with my life and things and the life this child's going to have, and I can't see it. There's a hole where you should be. I'm afraid you're not in the picture. Sorry, you didn't get the part.'

'Was it the sex?'

'Oh, for Christ's sake, John, you know it wasn't the sex.'

'When did you decide to dump me?'

'I didn't decide to dump you; we just reached a fork in the road.'

'It was after the opening party, that crowd in the street; it was that night, wasn't it?'

Lee went back to wiping her face. John took deep, ragged breaths.

'Yeah, I suppose it was. How did you know? Of course you knew; you're a poet, you know things like that. See, when I see the future it's got to be with someone who's stronger than me, who's going to protect me, or at least face it with me on equal terms. You let me go. I needed you and you weren't there, and I don't blame you, it wasn't your fault, no harm was done, and if we were just Jack and Jill it wouldn't matter, but I'm not, we're not. I'm Lee Montana, and the bottom line is that there probably isn't anyone who's going to be up to this, up to me. You know, for me the world's a really frightening place, John. I'm always frightened, and you're not up to that. The bummer is that what I really love about you is that you're not up to it. I'm starting to understand why so many stars marry their bodyguards or personal trainers. John, I'm sorry, I'm all out of explanations. This chapter's over. I know it's bleak, but there is an upside. I don't hate you or despise you, I haven't found you in bed with the maid or Isis, I'm not leaving you for another man, unless this child of ours is a boy, and we'll always have the baby, and I hope a friendship.'

'"We'll always have Paris."'

'Yeah, and we'll always have Paris.'

She got up and knelt in front of him and tried to kiss him, but John, with a *faux*-gallant act of bravado, pushed her away.

'Well, that's that then. When are you going?'

'The day after tomorrow, in the morning.'

'So soon?' His stomach churned. 'Shall I go to a hotel?'

'Don't be silly. Let's have a last day together, and there's some practical stuff I've got to sort out. Come on, I feel miserable as hell. This is the worst day of my life in England and that's saying something.'

'You should try it from my side, and I've been living here a lot longer than you.'

They got home, making tiny talk, smiling at each other when their glances collided. Lee went up to bed and John went to the spare room and lay awake and cried. The sadness was all, everywhere. It broke over him without ceasing, waves of unhappiness crashing rhythmically, dark and fathomless, stretching over the horizon. By seven he'd wept himself dry, and, shivering with exhaustion but still wide awake, he got up and went out into the city. Movement had a mild analgesic effect, so he strode across West London. The city was beautiful in the early light, the long white streets swagged and muffled with tiny squares of elaborate greenery, like a sober man with a passion for exuberant ties and handkerchiefs. There was a comfort in its permanence and age. How much despair had been absorbed by this brick and stone? How many tiny personal tragedies had been trudged across these streets to be blissfully forgotten? The city had a thousand stories, but it was too grand and ancient and polite to remember any of them.

John walked through the crowds going to work, carrying small lunch boxes of care. He came to an empty taxi rank, where there was a girl in a bright-green ball gown; ridiculous. She wasn't particularly beautiful – pretty eyes in a mousy face. Her evening sandals hurt her feet and her hair had lost all its special-occasion, salon sheen and hung in a matted nest over her shoulders. Last night's make-up was smudged on her cheek. She wore a man's dinner jacket, which sagged over her shoulders. John stopped and looked at her. A first date, a charity ball, with big flowers and ghastly food, champagne and cheap red, an auction and a bright table, then a Seventies disco, and the falling strands of sweaty hair, the slow dances with . . . not with the boy who'd taken her, with another she'd seen across the table, arms around his shoulders. The first slobbery kiss, the taxi home, the bed, and then this morning, in the bright street in her ridiculous frock, splashing out on a cab to Crouch End or Streatham or Putney. The coy taking of his dinner jacket – perhaps he'd suggested it. Yes. She was pleased; it meant he would phone. The smell of wine and smoke in her hair, the memory of him between her thighs, the ache and tiredness and, oh, a bath. Where was the cab? She looked round and saw John staring at her. Her expression, a colliding of emotions, like dappled light through leaves: embarrassment, sensuality, vulnerability, excitement and hope. She turned away and smiled to herself. For this brief moment she was the most handsome, enviable girl in the city, anonymous, noticed only by a sad boy. All her life she would never understand that this was where she'd burned brightest, and John felt his heart break.

Lee didn't wake till late afternoon. She was quiet and self-contained. Already she'd moved on; her bags were in the hall. She sat at the kitchen table.

'The house. Keep it. Well, live here. I'll put it in the child's name. Paint a spare room a bright colour. We'll come and stay. I'll tell you when it's born, but I'm sure we'll speak before then. You've got all my numbers. There may be some press and stuff; don't talk to them. Now, money.'

'Lee, don't.'

'OK. Well, I expect you'll make out all right. You should go and see that record guy, and if you need anything you know I'll always . . . well, you know. That's about it.'

'Yes, that's just about it.'

'Oh, John, don't look so miserable, please.'

'I am miserable,'

'So am I, but let's just pretend.'

The last performance of *Antigone*. The cast acted up, tried to corpse one another, winked and gurned. Lee was hardly there at all, barely listening. When it came to the nude scene her hand went to her shoulder, then stopped, and she turned to the guards, linked arms and exited. The audience tittered.

Afterwards there was a traditional cast party on stage. Oliver made a pompous speech about the fellowship of the wooden 'O', and the sweet sorrow and other horse shit, and said for the umpty-tumth time how sorry he was that Lee's personal commitments forbade a Broadway transfer, and the cast, thinking of tomorrow's call to their agents and part-time bar work, growled approval. And then it was hugs and exchanged phone numbers and the deathless promises of lunch and future projects. The corny schmaltz was Lee's home ground and she joined in, offering her own cup of tears to the communal bucket, and almost meaning it. John stood apart and thought that as the essence of drama was illusion, so the heart of an actor was delusion, and he envied them that. He envied everyone, even the dead. Particularly the dead.

The last night at home. John and Lee ate a little, drank a little, said little and went to their separate beds. John stared at the ceiling, summoning the strength to face the night.

His door opened softly and she slid between the sheets.

'I know this is a really bad idea, and it'll only make everything a thousand times worse, but what the hell, just one last time.'

It did make things worse, but there was a sad splendour in their final hot farewell and he slept.

'I've decided. I'm going to come with you to the airport.'

'John, please don't. I hate goodbyes. We've said everything

and done everything. There's no more, I'm wrung out.'

'No, I know. For me. I've got to see you go. It's like a funeral; you've got to be there.'

She sighed. 'Well, if you must.'

They held hands in the car. Hamed played Isis, John told him to put on Lee and Lee said she didn't want to listen to anything.

'You know, this is the first time I've ever broken up with someone in Europe. In America it's always so quick; you throw something, shout something, slam a door, call a lawyer and it's all over. Close up, cut, dissolve. This is like one of those French films that are so slow you think there ought to be an Oscar for lingering, but the emotion falls like snow, and in the end the whole cinema is covered in drifts of it. You get a different type of sadness here. American sadness doesn't feel like this, this is older, deeper, softer. God, I feel sad.'

Airports know they're amphitheatres of emotion and, to stop the whole to-and-fro business grinding to a lachrymose, melancholy halt, they're designed to muffle feelings. They interrupt at every opportunity with technical business and mundanity. The VIP officer, cheery with chat, checked in the baggage. There were magazines and gum to be got and screens to be read.

'Look, darling, I'm going to check in now. I can't drag this out any longer.'

She turned to Hamed and put an arm on his shoulder. 'Thank you for everything. You've been a real treasure. See you next time.'

'Pleasure, Lee. Yeah, see you next time.'

'And keep an eye on him for me. Make sure he doesn't sit in the dark.'

'Sure. Have a good flight.' And he moved a little way off, still watching her.

'Goodbye, John.'

'Bye, Lee.'

'Oh, my beautiful boy.' She took his pale, serious face between her hands and kissed him with a gentle passion. 'My beautiful boy.'

'Will you miss me?'

'Of course I'll miss you.'

'I love you.'

'I know.' She turned, put on her glasses and walked to the gate of no return. Her film star's end-of-the-movie, into-the-sunset, into-the-future, sashaying walk, and the two men watched her, and she didn't look back.

'HOME, JOHN?' HAMED CHECKED OUT THE WING MIRROR AND filtered into the traffic.

'I suppose.'

'Look, mate, I'm sorry. Really. For what it's worth, you two were good together. I'm sorry.'

'Yes.'

'Look, technically that's me finished, but I've nothing on today. Why don't I drive you over to see Isis. I know where she is and I happen to know that she wouldn't be at all averse to seeing you, and I happen to know that it's the obvious move, mate. You've got to get on.'

'Thanks, Hamed, but no.'

The cheap modern suburban countryside chugged past.

'It was fate, wasn't it?' John was really talking to himself. 'It was fate, kismet, karma, inshallah, that it would end like this. It was pre-destined. I did know, but you keep hoping, you keep trying to wriggle out, but you can't. It's already been decided. Do you remember that first weekend, Hamed? When we went to Gloucestershire and Lee said she was going to do *Antigone*, and I wasn't quite enthusiastic enough and she sulked. I think I knew then. You make a choice. It can be nothing, inconsequential, hardly a decision at all; you turn this way instead of that, sit here, smile at them, choose the chicken instead of the beef, and somewhere it flicks a switch, the wheels begin to turn, the line runs out and you don't even feel it. The hook. But it's a done deal; it's fate.'

Hamed checked him in the rear-view mirror.

'No, mate. You see, John, this is where you and I part company. You're stuck in this predestiny shit, this ancient, classical, we're-all-playthings-of-the-gods stuff, as if one act leads inexorably to the next and the protagonist is an automaton. But you've got to move on; you're ignoring freedom of choice, the essential, individual majesty of man. You've got to own your life, not be a tenant in it. Get into the eighteenth century and go with the flow of the Age of Reason; you're responsible for your own life. Man is born free; it's down in black and white. You know what the problem with fate is, don't you? That you assume there's only one. Like in *Antigone*: there's one destiny that fits everyone; they've all got to die because it's her fate. Well, every one of them has a destiny – the main parts, the soldiers, the page boy – that's democracy. You see, you believe you're dictated to by Lee's destiny because she's a star. She says come and people come, go and people go, but that's not necessarily so, John. We've all got choices, and if you'd ever looked up from that classical pessimism you'd realize that you never played your strongest suit.'

'What are you talking about, Hamed?'

'Come on, John. Get with the programme. She's an American, she's a woman, she's a movie star. Happy endings, mate. Happy endings are her religion, John. Optimism and hope. The dream, John. Happy endings are the American way. The modern hubris. To be a plaything of the gods you've got to believe in gods, otherwise fate's just random and pointless, and that's a contradiction in terms. Happy endings are the religion of faithless people. The bottom line is, this is your story. I've sat here and listened and driven it around; it's yours. And you can write it any way you like.'

'Shut up, Hamed. Just shut up.' John looked out of the window and thought and felt and wondered why he hadn't fought harder for this thing, this love, his only great love; and for the nascent child, his child. Where was the small receptor, the link, the trigger, the tiny chemical transformer that should have tripped and flashed the message, "Here we stand"? Here we'd risk everything and stand and fight to the last tear, the last humiliation, for this, this great love thing? He wasn't a bolter, but then neither was he a slugger. He was an accommodator, an appeaser, a pushover, a negotiator, an explainer, a hand-wringer.

In the slurry of misery John came to a small node of unpleasant self-revelation: he had no bottom line. There was no wall for his back to press against, there was no bloody pass where he'd make a stand. If he wouldn't fight for love he'd fight for nothing at all. He would always stand on the shore and watch the boat slip away. That had been the defining moment when a complex pattern had been set, the kismet. If you wouldn't die for love, what was the value of the explanation? And if love were just another relative disposable, what was the point of poetry? Because, make no mistake, have no doubts, if poetry means anything, believes in anything, it's love. It's poetry that gives the life and language to love. Love is for ever betrothed to poetry. All else is a one-night stand.

Love is poetry's holy place, its temple, its fortress, its homeland, and as the car beat a retreat back to the lonely, solitary city, John realized that if he couldn't break the fateful cycle of his own self-ordaining, cowardly little capitulations, he'd fail as a poet, and worse, he'd fail poetry. A line bidden perhaps by a final sigh of despair swam clear as a clarion into his mouth: 'If this be error and upon me proved, I never writ nor no man ever loved.'

AIRPORTS KNOW THEY'RE AMPHITHEATRES OF EMOTION AND, TO stop the whole to-and-fro business grinding to a lachrymose, melancholy halt, they're designed to muffle feelings. They interrupt at every opportunity with technical business and mundanity. The VIP officer, cheery with chat, checked in the baggage. There were magazines and gum to be got and screens to be read.

'Look, darling, I'm going to check in now. I can't drag this out any longer.'

She turned to Hamed and put an arm on his shoulder. 'Thank you for everything. You've been a real treasure. See you next time.'

'Pleasure, Lee. Yeah, see you next time.'

'And keep an eye on him for me. Make sure he doesn't sit in the dark.'

'Sure. Have a good flight.' And he moved a little way off, still watching her.

'Goodbye, John.'

'Bye, Lee.'

'Oh, my beautiful boy.' She took his pale, serious face between her hands and kissed him with a gentle passion. 'My beautiful boy.'

'Will you miss me?'

'Of course I'll miss you.'

'I love you.'

'I know.' She turned, and put on her glasses and walked to the gate of no return. Her film star's end-of-the-movie, into-the-sunset, into-the-future, sashaying walk, and the two men watched her, and she didn't look back.

As she got to the gate a noisy family of Cypriots – a mother, father, kids, uncles, all holding bags and rucksacks and bursting, taped-up cardboard stereo boxes – pushed in front of her. They were all talking at once, waving their arms; things kept dropping off them, toddlers escaped. The untidy gaggle searched their pockets for tickets and passports.

Lee stood aside, one hand on her hip, her exit spoiled. Her chin dropped to her chest, and then slowly she turned her head and looked back. She took a step, indecisive, and then walked slowly back to John, grinning.

She stood in front of him.

'You know I can't do it. Fuck it.' And she kissed him again with hope and promise and relief. 'Fuck it. Let's go and see Leo. Is there a flight to Nice, Hamed?'

'In twenty minutes, love.'

'I haven't got my passport,' said John, ridiculously.

'Inside pocket,' said Hamed.

John felt and there it was.

'I make things 'appen, mate.'

'Lee, what does this mean? Um, why are we doing this?'

'Oh, who knows? Maybe it's just putting it off. I can't promise, but I do know there's more things I love collected here', and she wrapped her arms about him, 'than anywhere else. And I know that you're very rare and very handsome, and I'm doing it because, well, shit, because I can, because I'm Lee Montana.'

Encore

HAMED SETTLES INTO THE FAST LANE, HEADING WEST, HIS ARM OUT the window, smoking a small cigar. It's a beautiful day, scudding clouds, flowers, trees, sheep, Bruce Springsteen on the stereo. Everything's sweet and where it should be. He checks the back seat in the mirror.

'So that was that. Well, up to a point. There's no such thing as a happy ending, of course. All that living happily ever after. You know that always made me sad when I was a kid; it was like a cheat, as if everything stopped there. You had this adventure, and then it was just happy ever after, like nothing else ever happened. Life isn't a game of bridge, where you deal cards and play a neat hand and either win or lose and then shuffle. You can cut up stories into anecdotes because it makes them manageable, explainable, but really life's a lottery and it just drifts on. One thing slides into the next.

'So, anyway, John and Lee. They had a baby, a daughter. John was at the birth in Beverly Hills and Lee wanted to call it Antigone. Well, you can imagine, John said absolutely not, you can't go through life being called Antigone, so they called it Sophraclea instead, which by Hollywood standards is conservative. Sophy for short. Lee and John didn't end up together, sorry, but then they didn't end up apart, either.

'John stayed in London, he made a lot of money from "I Watched You Sleeping". Well, you'd have heard it, everyone knows

301

it. It spent a year in the top ten, number one in every country with electricity, used for movies and commercials and covered by every wobbly balladeer, played on jukeboxes and karaoke machines, at weddings and funerals and on *Desert Island Discs*. It's a classic and it made him famous, about as famous as you can be while remaining anonymous. Who wrote "I Watched You Sleeping"? was a double difficult pub-quiz question. The song ended up more famous than Lee. People will sing it for a hundred years. John used some of the money to buy the bookshop. Yeah, I know, would you believe it? Bought the shop. Opened a second-hand section and went in every day and read. He didn't have many friends, didn't go out much, never married, just loved Lee and his daughter. Two or three times a year they'd get together, go on holiday and have a big time. She's a good kid, Sophy, happy, clever. She wants to be a poet like her dad, and she can't sing a note. Lee and John speak a lot on the phone, usually late at night. Sometimes she'll get on a plane and they'll just lie there in that big bed in the white room and hold each other, like frightened people holding driftwood in a darkening sea.

'You know, they all became famous in this story. Everyone was touched. They all became stars of sorts and got their dose of happy ever after.

'Mrs Patience sold the shop to John and moved to a cottage in Norfolk; she finally wrote her grandmother's cookery book and made a television series, *From a Country Kitchen*; she's very popular with old ladies.

'Clive finished *Fins of Desire*, found a publisher and it sold by the van load. Clive adored being famous; he loved being rich and best of all he loved being flash. He was never off the television, having rows, in gossip columns; he married half a dozen times, always little tarts with improbable breasts. He wrote a shelf full of sexy, exuberant trash. He'd go and see John occasionally and complain that his books weren't displayed properly. They were friends out of habit rather than conviction.

'Isis was already famous but "I Watched You Sleeping" was the end of her career. It came to a stop; she never sang anything that approached it again, but she didn't mind. Finally she retired to the west of Ireland and bred horses and children. She'd see John on her infrequent visits to London. They did get it together briefly, mainly because it seemed to both of them like unfinished business, and a remembrance of something that had gone. Sometimes they'd get drunk and sleep together, but it isn't as important as it might have been. Isis thinks of John as one of her closest friends, and not seeing him that often makes it easier, makes her fonder.

'Dom and Pete, the performance artists, they got famous. They're very big in Germany; big gay following. They were nominated for a Turner Prize for some nonsense involving videos and ox hearts.

'Skye, Oliver's daughter, had the fat sucked out of her, her face rebuilt, got plastic tits and got pregnant. She had a baby that had cerebral palsy. The child was her redemption. She started a charity, got involved in health-service politics and was made a life peer. I know, miracles never cease.

'Stu finally went to Hollywood, made a forgettable movie and got caught up in a rent-boy scandal; she found God and wrote a screenplay in prison. He's a bit of a Christian icon now.

'And Petra. Well, Petra. Petra never became famous, except she sort of is famous. She was the inspiration behind "I Watched You Sleeping", but she doesn't know that. No-one knows that except John. John was the last person to see her, in the street. She disappeared into the traffic. Never went home, never picked up her things, never told Clive, broke his heart. Just disappeared into the city. Sometimes, you know, I think I see her on a corner, stepping off an escalator, a face on a late night bus. She's out there somewhere, anonymous, inquisitive, energetic, wilful, bitter, hopeful, cynical. They were her people, that crowd, she was their Marianne. You can sense her. Whenever five or six people gather together, when it gets a bit rowdy in the crush, that's her.

'And Lee. Lee. Lee was Lee Montana, the most famous woman in the world, a star that will never die, burned bright on a celluloid loop into eternity. If you never die, can you really say you've ever lived? That's the problem with gods, do they ever live?

'All that stuff I said to John in the car to gee him up about fate, well, it wasn't quite the truth, was it? We're living in the age of the atheist, a time that doesn't believe in gods, but if you don't believe in anything it doesn't mean you believe in nothing, it just means you'll believe anything, and mostly we believe in stardom, we believe in fame. The screen gods and goddesses, their fame is a destiny, a karma, a fate – deaf, blind and inescapable – and Lee rode hers with a deific grace and beauty. John was her time-out, her time out of time. What she felt for him was as close as a goddess can get to loving a mortal.

'Me, well, you know me. I'm the Chorus, the man that makes it 'appen.

'There's one last thing I haven't told you. It's about a box in a cupboard in an attic in a white house. There, in the darkness, are John's poems, unread, unpublished. He never wrote again. They sit there, civilization's seeds. One day they'll blossom and take their place in the garden. They're some of the most beautiful, poignant things ever said, but they can wait. There's no sell-by date on poetry.

'Here, look at that. I love this bit. Look, see how the road cuts through the chalk and stretches out across the vale, on and on over the horizon. I love that. It's like you can't see the end, but you trust it. The road just unfolds and you feel sort of secure. I always think, Who's making this journey? Me or the road? Well, that's the thing, isn't it? Predestination and free will. We need each other. What's a traveller without a road?'